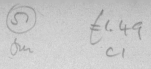

'For months I lay in bed and plotted how to kill my ex-husband. But I knew I'd bungle it and get caught, so I wrote it in a book instead.'

Thus began the twin careers of Sue Grafton and Kinsey Millhone. In 1982 Sue Grafton was a twice divorced screenwriter, mother of three, with visions of homicide dancing in her head. Now she is creator and alter-ego of one of America's most popular private investigators, Kinsey Millhone, star of the renowned 'alphabet' novels.

She was born in Louisville, Kentucky in 1940, her father was the mystery writer, C. W. Grafton, whose own work gave his daughter the initial inspiration to write herself. Since then, Sue Grafton has moved to Santa Barbara, where she writes full-time.

Sue Grafton

'D' IS FOR DEADBEAT

PAN BOOKS
In association with Macmillan London

The author wishes to acknowledge the invaluable assistance of the
following people: Stephen Humphrey, Florence Clark, Joyce Mackewich
Steve Stafford, Bob Ericson, Ann Hunnicutt, Charles and Mary Pope of
the Rescue Mission, Michael Thompson of the Santa Barbara Probation
Department, Michelle Bores and Bob Brandenburg of the Santa Barbara
Harbor Master's Office, Mary Louise Days of the Santa Barbara Building
Department, and Gerald Dow, Crime Analyst, Santa Barbara
Police Department.

First published in Great Britain 1987 by Macmillan London Ltd
This edition published 1990 by Pan Books Ltd,
Cavaye Place, London SW10 9PG
in association with Macmillan London Ltd
7 9 8 6
© Sue Grafton 1987
ISBN 0 330 31585 4

Printed and bound in Great Britain by Cox & Wyman Ltd, Reading, Berkshire

For my sister, Ann
and the memories of Maple Hill

1

Later, I found out his name was John Daggett, but that's not how he introduced himself the day he walked into my office. Even at the time, I sensed that something was off, but I couldn't figure out what it was. The job he hired me to do seemed simple enough, but then the bum tried to stiff me for my fee. When you're self-employed, you can't afford to let these things slide. Word gets out and first thing you know, everybody thinks you can be had. I went after him for the money and the next thing I knew, I was caught up in events I still haven't quite recovered from.

My name is Kinsey Millhone. I'm a private investigator, licensed by the state of California, operating a small office in Santa Teresa, which is where I've lived all my thirty-two years. I'm female, self-supporting, single now, having been married and divorced twice. I confess I'm sometimes testy, but for the most part I credit myself with an easygoing disposition, tempered (perhaps) by an exaggerated desire for independence. I'm also plagued with the sort of doggedness that makes private investigation a viable proposition for someone with a high school education, certification from the police academy, and a constitutional inability to work for anyone else. I pay my bills on time, obey most laws, and I feel that other people should do likewise . . . out of courtesy, if nothing else. I'm a purist when it comes to justice, but I'll lie at the drop of a hat. Inconsistency has never troubled me.

It was late October, the day before Halloween, and the weather was mimicking autumn in the Midwest—clear and sunny and cool. Driving into town, I could have sworn I smelled woodsmoke in the air and I half expected the leaves to be turning yellow and rust. All I actually saw were the same old palm trees, the same relentless green everywhere. The fires of summer had been contained and the rains hadn't started yet. It was a typical California *unseason*, but it *felt* like fall and I was responding with inordinate good cheer, thinking maybe I'd drive up the pass in the afternoon to the pistol range, which is what I do for laughs.

I'd come into the office that Saturday morning to take care of some bookkeeping chores—paying personal bills, getting out my statements for the month. I had my calculator out, a Redi-Receipt form in the typewriter, and four completed statements lined up, addressed and stamped, on the desk to my left. I was so intent on the task at hand that I didn't realize anyone was standing in the doorway until the man cleared his throat. I reacted with one of those little jumps you do when you open the evening paper and a spider runs out. He apparently found this amusing, but I was having to pat myself on the chest to get my heart rate down again.

"I'm Alvin Limardo," he said. "Sorry if I startled you."

"That's all right," I said, "I just had no idea you were standing there. Are you looking for me?"

"If you're Kinsey Millhone, I am."

I got up and shook hands with him across the desk and then suggested that he take a seat. My first fleeting impression had been that he was a derelict, but on second glance, I couldn't find anything in particular to support the idea.

He was in his fifties, too gaunt for good health. His face was long and narrow, his chin pronounced. His hair was an ash gray, clipped short, and he smelled of citrus cologne. His eyes were hazel, his gaze remote. The suit he wore was an odd shade of green. His hands seemed huge, fingers long and bony, the knuckles enlarged. The two inches of narrow wrist extending, cuffless, from his coat sleeves suggested shabbiness

2

though his clothing didn't really look worn. He held a slip of paper which he'd folded twice, and he fiddled with that self-consciously.

"What can I do for you?" I asked.

"I'd like for you to deliver this." He smoothed out the piece of paper then and placed it on my desk. It was a cashier's check drawn on a Los Angeles bank, dated October 29, and made out to someone named Tony Gahan for twenty-five thousand dollars.

I tried not to appear as surprised as I felt. He didn't look like a man with money to spare. Maybe he'd borrowed the sum from Gahan and was paying it back. "You want to tell me what this is about?"

"He did me a favor. I want to say thanks. That's all it is."

"It must have been quite a favor," I said. "Do you mind if I ask what he did?"

"He showed me a kindness when I was down on my luck."

"What do you need me for?"

He smiled briefly. "An attorney would charge me a hundred and twenty dollars an hour to handle it. I'm assuming you'd charge considerably less."

"So would a messenger service," I said. "It's cheaper still if you do it yourself." I wasn't being a smart-mouth about it. I really didn't understand why he needed a private detective.

He cleared his throat. "I tried that, but I'm not entirely certain of Mr. Gahan's current address. At one time, he lived on Stanley Place, but he's not there now. I went by this morning and the house is empty. It looks like it hasn't been lived in for a while. I want someone to track him down and make sure he gets the money. If you can estimate what that might run me, I'll pay you in advance."

"That depends on how elusive Mr. Gahan turns out to be. The credit bureau might have a current address, or the DMV. A lot of inquiries can be done by phone, but they still take time. At thirty bucks an hour, the fee does mount up."

He took out a checkbook and began to write out a check. "Two hundred dollars?"

"Let's make it four. I can always refund the balance if the charges turn out to be less," I said. "In the meantime, I've got a license to protect so this better be on the up and up. I'd be happier if you'd tell me what's going on."

This was where he hooked me, because what he said was just offbeat enough to be convincing. Liar that I am, it still didn't occur to me that there could be so much falsehood mixed in with the truth.

"I got into trouble with the law awhile back and served some time. Tony Gahan was helpful to me just before I was arrested. He had no idea of my circumstances so he wasn't an accessory to anything, nor would you be. I feel indebted."

"Why not take care of it yourself?"

He hesitated, almost shyly I thought. "It's sort of like that Charles Dickens book, *Great Expectations*. He might not like having a convicted felon for a benefactor. People have strange ideas about ex-cons."

"What if he won't accept an anonymous donation?"

"You can return the check in that case and keep the fee."

I shifted restlessly in my chair. What's wrong with this picture, I asked myself. "Where'd you get the money if you've been in jail?"

"Santa Anita. I'm still on parole and I shouldn't be playing the ponies at all, but I find it hard to resist. That's why I'd like to pass the money on to you. I'm a gambling man. I can't have that kind of cash around or I'll piss it away, if you'll pardon my French." He closed his mouth then and looked at me, waiting to see what else I might ask. Clearly, he didn't want to volunteer more than was necessary to satisfy my qualms, but he seemed amazingly patient. I realized later, of course, that his tolerance was probably the function of his feeding me so much bullshit. He must have been entertained by the

4

game he was playing. Lying is fun. I can do it all day myself.

"What was the felony?" I asked.

He dropped his gaze, addressing his reply to his oversized hands, which were folded in his lap. "I don't think that pertains. This money is clean and I came by it honestly. There's nothing illegal about the transaction if that's what's worrying you."

Of *course* it worried me, but I wondered if I was being too fastidious. There was nothing wrong with his request on the face of it. I chased the proposition around in my head with caution, wondering what Tony Gahan had done for Limardo that would net him this kind of payoff. None of my business, I supposed, as long as no laws had been broken in the process. Intuition was telling me to turn this guy down, but it happens that the rent on my apartment was due the next day. I had the money in my checking account, but it seemed providential to have a retainer drop in my lap unexpectedly. In any event, I didn't see a reason to refuse. "All right," I said.

He nodded once, pleased. "Good."

I sat and watched while he finished signing his name to the check. He tore it out and pushed it toward me, tucking the checkbook into the inner pocket of his suit coat. "My address and telephone number are on that in case you need to get in touch."

I pulled a standard contract form out of my desk drawer and took a few minutes to fill it in. I got his signature and then I made a note of Tony Gahan's last known address, a house in Colgate, the township just north of Santa Teresa. I was already feeling some low-level dread, wishing I hadn't agreed to do anything. Still, I'd committed myself, the contract was signed, and I figured I'd make the best of it. How much trouble could it be, thought I.

He stood up and I did too, moving with him as he walked toward the door. With both of us on our feet, I could see how

5

much taller he was than I . . . maybe six-four to my five-foot-six. He paused with his hand on the knob, gazing down at me with the same remote stare.

"One other thing you might need to know about Tony Gahan," he said.

"What's that?"

"He's fifteen years old."

I stood there and watched Alvin Limardo move off down the hall. I should have called him back, folks. I should have known right then that it wasn't going to turn out well. Instead I closed the office door and returned to my desk. On impulse, I opened the French doors and went out on the balcony. I scanned the street below, but there was no sign of him. I shook my head, dissatisfied.

I locked the cashier's check in my file cabinet. When the bank opened on Monday, I'd put it in my safe deposit box until I located Tony Gahan and then turn it over to him. Fifteen?

At noon, I closed up the office and went down the back stairs to the parking lot, where I retrieved my VW, a decaying sedan with more rust than paint. This is not the sort of vehicle you'd choose for a car chase, but then most of what a P.I. does for a living isn't that exciting anyway. I'm sometimes reduced to serving process papers, which gets hairy now and then, but much of the time I do preemployment background checks, skip-tracing, or case-and-trial preparation for a couple of attorneys here in town. My office is provided by California Fidelity Insurance, a former employer of mine. The company headquarters is right next door and I still do sporadic investigations for them in exchange for a modest two rooms (one inner, one outer) with a separate entrance and a balcony overlooking State Street.

I went by the post office and dropped the mail in the box and then I stopped by the bank and deposited Alvin Limardo's four hundred dollars in my checking account.

Four business days later, on a Thursday, I got a letter from the bank, informing me that the check had bounced. According to their records, Alvin Limardo had closed out his account. In proof of this, I was presented with the check itself stamped across the face with the sort of officious looking purple ink that makes it clear the bank is displeased.

So was I.

My account had been debited the four hundred dollars and I was charged an additional three bucks, apparently to remind me, in the future, not to deal with deadbeats. I picked up the phone and called Alvin Limardo's number in Los Angeles. A disconnect. I'd been canny enough to ignore the search for Tony Gahan until the check cleared, so it wasn't as if I'd done any work to date. But how was I going to get the check replaced? And what was I going to do with the twenty-five grand in the meantime? By then, the cashier's check was tucked away in my safe deposit box, but it was useless to me and I didn't want to proceed with delivery until I knew I'd be paid. In theory, I could have dropped Alvin Limardo a note, but it might have come bouncing back at me with all the jauntiness of his rubber check, and then where would I be? Crap. I was going to have to drive down to L.A. One thing I've learned about collections—the faster you move, the better your chances are.

I looked up his street address in my *Thomas Guide to Los Angeles Streets*. Even on the map, it didn't look like a nice neighborhood. I checked my watch. It was then 10:15. It was going to take me ninety minutes to reach L.A., probably another hour to locate Limardo, chew him out, get the check replaced, and grab a bite of lunch. Then I'd have to drive ninety minutes back, which would put me in the office again at 3:30 or 4:00. Well, that wasn't too bad. It was tedious, but necessary, so I decided I might as well quit bellyaching and get on with it.

By 10:30, I'd gassed up my car and I was on the road.

2

I left the Ventura Freeway at Sherman Oaks, taking the San Diego Freeway south as far as Venice Boulevard. I exited, turning right at the bottom of the off-ramp. According to my calculations, the address I wanted was somewhere close. I doubled back toward Sawtelle, the street that hugs the freeway on a parallel route.

Once I saw the building, I realized that I'd spotted the rear of it from the freeway as I passed. It was painted the color of Pepto-Bismol and sported a sagging banner of Day-Glo orange that said NOW RENTING. The building was separated from the roadway by a concrete rain wash and protected from speeding vehicles by a ten-foot cinderblock wall sprayed with messages for passing motorists. Spiky weeds had sprung up along the base of the wall and trash had accumulated like hanging ornaments in the few hearty bushes that managed to survive the gas fumes. I had noted the building because it seemed so typical of L.A.: bald, cheaply constructed, badly defaced. There was something meanspirited about its backside, and the entrance turned out to be worse.

The street was largely made up of California "bungalows," small two-bedroom houses of wood and stucco with ragged yards and no trees. Most of them had been painted in pastel hues, odd shades of turquoise and mauve, suggestive of discount paints that hadn't quite covered the color underneath. I found a parking space across the street and locked my car, then crossed to the apartment complex.

The building was beginning to disintegrate. The stucco looked mealy and dry, the aluminum window frames pitted and buckling. The wrought-iron gate near the front had been pulled straight out of the supporting wall, leaving holes large enough to stick a fist into. Two apartments at street level were boarded up. The management had thoughtfully provided a number of garbage bins near the stairs, without (apparently) paying for adequate trash removal services. A big yellow dog was scratching through this pile of refuse with enthusiasm, though all he seemed to net for his efforts was a quarter moon of pizza. He trotted off, the rim of crust clenched in his jaws like a bone.

I moved into the shelter of the stairs. Most of the mailboxes had been ripped out and mail was scattered in the foyer like so much trash. According to the address on the face of the check, Limardo lived in apartment 26, which I surmised was somewhere above. There were apparently forty units, only a few marked with the occupants' names. That seemed curious to me. In Santa Teresa, the post office won't even deliver junk mail unless a box is provided, clearly marked, and in good repair. I pictured the postman, emptying out his mail pouch like a wastepaper basket, escaping on foot then before the inhabitants of the building swarmed over him like bugs.

The apartments were arranged in tiers around a courtyard "garden" of loose gravel, pink paving stones, and nut grass. I picked my way up the cracked concrete steps.

At the second-floor landing, a black man was seated in a rickety metal folding chair, whittling with a knife on a bar of Ivory soap. There was a magazine open on his lap to catch the shavings. He was heavyset and shapeless, maybe fifty years old, his short-cropped frizzy hair showing gray around his ears. His eyes were a muddy brown, the lid of one pulled askew by a vibrant track of stitches that cut down along his cheek.

He took me in at a glance, turning his attention then to the sculpture taking form in his hands. "You must be looking for Alvin Limardo," he said.

"That's right," I said, startled. "How'd you guess?"

He flashed a smile at me, showing perfect teeth, as snowy as the soap he carved. He tilted his face up at me, the injured eye creating the illusion of a wink. "Baby, you ain't live here. I know ever'body live here. And from the look on your face, you ain't thinkin' to rent. If you knew where you were going, you'd be headed straight there. Instead, you be lookin' all around like somethin' might jump out on you, including me," he said and then paused to survey me. "I'd say you do social work, parole, something like that. Maybe welfare."

"Not bad," I said. "But why Limardo? What made you think I was looking for him?"

He smiled then, his gums showing pink. "We *all* Alvin Limardo 'round here. It's a joke we play. Just a name we take when we jivin' folk. I been Alvin Limardo myself lass week at the food stamp line. He get welfare checks, disability, AFDC. Somebody show up lass week wid a warrant on him. I tole 'em, 'Alvin Limardo's done leff. He gone. Ain't nobody here by that name about now.' The Alvin Limardo you want . . . he be white or black?"

"White," I said and then described the man who'd come into my office on Saturday. The black man started nodding about halfway through, his knife blade still smoothing the surface of the soap. It looked like he'd carved a sow lying on her side with a litter of piglets scrambling over her to nurse. The whole of it couldn't have been more than four inches long.

"That's John Daggett. Whooee. He bad. He the one you want, but he gone for sure."

"Do you have any idea where he went?"

"Santa Teresa, I heard."

"Well, I know he was up there last Saturday. That's where I ran into him," I said. "Has he been back since then?"

The man's mouth drooped with skepticism. "I seen him on Monday and then he gone off again. Only other peoples must want him too. He ack like a man who's runnin' and don't want to be caught. What you want wid him?"

"He wrote me a bum check."

He shot me a look of astonishment. "You take a check from a man like that? Lord God, girl! What's the matter wid you?"

I had to laugh. "I know. It's my own damn fault. I thought maybe I could catch him before he skipped out permanently."

He shook his head, unable to sympathize. "Don't take nothin' from the likes of him. That's your first mistake. Comin' 'round this place may be the next."

"Is there anybody here who might know how to get in touch with him?"

He pointed the blade of his knife toward an apartment two doors down. "Axe Lovella. She might know. Then again, she might not."

"She's a friend of his?"

"Not hardly. She's his wife."

I felt somewhat more hopeful as I knocked at apartment 26. I was afraid he'd moved out altogether. The door was a hollowcore with a hole kicked into the bottom about shin high. The sliding glass window was open six inches, a fold of drapery sticking out. A crack ran diagonally across the pane, held together by a wide band of electrician's tape. I could smell something cooking inside, kale or collard greens, with a whisper of vinegar and bacon grease.

The door opened and a woman peered out at me. Her upper lip was puffy, like the kind of scrape children get falling off bicycles when they first learn to ride. Her left eye had been blackened not long ago and it was streaked now with midnight blue, the surrounding tissue a rainbow of green and yellow and gray. Her hair was the color of hay, parted in the middle and snagged up over each ear with a bobby pin. I couldn't even guess how old she might be. Younger than I expected, given John Daggett's age, which had to be fifty plus.

"Lovella Daggett?"

"That's right." She seemed reluctant to admit that much.

"I'm Kinsey Millhone. I'm looking for John."

She licked uneasily at her upper lip as if she was still unfamiliar with its new shape and size. Some of the scraped area had formed a scab, which resembled nothing so much as half a moustache. "He's not here. I don't know where he's at. What'd you want him for?"

"He hired me to do some work, but he paid me with a bum check. I was hoping we could get it straightened out."

She studied me while she processed the information. "Hired you to do what?"

"Deliver something."

She didn't believe a bit of that. "You a cop?"

"No."

"What are you, then?"

I showed her the photostat of my license by way of reply. She turned and walked away from the door, leaving it open behind her. I gathered this was her method of inviting me in.

I stepped into the living room and closed the door behind me. The carpeting was that green cotton shag so admired by apartment owners everywhere. The only furniture in the room was a card table and two plain wooden chairs. A six-foot rectangle of lighter carpeting along one wall suggested that there'd once been a couch on the spot, and a pattern of indentations in the rug indicated the former presence of two heavy chairs and a coffee table, arranged in what decorators refer to as "a conversational grouping." Instead of conversation these days, Daggett apparently got right down to busting her chops, breaking anything else that came to hand. The one lamp I saw had been snapped off at the socket and the wires were hanging out like torn ligaments.

"Where'd the furniture go?"

"He hocked it all last week. Turns out he used the payments for his bar bill. The car went before that. It was a piece of junk, anyway, but I'd paid for it. You ought to see what I've got for a bed these days. Some peed-on old mattress he found out on the street."

There were two bar stools at the counter and I perched on one, watching as Lovella ambled into the small space that served as a kitchen. An aluminum saucepan sat on a gas flame on the stove, the water in it boiling furiously. On one of the back burners, there was a battered aluminum kettle filled with simmering greens.

Lovella wore blue jeans and a plain white tee shirt wrong-side out, the Fruit of the Loom label visible at the back of her neck. The bottom of the shirt had been pulled tight and knotted to form a halter, leaving her midriff bare. "You want coffee? I was just fixing some."

"Yes, please," I said.

She rinsed a cup under the hot water faucet and gave it a quick swipe with a paper towel. She set it on the counter and spooned instant coffee into it and then used the same paper towel as a potholder when she reached for the saucepan. The water sputtered against the edge of the pan as she poured. She added water to a second cup, gave a quick stir to the contents, and pushed it toward me with the spoon still resting up against the rim.

"Daggert's a jerk. They should lock him up for life," she remarked, almost idly, I thought.

"Did he do that to you?" I asked, my gaze flicking across her bruised face.

She fixed a pair of dead gray eyes on me without bothering to reply. Up close, I could see that she wasn't much more than twenty-five. She leaned forward, resting her elbows on the counter, her coffee cup cradled in her hands. She wasn't wearing a bra and her breasts were big, as soft and droopy as balloons filled with water, her nipples pressing against the tee-shirt fabric like puckered knots. I wondered if she was a hooker. I'd known a few with the same careless sexuality—all surface, no feeling underneath.

"How long have you been married?"

"You care if I have a cigarette?"

"It's your place. You can do anything you want," I said.

That netted me a wan smile, the first I'd seen. She reached for a pack of Pall Mall 100s, flipped on the gas burner, and lit her cigarette from it, tilting her head so her hair wouldn't catch fire. She took a deep drag and exhaled it, blowing a cloud of smoke at me. "Six weeks," she said, answering my question belatedly. "We were pen pals after he got sent to San Luis. Wrote for a year and then I married him the minute he got out. Dumb? Jesus. Can you believe I did that?"

I shrugged noncommittally. She didn't really care if I believed it or not. "How'd you connect in the first place?"

"A buddy of his. Guy named Billy Polo I used to date. They'd sit and talk about women and my name came up. I guess Billy made me sound like real hot stuff, so Daggett got in touch."

I took a sip of my coffee. It had that flat, nearly sour taste of instant, with tiny clumps of coffee powder floating at the edge. "Do you have any milk for this?"

"Oh, sure. Sorry," she said. She moved over to the refrigerator where she took out a small can of Carnation.

It wasn't quite what I had in mind, but I added some to my coffee, intrigued as evaporated milk rose to the surface in a series of white dots. I wondered if a fortune teller could read the pattern, like tea leaves. I thought I spied some indigestion in my future, but I wasn't sure.

"Daggett's a charmer when he wants," she said. "Give him a couple drinks, though, and he's mean as a snake."

14

That was a story I'd heard before. "Why don't you leave?" said I, as I always do.

"Because he'd come after me is why," she said snappishly. "You don't know him. He'd kill me without giving it a second thought. Same thing if I called the cops. Talk back to that man and he'll punch your teeth down your throat. He hates women is what's the matter with him. Of course, when he sobers up, he can charm your socks off. Anyway, I'm hoping he's gone for good. He got a phone call Monday morning and he was out of here like a shot. I haven't heard from him since. Of course, the phone was disconnected yesterday so I don't know how he'd reach me even if he wanted to."

"Why don't you talk to his parole officer?"

"I guess I could," she said reluctantly. "He reports to the guy every time he turns around. For two days he had a job, but he quit that. Of course, he's not supposed to drink. I guess he tried to play by the rules at first, but it was too much."

"Why not get out while you have the chance?"

"And go where? I don't have a nickel to my name."

"There are shelters for battered women. Call the rape crisis center. They'll know."

She gestured dismissively. "Jesus, I love people like you. You ever had a guy punch you out?"

"Not one I was married to," I said. "I wouldn't put up with that shit."

"That's what I used to say, sister, but I'll tell you what. You don't get away as easy as all that. Not with a bastard like Daggett. He swears he'd follow me to the ends of the earth and he would."

"What was he in prison for?"

"He never said and I never asked. Which was also dumb. It didn't make any difference to me at first. He was fine for a couple weeks. Just like a kid, you know? And sweet? Lord, he trotted around after me like a puppy dog. We couldn't get enough of each other and it all seemed just like the letters we wrote. Then he got into the Jack Daniel's one night and the shit hit the fan."

"Did he ever mention the name Tony Gahan?"

"Nuh-uh. Who's he?"

"I'm not sure. Some kid he asked me to find."

"What'd he pay you with? Can I see the check?"

I took it out of my handbag and laid it on the counter. I thought it best not to mention the cashier's check. I didn't think she'd take kindly to his giving money away. "I understand Limardo is a fabricated name."

She studied the check. "Yeah, but Daggett did keep some money in this account. I think he cleaned it out just before he left." She took a drag of her cigarette as she handed back the check. I managed to turn my head before she blew smoke in my face again.

"That phone call he got Monday, what was it about? Do you know?"

"Beats me. I was off at the Laundromat. I got home and he was still on the phone, his face as gray as that dish rag. He hung up quick and then started shovin' stuff in a duffel. He turned the place upside down lookin' for his bank book. I was afraid he'd come after me, thinkin' I took it, but I guess he was too freaked out to worry about me."

"He told you that?"

"No, but he was cold sober and his hands were shaking *bad*."

"You have any idea where he might have gone?"

A look flashed through her eyes, some emotion she concealed by dropping her gaze. "He only had one friend and that was Billy Polo up in Santa Teresa. If he needed help, that's where he'd go. I think he used to have family up there too, but I don't know what happened to them. He never talked much about that."

"So Polo's out of prison?"

"I heard he got out just recently."

"Well, maybe I'll track him down since that's the only lead I have. In the meantime, would you find a phone and call me if you hear from either one?" I took out a business card and jotted my home address and phone on the back. "Call collect."

She looked at both sides of the card. "What do you think is goin' on?"

"I don't know and I don't much care. As soon as I run him down, I'll clean up this business and *bail out.*"

3

As long as I was in the area, I went by the bank. The woman in charge of customer service couldn't have been less helpful. She was dark haired, in her early twenties, and new at the job I gathered because she greeted my every request with the haunted look of someone who isn't quite sure of the rules and therefore says no to everything. She would not verify "Alvin Limardo's" account number or the fact that the account had been closed. She would not tell me if there was, perhaps, another account in John Daggett's name. I knew there had to be a registered copy of the cashier's check itself, but she refused to verify the information he'd given at the time. I kept thinking there was some other tack I might take, especially with that much money at stake. Surely, the bank must care what happened to twenty-five thousand dollars. I stood at the counter and stared at the woman, and she stared back. Maybe she hadn't understood.

I took out the photostat of my license and pointed. "Look," I said, "You see this? I'm a private investigator. I've got a real problem here. I was hired to deliver a cashier's check, but now I can't find the man who gave it to me and I don't know the whereabouts of the person who's supposed to receive it and I'm just trying to get a lead so I can do what I was hired to do."

"I understand that," she said.

"But you won't give me any information, right?"

"It's against bank regulations."

"Isn't it against bank regulations for Alvin Limardo to write me a bad check?"

"Yes."

"Then what am I supposed to do with it?" I said. I really knew the answer . . . eat it, dum-dum . . . but I was feeling stubborn and perverse.

"Take him to small claims court," she said.

"But I can't find him. He can't be hauled into court if nobody knows where he is."

She stared at me blankly, offering no comment.

"What about the twenty-five thousand?" I said. "What am I supposed to do with that?"

"I have no idea."

I stared down at the desk. When I was in kindergarten, I was a biter and I still struggle with the urge. It just feels good, you know? "I want to speak to your supervisor."

"Mr. Stallings? He's gone for the day."

"Well, is there anybody else here who might give me some help on this?"

She shook her head. "I'm in charge of customer service."

"But you're not doing a thing. How can you call it customer service when you don't do shit?"

Her mouth turned prim. "Please don't use language like that around me. It's very offensive."

"What do I have to do to get help around here?"

"Do you have an account with us?"

"If I did, would you help?"

"Not with this. We're not supposed to divulge information about bank customers."

This was silly. I walked away from her desk. I wanted to make a withering remark, but I couldn't think of one. I knew I was just mad at myself for taking the job to begin with, but I was hoping to lay a little ire off on her . . . a pointless enterprise. I got back in my car and headed toward the freeway.

When I reached Santa Teresa, it was 4:35. I bypassed the office altogether and went home. My disposition improved the minute I walked in. My apartment was once a single-car garage and consists now of one room, fifteen feet on a side, with a narrow extension on the right that serves as a kitchenette, separated from the living area by a counter. The space is arranged with cunning: a stackable washer-dryer tucked in beside the kitchenette, bookshelves, drawers and storage compartments built into the wall. It's tidy and self-contained and all of it suits me absolutely. I have a six-foot convertible sofa that I usually sleep on as is, a desk, a chair, an endtable, and plump pillows that serve as additional seating if anyone comes over to sit. My bathroom is one of those preformed fiberglass units with everything molded into it, including a towel bar, a soap holder, and a cutout for a window that looks out at the street. Sometimes I stand in the bathtub, elbows resting on the sill, and stare at passing cars, just thinking how lucky I am. I love being single. It's almost like being rich.

I dropped my handbag on the desk and hung my jacket on a peg. I sat on the couch and pulled off my boots, then padded over to the refrigerator and took out a bottle of white zinfandel and a corkscrew. At intervals, I try to behave like a person with class, which is to say I drink wine from a bottle instead of a cardboard box. I pulled the cork and poured myself a glass. I crossed to the desk, taking the telephone book from the top drawer, trailing telephone cord, directory, and wine glass over to the sofa. I set the wine glass on the endtable and thumbed through the book to see if Billy Polo was listed. Of course, he wasn't. I looked up the name Gahan. No dice. I drank some wine and tried to think what to do next.

On an impulse, I checked for the name Daggett. Lovella had mentioned that he once lived up here. Maybe he still had relatives in town.

There were four Daggetts listed. I started dialing them in

order, saying the same thing each time. "Oh, hi. I'm trying to reach a John Daggett, who used to live in this area. Can you tell me if this is the correct number?"

On the first two calls, I drew a blank, but with the third, the man who answered responded to my query with one of those odd silences that indicate that information is being processed.

"What did you want with him?" he asked. He sounded like he was in his sixties, his phrasing tentative, alert to my response, but undecided how much he was willing to reveal.

He was certainly skipping right down to the tricky part. From everything I'd heard about Daggett, he was a bum, so I didn't dare claim to be a friend of his. If I admitted he owed me money, I was going to have the phone slammed down in my ear. Ordinarily, in a situation like this, I'd insinuate that I had money for *him*, but somehow I didn't think that would fly. People are getting wise to that shit.

I laid out the first lie that occurred to me. "Well, to tell you the truth," I said, "I've only met John once, but I'm trying to get in touch with a mutual acquaintance and I think John has his address and telephone number."

"Who were you looking to get in touch with?"

That caught me off-guard, as I hadn't made that part up yet. "Who? Um . . . Alvin Limardo. Has John ever mentioned Alvin?"

"No, I don't believe so. But, now, you may have the wrong party. The John Daggett that used to live here is currently in prison and he's been there, oh I'd say nearly two years." His manner suggested a man whose retirement has invested even a wrong number with some interesting possibilities. Still, it was clear I'd hit pay dirt.

"That's the one I'm talking about," I said. "He was up in San Luis Obispo."

"He still is."

"Oh, no. He's out. He was released six weeks ago."

"John? *No*, ma'am. He's still in prison and I hope he stays there. I don't mean to speak ill of the man, but you'll find he's what I call a problematic person."

"Problematic?"

"Well, yes. That's how I'd have to put it. John is the type of person that creates problems and usually of a quite serious nature."

"Oh, really," I said. "I didn't realize that." I loved it that this man was willing to chat. As long as I could keep him going, I might figure out how to get a bead on Daggett. I took a flyer. "Are you his brother?"

"I'm his brother-in-law, Eugene Nickerson."

"You must be married to his sister then," I said.

He laughed. "No, he's married to *my* sister. She was a Nickerson before she became a Daggett."

"You're Lovella's brother?" I was trying to picture siblings with a forty-year age span.

"No, Essie's."

I held the receiver away from my ear and stared at it. What was he talking about? "Wait a minute. I'm confused. Maybe we're *not* talking about the same man." I gave a quick verbal sketch of the John Daggett I'd met. I didn't see how there could be two, but there was something going on here.

"That's him all right. How did you say you knew him?"

"I met him last Saturday, right here in Santa Teresa."

The silence on the other end of the line was profound.

I finally broke into it. "Is there some way I might stop by so we can talk about this?"

"I think you'd best," he said. "What would your name be?"

"Kinsey Millhone."

He told me how to get to the place.

The house was white frame with a small wooden porch, tucked into the shadow of Capillo Hill on the west side of town. The street was abbreviated, only three houses on each side before the blacktop petered out into the gravel patch that formed a parking pad beside the Daggett residence. Beyond the house, the hill angled upward into sparse trees and underbrush. No sunlight whatever penetrated the yard. A sagging chicken wire fence cut along the lot lines. Bushes had been planted at intervals, but had failed to thrive, so that now there were only globes of dried twigs. The house had a hangdog look, like a stray being penned up until the dogcatcher comes.

I climbed the steep wooden steps and knocked. Eugene Nickerson opened the door. He was much as I had pictured him: in his sixties, of medium height, with wiry gray hair and eyebrows drawn together in a knot. His eyes were small and pale, his lashes nearly white. Narrow shoulders, thick waist, suspenders, flannel shirt. He carried a Bible in his left hand, his index finger closed between the covers, keeping his place.

Uh-oh, I thought.

"I'll have to ask your name again," he said as he admitted me. "My memory's not what it was."

I shook his hand. "Kinsey Millhone," I said. "Nice to meet you, Mr. Nickerson. I hope I didn't interrupt anything."

"Not at all. We're preparing for our Bible class. We usually get together on Wednesday nights, but our pastor has been down with the flu this week, so the meeting was postponed. This is my sister, Essie Daggett. John's wife," he said, indicating the woman seated on the couch. "You can call me Eugene if you like," he added. I smiled briefly in assent and then concentrated on her.

"Hello. How are you? I appreciate your letting me stop by like this." I moved over and offered my hand. She allowed a few fingers to rest in mine briefly. It was like shaking hands with a Playtex rubber glove.

She was broad-faced and colorless, with graying hair in an unbecoming cut and glasses with thick lenses and heavy plastic frames. She had a wen on the right side of her nose about the size of a kernel of popcorn. Her lower jaw jutted forward aggressively, with protrusive cuspids on either side. She smelled virulently of lilies of the valley.

Eugene indicated that I should have a seat, my choice being the couch where Essie sat, or a Windsor chair with one of the wooden spokes popped out. I opted for the chair, sitting forward slightly so as not to pop anything else. Eugene seated himself in a wicker rocker that creaked under his weight. He took up the narrow purple ribbon hanging out of the Bible and marked his place, then set the book on the table in front of him. Essie had said nothing, her gaze fixed on her lap.

"May I get you a glass of water?" he asked. "We don't hold with caffeinated beverages, but I'd be happy to pour you some 7-Up, if you like."

"I'm fine, thanks," I said. I was seriously alarmed. Being with devout Christians is like being with the very rich. One senses that there are rules at work, some strange etiquette that one might inadvertently breech. I tried to hold bland and harmless thoughts, hoping I wouldn't blurt out any four-letter words. How *could* John Daggett be related to these two?

Eugene cleared his throat. "I was explaining to Essie this confusion we're having over John Daggett's whereabouts. Our understanding is that John is still incarcerated, but now you seem to have a different point of view."

"I'm as baffled as you are," I said. I was thinking fast, wondering how much information I might elicit without giving anything away. As bugged as I was with Daggett, I still didn't feel I should be indiscreet. Not only was there the issue of his being out on parole—there was Lovella. I didn't want to be the one to spill the beans about this new bride of his to a woman he was apparently still married to. "Do you happen to have a picture of him?" I asked. "I suppose it's possible the man I talked to was simply claiming to be your brother-in-law."

"I don't know," Eugene said, dubiously. "It surely sounded like him from what you described."

Essie reached over and picked up a color studio photograph in an ornate silver frame. "This was taken on our thirty-fifth wedding anniversary," she said. Her voice had a nasal cast and a grudging undertone. She passed the photograph to her brother as though he'd never seen it before and might like to have a peek.

"Shortly before John left for San Luis," Eugene amended, passing the photo to me. His tone suggested John was off on a business trip.

I studied the picture. It was Daggett all right, looking as self-conscious as someone in one of those booths where you dress up as a Confederate soldier or a Victorian gent. His collar looked too tight, his hair too slicked down with pomade. His face looked tight too, as if any minute he might cut and run. Essie was seated beside him, as placid as a blancmange. She was wearing what looked like a crepe de chine dress in lilac, with shoulder pads and glass buttons, a big orchid corsage pinned to her left shoulder.

"Lovely," I murmured, feeling guilty and false. It was a terrible picture. She looked like a bulldog and John looked like he was suppressing a fart.

I handed the picture to Essie again. "What sort of crime did he commit?"

Essie inhaled audibly.

"We prefer not to speak of that," Eugene interjected smoothly. "Perhaps you should tell us of your own acquaintance with him."

"Well, of course, I don't know him well. I think I mentioned that on the phone. We have a mutual friend and he's the one I was hoping to get in touch with. John mentioned that he had family in this area and I just took a chance. I'm assuming you haven't spoken to him recently."

Essie shifted on the couch. "We stuck by him as long as we could. The pastor said in his opinion we'd done enough. We don't know what John might be wrestling with in the dark of his soul, but there's a limit to what others can *take*." The edge was there in her voice and I wondered what it was made of: rage, humiliation perhaps, the martyrdom of the meek at the hands of the wretched.

I said, "I gather John's been a bit of a trial."

Essie pressed her lips together, clutching her hands in her lap. "Well, it's just like the Bible says. '*Love* your enemies, *bless* them that curse you, do *good* to them that hate you, and pray for them which despitefully use you and persecute you'!" Her tone was accusatory. She began to rock with agitation.

Whoa, I thought, this lady's heat gauge has shot right up into the red.

Eugene creaked in his chair, snagging my attention with a gentle clearing of his throat. "You said you saw him on Saturday. May I ask what the occasion was?"

I realized then that I should have devoted a lot more time to the fib I'd told because I couldn't think how to respond, I was so unnerved by Essie Daggett's outburst that my mind went blank.

She leaned forward then. "Have you been saved?"

"Excuse me, what?" I said, squinting.

"Have you taken Jesus into your heart? Have you set aside *sin*? Have you *repented*? Have you been washed in the Blood of the *Lamb*?"

A spark of spit landed on my face, but I didn't dare react. "Not lately," I said. What is it about me that attracts women like this?

"Now Essie, I'm sure she didn't come by to ponder the state of her soul," Eugene said. He glanced at his watch. "My goodness, I believe it's time for your medication."

I took the opportunity to rise. "I don't want to take up any more of your time," I said, conversationally. "I really appreciate your help on this and if I need any more information, I'll give you a call." I fumbled in my handbag for a business card and left it on the table.

Essie had kicked into high gear by now. " 'And they shall stone thee with stones, and *thrust* thee through with their swords. And they shall burn thine houses with fire, and execute judgments upon thee in the sight of many women; and I will cause thee to *cease* from playing harlot, and thou also shalt give no hire anymore . . .' "

"Well, okay now, thanks a lot," I called, easing toward the door. Eugene was patting Essie's hands, too distracted to worry about my departure.

I closed the door and trotted back to my car at a quick clip. It was getting dark and I didn't like the neighborhood.

4

Friday morning I got up at 6:00 and headed over to the beach for my run. For much of the summer, I'd been unable to jog because of an injury, but I'd been back at it for two months and I was feeling good. I've never rhapsodized about exercise and I'd avoid it if I could, but I notice the older I get, the more my body seems to soften, like butter left out at room temp. I don't like to watch my ass drop and my thighs spread outward like jodhpurs made of flesh. In the interest of tight-fitting jeans, my standard garb, I jog three miles a day on the bicycle path that winds along the beach front.

The dawn was laid out on the eastern skyline like water-colors on a matte board: cobalt blue, violet, and rose bleeding together in horizontal stripes. Clouds were visible out on the ocean, plump and dark, pushing the scent of distant seas toward the tumbling surf. It was cold and I ran as much to keep warm as I did to keep in shape.

I got back to my apartment at 6:25, showered, pulled on a pair of jeans, a sweater, and my boots, and then ate a bowl of cereal, I read the paper from front to back, noting with interest the weather map, which showed the radiating spiral of a storm sweeping toward us from Alaska. An 80 percent chance of showers was forecast for the afternoon, with scattered showers through the weekend, clearing by Monday night. In Santa Teresa, rain is not a common event, and it takes on a festive air when it comes. My impulse, always, is to shut myself inside and curl up with a good book. I'd just picked up a new Len Deighton novel and I was looking forward to reading it.

At 9:00, reluctantly, I dug out a windbreaker and picked up my handbag, locked the apartment, and headed over to the office. The sun was shining with a brief show of warmth while the bank of charcoal clouds crept in from the islands twenty-six miles out. I parked in the lot and went up the back stairs, passing the glass double doors of California Fidelity, where business was already under way.

I unlocked my office and dropped my bag on the chair. I really didn't have much to do. Maybe I'd put in a little bit of work and then head home again.

My answering machine showed no messages. I sorted through the mail from the day before and then typed up the notes from my visit with Lovella Daggett, Eugene Nickerson, and his sister, Essie. Since no one seemed to know where John Daggett was, I decided I'd try to get a line on Billy Polo instead. I was going to need data for an effective paper search. I put a call through to the Santa Teresa Police Department and asked to be connected to Sergeant Robb.

I'd met Jonah back in June when I was working on a missing persons case. His erratic marital status made a relationship between us inadvisable from my point of view, but I still eyed him with interest. He was what they call Black Irish: dark-haired, blue-eyed, with (perhaps) a streak of masochism. I didn't know him well enough to determine how much of his suffering was of his own devising and I wasn't sure I wanted to find out. Sometimes I think an unconsummated affair is the wisest course, in any event. No hassles, no demands, no disappointments, and both partners keep all their neuroses under wraps. Whatever the surface appearances, most human beings come equipped with convoluted emotional machinery. With intimacy, the wreckage starts to show, damage rendered in the course of passions colliding like freight trains on the same track. I'd had enough of that over the years. I wasn't in any better shape than he was, so why complicate life?

Two rings and the call was picked up.

"Missing Persons, Sergeant Robb."

"Hello, Jonah. It's Kinsey."

"Hey, babe," he said, "What can I do for you that's legal in this state?"

I smiled. "How about a field check on a couple of ex-cons?"

"Sure, no sweat," he said.

I gave him both names and what little information I had. He took it down and said he'd get back to me. He'd fill out a form and have the inquiry run through the National Crime Information Computer, a federal offense since I'm really not entitled to access. Generally, a private investigator has no more rights than the average citizen and relies on ingenuity, patience, and resourcefulness for facts that law enforcement agencies have available as a matter of course. It's a frustrating, but not impossible, state of affairs. I simply cultivate relationships with people plugged into the system at various points. I have contacts at the telephone company, the credit bureau, Southern California Gas, Southern Cal Edison, and the DMV. Occasionally I can make a raid on certain government offices, but only if I have something worthwhile to trade. As for information of a more personal sort, I can usually depend on people's tendencies to rat on one another at the drop of a hat.

I made up a check sheet for Billy Polo and went to work. Knowing Jonah, he'd call Probation and pick up Polo's current address. In the meantime, I wanted to tag some bases of my own. A personal search always pays unexpected dividends. I didn't want to bypass the possibility of surprise, as that's half the fun. I knew Polo wasn't listed in the current phone book, but I tried information, thinking he might have had a phone put in. There was no new listing for him.

I put a call through to my pal at the utility company, inquiring about a possible service connection. Their records showed nothing. Apparently he hadn't applied for water, gas, or electricity in the area in his own name, but he could be renting a room somewhere, paying a flat rate, with utilities thrown in.

I put calls through to five or six fleabag hotels on lower State Street. Polo wasn't registered and nobody seemed to spark to the name. While I was at it, I tried John Daggett's name and got nowhere.

I knew I wouldn't get so much as a by-your-leave from the local Social Security office and I doubted I'd find Billy Polo's name among the voter registration files.

Which left what?

I checked my watch. Only thirty minutes had passed since I talked to Jonah. I wasn't sure how long it would take him to call back and I didn't want to waste time sitting around until I heard from him. I grabbed my windbreaker, locked the office, and went down the front stairs to State Street, walking two blocks over and two blocks up to the public library.

I found an empty table in the reference department and hauled out Santa Teresa telephone directories for the past five years, checking back year by year. Four books back, I found Polo. Great. I made a note of the Merced Street address, wondering if his prison sentence accounted for the absence of a listing since then.

I went over to the section on Santa Teresa history and pulled out the city directory for that year. In addition to an alphabetical listing by name, the city directory lists *addresses* alphabetically so that if you have an address and want to know the resident, you can thumb to the street and number and pick up the name of the occupant and a telephone number. In the back half, telephone numbers are listed sequentially. If all you have is a telephone number, the city directory will provide you with a name and address. By cross referencing the address, you can come up with the name again, an occupation, and the names of neighbors all up and down the same street. In ten minutes, I had a list of seven people who had lived in range of Billy Polo on Merced. By checking for those seven in the current directory, I determined that two were still living there. I jotted down both current telephone numbers, returned the books to their proper places, and headed back toward my office.

The sunlight, intermittent for the last hour, was now largely blocked by incoming clouds which had crowded out blue sky, leaving only an occasional patch, like a hole in a blanket. The air was beginning to cool rapidly, a damp breeze worrying at women's hems. I looked toward the ocean and spotted that silent veil of gray that betokens rain already falling some miles out. I quickened my pace.

Once in my office again, I entered the new information in the file I'd opened. I was just on the verge of closing up for the day when I heard a tap at the door. I hesitated, then crossed to the door and peered out.

There was a woman standing in the corridor, late thirties, expressionless and pale.

"Can I help you?" I said.

"I'm Barbara Daggett."

Quickly, I prayed this wasn't wife number three. I tried the optimistic approach. "John Daggett's daughter?"

"Yes."

She was one of those icy blondes, with skin as finely textured as a percale bedsheet, tall, substantially built, with short coarse hair fanning straight back from her face. She had high cheekbones, a delicate brow, and her father's piercing gaze. Her right eye was green, her left eye blue. I'd seen a white cat like that once and it had had the same disconcerting effect. She was wearing a gray wool business suit and a prim, high-necked white blouse with a froth of lace at the throat. Her heels were a burgundy leather and matched her shoulder bag. She looked like an attorney or a stockbroker, someone accustomed to power.

"Come on in," I said, "I was just trying to figure out how to get in touch with him. I take it your mother told you I stopped by."

I was making small talk. She wasn't having any of it. She sat down, turning those riveting eyes on me as I moved around to my side of the desk and took a seat. I thought of offering her coffee, but I really didn't want her to stay that long. Even the air around her seemed chilly and I didn't like the way she looked at me. I rocked back in my swivel chair. "What can I do for you?"

"I want to know why you're looking for my father."

I shrugged, underplaying it, sticking to the story I'd started with. "I'm not really. I'm looking for a friend of his."

"Why weren't we told Daddy was out of prison? My mother's in a state of collapse. We had to call the doctor and have her sedated."

"I'm sorry to hear that," I said.

Barbara Daggett crossed her legs and smoothed her skirt, her movements agitated. "Sorry? You don't know what this has done to her. She was just beginning to feel safe. Now we find out he's in town somewhere and she's very upset. I don't understand what's going on."

"Miss Daggett, I'm not a parole officer," I said. "I don't know when he got out or why nobody notified you. Your mother's problems didn't start yesterday."

A bit of color came to her cheeks. "That's true. Her problems started the day she married him. He's ruined her life. He's ruined life for all of us."

"Are you referring to his drinking?"

She brushed right over that. "I want to know where he's staying. I have to talk to him."

"At the moment, I have no idea where he is. If I find him, I'll tell him you're interested. That's the best I can do."

"My uncle tells me you saw him on Saturday."

"Only briefly."

"What was he doing in town?"

"We didn't discuss that," I said.

"But what did you talk about? What possible business could he have had with a private detective?"

I had no intention of giving her information, so I tried her technique and ignored the question.

I pulled a legal pad over and picked up a pen. "Is there a number where you can be reached?"

She opened her handbag and took out a business card which she passed across the desk to me. Her office address was three blocks away on State and her title indicated that she was chairman and chief executive officer of a company called FMS.

As if in response to a question, she said, "I develop financial management software systems for manufacturing firms. That's my office number. I'm not listed in the book. If you need to reach me at home, this is the number."

"Sounds interesting," I remarked. "What's your background?"

"I have a math and chemistry degree from Stanford and a double masters in computer sciences and engineering from USC."

I felt my brows lift appreciatively. I couldn't see any evidence that Daggett had ruined *her* life, but I kept the observation to myself. There was clearly more to Barbara Daggett than her professional status indicated. Maybe she was one of those women who succeeds in business and fails in relationships with men. As I'd been accused of that myself, I decided not to make a judgment. Where is it written that being part of a couple is a measure of anything?

She glanced at her watch and stood up. "I have an appointment. Please let me know if you hear from him."

"May I ask what you want with him?"

"I've been urging Mother to file for divorce, but so far she's refused. Maybe I can persuade him instead."

"I'm surprised she didn't divorce him years ago."

Her smile was cold. "She says she married him 'for better or for worse.' To date, there hasn't been any 'better.' Maybe she's hoping for a taste of that before she gives up."

"What about his imprisonment? What was that for?"

Something flickered in her face and I thought at first she wouldn't answer me. "Vehicular manslaughter," she said, finally. "He was drunk and there was an accident. Five people were killed, two of them kids."

I couldn't think of a response and she didn't seem to expect one. She stood up, closed the conversation with a perfunctory handshake, and then she was gone. I could hear her high heels tapping away down the corridor.

5

By the time I closed up the office and got down to my car, the clouds overhead looked like dark gray vacuum cleaner fluff and the rain had begun to splatter the sidewalk with polka dots. I stuck Daggett's file on the passenger seat and backed out of my space, turning right from the parking lot onto Cannon, and right again onto Chapel. Three blocks up, I made a stop, ducking into the supermarket to pick up milk, Diet Pepsi, bread, eggs, and toilet paper. I was into my siege mentality, looking forward to pulling up the drawbridge and waiting out the rain. With luck, I wouldn't have to go out for days.

The phone was ringing as I let myself in. I put the grocery bag on the counter and snatched up the receiver.

"God, I was just about to give up," Jonah said. "I tried the office, but all I got was your answering machine."

"I closed up for the day. I can work at home if I'm in the mood, which I'm not. Have you seen the rain?"

"Rain? Oh yeah, so there is. I haven't even looked out the window since I got in. God, that's great," he said. "Listen, I have some of the information you're looking for and the rest will have to wait. Woody's got a priority request and I had to back off. I'm working tomorrow so I can pick it up then."

"You're working Saturday?"

"I'm filling in for Sobel. My good deed for the week," he said. "Got a pencil? Polo's the one I got a line on."

He rattled out Billy Polo's age, date of birth, height, weight, hair and eye color, his a.k.a, and a hasty rundown of his record, all of which I noted automatically. He'd picked up the name of Billy's parole officer, but the guy was out of the office and wouldn't be available until Monday afternoon.

"Thanks. In the meantime, I'm nosing around on my own," I said. "I bet I'll get a line on him before you do." He laughed and hung up.

I put groceries away and then sat down at my desk, hauling out the little portable Smith-Corona I keep in the knee hole. I consigned the data Jonah'd given me to index cards and then sat and stared at it. Billy Polo, born William Polokowski, was thirty years old, five-foot-eight, a hundred and sixty pounds, brown hair, brown eyes, no scars, tattoos, or "observable physical oddities." His rap sheet sounded like a pop quiz on the California Penal Code, with arrests that ranged from misdemeanors to felonies. Assault, forgery, receiving stolen property, grand theft, narcotics violations. Once he was even convicted of "injuring a public jail," a misdemeanor in this state. Had this occurred in the course of an escape attempt, the charge would have been bumped up to a felony. As it was, he'd probably been caught scratching naughty words on the jail house walls. A real champ, this one.

Apparently, Billy Polo was pretty shiftless when it came to breaking the law and had never even settled on an area of expertise. He'd been arrested sixteen times, with nine convictions, two acquittals, five dismissals. Twice, he'd been put on probation, but nothing seemed to have affected the nature of his behavior, which appeared nearly pathological in its thrust. The man was determined to screw up. Since the age of eighteen, he'd spent an accumulated nine years in jail. No telling what his juvenile record looked like. I assumed his acquaintance with John Daggett dated from his latest offense, an armed robbery conviction, for which he'd served two years and ten months at the California Men's Colony at San Luis Obispo, a medium security facility about ninety miles north of Santa Teresa.

I pulled out the telephone book again and checked for a listing under the name Polokowski. Nothing. God, why can't anything be simple in this business? Oh well. I wasn't going to worry about it for the moment.

By now, I could hear the rain tapping on the glass-enclosed breezeway that connects my place to Henry Pitt's house. He's my landlord and has been for nearly two years. In dry weather, he places an old Shaker cradle out there, filled with rising bread. When the sun is out, the space is like a solar oven, warm and sheltered, dough puffing up above the rim of the cradle like a feather pillow. He can proof twenty loaves at a time, then bake them in the big industrial-sized oven he had installed when he retired from commercial baking. Now he trades fresh bread and pastries for services in the neighborhood and stretches his Social Security payments by clipping coupons avidly. He picks up additional income constructing crossword puzzles which he sells to a couple of those pint-sized "magazines" you can purchase in a supermarket checkout line. Henry Pitt is eighty-one years old and everyone knows I'm half in love with him.

I considered popping over to see him, but even the fifty-foot walk seemed like too much to deal with in the wet. I put some tea water on and picked up my book, stretching out on the sofa with a quilt pulled over me. And that's how I spent the rest of the day.

During the night, the rain escalated and I woke up twice to hear it lashing at the windows. It sounded like somebody spraying the side of the place with a hose. At intervals, thunder rumbled in the distance and my windows flickered with blue light, tree branches illuminated briefly before the room went black again. It was clear I'd have to cancel my 6:00 A.M. run, an obligatory day off, so I burrowed into the depths of my quilt like a little animal, delighted at the idea of sleeping late.

I woke at 8:00, showered, dressed, and fixed myself a soft-boiled egg on toast with lots of Lawry's Seasoned Salt. I'm not going to give up salt. I don't care what they say.

Jonah called as I was washing my plate. He said, "Hey, guess what? Your friend Daggett showed."

I tucked the receiver into the crook of my neck, turning off the water and drying my hands. "What happened? Did he get picked up?"

"More or less. A scruffy drifter spotted him face down in the surf this morning, tangled up in a fishing net. A skiff washed ashore about two hundred yards away. We're pretty sure it connects."

"He died last night?"

"Looks like it. The coroner estimates he went into the water sometime between midnight and five A.M. We don't have a determination yet on the cause and manner of death. We'll know more after the autopsy's done, of course."

"How'd you find out it was him?"

"Fingerprints. He was over at the morgue listed as a John Doe until we ran the computer check. You want to take a look?"

"I'll be right there. What about next of kin? Have they been notified?"

"Yeah, the beat officer went over as soon as we made the I.D. You know the family?"

"Not well, but we've met. I wouldn't want to be quoted on this, but I think you'll find out he's a bigamist. There's a woman down in L.A. who also claims she's married to him."

"Cute. You better come talk to us when you leave St. Terry's," he said and hung up.

The Santa Teresa Police Department doesn't really have a morgue of its own. There's a coroner-sheriff, an elected office in this county, but the actual forensic work is contracted out among various pathologists in the tri-county area. The morgue space itself is divided between Santa Teresa Hospital (commonly referred to as St. Terry's) and the former County General Hospital facility on the frontage road off 101. Daggett was apparently at St. Terry's, which was where I headed as soon as I'd rounded up my slicker, an umbrella, and my handbag.

The visitors' lot at the hospital was half empty. It was Saturday and doctors would probably be making rounds later in the day. The sky was thick with clouds and, high up, I could see the wind whipping through like a fan, blowing white mist across the gray. The pavement was littered with small branches, leaves plastered flat against the ground. Puddles had formed everywhere, pockmarked by the steady rainfall. I parked as close to the rear entrance as I could and then locked my car and made a dash for it.

"Kinsey!"

I turned as I reached the shelter of the building. Barbara Daggett hurried toward me from the far side of the lot, her umbrella tilted against the slant of the rain. She was wearing a raincoat and spike-heeled boots, her white-blonde hair forming a halo around her face. I held the door open for her and we ducked into the foyer.

"You heard about my father?"

"That's why I'm here. Do you know how it happened?"

"Not really. Uncle Eugene called me at eight-fifteen. I guess they tried to notify Mother and he interceded. The doctor has her so doped up it doesn't make any sense to tell her yet. He's worried about how she'll take it, as unstable as she is."

"Is your uncle coming down?"

She shook her head. "I said I'd do it. There's no doubt it's Daddy, but somebody has to sign for the body so the mortuary can come pick it up. Of course, they'll autopsy first. How did you find out?"

"Through a cop I know. I'd told him I was trying to get a line on your father, so he called me when they got a match on the fingerprints. Did you manage to locate him yesterday?"

"No, but it's clear someone did." She closed her umbrella and gave it a shake, then glanced at me. "Frankly, I'm assuming somebody killed him."

"Let's not be too quick off the mark," I said, though privately, I agreed.

The two of us moved through the inner door and into the corridor. The air was warmer here and smelled of latex paint.

"I want you to look into it for me, in any event," she said.

"Hey, listen. That's what the police are for. I don't have the scope for that. Why don't you wait and see what they have to say first?"

She studied me briefly and then moved on. "They don't give a damn what happened to him. Why would they care? He was a drunken bum."

"Oh come on. Cops don't have to *care*," I said. "If it's homicide, they have a job to do and they'll do it well."

When we reached the autopsy room, I knocked and a young black morgue attendant came out, dressed in surgical greens. His name tag indicated that his name was Hall Ingraham. He was lean, his skin the color of pecan wood with a high-gloss finish. His hair was cropped close and gave him the look of a piece of sculpture, his elongated face nearly stylized in its perfection.

"This is Barbara Daggett," I said.

He looked in her direction without meeting her eyes. "You can wait right down here," he said. He moved two doors down and we followed, pausing politely while he unlocked a viewing room and ushered us in.

"It'll be just a minute," he said.

He disappeared and we took a seat. The room was small, maybe nine by nine, with four blue molded-plastic chairs hooked together at the base, a low wooden table covered with old magazines, and a television screen affixed, at an angle, up in one corner of the room. I saw her gaze flick to it.

"Closed circuit," I said. "They'll show him up there."

She picked up a magazine and began to flip through it distractedly. "You never really told me why he hired you," she said. An ad for pantyhose had apparently caught her eye and she studied it as if my reply were of no particular concern.

I couldn't think of a reason not to tell her at this point, but I noticed that I censored myself to some extent, a habit of long standing. I like to hold something back. Once information is out, it can't be recalled so it's better to exercise caution before you flap your mouth. "He wanted me to find a kid named Tony Gahan," I said.

That remarkable two-toned gaze came up to meet mine and I found myself trying to decide which eye color I preferred. The green was more unusual, but the blue was clear and stark. The two together presented a contradiction, like the signal at a street corner, flashing Walk and Don't Walk simultaneously.

"You know him?" I asked.

"His parents and a younger sister were the ones killed in the accident, along with two other people in the car with them. What did Daddy want with him?"

"He said Tony Gahan helped him once when he was on the run from the cops. He wanted to thank him."

Her look was incredulous. "But that's bullshit!"

"So I gather," I said.

She might have pressed for more information, but the television screen flashed with snow at that moment and then flipped over to a closeup of John Daggett. He was lying on a gurney, a sheet neatly pulled up to his neck. He had the blank, plastic look that death sometimes brings, as if the human face were no more than an empty page on which the lines of emotion and experience are transcribed and then erased. He looked closer to twenty years old than fifty-five, with a stubble of beard and hair carelessly arranged. His face was unmarked.

Barbara stared at him, her lips parting, her face diffused with pink. Tears rose in her eyes and hung there, captured in the well of her lower lids. I looked away from her, unwilling to intrude any more than I had to. The morgue attendant's voice reached us through the intercom.

"Let me know when you're done."

Barbara turned away abruptly.

"Thank you. That's fine," I called. The television screen went dark.

Moments later, there was a tap at the door and he reappeared with a sealed manila envelope and a clipboard in hand.

"We'll need to know what arrangements you want made," he said. He was using that tone of studied neutrality I've heard before from those who deal with the bereaved. Its effect is impersonal and soothing, liberating one to transact business without intrusive emotionalism. He needn't have bothered. Barbara Daggett was a businesswoman, bred to that awesome poise that so unsettles men accustomed to female subservience. Her manner now was smooth and detached, her tone as impassive as his.

"I've talked to Wynington-Blake," she said, indicating one of the funeral homes in town. "If you'll notify them once the autopsy's done, they'll take care of everything. Is that form for me?"

He nodded and held the clipboard out to her with a pen attached. "A release for his personal effects," he said.

She dashed off a signature as if she were signing an autograph for a pesky fan. "When will you have the autopsy results?"

He handed her the envelope, which apparently contained Daggett's odds and ends. "Probably by late afternoon."

"Who's doing the post?" I asked.

"Dr. Yee. He's scheduled it for two-thirty."

Barbara Daggett glanced at me. "She's a private investigator. I want all information released to her. Will I need to sign a separate authorization for that?"

"I don't know. There's probably some procedure, but it's a new one on me. I can check into it and contact you later, if you like."

She slipped her business card under the clamp as she handed the clipboard back to him. "Do that."

His eyes met hers for the first time and I could see him register the oddity of the mismatched irises. She brushed past him, moving out of the room. He stared after her. The door closed.

I held my hand out. "I'm Kinsey Millhone, Mr. Ingraham."

He smiled for the first time. "Oh yeah. I heard about you from Kelly Borden. Nice to meet you."

Kelly Borden was a morgue attendant I'd met during a homicide investigation I'd worked on in August.

"Nice to meet you too," I said. "What's the story on this one?"

"I can't tell you much. They brought him in about seven, just as I was coming to work."

"Do you have any idea how long he'd been dead?"

"I don't know for sure, but it couldn't have been long. The body wasn't bloated and there wasn't any putrefaction. From what I've seen of drowning victims, I'd guess he went in the water late last night. Don't quote me on that. The watch he had on was stopped at two thirty-seven, but it could have been broken. It's a crummy watch and looks all beat up. It's in with his effects. Hell, what do I know? I'm just a flunkie, lowest of the low. Dr. Yee hates it if we talk to people like this."

"Believe me, I'm not going to say anything. I'm just asking for my own purposes. What about his clothing? How was he dressed?"

"Jacket, pants, shirt."

"Shoes and socks?"

"Well, shoes. He didn't have socks on and he didn't have a wallet or anything like that."

"Any signs of injury?"

44

"None that I've seen."

I couldn't think of anything else I wanted to ask for the moment so I thanked him and said I'd be in touch.

Then I went out to look for Barbara Daggett. If I was going to work for her, we needed to get business squared away.

6

I found her standing in the foyer, looking out at the parking lot. The rain was falling monotonously, occasional gusts of wind tossing the treetops. Cozy-looking lights were on in all the buildings that rimmed the parking lot, which only emphasized the dampness and the chill outside. A nurse, her white uniform flashing from the flaps of a dark blue raincoat, approached the doorway, leaping over puddles like a kid playing hopscotch. Her white hose were speckled with flesh-colored blotches where the rain had soaked through and the tops of her white shoes were spattered with mud. She reached the entrance and I held the door for her.

She flashed me a smile. "Whoo! Thanks. It's like an obstacle course out there." She shook the water from her raincoat and padded down the hallway, crepe soles leaving a pattern of damp footprints in her wake.

Barbara Daggett seemed rooted to the spot. "I have to go to Mother's," she said. "Somebody has to tell her." She turned and looked at me. "How much do you charge for your services?"

"Thirty an hour, plus expenses, which is standard for the area. If you're serious, I can drop a contract off at your office this afternoon."

"What about a retainer?"

I made a quick assessment. I usually ask for an advance, especially in a situation like this, when I know I'll be talking to the cops. There's no concept of privilege between a P.I.

and a client, but at least the front money makes it clear where my loyalties lie.

"Four hundred should cover it," I said. I wondered if the figure came to mind because of Daggett's bounced check. Oddly enough, I felt protective of him. He'd conned me—there was no doubt of that—but I *had* agreed to work for him, and in my mind, I still had a duty to discharge. Of course, I might not have felt as charitable if he were still alive, but the dead are defenseless, and somebody in this world has to look out for them.

"I'll have my secretary cut you a check first thing Monday morning," she said. She turned back, looking out the double doors into the gloom. She leaned her head against the glass.

"Are you okay?"

"You don't know how many times I've wished him dead," she said. "Have you ever dealt with an alcoholic?"

I shook my head.

"They're so maddening. I used to look at him and I was convinced he could quit drinking if he wanted to. I don't know how many times I talked to him, begging him to stop. I thought he didn't understand. I thought he just wasn't aware of what we were going through, my mother and me. I can remember the look he'd get in his eyes when he was drunk. Little pink piggy eyes. His whole body radiated this odor. Bourbon. God, I hate that stuff. He smelled like somebody'd dropped a bottle of Early Times down a heater vent . . . waves of smell. He reeked of it."

She looked over at me, her eyes dry and pitiless. "I'm thirty-four and I've hated him with every cell in my body for as long as I can remember. And now I'm stuck with it. He won, didn't he? He never changed, never straightened up, never gave us an inch. He was such a shitheel. It makes me want to smash this glass door out. I don't even know why I care how he died.

I should be relieved, but I'm pissed. The irony is that he's probably still going to dominate my life."

"How so?"

"Look what he's done to me already. I think of him every time I have a drink. I think of him if I decide *not* to have a drink. If I even *meet* a man who drinks or if I see a bum on the street or smell bourbon, his face is the first thing that comes to mind. Oh God, and if I'm around someone who's had too much, I can't stand it. I disconnect. My life is filled with reminders of him. His apologies and his phony, wheedling charm, his boo-hooing when the booze got to him. The times he fell, the times he got put in jail, the times he spent every dime we had. When I was twelve, Mother got religion and I don't know which was worse. At least Daddy woke up most days in okay shape. She had Jesus for breakfast, lunch, and dinner. It was grotesque. And then there were the joys of being an only child."

She broke off abruptly and seemed to shake herself. "Oh hell. What difference does it make? I know I sound sorry for myself, but it's been such a bitch and there's no end in sight."

"Actually, you look like you've done pretty well," I said.

She turned her gaze back to the parking lot and I could see her faint, bitter smile reflected in the glass. "You know what they say about living well as the best revenge. I did well because it was the one defense I had. Escape has been the motivating force in my life. Getting away from him, getting away from her, putting that household behind me. The funny thing is, I haven't moved an inch, and the harder I run, the faster I keep slipping back to them. There are spiders that work like that. They bury themselves and create a little pocket of loose dirt. Then when their prey comes along, the soil gives way and the victim slides right down into the trap. There are laws for everything except the harm families do."

She turned, shoving her hands down in her raincoat pockets. She pushed the door open with her backside and a draft of cold air rushed in. "What about you? Are you leaving or will you stick around?"

"I guess I'll hit the office as long as I'm out," I said.

She pressed a button on the handle of her umbrella and it lifted into the open position with a muffled *thunk*. She held it for me and we walked toward my car together. The raindrops tapping on the umbrella fabric made a muted sound, like popcorn in a covered saucepan.

I unlocked my car and got in, while she moved off toward hers, calling back over her shoulder. "Try me at the office as soon as you hear anything. I should be there by two."

My office building was deserted. California Fidelity is closed on weekends so their offices were dark. I let myself in, picking up the batch of morning mail that had been shoved through the slot. There were no messages on my answering machine. I pulled a contract out of my top drawer and spent a few minutes filling in the blanks. I checked Barbara Daggett's business card to verify the address, then I locked up again and went down the front stairs.

I walked the three blocks and dropped the contract off at her office, then headed over to the police station on Floresta. The combination of the weekend and the bad weather lent the station much the same deserted air as my office building. Crime doesn't adhere to a forty-hour week, but there are days when even the criminals don't seem to feel like doing much. The linoleum showed a gridwork of wet footprints, like a pattern of dance steps too complex to learn. The air smelled of cigarette smoke and damp uniforms. I could see where someone had fashioned a folded newspaper into a rain hat and then abandoned it on the wooden bench just inside the door.

One of the clerks in the identification and records section buzzed Jonah and he came out to the locked foyer door and admitted me.

He wasn't looking good. During the summer, he'd shed an excess twenty pounds and he'd told me he was still working out at the gym, so it wasn't that. His dark hair seemed poorly trimmed and the lines around his eyes were pronounced. He also had that weary aura that unhappiness seems to breed.

"What happened to you?" I asked as we walked back to his office. He'd been reconciled with his wife since June, after a year's separation, and from what I'd gathered, it was not going well.

"She wants an open relationship," he remarked.

"Oh come *on*," I said, with disbelief.

That netted me a tired smile. "That's what the lady says." He held the door open for me and we passed into an L-shaped room, furnished with big wooden desks.

Missing Persons is included in Crimes Against Persons, which in turn is considered part of the Investigations Division, along with Crimes Against Property, Narcotics, and Special Investigations. The room was deserted at the moment, but people came and went at intervals. From the interview room off the inside corridor, I could hear the rise and fall of a shrill female voice and I guessed that an interrogation was under way. Jonah closed the hall door, automatically protective of department business.

He filled two Styrofoam cups with coffee and brought them over, handing me packets of Cremora and Equal. Just what I needed, a cup of hot chemicals. We went through the motions of doctoring the coffee, which smelled like it'd been on the burner too long.

I took a few minutes to lay out the Daggett situation. At this point, we didn't have the results of the autopsy, so the idea of murder was purely theoretical. Still, I told Jonah what had gone on to date, detailing the principal characters. I was talking to him as a friend instead of a cop and he listened as an interested, but unofficial, party.

"So how long was he up here before he died?" Jonah asked.

"Since Monday presumably," I said. "It's possible he went

somewhere else first, but Lovella seemed to think he'd head straight for Billy Polo if he needed help."

"Did that information on Polo do you any good?"

"Not yet, but it will. I'm just waiting to see what we've got on our hands before I proceed. Even if the death was accidental, I suspect Barbara Daggett will want me to look into it. I mean, for starters, what was he doing on a boat in a rainstorm? And where has he been all this time?"

"Where have *you* been?" Jonah asked.

I focused on him and realized he'd shifted the subject. "Who, me? I've been around."

He picked up a pencil and began to tap out a beat, like a man auditioning for a tiny blues band. He was giving me a look I'd seen before, full of heat and speculation. "Are you dating anyone?"

I shook my head, smiling slightly. "The only good men I know are married." I was being flirtatious and he seemed to like that.

His blue eyes locked into mine and the color rose in his face. "What do you do for sex?"

"Jog on the beach. How about you?"

He smiled, breaking off eye contact. "In other words, it's none of my business."

I laughed. "I'm not avoiding the question. I'm telling the truth."

"Really? That's funny. I always pictured you out raising hell."

"I did some of that years ago, but I can't stand it these days. Sex is a bonding process. I'm careful who I connect up with. Besides, you don't know what the marketplace is like. A one-night stand is more like a wrestling match with a couple of quick take-downs. Talk about demoralizing. I'd rather be alone."

"I know what you mean. I was out there hustling some the year she was gone, but I never got the hang of it. I'd go in a bar and some babe would sidle up to me, but I never made the right moves. Couple of times, women told me I was rude when I just thought I was making small talk."

"It's worse if you're successful at it," I said. "Be grateful you never learned the gamesmanship. I know a couple of guys on the circuit and they're hard as nails, you know? Unhappy. Hostile toward women. They get laid, but that's about all they get."

Behind him, Lieutenant Becker came in and took a seat at a desk across the room. Jonah's pencil tapping started again and then stopped. He tossed it aside and rocked back in his chair.

"I wish life were simple," he said.

I kept my tone of voice mild. "Life *is* simple. You're the one making things complex. You were doing great without Camilla, as far as I could see. She crooks her finger, though, and you go running back. And now you can't figure out what went wrong. Quit acting like a victim when you did it to yourself."

This time he laughed. "God, Kinsey. Why don't you just say what's on your mind."

"Well, I don't understand voluntary suffering. If you're unhappy, change something. If you can't make it work, then bail out. What's the big deal?"

"Is that what you did?"

"Not quite. I dumped the first and the second one dumped me. With both, I did my share of suffering, but when I look back on it, I can't understand why I endured so long. It was dumb. It was a big waste of time and cost me a lot."

"I've never even heard you mention those guys."

"Yeah, well I'll tell you about them sometime."

"You want to have a drink when I get off work?"

I looked at him briefly and then shook my head. "We'd end up in bed, Jonah."

"That's the point, isn't it?" He smiled and did a Groucho Marx wiggle with his eyebrows.

I laughed and turned the subject back to Daggett as I got up. "Call me when Dr. Yee has results on the post."

"I'll call for more than that."

"Get your life squared away first."

When I left, he was still staring after me, and it was all I could do to get out of there. I had this troubling urge to gallop over and leap onto his lap, laughing while I covered his face with licks, but I didn't think the department would ever be the same. As I glanced back, I could see Becker giving us a speculative look while he pretended to check his "in" box.

7

Daggett's death was ruled accidental. Jonah called me at home at 4:00 to give me the news. I'd spent the afternoon again wrapped up in a quilt, hoping to finish the book. I'd just put on a fresh pot of coffee and I was scurrying back under the covers as the phone rang. When he told me, I was puzzled, but I wasn't convinced. I kept waiting for the punchline, but there wasn't one.

"I don't get it," I said. "Does Yee know the background on this?"

"Babe, Daggett's blood alcohol was point three-five. You're talking acute ethanol intoxication, almost coma stage."

"And that was the cause of death?"

"Well no, he drowned, but Yee says there's no evidence of foul play. None. Daggett went out in a boat, got tangled up in a fishing net, and fell overboard, too drunk to save himself."

"Bullshit!"

"Kinsey, some people die accidentally. It's a fact."

"I don't believe it. Not this one."

"The crime scene investigation unit didn't find a thing. Not even a *hint*. What can I say? You know these guys. They're as good as they come. If you think it's murder, come up with some evidence. In the meantime, we're calling it an accident. As far as we're concerned, the case is closed."

"What was he doing dead drunk in a boat?" I asked. "The man was broke and it was raining cats and dogs. Who'd he rent the boat from?"

I could hear Jonah sigh. "He didn't. Apparently, he took

a little ten-foot skiff from its mooring off the dock at Marina One. The harbor master identified the boat and you can see where the line was cut."

"Where'd they find it?"

"On the beach near the pier. There weren't any usable prints."

"I don't like it."

"Look, I know what you're saying and you've got a point. I tend to agree, if that makes you feel any better, but who's asking us? Look at it as a gift. If the death is ruled a homicide, you can't get near it. This way, you've got carte blanche . . . within limits, of course."

"Does Dolan know I'm interested?" Lieutenant Dolan was an assistant division commander and an old antagonist of mine. He hated private investigators getting involved in police business.

"The case is Feldman's. He won't give a shit. You want me to talk to him?"

"Yeah, do that," I said. "And clear it with Dolan, while you're at it. I'm tired of getting my hand smacked."

"Okay. I'll get back to you first thing Monday then," Jonah said. "In the meantime, let me know if anything turns up."

"Right. Thanks."

I put a call through to Barbara Daggett, repeating the information I'd just received. When I finished, she was silent.

"What do you think?" she asked, finally.

"Let's put it this way. *I'm* not satisfied, but it's your money. If you like, I can nose around for a couple of days and if nothing turns up, we'll dump the whole business and you'll just have to live with it."

"What are the odds?"

"I have no idea. All I know to do is pick up a thread and see where it leads. We may come up with six dead ends, but at least you'll know we gave it a shot."

"Let's do it."

"Great. I'll be in touch."

I pushed the quilt aside and got up. I hoped Billy Polo was still around. I didn't know where else to start.

I unplugged the coffeepot, poured the balance of the coffee into a thermos, and then made myself a peanut butter and dill pickle sandwich, which I put in a brown paper bag like a school kid. I had just about that same feeling in my gut too . . . the dull dread I'd experienced when I was eight, trudging off to Woodrow Wilson Elementary. I didn't want to go out in the rain. I didn't want to connect up with Billy Polo, who was probably a creep. He sounded like one of the sixth-grade boys I'd been so fearful of . . . lawless, out of control, and mean.

I searched through my closet until I found my slicker and an umbrella. I left my warm apartment behind and drove over to Billy Polo's old address on Merced. It was 4:15 and getting prematurely dark. The neighborhood had probably been charming once, but it was gradually being overtaken by apartment buildings and was now no more than a hapless mix of the down-at-the-heel and the bland. The little gingerbread structures were wedged between three-story stucco boxes with tenant parking underneath and everywhere there was evidence of the same tasteless disregard for history.

I parked under a pepper tree, using the overhanging branches as brief shelter while I put up my umbrella. I checked the names and house numbers of the two former neighbors, hoping one of them could give me a lead on Polo's current whereabouts.

The first door I knocked on was answered by an elderly woman in a wheelchair, her legs wrapped in Ace bandages and stuffed into lace-up shoes with slices cut out of the sides to accommodate her bunions. I stood on her leaky front porch, talking to her through the screen door, which she kept latched. She had a vague recollection of Billy, but had no idea what had happened to him or where he'd gone. She did direct me to a little rental unit at the rear of the property next door. This was not one of the addresses I'd picked up from the city directory. She said Billy's family had lived in the front house, while the rear was still occupied by an old gent named Talbot, who had been there for the last thirty years. I thanked her and picked my way down the rain-slicked stairs and back along the driveway.

The front unit must have been one of the early houses in the area—a story and a half of white frame, with a peaked roof, two dormers, and a front porch that was screened in now and furnished with junk. I could see the coils on the backside of an old refrigerator and beside it, what looked like a pillar of milk cartons, filled with paperback books. Hydrangeas and bougainvillea grew together in a tangle along the side of the house and the runoff from the rain gutter threw a gush of water out on the drive, forcing me to cut wide to the right.

The rear unit looked like it was originally a tool shed, with a lean-to attached to the left side and a tiny carport on the right. There was no car visible and most of the sheltered space was taken up by a cord of firewood, stacked against the wall. There was room left for a bicycle maybe, but not much else.

The structure was white frame, propped up on cinderblocks, with a window on either side of a central door, and a tiny chimney poking up through the roof. It looked like the drawing we all did in grade school, even to the smoke curling up from the chimney pipe.

I knocked and the door was opened by a wizened old man with no teeth. His mouth was a wide line barely separating the tip of his nose from the upward thrust of his chin. When he caught sight of me and realized that I was no one he knew, he left the doorway briefly and returned with his dentures, smiling slightly as he shifted them into place. His false teeth made a crunching sound like a horse chewing on a bit. He looked to be in his seventies, frail, his pale skin speckled with red and blue. His white hair was brushed into a pompadour in front, shaggy over his ears and touching his collar in the back. He wore a shirt that looked soft from years of washing and a cardigan sweater that probably belonged to a woman at some point. The buttons were rhinestone and the button-holes were on the wrong side. He smoothed his hair back with a trembling hand and waited to see what I could possibly want.

"Are you Mr. Talbot?"

"Depends on who's asking," he said.

"I'm Kinsey Millhone. The woman next door suggested that I talk to you. I'm looking for Billy Polo. His family lived in that front house about five years ago."

"I know Billy quite well. Why are you looking for him?"

"I need some information about a friend of his," I said and then gave him a brief explanation. I couldn't see any reason to prevaricate so I simply stated my purpose and left it at that.

He blinked at me. "Billy Polo's a very bad fella. I wonder if you're aware of that." His voice was powdery and I noticed that he had a tremor, his head oscillating as he spoke. I guessed that he suffered from some form of parkinsonism.

"Yeah, I am. I heard he was up at the California Men's Colony until recently. I think that's where he met the man I'm referring to. Do you have any idea how I might reach him?"

"Well, you know, his mother is the one who owned that place," he said, nodding toward the front house. "She sold it about two years ago when she remarried."

"Is she still here in town?"

"Yes, and I believe she's living on Tranvia. Her married name is Christopher. Just a minute and I'll give you the address." He shuffled away and a few moments later was back with a small address book in hand. "She's a lovely woman. Sends me a card every year at Christmastime. Yes, here it is.

Bertha Christopher. Goes by the nickname of Betty. If you chance to see her, I wish you'd give her my best."

"I'll do that, Mr. Talbot. Thanks so much."

Tranvia turned out to be a wide, treeless street off Milagro on the east side of town, a neighborhood of one-story frame houses on small lots, with chicken wire fences, unruly head-high poinsettia bushes pelted by the rain, and soggy children's toys abandoned in driveways paved with parallel strips of concrete. The level of maintenance here seemed erratic, but the address I now had for Bertha Christopher showed one of the better-kept houses on the block, mustard-colored with dark brown trim. I parked my VW on the opposite side of the street, about fifty yards away, so I could sit and watch the place inconspicuously. Most of the parked cars were crummy so mine fit right in.

It was now after 5:00 and the light was fading fast, the chill in the air more pronounced. The rain had eased somewhat so I left my umbrella where it was. I grabbed my yellow slicker and slipped into it, pulling up the hood. I locked the car and crossed the street, splashing through puddles that darkened the leather of my boots. The rain drummed against the fabric of the slicker with a pocking sound that made me feel like I was in a pup tent.

The Christopher property was surrounded by a low rock wall, constructed with sandstone boulders the size of canta-loupes, held together with concrete. A row of hanging plant-ers screened the front windows from the street and a set of glass windchimes, suspended in one corner of the porch, tin-kled with the wind. There were two lightweight aluminum lawn chairs arranged on either side of a metal table. Every-thing was soggy and smelled of wet grass.

There was no doorbell, but I tapped on the pane of glass in the front door, cupping a hand so I could peer in. The interior was in shadow, no lights showing from the rear of the house. I moved to the porch rail and checked the adjacent houses, both of which were dark. My guess was that many of these people were off at work. After a few minutes, I went back to my car.

I started the engine and ran the heater for a while, fogging up the windows until I could barely see. I rubbed a clear spot in the middle of the windshield and then sat and stared. Streetlights came on. At 5:45, I ate my sandwich just for something to do. At 6:15, I drank some coffee and flipped on my car radio, listening to a talk-show host interview a psychic. Fifteen minutes later, right after the 6:30 news, a car approached and slowed, turning into the Christophers' driveway.

A woman got out, dimly illuminated by the street light. She paused as if to raise her umbrella and then apparently decided to make a dash for it. I watched her scuttle up the driveway and around toward the back of the house. Moments later, the lights went on in sequence . . . first the rear left room, probably a kitchen, then the living room, and finally the front porch light. I gave her a few minutes to get her coat hung up and then I returned to her front door.

I knocked again. I could see her peer into the hallway from the rear of the house and then approach the front door. She stared at me blankly, then leaned her head close to the glass for a better look.

She appeared to be in her fifties, with a sallow complexion and a deeply creased face. Her hair was too uniform a shade to be a natural brown. She wore it parted on the side with big puffy bangs across her lined forehead. Her eyes were the size and color of old pennies and her makeup looked like it needed renewing at this hour of the day. She wore a uniform I'd seen before, brown pants and a brown-and-yellow-checked tunic. I couldn't place the outfit offhand.

"Yes?" she called through the glass.

I raised my voice against the sound of the rain. "I'm looking for Billy. Is he back yet?"

"He don't live here, hon, but he said he'd be by at eight o'clock. Who are you?"

I picked a name at random. "Charlene. Are you his mother?"

"Charlene who?"

"A friend of his said I should look him up if I was ever in Santa Teresa. Is he at work?"

She gave me an odd look, as if the notion of Billy working had never crossed her mind. "He's out checking the used car lots for an automobile."

She had one of those faces that seemed tantalizingly familiar and it dawned on me, belatedly, that she was a checker at the supermarket where I shop now and then. We'd even chatted idly about the fact that I was a P.I. I eased back out of the porch light, hoping she hadn't recognized me at the same time I recognized her. I held the corner of the slicker up as though to shield my face from the wind.

She seemed to pick up on the fact that something odd was going on. "What'd you want him for?"

I ignored that, pretending I couldn't hear. "Why don't I come back when he gets home?" I hollered. "Just tell him Charlene stopped by and I'll catch up with him when I can."

"Well, all right," she said reluctantly. I gave her a casual wave as I turned. I went down the porch steps and into the dark, aware that she was peering after me suspiciously. I must have disappeared from her field of vision then because she turned the porch light off.

I got back in my car with one of those quick, involuntary shudders that racks you from head to toe. When I caught up with Billy, I might well admit who I was and what I wanted with him, but for the moment, I didn't want to tip my hand. I checked my watch and settled in, prepared to wait. Already, it was feeling like a long night.

8

Four hours passed. The rain stopped. It became apparent that Billy was not only late, but possibly not coming at all. Maybe he'd bought a car and hightailed it out of town, or maybe at some point he'd phoned his mother and decided to skip the visit when he heard about "Charlene." I finished all the coffee in the thermos, my brain fairly crackling from caffeine. If I smoked cigarettes, I could have gone through a pack. Instead, I listened to eight more installments of the news, the farm report, and an hour of Hispanic music. I pondered the possibility of learning the Spanish language by simply listening to these gut-wrenching tunes. I thought about Jonah and the husbands I'd known. Surely, if my heart broke again, it would sound just like this, though for all I knew, the lyrics were about cut worms and inguinal hernias, matters only made soulful through soaring harmonies. Altogether, I came perilously close to boring myself insensible with my own mental processes, so it was with real relief that I saw the car approach and pull into the curb in front of the house across the street. It looked like a 1967 Chevrolet, white, with a temporary registration sticker on the windshield. I couldn't tell much about the guy who got out, but I watched with interest as he took the porch steps in two bounds and rang the bell.

Betty Christopher came to the door to let him in. The two of them disappeared. A moment later, shadows wavered against the kitchen light. I figured they'd sit down for a couple of beers and a heart-to-heart talk. The next thing I knew, however, the front door opened again and he came out. I slipped down on the car seat until my eyes were level with the bottom of the window. The cloud cover was still heavy, obscuring the moon, and the cars along the curb created deeper shadows still. He stared out at the street, taking in the line of parked cars one by one. I felt my heart start to thump as I watched him come down the steps and head in my direction.

He paused in the middle of the street. He moved over to a van parked two cars away from mine. He flicked on a flashlight and opened the door on the driver's side, apparently to check the registration. I lost sight of him. Moments went by. I watched the shadows, wondering if he'd crept around the other side and was coming up on my right. I heard a muffled sound as he closed the door to the van. The beam from his flashlight swept over the car in front of me and flashed across my windshield, the light too diffused by the time it reached me to illuminate much. He flicked it off. He waited, scanning the street on both sides. Apparently, he decided there was nothing to worry about. He crossed back to the house. As he reached the porch, she came out, clutching a robe around her. They talked for a few minutes and then he got in his car and took off. The minute she went inside, I started the VW and did a big U-turn, following. I hoped this wasn't all some elaborate ruse to flush me into the open.

He had already made a left turn and then a right by the time I caught sight of him two blocks ahead of me. We were driving along the back streets with no traffic lights at all and only an occasional stop sign to slow our progress. I had to close the gap or risk losing him. A "one-man" tail is nearly pointless unless you know who you're following and where he's going to begin with. At this hour, there were very few cars on the road, and if he drove far, he'd realize the presence of my VW was no accident.

I thought he was headed toward the freeway, but before he reached the northbound on-ramp, he slowed and made a right-hand turn. By then, I was only half a block back so I whipped over to the curb and parked, killing the engine. I locked the car and took off on foot, heading diagonally across the corner lot at a dead run. I caught sight of his taillights half a block ahead. The car was making a left-hand turn into a shabby trailer park.

Puente is a narrow street that parallels Highway 101 on the east side of town, with the trailer park itself squeezed into the space between the two roadways, screened off from the highway by a ten-foot board fence and masses of oleander. I was covering ground at a quick clip. The houses I passed were dark, driveways crowded with old cars, most of them sporting dents. The street lighting here was poor, but ahead of me I caught traces of light from the trailer park, which was strung with small multicolored bulbs.

By the time I got to the entrance, there was no sign of the Chevrolet, but the place was small and I didn't think the car would be hard to spot. The road twisting through the trailer park was two lanes wide. The blacktop still glistened from the rain and water was dripping from the eucalyptus trees that towered at intervals. There were signs posted everywhere: SLOW. SPEED BUMPS. TENANT PARKING ONLY. DO NOT BLOCK DRIVEWAY.

Most of the trailers were "single-wides," fifteen to twenty feet long, the kind that once upon a time you could actually hitch to your car and travel in. Nomad, Airstream, and Concord seemed to predominate. Each had a numbered cardboard sign in the window, indicating the number of the lot on which it sat. Some were moored in narrow patches of grass, temporary camper spaces for RVs passing through, but many were permanent and, by the look of them, had been there for years. The lots were stingy squares of poured concrete, surrounded by sections of white picket fence two feet high, or separated from one another by sagging lengths of bamboo matting. The yards, when they existed, harbored an assortment of plastic deer and flamingos.

It was almost eleven and many of the trailers were dark. Occasionally, I could see the blue-gray flicker of a TV set. I found the Chevrolet, hood warm, the engine still ticking, parked beside a dark green battered trailer with a torn awning and half the aluminum skirting ripped away. From inside, I could hear the dull thump of rock and roll music being played too loudly in too small a space.

The trailer windows were ovals of hot yellow light, positioned about a foot higher than eye level. I edged around to the right-hand side, easing in as close as I could, checking the area to see if any of the neighbors had spotted me. The trailer next door had a FOR RENT sign taped to the siding, and the one across the lane had the curtains pulled. I turned back to the window and got up on tiptoe, peering in. The window was opened slightly and the air seeping out was hot and smelled of fried onions. The curtains consisted of old cotton dish towels, with a brass rod threaded through one end, hanging crookedly enough to provide a clear view of Billy Polo and the woman he was talking to. They were both seated at a flop-down table in the galley, drinking beer, mouths working, words inaudible in the thumping din of music. The interior of the trailer was a depressing collage of cheap paneled walls, dirty dishes, junk, torn upholstery, newspapers, and canned goods stacked on counter tops. A bumper sticker pasted above the front door said, I'VE BEEN TO ALL 48 STATES!

There was a small black-and-white television set perched on a cardboard box, tuned to what looked like the tag end of a prime-time private-eye show. The action was speeding up. A car careened out of control, flipping end over end before it went off a cliff, exploding in midair. The picture cut to two men in an office, one talking on the phone. Neither Billy nor his companion seemed to be watching and the music must have made it impossible for them to hear the dialogue anyway.

I could feel a cramp forming in my right calf. I cast about for something to stand on to ease the strain. The yard next door was a jungle of overgrown shrubs, the parking space choked with discards. There was a set of detached wooden steps tucked up under the trailer door. I blundered through the bushes, my jeans and boots getting drenched in the process. I was counting on the thunder of music to cover the sound of my labors as I hefted the box steps, tramped back through the shrubs, and set the steps under the window.

Cautiously, I mounted, peering in again. Billy Polo had a surprisingly boyish face for a man who'd lived his thirty years as a thug. His hair was dark, a curly mass standing out around his face. His nose was small, his mouth generous, and he had a dimple in his chin that looked like a puncture wound. He wasn't a big man, but he had a wiry musculature that suggested strength. There was something manic about him, a hint of tension in his gestures. His eyes were restless and he tended to stare off to one side when he spoke, as if direct eye contact made him anxious.

The woman was in her early twenties, with a wide mouth, strong chin, and a pug nose that looked as if it was made of putty. She wore no makeup and her fair hair was dense, a series of tight ripples that she wore shoulder length, brittle and illcut. Her skin was very pale, mottled with freckles. She was wearing a man's oversized silk bathrobe and apparently nursing a cold. She kept a wad of Kleenex in her pocket which she honked into from time to time. She was so close to me I could see the chapping where the frequent blowing had reddened her nose and upper lip. I wondered if she was an old girlfriend of Billy's. There was no overt sexuality in the way they related to one another, but there was a curious intimacy. An old love affair gone flat perhaps.

The continuous rock and roll music was driving me nuts. I was never going to hear what they were saying with that stuff booming out all over the place. I got down off the steps and went around the other side of the trailer to the front door. The window to the right was wide open, though the curtains were pinned shut.

I waited until there was a brief pause between cuts. I took a deep breath and pounded on the door. "Hey! Could you cut the goddamn noise," I yelled. "We're tryin' to get some sleep over here!"

From inside the trailer, the woman hollered, "Sorry!" The music ceased abruptly and I went back around to the other side to see how much of their conversation I could pick up.

The quiet was divine. The volume on the television set must have been turned all the way down, because the string of commercials that now appeared was antic with silence and I could actually catch snatches of what they were saying, though they mumbled unmercifully.

". . . course, she's going to say that. What did you expect?" she said.

"I don't like the pressure. I don't like havin' her on my back . . ." He said something else I couldn't make out.

"What difference does it make? Nobody forced her. Shit, she's free, white, and twenty-one . . . the point is . . . getting into . . . just so she doesn't think . . . the whole thing, right?"

Her voice had dropped and when Billy answered, he had one hand across his mouth so I couldn't understand him at all. He was only half attentive anyway, talking to her with his gaze straying to the television picture. It must have been 11:00 because the local news came on. There was the usual lead-in, a long shot of the news desk with two male newscasters, one black, one white, like a matched set, sitting there in suits. Both looked properly solemn. The camera cut to a head shot of the black man. A photograph of John Daggett appeared briefly behind him. There was a quick shot of the beach. It took me a moment to realize that it must have been the spot where Daggett's body had been found. In the background, I could see the mouth of the harbor and the dredge.

Billy jerked upright, grabbing the woman's arm. She swiveled around to see what he was pointing to. The announcer talked on, smoothly moving the top sheet of paper aside. The camera cut to the co-anchor and the picture shifted to a still shot of a local waste disposal site.

Billy and the woman traded a long, anxious look. Billy started cracking his knuckles. "Christ!"

The woman snatched up the paper and tossed it at him. "I told you it was him the minute I read some bum washed up on the beach. Goddamn it, Billy! Everything with you comes down to the same old bullshit. You think you're so smart. You got all the angles covered. Oh sure. Turns out you don't even know what you're talking about!"

"They don't even know we knew him. How would they know that?"

She gave him a scornful look, exasperated that he'd try to defend himself. "Give the cops some credit! They probably identified him by his fingerprints, right? So they know he was up in San Luis. It's not going to take a genius to figure out you were up there with him. Next thing we know somebody's coming around knocking at the door. 'When'd you last see this guy?' Shit like that."

He got up abruptly. He crossed to a kitchen cabinet and opened it. "You got any Black Jack?"

"No, I don't have any Black Jack. You drank it all last night."

"Get some clothes on. Let's go over to the Hub."

"Billy, I've got a cold! I'm not going out at this hour. You go. Why do you need a drink anyway?"

He reached for his jacket, hunching into it. "You have any cash? All I got on me is a buck."

"Get a job. Pay your own way. I'm tired of givin' you money."

"I said you'd get it back. What are you worried about? Come on, come on," he said, snapping his fingers impatiently.

She took her time about it, but she did root through her

purse, coming up with a crumpled five-dollar bill, which he took without comment.

"Are you crashing here?" she asked.

"I don't know yet. Probably. Don't lock up."

"Well, just keep it down, okay? I feel like hell and I don't want to be woke up."

He put his hands on her arms. "Hey," he said. "Cool it. You worry too much."

"You know what your problem is? You think all you have to do is say shit like that and it's all okay. The world doesn't work that way. It never did."

"Yeah, well there's always a first time. Your problem is you're a pessimist. . . ."

At that point, I figured I'd better cut out and head back to my car. I eased down off my perch, debating briefly about whether I should move the steps or leave them there. Better to move them. I hefted them, swiftly pushing through the undergrowth to a cleared space where the junk was stacked up. I set the box down and then took off through the darkened trailer park and out to the street.

I jogged to my car, started it, and did another U-turn, anticipating that Billy would head back the same way he came. Sure enough, in my rearview mirror I saw the Chevrolet make a left turn onto the main thoroughfare, coming up behind me. He followed me for a block and a half, tailgating, a real A-type. With an impatient toot of the horn, he passed me, squealed into another left-hand turn, and zoomed off toward Milagro. I knew where he was headed so I took my time. There's a bar called the Hub about three blocks up. I walked into the place maybe ten minutes after he did. He'd already bought his Jack Daniel's, which he was nursing while he played pool.

9

The Hub is a bar with all the ambience of a converted ware-house. The space is too vast for camaraderie, the air too chill for relaxation. The ceiling is high, painted black, and covered with a gridwork of pipes and electrical conduits. The tables in the main room are sparse, the walls lined with old black-and-white photographs of the bar and its various clientele over the years. Through a wide archway is a smaller room with four pool tables. The juke box is massive, outlined in bands of yellow, green, and cherry red, with bubbles blipping through the seams. The place was curiously empty for a Sat-urday night. A Willie Nelson single was playing, but it wasn't one I knew.

I was the only woman in the bar and I could sense the male attention shift to me with a bristling caution. I paused, feeling sniffed at, as if I were a dog in an alien neighborhood. Cig-arette smoke hung in the air, and the men with their pool cues were caught in the hazy light, bent above the tables in silhouette. I identified Billy Polo by the great puff of hair around his head. Upright, he was taller than I'd pictured him, with wide, hard shoulders and slim hips. He was playing pool with a Mexican kid, maybe twenty-two, with a gaunt face, tattooed arms, and a strip of pinched-looking chest which was visible in the gap of the Hawaiian shirt he wore unbuttoned to the waist. He sported maybe six chest hairs in a shallow depression in the middle of his sternum.

I crossed to the table and stood there, waiting for Billy to finish his game. He glanced at me with disinterest and lined up the cue ball with the six ball, which he smacked smartly into a side pocket. He moved around the table without pause, lining up the two ball which he fired like a shot into the corner pocket. He chalked his cue, eyeing the three ball. He tested an angle and rejected it, leaning into the table then with a shot that sent the three ball rocketing into the side pocket, while the five ball glanced off the side, rolled into range of the corner pocket, hung there, and finally dropped in. A trace of a smile crossed Billy's face, but he didn't look up.

Meanwhile, the Mexican kid stood there and grinned at me, leaning on his cue stick. He mouthed, "I love you." One of his front teeth was rimmed in gold, like a picture frame, and there was a smudge of blue chalk near his chin. Behind him, Billy cleaned up the table and put his cue stick back in the rack on the wall. As he passed, he plucked a twenty from the kid's shirt pocket and tucked it into his own. Then, with his face averted, he said, "You the chick came looking for me at my mom's house earlier?"

"That's right. I'm a friend of John Daggett's."

He cocked his head, squinting, his right hand cupped behind his ear. "Who?"

I smiled lazily. We were apparently playing charades. I raised my voice, enunciating. "Daggett. John."

"Oh, yeah, him. How's he doing these days?" He started snapping his fingers lightly to the music, which had switched from Willie Nelson to a George Benson tune.

"He's dead."

I have to credit him. He did a nice imitation of casual surprise, not overdoing it. "You're shittin' me. Daggett's dead? Too bad. What happened to the dude, heart attack?"

"Drowned. It just happened last night, down at the marina." I wagged a thumb over my shoulder in the direction of the beach so he'd know which marina I meant.

"Here in town? Hey, that's tough. I didn't know that. He was in L.A. last I heard."

"I'm surprised you didn't see it on the news."

"Yeah, well I never pay attention to that shit, you know? Bums me out. I got better things to do with my time."

His eyes were all over the place and his body was half turned away. I had to guess that he was busy trying to figure out who I was and what I was up to. He flicked a look at me. "I'm sorry. I didn't catch your name."

"Kinsey Millhone."

He studied me fleetingly. "I thought my mom said the name was Charlene."

I shook my head. "I don't know where she got that."

"And you do what?"

"Basic research. I free-lance. What's that got to do with it?"

"You don't look like a friend of Daggett's. He was kind of a lowlife. You got too much class for a scumbag like him."

"I didn't say we were close. I met him recently through a friend of a friend."

"Why tell me about it? I don't give a damn."

"I'm sorry to hear that. Daggett said if anything happened to him, I should talk to you."

"Me? Naww," he said with disbelief. "That's fuckin' weird. You must have got me mixed up with somebody else. I mean, I knew Daggett, but I didn't *know* him, you dig?"

"That's funny. He told me you were the best of friends."

He smiled and shook his head. "Old Daggett gave you a bum steer, baby doll. I don't know nothin' about it. I don't even remember when I saw him last. Long time."

"What was the occasion?"

He glanced at the Mexican kid who was eavesdropping shamelessly. "Catch you later, man," he said to him. Then under his breath, with contempt, he said, "Paco." Apparently, this was a generic insult that applied to all Hispanics.

He touched my elbow, steering me into the other room. "These beaners are all the same," he confided. "Think they know how to play pool, but they can't do shit. I don't like talking personal in front of spics. Can I buy you a beer?"

"Sure."

He indicated an empty table and held a chair out for me. I hung my slicker over the back and sat down. He caught the bartender's eye and held up two fingers. The bartender pulled out two bottles of beer which he opened and set on the bar.

Billy said, "You want anything else? Potato chips? They make real nice french fries. Kinda greasy, but good."

I shook my head, watching him with interest. At close range, he had a curious charisma . . . a crude sexuality that he probably wasn't even aware of. I meet men like that occasionally and I'm always startled by the phenomenon.

He ambled over and picked up the beers, dropping a couple of crumpled bills on the bar. He said something to the bartender and then waited while the guy placed a glass upside down on each bottle, shooting a smirk in my direction.

He came back to the table and sat down. "Jesus, ask for a glass in this place and they act like you're puttin' on airs. Bunch of bohunks. I only hang out here because I got a sister works here three nights a week."

Ah, I thought, the woman in the trailer.

He poured one of the beers and pushed it over to me, taking his time then as he poured his own. His eyes were deepset, and he had dimples that formed a crease on either side of his mouth. "Look," he said, "I can see you got your mind made up I know something I don't. The truth is, I didn't like Daggett much and I don't think he liked me. Where you got this yarn about me bein' some pal of his, I don't know, but it wasn't from him."

"You called him Monday morning, didn't you?"

"Nuh-uh. Not me. Why would I call him?"

I went on as though he hadn't said anything. "I don't know what you told him, but he was scared."

"Sorry I can't help you out. Must have been somebody else. What was he doin' up here anyway?"

"I don't know. His body washed up in the surf this morning. I thought maybe you could fill me in on the rest. Do you have any idea where he was last night?"

"Nope. Not a clue." He'd gotten interested in a speck of dust in the foam on his beer and he had to pick that out.

"When did you see him last? I don't think you said."

His tone became facetious. "Geez, I don't have my Day-Timer with me. Otherwise, I could pin it down. We might've had lunch at some little out of the way place, just him and me."

"San Luis perhaps?"

There was a slight pause and his smile dimmed a couple of watts. "I was at San Luis with him," he said, cautiously. "Me and thirty-seven hundred other guys. So what?"

"I thought maybe you'd kept in touch."

"I can tell you didn't know Daggett too good. Being with him is like walking around with dog-do on your shoe, you know? It's not something you'd seek out."

"Who else did he know here in town?"

"Can't help you there. It's not my week to keep track."

"What about your sister? Did he know her?"

"Coral? No way. She don't hang out with bums like that. I'd break her neck. I don't get why you're goin' on and on about this. I told you I don't know nothin'. I didn't see him, didn't hear from him. Why can't you just take my word for it?"

"Because I don't think you're telling the truth."

"Says who? I mean, you came lookin' for me, remember? I don't have to talk to you. I'm doin' you a favor. I don't know who you are. I don't even know what the fuck you're up to."

I shook my head, smiling slightly. "God, Billy. Such foul talk. I didn't think you dealt with women that way. I'm shocked."

"Now you're makin' fun of me, right?" He scrutinized my face. "You some kind of cop?"

I ran my thumbnail down the bottle, snagging an accordion strip of label, which I picked off. "Actually I am."

He snorted. Now he'd heard everything. "Come on. Like what," he said.

"I'm a private investigator."

"Bullshit."

"It's a fact."

He tipped back in his chair, amused that I'd try to lay such a line on him. "Jesus, you're too much. Who do you think you're talkin' to? I might have been born at night, but it wasn't *last* night. I know the private eyes around town and you ain't one, so try somethin' else."

I laughed. "All right, I'm not. Maybe I'm just a nosy chick looking into the death of a man I once met."

"Now, that I'd buy, but it still don't explain why you're crankin' on my case."

"You introduced him to Lovella, didn't you?"

That stopped him momentarily. "You know Lovella?"

"Sure. I met her down in L.A. She has an apartment on Sawtelle."

"When was this?"

"Day before yesterday."

"No foolin'. And she told you to look me up?"

"How else would I know where you were?"

He stared at me, going through some sort of mental debate.

I thought a little coaxing might loosen his tongue. "Are you aware that Daggett's been beating the shit out of her?"

That made him restless and his eyes dropped away from mine. "Yeah, well Lovella's a big girl. She has to learn how to take care of herself."

"Why don't you help her out?"

He smiled bitterly. "I know people who'd laugh at the notion of me helping anyone," he said. "Besides, she's tough. You don't want to underestimate that one, I'm tellin' you."

"You've known her a long time, haven't you?"

His knee had started to jump. "Seven years, eight. I met her when she was seventeen. We lived together for a while, but it didn't work out. We used to knock heads too much. She's a bullheaded bitch, but I loved her a lot. Then I got busted on a burglary rap and me and her, hell, I don't know what it was. We wrote to each other for a while, but you can't go back to something once it's dead, you know? Anyway, now we're friends, I guess. At least I dig her. I don't know how she feels about me."

"Have you seen her recently?"

The knee stopped. "No, I haven't seen her recently," he said. "What about you? Why'd you go down there?"

"I was looking for Daggett. The phone was disconnected."

"What exactly did she say?"

I shrugged. "Nothing much. I wasn't there long and she wasn't feeling that good. She was nursing a big black eye."

"Jesus," he said. He rocked back in his chair. "Tell me something. How come women do that? Let guys punch 'em out?"

"I have no idea."

He drained his beer glass and set it down. "I bet you don't take crap from anyone, am I right?"

"We all take crap from someone," I said.

Billy got up. "Sorry to cut this off, but I gotta split." He turned, tucking his shirt down into his pants more securely. His body language said he'd already taken off and hoped his clothing would catch up with him by the time he hit the street.

I got up, reaching for my slicker. "You're not leaving town, are you?"

"What business is it of yours?"

"It doesn't seem like a good idea with Daggett's death hanging fire. Suppose the cops want to talk to you."

"About what?"

"Where you were last night, for starters."

His tone rose. "Where *I* was? What are you talkin' about?"

"They might want to know about the connection between Daggett and you."

"What connection? That's a crock. I don't know where you come up with that."

"It's not me you have to worry about. It's the cops who count."

"What cops?"

I shook my head. "You know who your friendly local cops are," I said. "If somebody puts a bug in the wrong ear, you'll be sitting in the hot seat."

He was all outrage. "Why would you do that to me?"

"Because you're not leveling with me, William."

"I *am* leveling with you! I've told you everything I know."

"I don't think so. I think you knew about Daggett's death. I think you saw him this week."

He put his hands on his hips and looked off across the room, shaking his head. "Man, this is all I need. This is no lie. I've been straight. I'm minding my own business, doing like I been told. I didn't even know the dude was up here."

"You can stick to your story if you like," I said, "but I'll give you a word of advice. I've got the license number of that car you bought. You bolt and I'm calling Lieutenant Dolan down at Homicide."

He seemed as much puzzled as dismayed. "What is this? A shakedown? Is that what this is about?"

"What's to shake? You don't have a cent. I want information, that's all."

"I don't *have* any information. How many times I gotta tell you that?"

"Look," I said patiently. "Why don't I let you think about the situation and then we can talk again."

"Why don't you go fuck yourself!"

I put my slicker on, tucking the strap of my handbag over my shoulder. "Thanks for the beer. I'll buy yours next time."

He made an exaggerated gesture of dismissal, too pissed

off to reply. He headed toward the door and I watched him go. I glanced at my watch. It was well after midnight and I was exhausted. My head was starting to ache and I knew everything about me smelled like stale cigarette smoke. I wanted to go home, strip down, shower, and then crawl into the folds of my quilt. Instead, I took a deep breath and went after him.

10

I gave him a good head start, then followed him back to the trailer. The temperature felt like it had dropped into the fifties. The eucalyptus trees were still tossing occasional showers at me when the wind cut through, but for the most part, the night was clear. Above me, I could see pale puffs of rain cloud receding, wide patches of starry sky breaking through. I parked half a block away and padded into the park on foot as I had before. Billy's car was parked beside the trailer. I was getting bored, but I had to be certain he wasn't heading off to consult with some confederate I didn't know about.

The same lights were on in the galley, but a dim light now glowed at the rear of the trailer, where I imagined the bedroom to be. I picked my way through the bushes to that end. Curtains were pulled across the windows, but the venting system was piping a murmured conversation right out through a mesh-covered opening. I hunkered down by the torn skirting, leaning my head against the aluminum. I could smell cigarette smoke, which I guessed was Coral's.

". . . want to know why she showed up now," she was saying. "That's what we have to worry about. For all we know, they're in it together."

"Yeah, but doin' what? That's what I can't figure out."

"When'd she say she'd get in touch?"

"She didn't. Said I should think about the situation. Jesus. How'd she get a bead on the Chevy so fast? That's what bugs me. I had that car two hours."

"Maybe she followed you, dimwit."

The silence was profound. "Goddamn it," he said.

I heard footsteps thump toward the front of the trailer. By the time the door banged open I was easing my way around the end. I peered out into the carport. The nose of the Chevy was about six feet away, the space on either side of it crowded with junk.

The door to the trailer had been flung open. Light poured out, washing as far as the point where the asphalt began. With a quick look over my shoulder, I waded into the refuse, picking my way around to the far side of the car, where I crouched, listening intently. Sometimes I feel like I spend half my life this way. I heard Billy fumble his way around the bedroom end of the trailer just as I had.

"Jesus!" he hissed.

Coral peered out the side window, whispering hoarsely. "What's wrong?"

"Shut up! Nothing. I banged my goddamn shin on the trailer hitch. Why don't you clean up this crap?"

My sentiments exactly.

Coral laughed and the curtain dropped back into place.

Billy appeared again at the far end of the carport, rubbing his left shin. He did a quick visual survey, apparently convinced by then there wasn't anybody lurking about the premises. He shook his head and thumped up the steps, banging the door shut behind him. The carport went dark. I let out my breath.

I could hear them murmuring together, but by then I didn't really care what else they discussed. As soon as I was convinced it was safe, I crept out of the driveway and headed for my car.

Sunday morning was overcast. The very air looked gray, and dampness seemed to rise up out of the earth like a mist. I went through my usual morning routine, getting a three-mile run in before the skies opened up again. At 9:00, I put a call through to Barbara Daggett at home. I brought her up to date, filling her in on my night's activities.

"What now?" she asked.

"I'm going to let Billy Polo stew for a day or two and then get back to him."

"What makes you think he won't skip?"

"Well, he *is* on parole and I'm hoping he won't want to mess that up. Besides, it feels like a waste of money to pay me to sit there all day."

"I thought you said he was the only lead you had."

"Maybe not," I said cautiously. "I've been thinking about Tony Gahan and the other people killed in the accident."

"Tony Gahan?" she said with surprise. "How could he be involved in this?"

"I don't know. Your father hired me originally to track him down. Maybe he found the kid himself and that's where he was early in the week."

"But Kinsey, why would Daddy want to track him down? That boy must hate his guts. His whole family was wiped out."

"That's my point."

"Oh."

"Do you have any idea how to locate him? Your father had an address on Stanley Place, but the house was apparently empty. I can't find a Gahan listed in the telephone book."

"He lives with his aunt now, I think, somewhere in Colgate. Let me see if I've got an address."

Colgate is the bedroom community, attached to Santa Teresa like a double star. The two are just about the same size, but Santa Teresa has all the character and Colgate has the affordable housing, along with hardware stores, paint companies, bowling alleys, and drive-in theaters. Colgate is the Frostee-Freeze capital of the world.

There was a pause and I could hear pages rattle. She came back on the line. "My mistake. They live near the Museum. Her last name is Westfall. Ramona."

"I wonder why your father didn't know about her."

"I don't know. She was there for the trial. I do remember that, because someone pointed her out to me. I wrote her a note afterwards, saying that of course we'd do anything we could to help, but I never heard back."

"You know anything else about her? Is she married, for instance?"

"I think so, yes. Her husband manufactures industrial supplies or something like that. Actually, now that I think about it, she *was* working at that kitchenware place on Capilla because I spotted her when I was in there shopping a couple of months ago. Maybe you could catch her this afternoon if she still works there."

"On Sunday?"

"Sure, they're open from twelve to five."

"I'll try her first and see how far I get," I said. "What about your mother? How's she holding up?"

"Surprisingly well. Turns out she handles death like a champ. If it's covered in the Bible, she trots out all the appropriate attitudes and goes through the sequence automatically. I thought she'd flip out, but it seems to have put her back on her feet. She's got church women sitting with her, and the pastor's there. The kitchen table's stacked with tuna casseroles and chocolate cakes. I don't know how long it will last, but for now, she's in her element."

"When's the funeral?"

"Tuesday afternoon. The body's been transported to the mortuary. I think they said he'd be ready for viewing early this afternoon. Are you coming by?"

"Yes, I think I will. I can tell you then if I've talked to this Westfall woman or the kid."

Jorden's is a gourmet cook's fantasy, with every imaginable food preparation device. Rack after rack of cookware, utensils, cookbooks, linens, spices, coffees, and condiments; chafing dishes, wicker baskets, exotic vinegars and oils, knives, baking pans, glassware. I stood in the entrance for a moment, amazed by the number and variety of food-related implements. Pasta machines, cappuccino makers, food warmers, coffee grinders, ice cream freezers, food processors. The air smelled of chocolate and made me wish I had a mother. I spotted three saleswomen, all wearing wraparound aprons made of mattress ticking, with the store's name embroidered in maroon across the bib.

I asked for Ramona Westfall and was directed toward the rear aisle. She was apparently doing a shelf count. I found her perched on a small wooden stool, clipboard in hand, checking off items on a list that included most of the non-electrical gadgets. She was sorting through a bin of what looked like small stainless steel sliding boards with a blade across the center that would slice your tiny ass off.

"What are those?" I asked.

She glanced up at me with a pleasant smile. She appeared to be in her late forties, with short, pale sandy hair streaked with gray, hazel eyes peering at me over a pair of half-glasses which she wore low on her nose. She used little if any makeup, and even seated, I could tell she was small and slim. Under the apron, she wore a white, long-sleeved blouse with a Peter Pan collar, a gray tweed skirt, hose, and penny loafers.

"That's a mandoline. It's made in West Germany."

"I thought a mandolin was a musical instrument."

"The spelling's different. This is for slicing raw vegetables. You can waffle-cut or julienne."

"Really?" I said. I had sudden visions of homemade French fries and cole slaw, neither of which I've ever prepared. "How much is that?"

"A hundred and ten dollars. With the slicing guard, it's one thirty-eight. Would you like a demonstration?"

I shook my head, unwilling to spend that much money on behalf of a potato. She got to her feet, smoothing the front of her apron. She was half a head shorter than I and smelled like a perfume sample I'd gotten in the mail the week before. Lavender and crushed jasmine. I was impressed with the price of the stuff, if not the scent. I stuck it in a drawer and I'm assailed with the fragrance now every time I pull out fresh underwear.

"You're Ramona Westfall, aren't you?"

Her smile was modified to a look of expectancy. "That's right. Have we met?"

I shook my head. "I'm Kinsey Millhone. I'm a private investigator here in town."

"Is there something I can help you with?"

"I'm looking for Tony Gahan. I understand you're his aunt."

"Tony? Good heavens, what for?"

"I was asked to locate him on a personal matter. I didn't know how else to get in touch with him."

"What personal matter? I don't understand."

"I was asked to deliver something to him. A check from a man who's recently deceased."

She looked at me blankly for a moment and then I saw recognition leap in her eyes. "You're referring to John Daggett, aren't you? Someone told me it was on the news last night. I assumed he was still in prison."

"He's been out for six weeks."

Her face flooded with color. "Well, isn't that typical," she snapped. "Five people dead and he's back on the streets."

"Not quite," I said. "Could we go someplace and talk?"

"About what? About my sister? She was thirty-eight, a beautiful person. She was decapitated when he ran a stoplight and plowed into them. Her husband was killed. Tony's sister was crushed. She was six, just a baby. . . ." She bit off her sentence abruptly, suddenly aware that her voice had risen. Nearby, several people paused, looking over at us.

"Who were the others? Did you know them?" I asked.

"You're the detective. You figure it out."

In the next aisle, a dark-haired woman in a striped apron

caught her eye. She didn't open her mouth, but her expression said, "Is everything all right?"

"I'm taking a break," Ramona said to her. "I'll be in the back room if Tricia's looking for me."

The dark-haired woman glanced at me briefly and then dropped her gaze. Ramona was moving toward a doorway on the far side of the room. I followed. The other customers had lost interest, but I had a feeling that I'd be facing an unpleasant scene.

By the time I entered the back room, Ramona was fumbling in her handbag with shaking hands. She opened a zippered compartment and took out a vial of pills. She extracted a tablet and broke it in half, downing it with a slug of cold coffee from a white mug with her name on the side. On second thought, she took the second half of the tablet as well.

I said, "Look, I'm sorry to have to bring this up . . ."

"Don't apologize," she spat. "It doesn't do any good." She searched through the bag and came up with a hard pack of Winston's. She pulled out a cigarette and tamped it repeatedly on her thumbnail, then lit it with a Bic disposable lighter she'd tucked in her apron pocket. She hugged her waist with her left arm, propping the right elbow on it so she could hold the cigarette near her face. Her eyes seemed to have darkened and she fixed me with a blank, rude stare. "What is it you want?"

I could feel my face warm. Somehow the money was suddenly beside the point and seemed like too paltry a sum in any event. "I have a cashier's check for Tony. John Daggett asked me to deliver it."

Her smile was supercilious. "Oh, a *check*. Well, how much is it for? Is it per *head* or some sort of lump sum payment by the carload?"

"Mrs. Westfall," I said patiently.

"You can call me Ramona, dear, since the subject matter's so intimate. We're talking about the people I loved best in this world." She took a deep drag of her cigarette and blew smoke toward the ceiling.

I clamped down on my temper, controlling my response. "I understand that the subject is painful," I said. "I know there's no way to compensate for what happened, but John Daggett was making a gesture, and regardless of your opinion of him, it's possible that Tony might have a use for the money."

"We provide for him very nicely, thanks. We don't need anything from John Daggett *or* his daughter or from *you*."

I plowed on, heading into the face of her wrath like a swimmer through churning surf. "Let me just say something first. Daggett came to me last week with a cashier's check made out to Tony."

She started to speak, but I held up one hand. "Please," I said.

She subsided, allowing me to continue.

"I put the check in a safe deposit box until I could figure out how to deliver it, as agreed. You can toss it in the trash for all I care, but I'd like to do what I said I'd do, which is to see that Tony Gahan gets it. In theory, it's Tony's to do with as he sees fit, so I'd appreciate it if you'd talk to him before you do anything else."

She thought about that one, her eyes locked on mine. "How much?"

"Twenty-five thousand. That's a good chunk of education for Tony, or a trip abroad. . . ."

"I get the point," she cut in. "Now maybe you'll allow me to have my say. That boy has been with us for almost three years now. He's fifteen years old and I don't think he's slept a full eight hours since the accident. He has migraines, he bites his nails. His grades are poor, school attendance is *shit*. We're talking about a kid with an I.Q. right off the charts. He's a wreck and John Daggett did that to him. There's no way . . . no *way* anyone can ever make up to Tony for what that man did."

"I understand that."

"No, you don't." Her eyes filled suddenly with tears. She was silent, hands shaking again so badly now that she could scarcely get the Winston to her lips. She managed to take another drag, fighting for control. The silence lengthened. She seemed to shudder and I could almost see the tranquilizer kick in. She turned away abruptly, dropped the cigarette, and stepped on it. "Give me a number where I can reach you. I'll talk to my husband and see what he says."

I handed her my card, taking a moment to jot down my home address and telephone number on the back, in case she needed to reach me there.

11

After I left Ramona Westfall, I stopped by my apartment and changed into pantyhose, low heels, and my all-purpose dress. This garment, which I've owned for five years, is made of some magic fabric that doesn't wilt, wrinkle, or show dirt. It can be squashed down to the size of a rain hat and shoved in the bottom of my handbag without harm. It can also be rinsed out in any bathroom sink and hung to dry overnight. It's black, lightweight, has long sleeves, zips up the back, and should probably be "accessorized," a women's clothing concept I've never understood. I wear the dress "as is" and it always looks okay to me. Once in a while I see this look of recognition in someone's eye, but maybe it's just a moment of surprise at seeing me in something other than jeans and boots.

The Wynington-Blake Mortuary—Burials, Cremation, and Shipping, Serving All Faiths—is located on the east side of town on a shady side street with ample parking. It was originally built as a residence and retains the feeling of a substantial single-family dwelling. Now, of course, the entire first floor has been converted into the equivalent of six spacious living rooms, each furnished with metal folding chairs and labeled with some serene-sounding word.

The gentleman who greeted me, a Mr. Sharonson, wore a subdued navy blue suit, a neutral expression, and used a public library voice. John Daggett was laid out in "Meditation," which was just down the corridor and to my left. The family, he murmured, was in the Sunrise Chapel if I cared to wait.

I signed in. Mr. Sharonson removed himself discreetly and I was left to do as I pleased. The room was rimmed with chairs, the casket at the apex. There were two sprays of white gladioli that looked somehow like pristine fakes provided by the mortuary, instead of wreaths sent by those who mourned Daggett's passing. Organ music was being piped in, a nearly subliminal auditory cue meant to trigger thoughts about the brevity of life.

I tiptoed across the room to have a peek at him. The color and texture of Daggett's skin looked about like a Betsy-Wetsy doll I'd had as a kid. His features had a flattened appearance, which I suspected was a side effect of the autopsy process. Peel somebody's face back and it's hard to line it all up again. Daggett's nose looked crooked, like a pillowcase put on with the seam slightly skewed.

I was aware of a rustling behind me and Barbara Daggett appeared on my right. We stood together for a moment without a word. I don't know why people stand and study the dead that way. It makes about as much sense as paying homage to the cardboard box your favorite shoes once came in. Finally, she murmured something and turned away, moving toward the entrance where Eugene Nickerson and Essie Daggett were just coming in through the archway.

Essie was wearing a dark navy dress of rayon jersey, her massive arms dimpled with pale flesh. Her hair looked freshly "done," puffed and thick, sprayed into a turban of undulating gray. Eugene, in a dark suit, steered her by the elbow, working her arm as if it were the rudder on a ship. She took one look at the casket and her wide knees buckled. Barbara and Eugene caught her before she actually hit the floor. They guided her to an upholstered chair and lowered her into the seat. She fumbled for a handkerchief, which she pressed to her mouth as if she meant to chloroform herself.

"Sweet Jesus Lord," she mewed, her eyes turned up piteously. "Lamb of God . . ." Eugene began to pat at her hand and Barbara sat down beside her, putting one arm around her protectively.

"You want me to bring her some water?" I asked.

Barbara nodded and I moved toward the doorway. Mr. Sharonson had sensed the disturbance and had appeared, his face forming a question. I passed the request along and he nodded. He left the room and I returned to Mrs. Daggett's side. She was having a pretty good time by now, rolling her head back and forth, reciting scriptures in a high-pitched voice. Barbara and Eugene were working to restrain her and I gathered that Essie had expressed a strong desire to fling herself into the coffin with her beloved. I might have given her a boost myself.

Mr. Sharonson returned with a paper envelope full of water, which Barbara took, holding it to Essie's lips. She jerked her head back, unwilling to accept even this small measure of solace. "By night on my bed, I sought him whom my soul loveth," she warbled. "I sought him, but I found him not. I will rise now, and go about the city in the streets, and in the broad ways I will seek him whom my soul loveth. The watchmen that go about the city found me . . . Lord in Heaven . . . O God. . . ."

With surprise, I realized she was quoting fragments from the Song of Solomon, which I recognized from my old Methodist Sunday School days. Little kids were never allowed to read that part of the Bible as it was considered too smutty, but I was real interested in the idea of a man with legs like pillars of marble set upon sockets of fine gold. There was some talk of swords and thighs that caught my attention too. I believe I lasted three Sundays before my aunt was asked to take me down the street to the Presbyterians.

Essie was rapidly losing control, whipping herself into such an agitated state that Eugene and Mr. Sharonson had to assist her to her feet and help her out of the room. I could hear her cries becoming feebler as she was moved down the hall. Barbara rubbed her face wearily. "Oh God. Count on Mother," she said. "How has your day been?"

I sat down beside her. "This doesn't seem like the best time to talk," I said.

"Oh, don't worry about it. She'll calm down. This is the first she's seen of him. There's some kind of lounge upstairs. She can rest for a while and she'll be fine. What about Ramona Westfall? Did you talk to her?"

I filled her in on my brief interview, bringing the subject around to my real question at this point, which had to do with the two other victims in the accident. Barbara closed her eyes, the matter clearly causing her pain.

"One was a little friend of Hilary Gahan's. Her name was Megan Smith. I'm sure her parents are still in the area. I'll check the address and telephone number when I get home. Her father's name is Wayne. I forget the name of the street, but it's probably listed."

I took my notebook out and jotted the name down. "And the fifth?"

"Some kid who'd bummed a ride with them. They picked him up at the on-ramp to the freeway to give him a lift into town."

"What was his name?"

"Doug Polokowski."

I stared at her. "You're kidding."

"Why? Do you know him?"

"Polokowski is Billy Polo's real last name. It's on his rap sheet."

"You think they're related?"

"They'd almost have to be. There's only one Polokowski family in town. It's got to be a cousin or a brother, *something*."

"But I thought Billy Polo was supposed to be Daddy's best friend. That doesn't make sense."

Mr. Sharonson returned to the room and caught her eye. "Your mother is asking for you, Miss Daggett."

"You go ahead," I said. "I've got plenty to work on at this point. I'll call you later at home."

Barbara followed Mr. Sharonson while I headed out to the foyer and hustled up a telephone book. Wayne and Marilyn Smith were listed on Tupelo Drive out in Colgate, right around the corner from Stanley Place, if my memory served me correctly. I considered calling first, but I was curious what the reaction would be to the fact of Daggett's death, if the news hadn't already reached them. I stopped to get gas in the VW and then headed out to the freeway.

The Smiths' house was the single odd one in a twelve-block radius of identical tract homes and I guessed that theirs was the original farmhouse at the heart of what had once been a citrus grove. I could still spot orange trees in irregular rows, broken up now by winding roads, fenced lots, and an elementary school. The Smiths' mailbox was a small replica of the house and the street number was gouged out of a thick plank of pine, stained dark and hung above the porch steps. The house itself was a two-story white frame with tall, narrow windows and a slate roof. A sprawling vegetable garden stretched out behind the house, with the garage beyond that. A tire swing hung by a rope from a sycamore that grew in the yard. Orange trees extended on all sides, looking twisted and barren, their producing years long past. It was probably cheaper to leave them there than to tear them out. An assortment of boys' bicycles in a rack on the porch suggested the presence of male offspring or an in-progress meeting of a cycling club.

The bell consisted of a metal twist in the middle of the door. I cranked it once and it trilled harshly. As with the Christopher house, the upper portion of the door was glass, allowing me a glimpse of the interior—high ceilings, waxed pine floors, a scattering of rag rugs, and Early American antiques that looked authentic to my untrained eye. The walls were covered with patchwork quilts, the colors washed out to pale shades of mauve and blue. Numerous children's jackets hung from a row of pegs to the left, rainboots lined up underneath.

A woman in jeans and an oversized white shirt trotted down the stairs, trailing one hand along the banister. She gave me a quick smile and opened the front door.

"Oh hi. Are you Larry's mom?" She read instantly from my expression that I hadn't the faintest idea what she was talking about. She gave a quick laugh. "I guess not. The boys got back from the movie half an hour ago and we've been waiting for Larry's mother to pick him up. Sorry."

"That's all right. I'm Kinsey Millhone," I said. "I'm a private investigator here in town." I handed her my card.

"Can I help you with something?" She was in her mid-thirties, her blonde hair pulled straight back from her face in a clumsy knot. She was dark-eyed, with the tanned good looks of someone who works outdoors. I imagined her to be the kind of mother who forbade her children to eat refined sugar and supervised the television shows they watched. Whether such vigilance pays off or not, I'm never sure. I tend to place kids in a class with dogs, preferring the quiet, the smart, and the well trained.

"John Daggett was killed here in town Friday night," I said.

Something flickered across her face, but maybe it was just the realization that a painful subject was coming up again. "I hadn't heard about that. What happened?"

"He fell out of a boat and drowned."

She thought about that briefly. "Well, that's not too bad. Drowning's supposed to be fairly easy, isn't it?" Her tone of voice was light, her expression pleasant. It took me a minute to realize the savagery of the sentiment. I wondered what kind of torture she'd wished on him.

"Most of us don't get to choose our death," I said.

"My daughter certainly didn't," she said tartly. "Was it an accident or did someone give him a nice push?"

"That's what I'm trying to find out," I said. "I heard he came up from L.A. on Monday, but nobody seems to know where he spent the week."

"Not here, I can assure you. If Wayne so much as set eyes on him, he'd have. . . ." The words tapered off to a faint smile and her tone became almost bantering. "I was going to say, he'd have killed him, but I didn't mean that literally. Or maybe I did. I guess I shouldn't speak for Wayne."

"What about you? When did you see him last?"

"I have no idea. Two years ago at least."

"At the trial?"

She shook her head. "I wasn't there. Wayne sat in for a day, but he couldn't take it after that. He talked to Barbara Daggett once, I think, but I'm sure there's been nothing since. I'm assuming somehow that the man was murdered. Is that what you're getting at?"

"It's possible. The police don't seem to think so, but I'm hoping they'll revise their opinion if I can come up with some evidence. I get the impression a lot of people wanted Daggett dead."

"Well, I sure did. I'm thrilled to hear the news. Somebody should have killed him at birth," she said. "Would you like to come in? I don't know what I can tell you, but we might as well be comfortable." She glanced at my business card again, double-checking the name and then tucking it in her shirt pocket.

She held the door and I passed over the threshold, pausing to see where she meant for us to go. She led me into the living room.

"You and your husband were home Friday night?"

"Why? Are we suspects?"

"There isn't even a formal investigation yet," I said.

"I was here. Wayne was working late. He's a C.P.A."

She indicated a chair and I sat down. She took a seat on the couch, her manner relaxed. She was wearing a thin gold bracelet on her right wrist and she began to turn that, straightening a kink in the chain. "Did you ever meet John Daggett yourself?" she asked.

"Once. He came to my office a week ago Saturday."

"Ah. Out on parole, no doubt. He must have served his ten minutes."

I made no comment, so she went on.

"What was he doing in Santa Teresa? Returning to the scene of the slaughter?"

"He was trying to locate Tony Gahan."

This seemed to amuse her. "To what end? It's probably none of my business, but I'm curious."

I was discomfited by her attitude, which seemed an odd mix of the wrathful and the jocular. "I'm not really sure what his intentions were," I said carefully. "The story he told me wasn't true anyway, so it's probably not worth repeating. I gathered he wanted to make restitution."

Her smile faded, dark eyes boring into mine with a look that chilled me. "There's no such thing as 'restitution' for what that man did. Megan died horribly. Five-and-a-half years old. Has anyone given you the details?"

"I have the newspaper clippings in the car. I talked to Ramona Westfall too, and she filled me in," I said, lying through my teeth. I didn't want to hear about Megan's death. I didn't think I could bear it, whatever it was. "Have you kept in touch with the other families?"

For a moment, I didn't think I could distract her. She was going to sit there and tell me some blood-curdling tale that I was never going to forget. Cruel images seemed to play across her face. She faltered and her expression underwent that transformation that precedes tears—her nose reddening, mouth changing shape, lines drawing down on either side. Then her self-control descended and she looked at me with clouded eyes. "I'm sorry. What?"

"I was wondering if you'd talked to the others recently. Mrs. Westfall or the Polokowskis."

"I've hardly even talked to Wayne. Megan's death has just about done us in."

"What about your other children? How are they handling it?"

"Better than we are, certainly. People always say, 'Well, you still have the boys.' But it doesn't work that way. It's not like you can substitute one child for another." Belatedly, she took out a Kleenex and blew her nose.

"I'm sorry I had to bring it all up again," I said. "I've never had children, but I can't imagine anything more painful than losing one."

Her smile returned, fleeting and bitter. "I'll tell you what's worse. Knowing there's a man out there doing a few months in jail for 'vehicular manslaughter' when he murdered five people. Do you know how many times he got picked up for drunk driving before that accident? Fifteen. He paid a few fines. He got his hand smacked. Once he did thirty days, but most of the time. : . ." She broke off, then changed her tone. "Oh hell. What difference does it make? Nothing changes anyway and it never ends. I'll tell Wayne you stopped by. Maybe he knows where Daggett was."

12

I sat in the car and shuddered. I couldn't think when an interview had made me feel so tense. Daggett *had* to have been murdered. I just didn't see how it could come down any other way. What I couldn't figure out was how to get my thinking straight. Usually the morality of homicide seems clear to me. Whatever the shortcomings of the victim, murder is wrong and the penalties levied against the perpetrator had better be substantial to balance out the gravity of the crime. In this case, that seemed like a simplistic point of view. It was *Daggett* who had caused the world to tilt on its axis. Because of him, five people had died, so that his death, whatever the instrument, was swinging the planet upright again, restoring a moral order of sorts. At the moment, I still didn't know whether his desire to make restitution was sincere or part of some elaborate con. All I knew was that I'd been caught up in the loop and I had a part to play, though I had no idea yet what it was.

I started the car and headed back to my place. The sky was clouding over again. It was after 5:00 and a premature twilight already seemed to be spilling down the mountainside. I pulled up in front of my apartment and switched off the ignition. I glanced over at my windows, which were dark. I was feeling edgy and I wasn't ready to go home yet. On impulse, I started the car again and headed for the beach, drawn by the scent of salt in the air. Maybe a walk would ease my restlessness.

I pulled into one of the municipal lots and parked, slipping out of my shoes and pantyhose, which I tossed in the back seat along with my handbag. I zipped up my windbreaker and locked the car, tucking my keys in my jacket pocket as I crossed the bike path to the beach. The ocean was silver, but the breaking waves were a muddy brown and the sand along the surf line was peppered with rocks. This was the winter beach, dark boulders having surfaced with the shifting coastal sands. Gulls hovered overhead, eyeing the thundering waves for signs of edible sea life.

I walked along the wet sand with a buffeting wind at my back. A windsurfer clung to the crossbar on a bright green sail, arching himself against the force of the wind, his board streaking toward the beach. Two big fishing boats were chugging into the marina. Everywhere there was the sense of urgency and threat—the torn white of storm surf, the darkening gray of the sky. Across the harbor, the ocean drove at the shore without pity, pounding at the breakwater with a grudging monotony. A rocketing spray shot straight up on impact, fanning along the seawall. I could almost hear the splats as successive waves hit the concrete walkway on the landward side.

I passed the entrance to the wharf. Ahead the beach widened, curving left toward the marina where the bare masts of sailboats tilted in the wind like metronomes. The sand was softer here, deeper too, so that walking became a labor. I turned and walked backwards for a few steps, trying to get my bearings. Somewhere along this part of the beach was the spot where Daggett's body had been found. A brief glimpse of the site had appeared on the newscast and I was hoping now to get a fix on the place. I thought it was probably this side of the boat launch. Ahead and to my right was the kiddie park with its playground equipment and a fenced-in area with a wading pool.

The newscast had shown a portion of the dredge in the background, intersected by the breakwater and a line of rocks. I trudged on until I had the three lined up in the same configuration. The dry sand was trampled and there were signs that vehicles had crossed the beach. Where waves slapped against the shore, all traces of activity had been erased. The crime scene investigators had, no doubt, done at least a cursory search. I scanned the area without any expectation of finding "evidence." If you murder a man by tossing him, dead drunk, out of a rowboat, there aren't any telltale clues to dispose of afterward. The boat itself had been left to drift and, from what Jonah said, must have washed ashore closer to the pier.

I drank in the heady perfume of the sea, watching the restless surge of the waves, turning myself slowly until the ocean was at my back and I was staring at the line of motels across the boulevard. Daggett had apparently died sometime between midnight and 5:00 A.M. I wondered if it would be productive to canvas the neighborhood for witnesses. It was possible, of course, that Daggett had actually cut the line on the skiff himself, rowing out of the harbor alone. With a 0.35 blood alcohol level, it seemed unlikely. By the time blood alcohol concentrations reach 0.40 percent, a drunk is essentially in a state of deep anesthesia, incapable of anything so athletic as working an oar. He might have maneuvered his way out of the harbor first and *then* sat in the bobbing boat, drinking himself insensible, but I couldn't picture that. I kept visualizing somebody with him . . . waiting, watching . . . finally hefting his feet and toppling him backwards. "A lesson in the back flip, Daggett. Oh shit, you blew it. Too bad, sucker. You die."

Getting him in the boat in the first place might have been a trick, as drunk as he was, but the rest of it must have been a snap.

I glanced to my right. An old bum with a shopping cart was picking through a trash container. I crossed the sand, heading toward him. As I approached, I could see that his skin was nearly gray with accumulated filth, tanned by the wind, with an overlay of rosiness from recent sunburn or

Mogen David wine . . . Mad Dog 20–20, as it's better known among the scruffy drifters. He looked in his seventies and was bulked up by layers of clothing. He wore a watch cap, his gray hair hanging out of it like mop strings. He smelled as musky as an old buffalo. The odor radiated from his body in nearly visible wavy lines, like a cartoon rendition of a skunk.

"Hello," I said.

He went about his business, ignoring me. He pulled out a pair of spike heels, inspecting them briefly before he tucked them into one of his plastic trash bags. A two-day-old newspaper didn't interest him. Beer cans? Yes, he seemed to like those. A Kentucky Fried Chicken barrel was a reject. A skirt? He held it up with a critical eye and then shoved it into the trash bag with the shoes. Someone had discarded a plastic beach ball with a hole punched in it. The old man set that aside.

"Did you hear about the guy they found in the surf yesterday?" I asked. No response. I felt like an apparition, calling to him from the netherworld. I raised my voice. "I heard somebody down here spotted him and called the cops. Do you happen to know who?"

I guess he didn't care to discuss it. He resolutely avoided eye contact. I didn't have my handbag with me so I didn't have a business card or even a dollar bill as a letter of reference. I had no choice but to let it drop. I moved away. By then, he had worked his way down in the bin, his head almost out of sight. So much for my interviewing techniques.

By the time I got back to the parking lot, the light had faded, so I registered the fact that something was wrong long before I realized what it was. The door on the passenger side of my car was ajar. I stopped in my tracks.

"Oh no," I said.

I approached with caution, as if the vehicle might be booby-trapped. It looked like someone had run a coathanger in through the wind-wing in an attempt to jimmy the lock. Failing that, the shitheel had simply smashed the window out on the passenger side and had opened the door. The glove compartment hung open, the contents spilling out across the front seat. My handbag was missing. *That* generated a flash of irritation, swiftly followed by dread. I jerked the seat forward and hauled out my briefcase. The strap that secured the opening had been cut and my gun was gone.

"Oh nooo," I wailed. I gave vent to a string of expletives. In high school, I had hung out with some bad-ass boys who taught me to cuss to perfection. I tried some combinations I hadn't thought of in years. I was mad at myself for leaving the stuff in plain sight on the seat and mad at the jerk who ripped me off. Mine was one of the last cars left in the lot and had probably stood out like a beacon. I slammed the car door shut and headed off across the street, still barefoot, gesturing and muttering to myself like a mental case. I didn't even have the spare change to call the cops.

There was a hamburger stand close by and I conned the fry cook into making the call for me. Then I went back and waited until the black-and-white arrived. The beat officers, Pettigrew and Gutierrez (Gerald and Maria, respectively), I'd encountered some months before when they made an arrest in my neighborhood.

She took the report now, while he made sympathetic noises. Somehow the two of them managed to console me insofar as that was possible, calling for a crime scene investigator who obligingly came out and dusted for prints. We all knew it was pointless, but it made me feel better. Pettigrew said he'd check the computer for the serial number on my gun, which was registered, thank God. Maybe it would turn up later in a pawn shop and I'd get it back.

I love my little semiautomatic, which I've had for years . . . a gift from the aunt who raised me after my parents' death. That gun was my legacy, representing the odd bond between us. She'd taught me to shoot when I was eight. She had never married, never had children of her own. With me, she'd exercised her many odd notions about the formation of female character. Firing a handgun, she felt, would teach me to appreciate both safety and accuracy. It would also help me develop good hand-eye coordination, which she thought was useful. She'd taught me to knit and crochet so that I'd learn patience and an eye for detail. She'd refused to teach me to cook as she felt it was boring and would only make me fat. Cussing was okay around the house, though we were expected to monitor our language in the company of those who might take offense. Exercise was important. Fashion was not. Reading was essential. Two out of three illnesses would cure themselves, said she, so doctors could generally be ignored except in case of accident. On the other hand, there was no excuse for having bad teeth, though she viewed dentists as the persons who came up with ludicrous schemes for the human mouth. Drilling out all of your old fillings and replacing them with gold, was one. She had dozens of these precepts and most are still with me.

Rule Number One, first and foremost, above and beyond all else, was financial independence. A woman should never, never, never be financially dependent on anyone, especially a man, because the minute you were dependent, you could be abused. Financially dependent persons (the young, the old, the indigent) were inevitably treated badly and had no recourse. A woman should *always* have recourse. My aunt believed that every woman should develop marketable skills, and the more money she was paid for them the better. Any feminine pursuit that did not have as its ultimate goal increased self-sufficiency could be disregarded. "How to Get Your Man" didn't even appear on the list.

When I was in high school, she'd called Home Ec "Home Ick" and applauded when I got a D. She thought it would make a lot more sense if the boys took Home Ec and the girls took Auto Mechanics and Wood Shop. Make no mistake about it, she liked (some) men a lot, but she wasn't interested in tending to one like a charwoman or a nurse. She was nobody's mother, said she, not even mine, and she didn't intend to behave like one. All of which constitutes a long-winded account of why I wanted my gun back, but there it is. I didn't have to explain any of this to G. Pettigrew or M. Gutierrez. They both knew I'd been a cop for two years and they both understood the value of a gun.

By the time everyone left the parking lot, it was fully dark and starting to rain again. Oh perfect.

I drove home and started making out a list of items I'd have to replace, including my driver's license, gasoline charge card, checkbook, and God knows what else. While I was at it, I looked up three "800" numbers, phoning in the loss of my credit cards from the Xerox copy I keep in my file drawer at home. I'd only been carrying about twenty bucks in cash, but I resented the loss. It was all too irritating to contemplate for long. I showered, pulled on jeans, boots, and a sweater, and headed up to Rosie's for a bite to eat.

Rosie's is the tavern in my neighborhood, run by herself, a Hungarian woman in her sixties, short and top-heavy, with dyed red hair that recently had looked like a cross between terra cotta floor tile and canned pumpkin pie filling. Rosie is an autocrat—outspoken, overbearing, suspicious of strangers. She cooks like a dream when it suits her, but she usually wants to dictate what you should eat at any given meal. She's protective, sometimes generous, often irritating. Like your best friend's cranky grandmother, she's someone you endure for the sake of peace. I hang out at her establishment because it's unpretentious and it's only half a block away from my place. Rosie apparently feels that my patronage entitles her to boss me around . . . which is generally true.

That night when I walked in, she took one look at my face and poured me a glass of white wine from her personal supply. I moved to my favorite booth at the rear. The backs are high, cut from construction grade plywood and stained dark, with side pieces shaped like the curve of a wingback chair. Within moments, Rosie materialized at the table and set the glass of wine in front of me.

"Somebody just busted out the window of my car and stole everything I hold dear, including my gun," I said.

"I've got some *sóska leves* for you," she announced. "And after that, you gonna have a salad made with celery root, some chicken paprikas, some of Henry's good rolls, cabbage strudel, and deep-fried cherries if you're good and clean up your plate. It's on the house, on account of your troubles, only think about this one thing while you eat. If you had a good man in your life, this would never happen to you and that's all I'm gonna say."

I laughed for the first time in days.

13

The next morning, Monday, I began the laborious process of replacing the contents of my handbag. I hit the DMV first, since the offices opened at 8:00 A.M. I set in motion the paperwork for a new driver's license, paying three dollars for a duplicate. The minute the bank opened, I closed out my checking account and opened a new one. I stopped by the apartment then and put a call through to Sacramento to the Bureau of Collection and Investigative Services, Department of Consumer Affairs, requesting application for a certified replacement for my private investigator's registration card. I armed myself with a batch of business cards from my ready supply and hunted up an old handbag to use until I could buy a new one. I drove over to the drugstore and made purchases to replace at least a few of the odds and ends I carry with me as a matter of course, birth control pills being one. At some point, I'd have to have my car window replaced, too. Irksome, all of it.

I didn't reach the office until almost noon and the message light on my answering machine was blinking insistently. I tossed the morning mail aside and punched the playback button as I passed the desk, listening to the caller as I opened the French doors to let in some fresh air.

"Miss Millhone, this is Ferrin Westfall at 555-6790. My wife and I have discussed your request to speak with our nephew, Tony, and if you'll get in touch, we'll see what we can work out. Please understand, we don't want the boy upset. We trust you'll conduct whatever business you have with him discreetly." There was a click, breaking the connection. His tone had been cold, perfectly suited to his formal, well-organized speaking voice. No "uh"s, no hesitations, no hiccups in the presentation. I lifted my brows appreciatively. Tony Gahan was in capable hands. Poor kid.

I made myself a pot of coffee and waited until I'd downed half a cup before I returned the call. The phone rang twice.

"Good morning. PFC," the woman said.

PFC turned out to be Perforated Formanek Corporation, a supplier of industrial abrasives, grinders, clamps, epoxy, cutters, end mills, and precision tools. I know this because I asked and she recited the entire inventory in a sing-song tone, thinking perhaps that I was in the market for one of the above. I asked to speak to Ferrin Westfall and was thanked for my request.

There was a click. "Westfall," said he.

I identified myself. There was a silence, meant (perhaps) to intimidate. I resisted the urge to rush in with a lot of unnecessary chatter, allowing the pause to go on for as long as it suited him.

Finally, he said, "We'll see that Tony's available this evening between seven and eight if that's acceptable." He gave me the address.

"Fine," I said. "Thank you." Ass, I added mentally. Then I hung up.

I tipped back in my swivel chair and propped my feet up. So far, it was a crummy day. I wanted my handbag back. I wanted my gun. I wanted to get on with life and quit wasting time with all this clerical nonsense. I glanced out at the balcony. At least it wasn't raining at the moment. I pulled the mail over and started going through it. Most of it was junk.

I was feeling restless again, thinking about John Daggett and his boat trip across the harbor. Yesterday, at the beach, the notion of canvassing the neighborhood for witnesses had seemed pointless. Now I wasn't so sure. Somebody might have seen him. Public drunkenness is usually conspicuous, especially at an hour when not many people are about. Weekend guests at the beach motels had probably checked out by now, but it might still be worth a shot. I grabbed my jacket and my car keys, locked the office, and headed down the back stairs.

My VW was looking worse every time I turned around. It's fourteen years old, an oxidized beige model with dents. Now the window was smashed out on the passenger side. Not a class act by any stretch of the imagination, but it was paid for. Every time I think about a new car, it makes my stomach do a flip-flop. I don't want to be saddled with car payments, a jump in insurance premiums, and hefty registration fees. My current registration costs me twenty-five dollars a year, which suits me just fine. I turned the ignition key and the engine fired right up. I patted the dashboard and backed out of the space, taking State Street south toward the beach.

I parked on Cabana, just across from the entrance to the wharf. There are eight motels strung out along the boulevard, none with rooms for under sixty dollars a night. This was the "off" season and there were still no vacancies. I started with the first, the Sea Voyager, where I identified myself to the manager, found out who'd been working the night desk the previous Friday, jotted down the name, and left my card with a handwritten note on the back. As with many other aspects of the job I do, this door-to-door inquiry requires dogged patience and a fondness for repetition that doesn't really come naturally. The effort has to be made, however, on the off chance that someone, somewhere can fill in a detail that might help. Having worked my way to the last motel, I returned to my car and headed on down the boulevard toward the marina, half a mile away.

I parked this time near the Naval Reserve Building, in the lot adjacent to the harbor. There didn't seem to be much foot traffic in the area. The sky was overcast, the air heavy with the staunch smells of fresh fish and diesel fuel. I ambled along the walk that skirts the waterfront, with its eighty-four acres of slips for eleven hundred boats. A wooden pier, two lanes wide, juts out into the water topped with a crane and pulleys for hoisting boats. I could see the fuel dock and the city guest dock, where two men were securing the lines on a big power boat that they'd apparently just brought in.

On my right, there was a row of waterfront businesses—a fish market with a seafood restaurant above, a shop selling marine and fishing supplies, a commercial diving center, two yacht brokers. The building fronts are all weathered gray wood, with bright royal blue awnings that echo the blue canvas sail covers on boats all through the harbor. For a moment, I paused before a plate glass window, scanning the snapshots of boats for sale—catamarans, luxury cabin cruisers, sailboats designed to sleep six. There's a small population of "live-aboards" in the harbor—people who actually use their boats as a primary residence. The idea is mildly appealing to me, though I wonder about the reality of chemical toilets in the dead of night and showering in marina restrooms. I crossed the walk and leaned on the iron railing, looking out across the airy forest of bare boat masts.

The water itself was a dark hunter green. Big rocks were submerged in the gloomy depths, looking like sunken ruins. Few fish were visible. I spotted two little crabs scuttling along the boulders at the water's edge, but for the most part, the shallows seemed cold and sterile, empty of sea life. A beer bottle rested on a shelf of sand and mud. Two harbor patrol boats were moored not far away.

I spotted a line of skiffs tied up at one of the docks below and my interest perked up. Four of the marinas are kept locked and can only be entered with a card key issued by the Harbor Master's Office, but this one was accessible to the public. I moved down the ramp for a closer look. There were maybe twenty-five small skiffs, wood and fiberglass, most of them eight to ten feet long. I had no way of knowing if one of these was the boat Daggett had taken, but this much seemed clear: if you cut the line on one of these boats, you'd have to row it out around the end of the dock and through the harbor. There was no current here and a boat left to drift would simply bump aimlessly against the pilings without going anyplace.

I went up the ramp again and turned left along the walkway until I reached Marina One. At the bottom of the ramp, I could see the chain-link fence and locked gate. I loitered on the walk, keeping an eye on passersby. Finally, a middle-aged man approached, his card key in one hand, a bag of groceries in the other. He was trim and muscular, tanned to the color of rawhide. He wore Bermuda shorts, Topsiders, and a loose cotton sweater, a mat of graying chest hairs visible in the V.

"Excuse me," I said. "Do you live down there?"

He paused, looking at me with curiosity. "Yes." His face was as lined as a crumpled brown grocery bag pressed into service again.

"Do you mind if I follow you out onto Marina One? I'm trying to get a line on the man who washed up on the beach Saturday."

"Sure, come on. I heard about that. The skiff he stole belongs to a friend of mine. By the way, I'm Aaron. You are?"

"Kinsey Millhone," I said, trotting down the ramp after him. "How long have you lived down here?"

"Six months. My wife and I split up and she kept the house. Nice change, boat life. Lot of nice people. You a cop?"

"Private investigator," I said. "What sort of work do you do?"

"Real estate," he said. "How'd you get into it?" He inserted his card and pushed the gate open. He held it while I passed through. I paused on the other side so he could lead the way.

"I was hired by the dead man's daughter," I said.

"I meant how'd you get into investigative work."

"Oh. I used to be a cop, but I didn't like it much. The law enforcement part of it was fine, but not the bureaucracy. Now I'm self-employed. I'm happier that way."

We passed a cloud of sea gulls converging rapidly on an object bobbing in the water. The screeches from the birds were attracting gulls from a quarter of a mile away, streaking through the air like missiles.

"Avocado," Aaron said idly. "The gulls love them. This is me." He had paused near a thirty-seven-foot twin-diesel trawler, a Chris Craft, with a flying bridge.

"God, it's a beautiful boat."

"You like it? I can sleep eight," he said, pleased. He hopped down into the cockpit and turned, holding a hand out to me. "Pop your boots off and you can come on board and take a look around. Want a drink?"

"I better not, thanks. I've got a lot of ground to cover yet. Is there any way you can introduce me to the guy whose skiff was stolen?"

Aaron shrugged. "Can't help you there. He's out on a fishing boat all day, but I can give him your name and telephone number if you like. I think the police impounded the skiff, so if you want to see that, you better talk to them."

I didn't expect anything to come of it, but I thought I'd leave the door open just in case. I took out a business card, jotting down my home number on the back before I passed it on to him. "Have him give me a call if he knows anything," I said.

"I'll tell you who you might want to talk to. Go down here six slips and see if that guy's in. *The Seascape* is the name of the boat. His is Phillip Rosen. He knows all the gossip down here. Maybe he can help."

"Thanks."

The Seascape was a twenty-four-foot Flicka, a gaff-rigged sloop with a twenty-foot mast, teak deck, and a fiberglass hull that mimicked wood.

I tapped on the cabin roof, calling a hello toward the open doorway. Phillip Rosen appeared, ducking his head as he came up from down below. His emerging was like a visual joke: he was one of the tallest men I'd seen except on a basketball court. He was probably six-foot-ten and built on a grand scale—big hands and feet, big head with a full head of red hair, a big face with red beard and moustache, bare-chested and barefoot. Except for the ragged blue jean cut-offs, he looked like a Viking reincarnated cruelly into a vessel unworthy of him. I introduced myself, mentioning that Aaron had suggested that I talk to him. I told him briefly what I wanted.

"Well, I didn't see them, but a friend of mine did. She was coming down here to meet me and passed 'em in the parking lot. Man and a woman. She said the old guy was drunk as a skunk, staggering all over the place. The little gal with him had a hell of a time trying to keep him upright."

"Do you have any idea what she looked like?"

"Nope. Dinah never said. I can give you her number though, if you want to ask her about it yourself."

"I'd like that," I said. "What time was this?"

"I'd say two-fifteen. Dinah's a waitress over at the Wharf and she gets off at two. I know she didn't close up that night and it only takes five minutes to get here. Shoot, if she walked on water, she could skip across the harbor in the time it takes her to get to the parking lot."

"Is she at work now by any chance?"

"Monday afternoon? Could be. I never heard what her schedule was this week, but you can always try. She'd be up in the cocktail lounge. A redhead. You can't miss her if she's there."

Which turned out to be true. I drove the half mile from the marina to the wharf, leaving my car with the valet who handles restaurant parking. Then I went up the outside staircase to the wooden deck above. Dinah was crossing from the bar to a table in the corner, balancing a tray of margaritas. Her hair was more orange than red, too carroty a shade to be anything but natural. She was probably six feet tall in heels, wearing dark mesh hose, and a navy blue "sailor" suit with a skirt that skimmed her crotch. She had a little sailor cap pinned to her head and an air about her that suggested she'd known starboard from port since the day she reached puberty.

I waited until she'd served the drinks and was on her way back to the bar. "Dinah?"

She looked at me quizzically. Up close, I could see the overlay of pale red freckles on her face and a long, narrow nose. She wore false eyelashes, like a series of commas encircling her pale hazel eyes, lending her a look of startlement. I gave her a brief rundown, patiently repeating myself. "I know who the old guy is," I said. "What I'm trying to get a fix on is the woman he was with."

Dinah shrugged. "Well, I can't tell you much. I just saw them as I went past. I mean, the marina's got *some* lights, but not that great. Plus, it was raining like a son of a bitch."

"How old would you say she was?"

"On the young side. Twenties, maybe. Blonde. Not real big, at least compared to him."

"Long hair? Short? Buxom? Flat-chested?"

"The build, I don't know. She was wearing a raincoat. Some kind of coat, anyway. Hair was maybe shoulder length, not a lot of curl. Kind of bushy."

"Pretty?"

She thought briefly. "God, all I remember thinking was there was something off, you know? For starters, he was such a mess. I could smell him ten feet away. Bourbon fumes. Phew! Actually, I kind of thought she might be a hooker on the verge of rolling him. I nearly said something to her, but then I decided it was none of my business. He was having a great old time, but you know how it is. Drunk as he was, she really could have ripped him off."

"Yeah, well, she did. *Dead* is about as ripped off as you can get."

14

By the time I pulled out of the restaurant parking lot, it was 2:00 and the air felt dank. Or maybe it was only the shadowy image of Daggett's companion that chilled me. I'd been half convinced there was someone with him that night and now I had confirmation—not proof of murder, surely, but some sense of the events leading up to his death, a tantalizing glimpse of his consort, that "other" whose ghostly passage I tracked.

From Dinah's description, Lovella Daggett was the first name that popped into my head. Her trashy blonde looks had made me think she was hooking when I met her in L.A. On the other hand, most of the women I'd run across to date were on the young side and fair-haired—Barbara Daggett, Billy Polo's sister Coral, Ramona Westfall, even Marilyn Smith, the mother of the other dead child. I'd have to start pinning people down as to their whereabouts the night of the murder, a tricky matter as I had no way to coerce a reply. Cops have some leverage. A P.I. has none.

In the meantime, I went by the bank and removed the cashier's check from my safe deposit box. I ducked into a coffee shop and grabbed a quick lunch, then spent the afternoon in the office catching up on paperwork. At 5:00, I locked up and went home, puttering around until 6:30 when I left for Ferrin and Ramona Westfall's house to meet Tony Gahan.

The Westfalls lived in an area called the Close, a deadend street lined with live oaks over near the Natural History Museum. I drove through stone gates into the dim hush of privacy. There are only eight homes on the cul-de-sac, all Victorian, completely restored, immaculately kept. The neighborhood looks, even now, like a small, rural community inexplicably lifted out of the past. The properties are surrounded by low walls of fieldstone, the lots overgrown with bamboo, pampas grass, and fern. It was fully dark by then and the Close was wreathed in mist. The vegetation was dense, intensely scented, and lush from the recent rain. There was only one street light, its pale globe obscured by the branches of a tree.

I found the number I was looking for and parked on the street, picking my way up the path to the front. The house was a putty-colored, one-story wood frame with a wide porch, white shutters and trim. The porch furniture was white wicker with cushions covered in a white-and-putty print. Two Victorian wicker plant stands held massive Boston ferns. All too perfect for my taste.

I rang the bell, refusing to peer in through the etched glass oval in the door. I suspected the interior was going to look like something out of *House and Garden* magazine, an elegant blend of the old, the new, and the offbeat. Of course, my perception was probably colored by Ferrin Westfall's curt treatment of me and Ramona's outright hostility. I'm not above holding grudges.

Ramona Westfall came to the door and admitted me. I kept my tone pleasant, but I didn't fall all over myself admiring the place, which, at a glance, did appear to be flawlessly done. She showed me into the front parlor and removed herself, closing the oak-paneled sliding doors behind her. I waited, staring resolutely at the floor. I could hear murmuring in the hall. After a moment, the doors slid open and a man entered, introducing himself as Ferrin Westfall . . . as if I hadn't guessed. We shook hands.

He was tall and slim, with a cold, handsome face and silver hair. His eyes were a dark green, as empty of warmth as the harbor. There were hints of something submerged in the depths, but no signs of life. He wore charcoal gray pants and a soft gray cashmere sweater that fairly begged to be stroked. He indicated that I should have a seat, which I did.

He surveyed me for a moment, taking in the boots, the faded jeans, the wool sweater beginning to pill at the elbows. I was determined not to let his disapproval get through to me, but it required an effort on my part. I stared at him impassively and warded off his withering assessment by picturing him on the toilet with his knickers down around his ankles.

Finally, he said, "Tony will be out in a moment. Ramona's told me about the check. I wonder if I might examine it."

I removed the check from my jeans pocket and smoothed it out, passing it to him for his inspection. I wondered if he thought it was forged, stolen, or in some way counterfeit. He scrutinized it, fore and aft, and returned it, apparently satisfied that it was legitimate.

"Why did Mr. Daggett come to you with this?" he asked.

"I'm not really sure," I said. "He told me he'd tried to find Tony at an old address. When he had no luck, he asked me to track him down and deliver it."

"Do you know how he acquired the money?"

Again, I found myself feeling protective. It was really none of this man's business. He probably wanted to assure himself that Daggett hadn't come by the money through some tacky enterprise—drugs, prostitutes, selling dogs and kitty cats to labs for medical experiments.

"He won it at the track," I said. Personally, I hadn't quite believed this part of Daggett's tale, but I didn't mind if Ferrin Westfall got sucked in. He didn't seem any more convinced than I. He shifted the subject.

"Would you prefer to be alone with Tony?"

I was surprised at the offer. "Yes, I would. I'd really like to go off somewhere with him and have a Coke."

"I suppose that would be all right, as long as you don't keep him too long. This is a school night."

"Sure. That's very nice of you."

There was a tap at the door. Mr. Westfall rose and crossed the room. "This will be Tony," he said.

The doors slid back and Tony Gahan came in. He looked like an immature fifteen. He was maybe five-foot-six, a hundred and twenty-five pounds. His uncle introduced me. I proferred my hand and we fumbled through a handshake. Tony's eyes were dark, his hair a medium brown, attractively cut, which struck me as odd. Most of the high school kids I've seen lately look like they're being treated for the same scalp disease. I suspected Tony's hairstyle was a concession to Ferrin Westfall's notions of good taste and I wondered how that sat with him.

His manner was anxious. He seemed like a kid trying desperately to please. He shot a cautious look at his uncle, searching for visual cues as to what was expected of him and how he was meant to behave. It was painful to watch.

"Miss Millhone would like to take you out for a Coke, so she can talk to you," Mr. Westfall said.

"How come?" he croaked. Tony looked like he was going to drop dead on the spot and I remembered in a flash how much I'd hated eating and drinking in the presence of strange adults when I was his age. Meals represent a series of traps when you haven't yet mastered the appropriate social skills. I hated adding to his distress, but I was convinced I'd never have a decent conversation with him in this house.

"She'll explain all that," Mr. Westfall said. "Obviously, you're not required to go. If you'd prefer to stay here, simply say so."

Tony seemed unable to get a reading from his uncle's statement, which was neutral on the surface, but contained some tricky side notes. It was the word "simply" that tripped him, I thought, and the "obviously" didn't help.

Tony glanced at me with a half shrug. "It's okay, I guess. Like, right now?"

Mr. Westfall nodded. "It won't be for long. You'll need a jacket, of course."

Tony moved out into the hall and I followed, waiting until he found his jacket in the hall closet.

At fifteen, I thought he could probably figure out if he needed a jacket or not, but neither of them consulted me on the subject. I opened the front door and held it while he went out. Mr. Westfall watched us for a moment and then closed the door behind us. God, it was just like a date. I nearly swore I'd have him home by 10:00. Absurd.

We made our way down the path in the dark. "You go to Santa Teresa High School?"

"Right."

"What year?"

"Sophomore."

We got in the car. Tony tried to roll down the smashed window on his side without much success. A shard of glass tinkled down into the door frame. He finally gave up.

"What happened to this?"

"I was careless," I said, and let it go at that.

I did a U-turn in the lane and I headed for the Clockworks on State Street, a teen hangout generally regarded as seedy, unclean, and corrupt, which it is ... a training ground for junior thugs. Kids come here (stoned, no doubt) to drink Cokes, smoke clove cigarettes, and behave like bad-asses. I'd been introduced to the place by a seventeen-year-old pink-haired dope dealer named Mike, who made more money than I did. I hadn't seen him since June, but I tend to look for him around town.

We parked in a small lot out back and went in through the rear entrance. The place is long and narrow, painted charcoal gray, the high ceiling rimmed with pink and purple neon. A series of mobiles, looking like big black clock gears, revolve in the smoky air. The noise level, on weekends, is deafening, the music so loud it makes the floor vibrate. On week nights, it's quiet and oddly intimate. We found a table and I went over to the counter to pick up a couple of Cokes. There was a tap on my shoulder and I turned to find Mike standing there. I felt a rush of warmth. "I was just thinking about you!" I said. "How are you?"

A pink tint crept across his cheeks and he gave me a slow seductive smile. "I'm okay. What are you doin' these days?"

"Nothing much," I said. "Great hair." Formerly, he'd sported a Mohawk, a great cockscomb of pink down the center of his head, with the sides shaved close. Now it was arranged in a series of purple spurts, each clump held together with a rubber band, the feathery tips bleached white. Aside from the hair, he was a good-looking kid, clear skin, green eyes, good teeth.

I said, "Actually, I'm about to have a talk with that guy over there . . . a schoolmate of yours."

"Yeah?" He turned and gave Tony a cursory inspection.

"You know him?"

"I've seen him. He doesn't hang out with the kind of people I do." His gaze returned to Tony and I thought he was going to say more, but he let it pass.

"What are you up to?" I asked. "Still dealing?"

"Who me? Hey, no. I told you I'd quit," he said, sounding faintly righteous. The look in his eyes, of course, suggested just the opposite. If he was doing something illegal, I didn't want to know about it anyway, so I bypassed the subject.

"What about school? You graduate this year?"

"June. I got college applications out and everything."

"Really?" I couldn't tell if he was putting me on or not.

He caught the look. "I get good grades," he protested. "I'm not just your average high school dunce, you know. The bucks I got, I could go anyplace I want. That's what private enterprise is about."

I had to laugh. "For sure," I said. The "bar maid" set two Cokes on the counter and I paid her. "I have to get back to my date."

"Nice seeing you," he said. "You ought to come in sometime and talk to me."

"Maybe I'll do that," I said. I smiled at him, mentally shaking my head. Flirtatious little shit. I moved over to the table where Tony was sitting. I handed him a Coke and sat down.

"You know that guy?" Tony asked cautiously.

"Who, Mike? Yes, I know him."

Tony's eyes strayed to Mike and back again, resting on my face with something close to respect. Maybe I wasn't such a geek after all.

"Did your uncle tell you what this is about?" I asked.

"Some. He said the accident and that old drunk."

"You feel okay discussing it?"

He shrugged by way of reply, avoiding eye contact.

"I take it you weren't in the car," I said.

He smoothed the front of his hair to the side. "Uh-uh. Me and my mom got into this argument. They were going to my granny's for this Easter egg hunt and I didn't want to go."

"Your grandmother's still in town someplace?"

He shifted in his chair. "In a rest home. She had a stroke."

"She's your mother's mother?" I didn't care particularly about any of this. I was just hoping the kid would relax and open up.

"Yeah."

"What's it like living with your aunt and uncle?"

"Fine. No big deal. He comes down on my case all the time, but she's nice."

"She said you were having some problems at school."

"So?"

"Just curious. She says you're very smart and your grades are in the toilet. I wondered what that was about."

"It's about school sucks," he said. "It's about I don't like people butting into my fuckin' business."

"Really," I said. I took a sip of Coke. His hostility was like a sewer backing up and I thought I'd give the efflux a chance to subside. I didn't care if he cussed. I could outcuss him any day of the week.

When I didn't react, he filled the silence. "I'm trying to get my grades pulled up," he said somewhat grudgingly. "I had to take all this bullshit math and chemistry. That's why I didn't do good."

"What's your preference? English? Art?"

He hesitated. "You some kind of shrink?"

"No. I'm a private investigator. I assumed you knew that."

He stared at me. "I don't get it. What's this got to do with the accident?"

I took out the check and laid it on the table. "The man responsible wanted me to look you up and give you this."

He picked the check up and glanced at it.

"It's a cashier's check for twenty-five thousand dollars," I said.

"What for?"

"I'm not really sure. I think John Daggett was hoping to make restitution for what he did."

Tony's confusion was clear and so was the anger that accompanied it. "I don't want this," he said. "Why give it to me? Megan Smith died too, you know, and so did that other guy, Doug. Are they gettin' money too, or just me?"

"Just you, as far as I know."

"Take it back then. I don't want it. I hate that old bastard." He tossed the check on the table and gave it a push.

"Look. Now just wait and let me say something first. It's your choice. Honestly. It's up to you. Your aunt was offended by the offer and I understand that. No one can force you to accept the money if you don't want it. But just hear me out, okay?"

Tony was staring off across the room, his face set.

I lowered my voice. "Tony, it's true John Daggett was a drunk, and maybe he was a totally worthless human being, but he did something he felt bad about and I think he was trying to make up for it. Give him credit for that much and don't say no without giving it consideration first."

"I don't *want* money for what he did."

"I'm not done yet. Just let me finish this."

His mouth trembled. He made a dash at his eyes with the sleeve of his jacket, but he didn't get up and walk away.

"People make mistakes," I said. "People do things they never meant to do. He didn't kill anyone deliberately . . ."

"He's a fuckin' drunk! He was out on the fuckin' street at fuckin' nine in the morning. Dad and Mom and Hilary . . ." His voice broke and he fought for control. "I don't want anything from him. I hate his guts and I don't want his crummy check."

"Why don't you cash it and give it all away?"

"No! You take it. Give it back to him. Tell him I said he could get fucked."

"I can't. He's dead. He was killed Friday night."

"Good. I'm glad. I hope somebody cut his heart out. He deserved it."

"Maybe so. But it's still possible that he felt something for you and wanted to give you back some of what he took away."

"Like what? It's done. They're all dead."

"But you're not, Tony. You have to find a way to get on with life . . ."

"Hey! I'm doing that, okay? But I don't have to listen to this bullshit! You said what you had to say and now I want to go home."

He got up, radiating rage, his whole body stiff. He moved swiftly toward the rear entrance, knocking chairs aside. I snatched up the check and followed.

When I reached the parking lot, he was kick-boxing the remaining glass out of the smashed window of my car. I started to protest and then I stopped myself.

Oh why not, I thought. I had to replace the damn thing anyway. I stood and watched him without a word. When he was done, he leaned against the car and wept.

15

By the time I got Tony home again, he was calm, shut down, as if nothing out of the ordinary had occurred. I pulled up in front of the house. He got out, slammed the door, and headed up the path without a word. I was reasonably certain he wouldn't mention his outburst to his aunt and uncle, which was fortunate as I'd sworn I could talk to him without his getting upset. I was, of course, still in possession of Daggett's check, wondering if I'd be toting it around for life, trying in vain to get someone to take it off my hands.

When I got back to my place, I spent twenty minutes unloading my VW. While I tend to maintain an admirable level of tidiness in the apartment, my organizational skills have never extended to my car. The back seat is usually crowded with files, law books, my briefcase, piles of miscellaneous clothing—shoes, pantyhose, jackets, hats, some of which I use as "disguises" in the various aspects of my trade.

I packed everything in a cardboard box and then proceeded around to the backyard where the entrance to my apartment is located. I opened the padlock on the storage bin attached to the service porch and stowed the box, snapping the padlock into place again.

As I reached my door, a dark shape loomed out of the shadows. "Kinsey?"

I jumped, realizing belatedly that it was Billy Polo. I couldn't distinguish his features in the dark, but his voice was distinctly his own.

"Oh Jesus, what are you doing here?" I said.

"Hey, I'm sorry. I didn't mean to scare you. I wanted to talk to you."

I was still trying to recover from the jolt he'd given me, my temper rising belatedly. "How'd you know where to find me?"

"I looked you up in the telephone book."

"My home address isn't in the book."

"Yeah, I know. I tried your office first. You weren't in, so I asked next door at that insurance place."

"California Fidelity gave you my home address?" I said. "Who'd you talk to?" I didn't believe for a minute that CF would release that kind of information to him.

"I didn't get her name. I told her I was a client and it was urgent."

"Bullshit."

"No, it's the truth. She only gave it to me because I leaned on her."

I could tell he wasn't going to budge on the point, so I let it pass. "All right, what is it?" I said. I knew I sounded cranky, but I didn't like his coming to my place and I didn't believe his tale about how he found out where it was.

"We're just gonna stand around out here?"

"That's right, Billy. Now get on with it."

"Well, you don't have to get so huffy."

"Huffy! What the hell are you talking about? You loom up out of the dark and scare me half to death! I don't know you from Jack the Ripper so why should I invite you in?"

"Okay, okay."

"Just say what you have to say. I'm beat."

He did some fidgeting around . . . for effect, I thought. Finally, he said, "I talked to my sister, Coral, and she told me I should be straight with you."

"Oh goody, what a treat. Straight about what?"

"Daggett," he mumbled. "He did get in touch."

"When was this?"

"Last Monday when he got to town."

"He called you?"

"Yeah, that's right."

"How'd he know where you were?"

"He tried my mom's house and talked to her. I wasn't home at the time, so she got his number and I called him back."

"Where'd he call from?"

"I don't know for sure. Some dive. There was all this noise in the background. He was drunk and I figured he must have parked himself in the first bar he found."

"What time of day was this?"

"Maybe eight at night. Around in there."

"Go on."

"He said he was scared and needed help. Somebody called him down in Los Angeles and told him he was dead meat on account of a scam he pulled up in prison just before he got out."

"What scam?"

"I don't know all the details. What I heard was his cellmate got snuffed and Daggett helped himself to a big wad of cash the guy had hidden in his bunk."

"How much?"

"Nearly thirty grand. It was some kind of drug deal went sour, which is why the guy got killed in the first place. Daggett walked off with the whole stash and somebody wanted it back. They were comin' after him. At least that's what they told him."

"Who?"

"I don't want to mention names. I got a fair idea and I could find out for sure if I wanted to, but I don't like puttin' my neck in a noose unless I have to. The point is I shined him on. I wasn't going to help that old coot. No way. He got himself in a hole, let him get himself out. I didn't want to be involved. Not with those guys after him. I'm too fond of my health."

"So what happened? You talked on the phone and that was it?"

"Well, no. I met him for a drink. Coral said I should level with you about that."

"Really," I said: "What for?"

"In case something came up later. She didn't want it to look like I was holding out."

"So you think they caught up with him?"

"He's dead, ain't he?"

"Proving what?"

"Don't ask me. I mean, all I know is what Daggett said. He was on the run and he thought I'd help."

"How?"

"A place to hide."

"When did you meet with him?"

"Not till Thursday. I was tied up."

"Pressing social engagements, no doubt."

"Hey, I was looking for work. I'm on parole and I got requirements to meet."

"You didn't see him Friday?"

"Uh-uh. I just saw him once and that was Thursday night."

"What'd he do in the meantime?"

"I don't know. He never said."

"Where'd you meet him?"

"At the bar where Coral works."

"Ah, now I see. She got worried I'd ask around and some-body'd say they saw you with him."

"Well, yeah. Coral don't like me to mess with the law, especially with me on parole anyway."

"How come it took the bad guys so long to catch up with him? He's been out of prison for six weeks."

"Maybe they didn't figure it was him at first. Daggett wasn't the brightest guy, you know. He never did nothin' right in his life. They prob'ly figured he was too dumb to stick his hand in a mattress and walk off with the cash."

"Did Daggett have the money with him when you talked to him?"

"Are you kidding? He tried to borrow ten bucks from me," Billy said, aggrieved.

"What was the deal?" I asked. "If he gave the money back, they'd let him off the hook?"

"Probably not. I doubt that."

"So do I," I said. "How do you think Lovella figures into this?"

"She doesn't. It's got nothing to do with her."

"I wouldn't be too sure about that. Somebody saw Daggett down at the marina last Friday night, dead drunk, in the company of a trashy-looking blonde."

Even in the dark, I could tell Billy Polo was staring at me.

"A blonde?"

"That's right. She was on the young side from what I was told. He was staggering, and she had to work to keep him on his feet."

"I don't know nothin' about that."

"Neither do I, but it sure sounded like Lovella to me."

"Ask her about it then."

"I intend to," I said. "So what happens next?"

"About what?"

"The thirty thousand, for starters. With Daggett dead, does the money go back to the guys who were after him?"

"If they found it, I guess it does," he said, uncomfortably.

"What if they didn't find it?"

Billy hesitated. "Well, I guess if it's stashed somewhere, it'd belong to his widow, wouldn't it? Part of his estate?"

I was beginning to get the drift here, but I wondered if he did. "You mean Essie?"

"Who?"

"Daggett's widow, Essie."

"He's divorced from her," Billy said.

"I don't think so. At least not as far as the law is concerned."

"He's married to Lovella," he said.

"Not legally."

"You're shittin' me."

"Come to the funeral tomorrow and see for yourself."

"This Essie has the money?"

"No, but I know where it is. Twenty-five thousand of it, at any rate."

"Where?" he said, with disbelief.

"In my pocket, sweetheart, in the form of a cashier's check made out to Tony Gahan. You remember Tony, don't you?"

Dead silence.

I lowered my voice. "You want to tell me who Doug Polokowski is?"

Billy Polo turned and walked away.

I stood there for a moment and then followed reluctantly, still pondering the fact that he had my home address. Last time I'd talked to him, he didn't even buy the fact that I was a private investigator. Now suddenly he was seeking me out, having confidential chats about Daggett on my front step. It didn't add up.

I heard his car door slam as I reached the street. I hung back in the shadows, watching as he swung the Chevrolet out of a parking place four doors down. He gunned it, speeding off toward the beach. I debated about whether to pursue him, but I couldn't bear the thought of lurking about outside Coral's trailer again. Enough of that stuff. I turned back and let myself into my apartment. I kept thinking about the fact that my car was broken into, my handbag stolen, along with all of my personal identification. Had Billy Polo done that? Is that how he came up with my home address? I couldn't figure out how he'd tracked me to the beach in the first place, but it would explain how he knew where to find me now.

I was sure he was maneuvering, but I couldn't figure out what he'd hoped to get. Why the yarn about Daggett and the bad guys in jail? It did fit with some of the facts, but it didn't have that nice, untidy ring of truth.

I hauled out a stack of index cards and wrote it all down anyway. Maybe it would make sense later, when other information came to light. It was 10:00 by the time I finished. I pulled the white wine out of the refrigerator, wiggled the cork loose, and poured myself a glass. I stripped my clothes off, turned the lights out, and toted the wine into the bathroom where I set it on the window sill in the bathtub and stared out at the darkened street. There's a streetlight out there, buried in the branches of a jacaranda tree, largely denuded now by the rain. The window was half opened and a damp slat of night wind wafted in, chilly and secretive. I could hear rain begin to rattle on my composition roof. I was restless. When I was a young girl, maybe twelve or so, I wandered the streets on nights like this, barefoot, in a raincoat, feeling anxious and strange. I don't think my aunt knew about my nocturnal excursions, but maybe she did. She had a restless streak of her own and she may have honored mine. I was thinking a lot about her, of late, perhaps because of Tony. His family had been wiped out in a car accident, just as mine had, and he was being raised now by an aunt. Sometimes, I had to admit to myself . . . especially on nights like this . . . that the death of my parents may not have been as tragic as it seemed. My aunt, for all her failings, was a perfect guardian for me . . . brazen, remote, eccentric, independent. Had my parents lived, my life would have taken an altogether different route. There was no doubt of that in my mind. I like my history just as it is, but there was something else going on as well.

Looking back on the evening, I realized how much I'd identified with Tony's kicking my car window out. The rage and defiance were hypnotic and touched off deep feelings of my own. Daggett's funeral was coming up the next afternoon and that touched off something else . . . old sorrows, good friends gone down into the earth. Sometimes I picture death as a wide stone staircase, filled with a silent procession of those being led away. I see death too often to worry about it much, but I miss the departed and I wonder if I'll be docile when my turn comes.

I finished my wine and went to bed, sliding naked into the warm folds of my quilt.

16

The dawn was accompanied by drizzle, dark gray sky gradually shading to a cold white light. Ordinarily, I don't run in the rain, but I hadn't slept well and I needed to clear away the dregs of nagging anxiety. I wasn't even sure what I was worried about. Sometimes I awaken uncomfortably aware of a low-level dread humming in my gut. Running is the only relief I can find short of drink and drugs, which at 6:00 A.M. don't appeal.

I pulled on a sweat suit and hit the bike path, jogging a mile and a half to the recreation center. The palm trees along the boulevard had shed dried fronds in the wind and they lay on the grass like soggy feathers. The ocean was silver, the surf rustling mildly like a taffeta skirt with a ruffle of white. The beach was a drab brown, populated by sea gulls snatching at sand fleas. Pigeons lifted in a cloud, looking on. I have to admit I'm not an outdoor person at heart. I'm always aware that under the spritely twitter of birds, bones are being crunched and ribbons of flesh are being stripped away, all of it the work of bright-eyed creatures without feeling or conscience. I don't look to Nature for comfort or serenity.

Traffic was light. There were no other joggers. I passed the public restrooms, housed in a cinderblock building painted flesh pink, where two bums huddled with a shopping cart. One I recognized from two nights before and he watched me now, indifferently. His friend was curled up under a cardboard comforter, looking like a pile of old rags. I reached the turnaround and ran the mile and a half back. By the time I got home, my Etonics were soaked, my sweat pants were darkened by the drizzle, and the mist had beaded in my hair like a net of seed pearls. I took a long hot shower, optimism returning now that I was safely home again.

After breakfast, I tidied up and then checked my automobile insurance policy and determined that the replacement of my car window was covered, after a fifty-dollar deductible. At 8:30, I started soliciting estimates from auto glass shops, trying to persuade someone to work me in before noon that day. I zipped myself into my all-purpose dress again, resurrected a decent-looking black leather shoulder bag that I use for "formal" wear and filled it with essentials, including the accursed cashier's check.

I dropped the car off at an auto glass shop not far from my office and hoofed it the rest of the way to work. Even with low-heeled pumps, my feet hurt and my pantyhose made me feel like I was walking around with a hot, moist hand in my crotch.

I let myself into the office and initiated my usual morning routines. The phone rang as I was plugging in the coffeepot.

"Miss Millhone, this is Ramona Westfall."

"Oh hello," I said. "How are you?" Secretly, my stomach did a little twist and I wondered if Tony Gahan had told her about his freak-out at the Clockworks the night before.

"I'm fine," she said. "I'm calling because there's something I'd like to discuss with you and I hoped you might have some time free this morning."

"Well, my schedule's clear, but I don't have a car. Can you come down here?"

"Yes, of course. I'd prefer that anyway. Is ten convenient? It's short notice, I know."

I glanced at my watch. Twenty minutes. "That's fine," I said. She made some good-bye noises and clicked off. I depressed the line and then put a call through to Barbara Daggett at her mother's house to verify the time of the funeral. She was unavailable to come to the phone, but Eugene Nickerson told me the services were at 2:00 and I said I'd be there.

I took a few minutes to open my mail from the day before, posting a couple of checks to accounts receivable, then made a quick call to my insurance agent, giving her the sketchy details about my car window. I'd no more than put the phone down when it rang again.

"Kinsey, this is Barbara Daggett. Something's come up. When I arrived here this morning, there was some woman sitting on the porch steps who says she's Daddy's wife."

"Oh God. Lovella."

"You know about her?"

"I met her last week when I was down in L.A., trying to get a line on your father's whereabouts."

"And you knew about this claim of hers?"

"I never heard the details, but I gathered they were living in some kind of common-law relationship."

"Kinsey, she has a marriage certificate. I saw it myself. Why didn't you tell me what was going on? I was speechless. She stood out on the front porch, screaming bloody murder until I finally had to call the police. I can't believe you didn't at least *mention* it."

"When was I supposed to do that? At the morgue? Over at the funeral home with your mother in a state of collapse?"

"You could have called me, Kinsey. Any time. You could have come to my office to discuss it."

"Barbara, I could have done half a dozen things, but I didn't. Frankly, I was feeling protective of your father and I was hoping you wouldn't have to find out about this 'alleged' marriage. That certificate could be a fake. The whole thing could be trumped up, and if not, you've still got problems enough without adding bigamy to his list of personal failings."

"That isn't yours to decide. Now Mother wants to know

what the ruckus was about and I have no idea what to say."

"Well, I can see why you're upset, but I'm not sure I'd do it any differently."

"I can't believe you'd take that attitude! I don't appreciate being kept in the dark," she said. "I hired you to investigate and I expect you to pass on whatever comes to light."

"Your father hired me long before you did," I said.

That silenced her for a moment and then she took off again. "To do what? You never did specify."

"Of course I didn't. He talked to me confidentially. It was all bullshit, but it's still not mine to flap around. I couldn't stay in business if I blabbed all the information that came my way."

"I'm his daughter. I have a right to know. Especially if my father's a *bigamist*. What else am I paying you for?"

"You might be paying me to exercise a little judgment of my own," I said. "Come on, Barbara. Be reasonable. Suppose I'd told you. What purpose would that have served? If your parents are still legally married, Lovella has no claim whatever and, for all I know, she's perfectly aware of that. Why add to your grief when she might well have slunk away without a word?"

"How did she know he died in the first place?"

"Not from me, I can tell you that. I'm not an idiot. The last thing in the world I wanted was her up here camping out on your doorstep. Maybe she read it in the paper. Maybe she heard it on the news."

She murmured something, temporarily mollified.

"What happened when the cops got there?" I asked.

There was another pause while she debated whether to move on or continue berating me. I sensed that she enjoyed chewing people out and it was hard for her to give up the opportunity. From my point of view, she wasn't paying me enough to take much guff. A little bit, perhaps. I probably should have told her.

"The two officers took her aside and had a talk with her. She left a few minutes ago."

"Well, if she shows up again, I'll take care of it," I said.

"Again? Why would she do that?"

I remembered then that aside from the matter of her father's apparent bigamy, I hadn't told her about the infamous twenty-five thousand dollars, which Billy Polo assumed was part of Daggett's "estate." Maybe Lovella had come up here to collect. "I think we better have a chat soon," I said.

"Why? Is there something *else*?"

I looked up. Ramona Westfall was standing in my doorway. "There's always something else," I said. "That's what makes life so much fun. I've got someone here. I'll talk to you this afternoon."

I hung up and rose to my feet, shaking hands with Mrs. Westfall across the desk. I invited her to take a seat and then poured coffee for us both, using social ritual as a way of setting her at ease, or so I hoped.

She was looking drawn, the fine skin under her mild eyes smudged with fatigue. She wore a tan poplin shirtwaist with shoulder epaulets and carried a mesh-and-canvas handbag that looked like it could be packed for a quick safari somewhere. Her pale hair had the sheen of a Breck shampoo ad in a magazine. I tried to picture her in a raincoat, lurching around the marina with Daggett's arm draped over her shoulder. Could she have flipped him, ass over teakettle, right out of that skiff? Hey, sure. Why not?

She stared at me uneasily, reaching out automatically to straighten some items on my desk. She lined up three pencils with the points facing me, like little ground-to-air missiles, and then she cleared her throat.

"Well. We were wondering. Tony never said anything so we thought perhaps we should ask you about it. Did you tell Tony about the money when you talked to him last night?"

"Sure," I said. "Not that it did any good. I got nowhere. He was adamant. He wouldn't even discuss it."

She colored slightly. "We're thinking to take it," she said. "Ferrin and I talked about it last night while Tony was out with you and we're beginning to believe we should put the money in a trustee account for him . . . at least until he's eighteen and really has a sense of what he might do with it."

"What brought about the change?"

"Oh everything, I guess. We've been in family counseling and the therapist keeps hoping we can work through some of the anger and the grief. He feels Tony's migraines are stress-related in part, a sort of index of his unwillingness . . . or maybe inability is a better word . . . to process his loss. I've been wondering how much I've contributed to that. I haven't dealt with Abby's death that well and it can't have helped him." She paused and then shook her head slightly as though embarrassed. "I know it's a reversal. I suppose we've been unnecessarily rude to you and I'm sorry."

"You don't have to apologize," I said. "Personally, I'd be delighted to have you take the check. At least then I could feel I'd discharged my responsibilities. If you change your mind later, you can always donate the money to a worthy cause. There are lots of those around."

"What about his family? Daggett's. They may feel they're entitled to the money, don't you think? I mean, I wouldn't want to take it if there are going to be any legal ramifications."

"You'd have to talk to an attorney about that," I said. "The check is made out to Tony, and Daggett hired me to deliver it to him. I don't think there's any question about his intention. There may be other legal issues I don't know about, but you're certainly welcome to talk to someone first." Secretly, I wanted her to take the damn thing and be done with it.

She stared at the floor for a moment. "Tony said . . . last night he mentioned that he might want to go to the funeral.

Do you think he should? I mean, does that seem like a good idea to you?"

"I don't know, Mrs. Westfall. That's way out of my line. Why don't you ask his therapist?"

"I tried, but he's out of town until tomorrow. I don't want Tony any more upset than he is."

"He's going to feel what he feels. You can't control that. Maybe it's something he has to go through."

"That's what Ferrin says, but I'm not sure."

"What's the story on the migraines? How long has that been going on?"

"Since the accident. He had one last night as a matter of fact. It's not your fault," she added hastily. "His head started bothering him about an hour after he got home. He threw up every twenty minutes or so from midnight until almost four A.M. We finally had to take him over to the emergency room at St. Terry's. They gave him a shot and that put him out, but he woke up a little while ago and he's talking now about going to the funeral. Did he mention it to you?"

"Not at all. I told him Daggett was dead, but he didn't react much at the time, except to say he was glad. Is he well enough to go?"

"He will be, I think. The migraines are odd. One minute you think he's never going to pull out of it and the next minute he's on his feet and starving to death. It happened last Friday night."

"Friday?" I said. The night of Daggett's death.

"That episode wasn't quite as bad. When he came home from school, he knew he was on the verge of a headache. We tried to get some medication down him to head it off, but no luck. Anyway, he pulled out of it after a while and I ended up fixing him two meatloaf sandwiches in the kitchen at two A.M. He was fine. Of course, he had another headache on Tuesday, and then the one last night. Two the week before that. Ferrin thinks maybe his going to the funeral will have some symbolic significance. You know, finish it off for him and set him free."

"That's always possible."

"Would Barbara Daggett object?"

"I don't see why she would," I said. "I suspect she feels as guilty as her father did, and she's offered to help."

"I guess I'll see how he's doing when I get home, then," she said. She glanced at her watch. "I better go."

"Let me give you the check." I pulled my handbag out of the bottom drawer and took out the check, which I passed across the desk to her. As her husband had done the night before, she smoothed out the folds, looking at it closely as if it might be some preposterous fake. She folded it up again and slipped it in her bag as she got to her feet. She hadn't touched her mug of coffee. I hadn't drunk mine either.

I told her the time and place of the services and walked her to the door. After she left, I sat down at my desk again, reviewing everything she'd said. At some point, I wanted to take Tony Gahan aside and see if he could verify her presence at the house the night Daggett died. It was hard to picture her as a killer, but I'd been fooled before.

17

John Daggett's funeral service took place in the sanctuary of some obscure outpost of the Christian church. The building itself was a one-story yellow stucco, devoid of ornament, located just off the freeway—the sort of chapel you glimpse through the bushes when you're going someplace else. I arrived late. I'd retrieved my VW from the auto glass shop at 1:45 after countless delays, and I confess I'd spent a few contented moments cranking my new car window up and down. The drizzle was beginning to turn serious and I was heartened by the notion that it wouldn't blow straight in on me.

When I reached the gravel parking lot beside the church, there were already fifty cars jammed into space for thirty-five. Some vehicles had nosed out into the vacant lot next door and some hugged the fence along the frontage road. I was forced to pass the place, snag a spot at the end of a long line of cars, and walk back. I could already hear electronic organ music thumping out in a style better suited to a skating rink than a house of God. I noticed from the sign out front that the minister was called a pastor instead of "Reverend" and I wondered if that was significant. Pastor Howard Bowen. The church name was composed of a long string of words and reminded me uneasily of the outfit that distributes pamphlets door-to-door. I hoped they weren't keen on converts.

Mr. Sharonson, from Wynington-Blake, was standing by himself on the low front steps and he gave me a pained look as he passed me a mimeographed copy of the program with a hand-drawn lily on the front. His manner suggested that the services were spiritually second-rate, this being the K mart of churches.

I went in. An usher peeled a metal folding chair from a stack near the door and flipped it open for me. The congregation had risen to its feet to sing so I stood in the back row, wedged in among other late arrivals. The woman on my left offered to share her hymnal and I took my half, my gaze sliding over the page in haste. They were on verse four of a ditty that went on and on about blood and sin. I made some mouth noises which I hoped were being lost in the general din. Aside from the fact I don't believe in this stuff, I don't sing too good and I was worried I might be denounced on both counts.

Way up at the front, I thought I spotted Barbara Daggett's blonde head, but I didn't see anyone else I knew. We sat down with a rustle of clothing and the scrape of metal chair legs. While Pastor Bowen, in a matte black suit, talked about what wretches we were, I stared at the brown vinyl tile floor and studied the staunch row of stained glass windows which depicted forms of spiritual torment that made me squirm. Already, I could feel a burgeoning urge to repent.

I could see Daggett's casket up by the altar, looking somehow like one of those boxes magicians use when they cut folk in half. I checked my program. We'd whipped through the opening prayer and the invocation, and now that we'd dispensed with the first hymn, we were apparently settling in for an energetic discourse on the temptations of the flesh, which put me in mind of the numerous and varied occasions on which I'd succumbed. That was entertaining.

Pastor Bowen was in his sixties, balding, a small man with a tight round face, who looked like he would suffer from denture breath. He'd chosen as his subject matter a passage from Deuteronomy: "The Lord shall smite thee in the knees, and in the legs, with a sore botch that cannot be healed, from the sole of thy foot unto the top of thy head," and I heard more on that subject than I thought possible without falling asleep. I was curious what he could find to say about John Daggett, whose transgressions were many and whose repentances were few, but he managed to tie Daggett's passing into "He shall lend to thee, and thou shalt not lend to him; he shall be the head, and thou shalt be the tail," and sailed right into an all-encompassing prayer.

When we stood for the final hymn, I felt someone's eyes on me and I looked over to spot Marilyn Smith two rows down, in the company of a man I assumed to be her husband, Wayne. She was wearing red. I wondered if she would leap up and do a tap dance on the coffin lid. The congregation by now was really getting into the spirit of things and hosannas were being called out on all sides, accompanied by amens, huzzahs, and much rending and tearing of clothes. I wanted to excuse myself, but I didn't dare. This was beginning to feel like soul-aerobics.

The woman next to me began to sway, her eyes closed, while she hooted out an occasional "Yes, Lord." I'm not given to this sort of orthodox public outburst and I commenced to edge my way to the door. I could see now that the minister, doing what looked like deltoid releases, was leading his merry band of church elders in the equivalent of a canonical conga line with Essie Daggett bringing up the rear.

At the exit, I came face to face with Billy Polo and his sister, Coral. He took me by the arm and pulled me aside as the service drew to a close behind me and people began to crowd through the door. Essie Daggett was wailing, nearly borne aloft like a football coach after a big win. Barbara Daggett and Eugene Nickerson had arranged themselves on either side, giving her what protection they could. For some reason, the other mourners were reaching out to touch and pat and grasp at Essie, as if her grief lent her healing powers.

The pallbearers came last, pulling the coffin along on a rolling cart instead of toting it. None of the six of them appeared to be under sixty-five and Wynington-Blake may have worried that they'd collapse, or topple their cargo right out into the aisle. As it was, the cart seemed to have one errant wheel which caused it to meander, squeaking energetically. The coffin, as though with a will of its own, headed for the chairs first on one side and then the other. I could see the pall-bearers struggle to maintain mournful expressions while correcting its course, dragging it up the aisle like a stubborn dog.

I caught sight of Tony Gahan briefly, but he was gone again before I could speak to him. The hearse pulled up in front and the coffin was angled down the low steps and into the rear. Behind it, the limousine pulled up and Essie was helped into the back seat. She was wearing a black suit, with a broad-brimmed black straw hat, swathed in veiling. She looked more like a beekeeper than anything else. Stung by the Holy Spirit, I thought. Barbara Daggett wore a charcoal gray suit and black pumps, her two-toned eyes looking almost electric in the pale oval of her face. The rain was falling steadily and Mr. Sharonson was distributing big black umbrellas as people ducked off the porch and hurried to the parking lot.

Cars were being started simultaneously in a rumble of exhaust fumes, gravel popping as we pulled out onto the frontage road and began the slow procession to the cemetery, maybe two miles away. Again, we parked in a long line, car doors slamming as we crossed the soggy grass. This was apparently a fairly new cemetery, with few trees—a wide flat field planted to an odd crop. The headstones were square cut and low, without any of the worn beauty of stone angels or granite lambs. The grounds were well kept, but consisted primarily of asphalt roadways winding among sections of burial plots that had apparently been sold "pre-need." I wondered if cemeteries, like golf courses, had to be designed by experts for maximum aesthetic effect. This one felt like a cut-rate country club, low membership fees for the upstart dead. The rich and respectable were buried someplace else and John

Daggett couldn't possibly qualify for inclusion among them.

Wynington-Blake had set up a canopy over the grave itself and, nearby, a second larger one with folding chairs arranged under it. No one seemed to know who was supposed to go where and there was a bit of milling around. Essie and Barbara Daggett were led into the big tent and placed in the front row, with Eugene Nickerson on one side and a fat woman on the other in a set of four folding chairs connected at the base. The back legs were already beginning to sink into the rain-softened soil, tilting the four of them backward at a slight angle. I had a brief image of them trapped like that, staring at the tent top, legs dangling, unable to right themselves again. Why is it that grief always seems edged with absurdity?

I eased over to one side, under shelter, but remained standing. Most of the mourners appeared to be elderly and (perhaps) needed folding chairs more than I. It looked like the entire church membership had turned out in Essie Daggett's behalf.

Pastor Bowen had declined a raincoat and he stood now in the open air, rain collecting on his balding head, waiting patiently for everyone to get settled. At this range, I saw evidence of a hearing aid tucked into the tiny ear cave on his right. Idly, he fiddled with the device, keeping his expression benign so as not to call attention to himself. I wondered if the battery was shorting out from the damp. I could see him tap on the aid with his index finger, flinching then as though it had suddenly barked to life again.

On the far side of the tent, I saw Marilyn and Wayne Smith, and behind them Tony Gahan, accompanied by his aunt Ramona. He looked like the perfect prep school gentleman in gray wool slacks, white shirt, navy blazer, rep tie. As though sensing that he was being watched, his eyes strayed to mine, his expression as empty as a robot's. If he was expunging raw hate or an old sorrow, there was no sign of it. Billy Polo and his sister stood outside the tent in the rain, sharing an umbrella. Coral looked miserable. She was apparently still caught up in the throes of a cold, clutching a fistful of Kleenex. She belonged in bed with a flannel rag on her chest reeking of Vick's Vaporub. Billy seemed restless, scanning the crowd with care. I followed his gaze, wondering if he was looking for someone in particular.

"Dear friends," the minister said in a powdery voice. "We are gathered here on the sad occasion of John Daggett's death, to witness his return to the earth from which he was formed, to acknowledge his passing, to celebrate his entry into the presence of our Lord Jesus. John Daggett has left us. He is free now of the cares and worries of this life, free of sin, free of his burdens, free of blame. . . ."

From somewhere near the back, a woman hollered out "Yes, Lord!" and a second woman yelled out "Buulllshiit!" in just about the same tone. The minister, not hearing that well, apparently took both as spiritual punctuation marks, Biblical whoopees to incite him to greater eloquence. He raised his voice, closing his eyes as he began quoting admonitions against sin, filth, defiled flesh, lasciviousness, and corruption.

"John Daggett was the biggest asshole who ever lived so get it straight!" came the jeering voice again. Heads whipped around. Lovella had gotten to her feet near the back. The people turned to stare, their faces blank with amazement.

She was drunk. She had the little bitty pink eyes that suggest some high-grade marijuana toked up in addition to the booze. Her left eye was still slightly puffy, but the bruising had lightened up to a mild yellow on that side and she looked more like she was suffering from an allergy than a rap up the side of the head from the dead man. Her hair was the same blonde bush I remembered, her mouth a slash of dark red. She'd been weeping copiously and her mascara was speckled under her lower lids like soot. Her skin was splotchy, her nose hot pink and running. For the occasion she'd chosen a black sequined cocktail dress, low cut. Her breasts looked almost transparent and bulged out like condoms inflated as a joke. I couldn't tell if she was weeping out of rage or grief and I didn't think this crowd was prepared to deal with either one.

I was already headed toward the rear. Out of the corner of my eye, I saw Billy Polo make a beeline toward her on the far side of the tent. The minister had figured out by now that she was not on his team and he shot a baffled look at Mr. Sharonson, who motioned the ushers to take charge. We all reached her just about at the same time. Billy grabbed her from behind, pinning her arms back. Lovella flung him off, kicking like a mule, yelling "Fuck-heads! You scum-sucking hypocrites!" One usher snagged her by the hair and the other took her feet. She shrieked and struggled as they carried her toward the road. I followed, glancing back briefly. Barbara Daggett was obscured by the mourners who'd stood up for a better look, but I saw that Marilyn Smith was loving every trashy minute of Lovella's performance.

By the time I reached Lovella, she was lying in the front seat of Billy Polo's Chevrolet, hands covering her face as she wept. The doors were open on both sides of the car and Billy knelt by her head, shushing and soothing her, smoothing her rain-tangled hair. The two ushers exchanged a look, apparently satisfied that she was under control at that point. Billy bristled at their intrusion.

"I got her, man. Just bug off. She's cool."

Coral came around the car and stood behind him, holding the umbrella. She seemed embarrassed by Billy's behavior, uncomfortable in the presence of Lovella's excess. The three of them formed an odd unit and I got the distinct impression that the connection between them was more recent than Billy'd led me to believe.

The graveside service, I gathered, was drawing to a close. From the tent came the thin, discordant voices of the mourners as they joined in an a cappella hymn. Lovella's sobs had taken on the intensity of a child's—artless, unself-conscious.

Was she truly grieving for Daggett or was something else going on?

"What's the story, Billy?" I said.

"No story," he said gruffly.

"Something's going on. How'd she find out about his death? From you?"

Billy laid his face against her hair, ignoring me.

Coral shifted her gaze to mine. "He doesn't know anything."

"How about you, Coral? You want to talk about it?"

Billy shot her a warning look and she shook her head.

Murmurs and activity from the tent. The crowd was breaking up and people were beginning to move toward us.

"Watch your head. I'm closing the car doors," Billy said to Lovella. He shut the door on the driver's side and moved around the front to catch the door on the passenger side. He paused with his hand on the handle, waiting for her to pull her knees up to make clearance. Idly, he surveyed the mourners still huddled under the cover of the tent. As the crowd shifted, I saw his gaze flicker. "Who's that?"

He was looking at a small group formed by Ramona Westfall, Tony, and the Smiths. The three adults were talking while Tony, his hands in his pockets, passed his shoe over the rung of a folding chair, scraping the mud from the sole. Barbara Daggett was just behind him, in conversation with someone else. I identified everyone by name. I thought Wayne was the one who seemed to hold his attention, but I wasn't positive. It might have been Marilyn.

"How come the Westfalls showed up for this?"

"Maybe the same reason you did."

"You don't know why I came," he said. He was agitated, jingling the car keys, his gaze drifting back to the mourners.

"Maybe you'll tell me one of these days."

His smirk said don't count on it. He signaled to Coral and she got in the back seat. He got in the car and started it, pulling out then without a backwards glance.

18

Barbara Daggett invited me back to her mother's house after the funeral, but I declined. I couldn't handle another emotional circus act. After I've spent a certain amount of time in the company of others, I need an intermission anyway. I retreated to my office and sat there with the lights out. It was only 4:00, but dark clouds were massing again as though for attack. I slipped my shoes off and put my feet up, clutching my jacket around me for warmth. John Daggett was in the ground now and the world was moving on. I wondered what would happen if we left it at that. I didn't think Barbara Daggett gave a damn about seeing justice done, whatever that consisted of. I hadn't come up with much. I thought I was on the right track, but I wasn't sure I really wanted an answer to the question Daggett's death had posed. Maybe it was better to forget this one, turn it under again like top soil, worms and all. The cops didn't consider it a homicide anyway and I knew I could talk Barbara Daggett out of pursuing the point. What was there to be gained? I wasn't in the business of avenging Daggett's death. Then what was I uneasy about? It was the only time in recent memory that I'd wanted to drop a case. Usually I'm dogged, but this time I wanted out. I think I could have talked myself into it if nothing else had occurred. As it happened, my phone rang about ten minutes later, nudging me into action again. I took my feet off the desk for form's sake and picked up on the first ring. "Millhone."

A young-sounding man said hesitantly: "Is this the office or an answering service?"

"The office."

"Is this Kinsey Millhone?"

"Yes. Can I help you?"

"Yeah, well my boss gave me this number. Mr. Donagle at the Spindrift Motel? He said you had some questions about Friday night. I think maybe I saw that guy you were asking about."

I reached for a lined yellow pad and a pen. "Great. I appreciate your getting in touch. Could you tell me your name first?"

"Paul Fisk," he said. "I read in the paper some guy drowned and it just sure seemed like an odd coincidence, but I didn't know if I should say anything or not."

"You saw him Friday night?"

"Well, I think it was him. This was about quarter of two, something like that. I'm on night desk and sometimes I step outside for some air, just to keep myself awake." He paused and I could hear him shift gears. "This is confidential, isn't it?"

"Of course. Strictly between us. Why? Did your girlfriend stop by or something like that?"

His laugh was nervous. "Naw, sometimes I smoke a little weed is all. Place gets boring at two A.M., so that's how I get through. Get loaded and watch old black-and-white movies on this little TV I got. I hope you don't have a problem with that."

"Hey, it's your business, not mine. How long have you worked at the Spindrift?"

"Just since March. It's not a great job, but I don't want to get fired. I'm trying to get myself out of debt and I need the bucks."

"I hear you," I said. "Tell me about Friday night."

"Well, I was on the porch and this drunk went by. It was raining pretty hard so I didn't get a real good look at him at the time, but when I saw the news, the age and stuff seemed pretty close."

"Did you see the picture of him by any chance?"

"Just a glimpse on TV, but I wasn't paying much attention so I couldn't say for sure it was him. I guess I should have called the cops, but I didn't have anything much to report and I was afraid it'd come out about the . . . about that other stuff."

"What was he doing, the drunk?"

"Nothing much. It was him and this girl. She had him by the arm. You know, kind of propped up. They were laughing like crazy, wandering all over the place on account of his being so screwed up. Alcohol'll do that, you know. Bad stuff. Not like weed," he said.

I bypassed the sales pitch. "What about the woman? Did you get a good look at her?"

"Not really. Not to describe."

"What about hair, clothing, things like that?"

"I noticed some. She had these real spiky heels and a raincoat, a skirt, and let's see . . . a shirt with this sweater over it. Like, what do you call 'em, preppies wear."

"A crewneck?"

"Yeah. Same color green as the skirt."

"You saw all that in the dark?"

"It's not that dark there," he said. "There's a streetlight right out in front. The two of them fell down in a heap they were laughing so hard. She got up first and kind of looked down to see if her stockings were torn. He just lay there in a puddle on his back till she helped him up."

"Did they see you?"

"I don't think so. I was standing in the shadow of this overhang, keeping out of the wet. I never saw 'em look my way."

"What happened after the fall?"

"They just went on toward the marina."

"Did you hear them say anything?"

"Not really. It sounded like she was teasing him about falling down, but other than that nothing in particular."

"Could they have had a car?"

"I don't think so. Anyway, not that I saw."

"What if they'd parked it in that municipal lot across the street?"

"I guess they could have, but I don't know why they'd walk to the marina in weather like that. Seems like if they had a car it'd be easier to drive and then park it down there."

"Unless he was too drunk. He'd had his driver's license yanked too."

"She could have driven. She was half sober at least."

"You've got a point there," I said. "What about public transportation? Could they have come by bus or cab?"

"I guess, except the buses don't run that late. A cab maybe. That'd make sense."

I was jotting down information as he gave it to me. "This is great. What's your home phone in case I need to get in touch?"

He gave me the number and then said, "I usually work eleven to seven on weekdays."

I made a quick note. "Do you think you'd recognize the girl if you saw her again?"

"I don't know. Probably. Do you know who she is?"

"Not yet. I'm working on that."

"Well, I wish you luck. You think this'll help?"

"I hope so. Thanks for calling. I really appreciate it."

"Sure thing, and if you catch up with her, let me know. Maybe you can do like a police lineup or something like that."

"Great and thanks."

He clicked off and I finished making notes, adding this information to what I had. Dinah had spotted Daggett and the girl at 2:15 and Paul Fisk's sighting placed them right on

Cabana thirty minutes before. I wondered where they'd been before that. If they'd arrived by cab, had she taken one home from the marina afterward? I didn't get it. Most killers don't take taxis to and from. It isn't good criminal etiquette.

I hauled out the telephone book and turned to the Yellow Pages to look up cab companies. Fortunately, Santa Teresa is a small town and there aren't that many. Aside from a couple of airport and touring services, there were six listed. I dialed each in turn, patiently explaining who I was and inquiring about a 2:00 A.M. Saturday fare with a Cabana Boulevard drop off. I was also asking about a pickup anywhere in that vicinity sometime between 3:00 and 6:00 A.M. According to the morgue attendant, the watch Daggett had been wearing was frozen at 2:37, but anybody could have jimmied that, breaking the watch to pinpoint the time, then attaching it to his wrist before he was dumped. If she'd left the boat and swum ashore or rowed to the wharf and abandoned it there, it was still going to take her a little time to organize herself for the cab ride home.

All the previous week's trip sheets, of course, had been filed and there were some heavy sighs and grumblings all around at the notion of having to look them up. Ron Coachella, the dispatcher for Tip Top, was the only cheerful soul in the lot, primarily because he'd done a records search for me once before with good results. I couldn't talk anyone into doing the file check right then, so I left my name and number and a promise that I'd call again. "Whoopee-do," said one.

While I was talking, I'd been doodling on the legal pad, running my pencil around idly so that the line formed a maze. I circled the note about the green skirt. Hadn't that old bum pulled a pair of spike heels and a green skirt out of a trash bin at the beach? I remembered his shoving discarded clothing into one of the plastic bags he kept in his shopping cart. Hers? Surely she hadn't made her way home in the buff. She did have the raincoat, but I wondered if she might have had a change of clothes stashed somewhere too. She'd sure gone to a lot of trouble if she were setting Daggett up. This didn't look like an impulsive act, done in the heat of the moment. Had she had help? Someone who picked her up afterward? If the cab companies didn't come up with a record of a fare, I'd have to consider the possibility of an accomplice.

In the meantime, I thought I'd better head down to the beach and look for my scruffy drifter friend. I'd seen him that morning near the public restrooms when I did my run. I tore the sheet off the legal pad and folded it, shoving it in my pocket as I grabbed up my handbag, locked the office, and headed down the back stairs to my car.

It was now nearly quarter to five, getting chillier by the minute, but at least it was dry temporarily. I cruised along Cabana, peering from my car window. There weren't many people at the beach. A couple of power walkers. A guy with a dog. The boulevard seemed deserted. I doubled back, heading toward my place, passing the wharf on the left and the string of motels across the street. Just beyond the boat launch and kiddie pool, I pulled up at a stoplight, scanning the park on the opposite corner. I could see the band shell where bums sometimes took refuge, but I didn't see any squatters. Where were all the transients?

I circled back, passing the train station. It occurred to me that this was probably the bums' dinner hour. I cut over another block and a half and sure enough, there they were—fifty or so on a quick count, lined up outside the Redemption Mission. The fellow I was looking for was near the end of the line, along with his pal. There was no sign of their shopping carts, which I thought of as a matched set of movable metal luggage, the derelict's Louis Vuitton. I slowed, looking for a place to park.

The neighborhood is characterized by light industry, factory outlets, welding shops, and quonset huts where auto body repair work is done. I found a parking spot in front of a place that made custom surfboards. I pulled in, watching in my rearview mirror until the group outside the mission had shuffled in. I locked the car then and crossed the street.

The Redemption Mission looks like it's made out of papier-mâché, a two-story oblong of fakey-looking fieldstone, with ivy clinging to one end. The roofline is as crenellated as a castle's, the "moat" a wide band of asphalt paving. City fire codes apparently necessitated the addition of fire escapes that angle down the building now on all sides, looking somehow more perilous than the possibility of fire. The property is considered prime real estate and I wondered who would house the poor if the bed space were bought out from under them. For most of the year, the climate in this part of California is mild enough to allow the drifters to sleep outdoors, which they seem to prefer. Seasonally, however, there are weeks of rain . . . even occasionally someone with a butcher knife intent on slitting their throats. The mission offers safe sleeping for the night, three hot meals a day, and a place to roll cigarettes out of the wind.

I picked up cooking odors as I approached—bulk hamburger with chili seasoning. As usual, I couldn't remember eating lunch and here it was nearly dinnertime again. The sign outside indicated prayer services at 7:00 every night and Hot Showers & Shaves on Mondays, Wednesdays, and Saturdays. I stepped inside. The walls were painted glossy beige on top and shoe brown down below. Hand-lettered signs pointed me to the dining room and chapel on the left. I followed the low murmur of conversation and the clatter of silverware.

On the right, through a doorway, I spotted the dining room— long metal folding tables covered with paper, metal folding chairs filled with men. Nobody paid any attention to me. I could see serving plates stacked high with soft white bread, bowls of applesauce sprinkled with cinnamon, salads of iceberg lettuce that glistened with bottled dressing. The table seated twenty, already bent to their evening meal of chili served over elbow macaroni. Another fifteen or twenty men sat obediently in the "chapel" to my left, which consisted of a lectern, an old upright piano, orange molded plastic chairs, and an imposing cross on the wall.

The scruffy drifter I was looking for sat in the back row with his friend. Slogans everywhere assured me that Jesus cared, and that certainly seemed true here. What impressed me most was the fact that Redemption Mission (according to the wall signs) was supported by private donations, with little or no connection to the government.

"May I help you?"

The man who'd approached me was in his sixties, heavyset, clean-shaven, wearing a red short-sleeved cotton shirt and baggy pants. He had one normal arm and one that ended at the elbow in a twist of flesh like the curled top of a Mr. Softee ice cream cone. I wanted to introduce myself, shaking hands, but the stump was on the right and I didn't have the nerve. I took out a business card instead, handing it to him.

"I wonder if I might have a word with one of your clients?"

His beefy brow furrowed. "What's this about?"

"Well, I think he retrieved some articles I'm looking for from a trash can at the beach. I want to find out if he still has them in his cart. It will only take a minute."

"You see him in here?"

I indicated the one who interested me.

"You'll have to talk to the both of them," the man said. "Delphi's the fellow you want, but he don't talk. His buddy does all the talking. His name is Clare. I'll bring them out if you'll wait out there in the corridor. They got their shopping carts on the back patio. I'd go easy about them carts. They get a might possessive of their treasures sometimes."

I thanked him and retraced my steps, lingering in the entranceway until Delphi and Clare appeared. Delphi had shed some of his overcoats, but he wore the same dark watch cap and his skin had the same dusky red tone. His friend Clare was tall and gaunt with a very pink tongue that crept out of his mouth through the gap left by his missing front teeth. His hair was a silky white, rather sparse, his arms long and stringy, hands huge. Delphi made no eye contact at all, but Clare turned out to have some residual charm, left over perhaps from the days before he started to drink.

I explained who I was and what I was looking for. I saw Delphi look at Clare with the haunted subservience of a dog accustomed to being hit. Clare may have been the only human being in the world who didn't frighten or abuse him and he evidently depended on Clare to handle interactions of this kind.

"Yep. I know the ones. High heels in black suede. Green wool skirt. Delphi here was pleased. Usually it's slim pickin's around that bin. Aluminum cans is about the best you can hope for, but he got lucky, I guess."

"Does he still have the items?"

The tongue crept out with a crafty life of its own, so pink it looked like Clare had been sucking red hots. "I can ask," he said.

"Would you do that?"

Clare turned to Delphi. "What do you think, Delph? Shall we give this little gal what she wants? Up to you."

Delphi gave no evidence whatever of hearing, absorbing, or assenting. Clare waited a decent interval.

"Now that's tough," Clare said to me. "That was his best day and he likes that green skirt."

"I could reimburse him," I said tentatively. I didn't want to insult these guys.

Out came the tongue, like some shy creature peering from its lair. Delphi's hearing seemed to improve. He shifted slightly. I left Clare to translate this movement into dollars and cents.

"A twenty might cover it," Clare said at length.

I only had a twenty on me, but I took it out of the zipped

compartment in my black handbag. I offered it to Delphi. Clare interceded. "Hold that until we've done our business. Let's step outside."

I filed after them along a short corridor to a back exit that opened on a small concrete patio surrounded on three sides by an openwork fence made of lathing. Someone had "landscaped" the entire area in annuals planted in coffee cans and big industrial-sized containers that had held green beans and applesauce. Delphi stood by, looking on anxiously, while Clare pawed through one of the shopping carts. He seemed to know exactly where the shoes and skirt were located, whisking them out in no time flat. He passed them over to me and I handed him the twenty. It felt somehow like an illicit drug sale and I had visions of them buying a jug of Mad Dog 20–20 after I'd left. Clare held the bill up for Delphi to inspect, then he glanced at me.

"Don't you worry. We'll put this in the collection plate," Clare said. "Delphi and me have give up drink." I thought Clare seemed happier about it than Delphi did.

19

My dinner that night was cheese and crackers, with a side of chili peppers just to keep my mouth awake. I'd changed out of my all-purpose dress into a tee shirt, jeans, and fuzzy slippers. I ate sitting at my desk, with a Diet Pepsi on the rocks. I studied the skirt and shoes. I tried the right shoe on. Too wide for me. The back of the heel was scuffed, the toe narrowing to a bunion-producing point. The manufacturer's name on the inner sole had been blurred by sweat. A pair of Odoreaters wouldn't have been out of line here. The skirt was a bit more informative, size 8, a brand I'd seen at the Village Store and the Post & Rail. Even the lining was in good shape, though wrinkled in a manner that suggested a recent soaking. I touched my tongue to the fabric. Salt. I checked the inseam pockets, which were empty. No cleaner's marks. I thought about the women connected, even peripherally, with Daggett's death. The skirt might fit any one of them, except for Barbara Daggett maybe, who was big-boned and didn't seem like the type for the preppy look, especially in green. Ramona Westfall was a good candidate. Marilyn Smith, perhaps. Lovella Daggett or Billy's sister, Coral, could probably both wear an 8, but the style seemed wrong . . . unless the outfit had been lifted from a Salvation Army donation box. Maybe in the morning I'd stop by a couple of clothing stores and see if any of the salesclerks recognized the skirt. Fat chance, I thought. A better plan would be to show it, along with the shoes, to all five women and see if anyone would admit ownership. Unlikely under the circumstances. Too bad I couldn't do a little breaking and entering. The matching green sweater might come to light in someone's dresser drawer.

I padded into the kitchen and rinsed my plate. Eating alone is one of the few drawbacks to single life. I've read those articles that claim you should prepare food just as carefully for yourself as you would for company. Which is why I do cheese and crackers. I don't cook. My notion of setting an elegant table is you don't leave the knife sticking out of the mayonnaise jar. Since I usually work while I eat, there isn't any point in candlelight. If I'm not working, I have *Time* magazine propped up against a stack of files and I read it back to front as I munch, starting with the sections on books and cinema, losing interest by the time I reach Economy & Business.

At 9:02, my phone rang. It was the night dispatcher for Tip Top Cab Company, a fellow who identified himself as Chuck. I could hear the two-way radio squawking in the background.

"I got this note from Ron says to call you," said he. "He pulled the trip sheets for last Friday night and said to give you the information you were asking about, but I'm not really sure what you want."

I filled him in and waited briefly while he ran his eye down the sheet. "Oh yeah. I guess this is it. He's got it circled right here. It was my fare. That's probably why he asked me to call. Friday night, one twenty-three . . . well, you'd call that early Saturday. I dropped a couple off at State and Cabana. Man and a woman. I figured they were booked into a motel down there."

"I've heard the man was drunk."

"Oh yeah, very. Looked like she'd been drinking too, but not like him. He was a mess. I mean, this guy smelled to high heaven. Stunk up the whole back seat and I got a pretty fair tolerance for that kind of thing."

"What about her? Can you tell me anything?"

"Can't help you on that. It was late and dark and raining to beat the band. I just took 'em where they said."

"Did you talk to them?"

"Nope. I'm not the kind of cabbie engages in small talk with a fare. Most people aren't interested and I get sick of repeating myself. Politics, weather, baseball scores. It's all bull. They don't want to talk to me and I don't want to talk to them. I mean, if they ask me something I'm polite, don't get me wrong, but I can't manufacture chitchat to save my neck."

"What about the two of them? They talk to each other?"

"Who knows? I tuned 'em out."

God, this was no help at all. "You remember anything else?"

"Not offhand. I'll give it some thought, but it wasn't any big deal. Sorry I can't be a help."

"Well, at least you've verified a hunch of mine and I appreciate that. Thanks for your time."

"No problem."

"Oh, one more thing. Where'd the fare originate?"

"Now *that* I got. You know that sleazeball bar on Milagro? That place. I picked 'em up at the Hub."

I sat and stared at the phone for a moment after he hung up. I felt like I was running a reel of film backwards, frame by frame. Daggett left the Hub Friday night in the company of a blonde. They apparently had a lot of drinks, a lot of laughs, staggered around in the rain together, fell down, and picked themselves up again. And little by little, block by block, she was steering him toward the marina, herding him toward the boat, guiding him out into the harbor on the last short ride of his life. She must have had a heart of stone and steadier nerves than mine.

I made some quick notes and tossed the index cards in the top drawer of my desk. I kicked off my slippers and laced up my tennies, then pulled on a sweatshirt. I snatched up the skirt and shoes, my handbag, and car keys and locked up, heading out to the VW. I'd start with Coral first. Maybe she'd know if Lovella was still in town. I was remembering now the fragment of conversation I'd overheard the night I eavesdropped on Billy and Coral. She'd been talking to Billy then about some woman. I couldn't remember exactly what she'd said, but I did remember that. Maybe Coral had seen the woman I was looking for.

When I reached the trailer park, I found the trailer dimly lighted, as if someone had gone out and left a lamp burning to keep the burglars at bay. Billy's Chevrolet was in the carport, the hood cold to the touch. I knocked on the door. After a moment, I heard footsteps bumping toward the front.

"Yeah?" Billy's muffled voice came through the door.

"It's Kinsey," I said. "Is Coral here?"

"Uh-uh. She's at work."

"Can I talk to you?"

He hesitated. "About what?"

"Friday night. It won't take long."

There was a pause. "Wait a sec. Let me throw some clothes on."

Moments later, he opened the door and let me in. He had pulled on a pair of jeans. Aside from that, he was barefoot and naked to the waist. His dark hair was tousled. He looked like he hadn't worked out recently, but his arms and chest were still well developed, overlaid by a fine mat of dark hair.

The trailer was disordered—newspapers, magazines, dinner dishes for two still out on the table, the counters covered with canned goods, cracker boxes, bags of flour, sugar, and corn meal. There wasn't a clear surface anywhere and no place to sit. The air was dense, smelling faintly of fresh cigarette smoke.

"Sorry to disturb you," I said. He looked like he'd been screwing his brains out and I wondered who was in the bedroom. "You have company?"

He glanced toward the rear, his dimples surfacing. "No, I don't. Why, are you interested?"

I smiled and shook my head, at the same time caught up in a flash fantasy of me and Billy Polo tangled up in sheets that smelled like him, musky and warm. His skin exuded a masculine perfume that conjured up images of all the trashy things we might do if the barriers went down. I kept my expression neutral, but I could feel my face tint with pink. "I have some questions I was hoping Coral might help me with."

"So you said. Try the Hub. She'll be there till closing time."

I laid the skirt and shoes across the television set, which was the only bare surface I could find. "Do you know if these are hers?"

He glanced at the items, too canny to bite. "Where'd you get 'em?"

"A friend of a friend. I thought you might know whose they were."

"I thought this was supposed to be about Friday night."

"It is. I talked to a cabbie who picked Daggett up at the Hub Friday night and dropped him off down near the wharf."

"I'll bite. So what?"

"A blonde was with him. The cabbie took them both. I figure she met him at the Hub, so I thought Coral might have had a look at her."

Billy knew something. I could see it in his face. He was processing the information, trying to decide what it meant.

I was getting impatient. "Goddamn it, Billy, level with me!"

"I am!"

"No, you're not. You've been lying to me since the first time you ever opened your mouth."

"I have not," he said hotly. "Name one thing."

"Let's start with Doug Polokowski. What's your relation to him? Brother?"

He was silent. I stared at him, waiting him out.

"Half-brother," he said grudgingly.

"Go on."

His tone of voice dropped, apparently with embarrassment.

"My mom and dad split up, but they were still legally married when she got pregnant by somebody else. I was ten and I hated the whole idea. I started gettin' in trouble right about then so I spent half my time in Juvenile Hall anyway, which suited me just fine. She finally had me declared a whaddyou call 'em. . . ."

"An out-of-control minor?"

"Yeah, one of them. Big deal. I didn't give a fat rat's ass. Let her dump us. Let her have a bunch more kids. She didn't have any more sense than that, then to hell with her."

"So you and Doug were never close?"

"Hardly. I used to see him now and then when I'd come home but we didn't have much of a relationship."

"What about you and your mother?"

"We're okay. I got over it some. After Doug got killed, we did better. Sometimes it happens that way."

"But you must have known Daggett was responsible."

"Sure I knew. Of course I did. Mom wrote and told me he was bein' sent up to San Luis. At first, I thought I'd get even with him. For her sake, if nothin' else. But it didn't work out like that. He was too pathetic. Know what I mean? Hell, I ended up almost feeling sorry for him. I despised him for the whiny little fucker that he was, but I couldn't leave him alone. It's like I had to torment him. I liked to watch him squirm, which maybe makes me weird but it don't make me a killer. I never murdered anybody in my life."

"What about Coral? Where was she in all this?"

"Hey, you ask her."

"Could she have been the one with Daggett that night? It sounds like Lovella to me, but I can't be sure."

"Why ask me? I wasn't there."

"Did Coral mention it?"

"I don't want to talk about this," he said, irritably.

"Come on. You talked to Daggett Thursday night. Did he mention this woman?"

"We didn't talk about women," Billy said. He began to snap the fingers of his right hand against his left palm, making a soft, hollow pop. I could feel myself going into a terrier pup mode, worrying the issue like a rawhide bone, knotted on both ends.

"He must have known who she was," I said. "She didn't just materialize out of the blue. She set him up. She knew what she was doing. It must have been a very carefully thought-out plan."

The popping sound stopped and Billy's tone took on a crafty note. "Maybe she was connected to the guys who wanted their money back," he said.

I looked at him with interest. That really hadn't occurred to me, but it didn't sound bad. "Did you tip them off?"

"Listen, babe, I'm not a killer and I'm not a snitch. If Daggett had a beef with somebody, that was his lookout, you know?"

"Then what's the debate? I don't understand what you're holding back."

He sighed and ran a hand through his hair. "Lay off, okay? I don't know nothin' else so just leave it alone."

"Come on, Billy. What's the rest of it?" I snapped.

"Oh, shit. It wasn't Thursday," he blurted out. "I met Daggett Tuesday night and that's when he asked me to help him out."

"So he could hide from the guys at San Luis," I said, making sure I was following.

"Well, yeah. I mean, they'd called him Monday morning and that's why he'd hightailed it up here. We talked on the phone late Monday. He was drunk. I didn't feel like putting myself out. I'd just got home and I was bushed so I said I'd meet him the next night."

"At the Hub?"

"Right."

"Which is what you did," I said, easing him along.

"Sure, we met and talked some. He was already in a panic so I kind of fanned the flames, just twitting him. There's no harm in that."

"Why lie about it? Why didn't you tell me this to begin with?" I was crowding him, but I thought it was time to persist.

"It didn't look right somehow. I didn't want my name tied to his. Thursday night sounded better. Like I wasn't all that hot to talk to him. You know, like I didn't rush right out. I can't explain it any better than that."

It was just lame enough to make sense to me. I said, "All right. I'll buy it for now. Then what?"

"That's all it was. That's the last I saw of him. He came in again Friday night and Coral spotted him, so she called me, but by the time I got there, he'd left."

"With the woman?"

"Yeah, right."

"So Coral did see her."

"Sure, but she didn't know who she was. She thought it was some babe hittin' on him, like a whore, something like that. The chick was buyin' him all these drinks and Daggett was lappin' 'em up. Coral got kind of worried. Not that either of us really gave a shit, but you know how it is. You don't want to see a guy get taken, even if you don't like him much."

"Especially if you've heard he's got thirty thousand dollars on him, right?" I said.

"It wasn't thirty. You said so yourself. It was twenty-five." Billy was apparently feeling churlish now that he'd opened up. "Anyway, what are you goin' on and on about? I told you everything I know."

"What about Coral? If you lied, maybe she's been lying too."

"She wouldn't do that."

"What'd she say when you got there?"

The look on Billy's face altered slightly and I thought I'd hit on something. I just didn't know what. My mind leapt ahead. "Did Coral *follow* them?" I asked.

"Of course not."

"What'd she say then?"

"Coral wasn't feeling so hot," he replied, uneasily.

"So she'd what, gone home?"

"Not really. She was coming down with this cold and she'd taken a cold cap. She was feeling zonked so she went back in the office and lay down on the couch. The bartender thought she'd left. I get there and I'm pissed because I can't find her, I can't find Daggett. I don't know what's goin' on. I hang around for a while and then I come back here, thinking she's home. Only she's not. It was a fuck-up, that's all. She was at the Hub the whole time."

"What time did she get home?"

"I don't know. Late. Three o'clock. She had to wait till the owner closed out the register and then he only gave her a lift partway so she had to walk six blocks in the rain. She's been sick as a dog ever since."

I stared at him, blinking, while the wheels went round and round. I was picturing her at the wharf with Daggett and the fit was nice.

"Why look at me like that?" he said.

"Let me say this. I'm just thinking out loud," I said. "It could have been Coral, couldn't it? The blonde who left the Hub with him? That's what's been worrying you all this time."

"No, uh-uh. No way," he said. His eyes had settled on me with fascination. He didn't like the line I was taking, but he'd probably thought about it himself.

"You only have her word for the fact that this other woman even exists," I said.

"The cabbie saw her."

"But it could have been Coral. She might have been the one buying Daggett all those drinks. He knew who she was and he trusted her too, because of you. She could have called the cab and then left with him. Maybe the reason the bartender thought she was gone was because he saw her leave."

"Get the hell out of here," Billy whispered.

His face had darkened and I saw his muscles tense. I'd been so caught up in my own speculation I hadn't been paying attention to the effect on him. I picked up the skirt and shoes, keeping an eye on him while I edged toward the door. He leaned over and opened it for me abruptly.

I had barely cleared the steps when the door slammed behind me hard. He shoved the curtain aside, staring at me belligerently as I backed out of the carport. The minute the curtain dropped, I cut around to the trailer window where I'd spied on him before. The louvers were closed, but the curtain on that side gaped open enough to allow me a truncated view.

Billy had sunk down on the couch with his head in his hands. He looked up. The woman who'd been in the back bedroom had now emerged and she leaned against the wall while she lit another cigarette. I could see a portion of her heavy thighs and the hem of a shortie nightgown in pale yellow nylon. Like a drowning man, Billy reached for her and pulled her close, burying his face between her breasts. Lovella. He began to nuzzle at her nipples through the nylon top, making wet spots. She stared down at him with that look new mothers have when they suckle an infant in public. Lazily, she leaned over and stubbed out her cigarette on a dinner plate, then wound her fingers into his hair. He grabbed her at the knees and lowered her to the floor, pushing her gown up around her waist. Down, down, down, he went.

I headed over to the Hub.

20

It looked like another slow night at the Hub. The rain had picked up again and business was off. The roof was leaking in two places and someone had put out galvanized pails to catch the drips . . . one on the bar, one by the ladies' room. The place, at its best, was populated by neighborhood drinkers—old women with fat ankles in heavy sweaters who started at 2:00 in the afternoon and consumed beer steadily until closing time, men with nasal voices and grating laughs whose noses were bulbous and sunburned from alcohol. The pool players were usually young Mexicans who smoked until their teeth turned yellow and squabbled among themselves like pups. That night the pool room was deserted and the green felt table tops seemed to glow as though lighted from within. I counted four customers in all and one was asleep with his head on his arms. The jukebox was suffering from some mechanical quirk that gave the music a warbling, underwater quality.

I approached the bar, where Coral was perched on a high-backed stool with a Naugahyde top. She was wearing a Western-cut shirt with a silver thread running through the brown plaid, tight jeans rolled up at the ankles, and heels with short white socks. She must have recognized me from the funeral because when I asked if I could talk to her, she hopped down without a word and went around to the other side of the bar.

"You want something to drink?"

"A wine spritzer. Thanks," I said.

She poured a spritzer for me and pulled a draft beer for

herself. We took a booth at the back so she could keep her eye on the clientele in case someone needed service. Up close, her hair looked so bushy and dry I worried about spontaneous combustion. Her makeup was too harsh for her fair coloring and her front teeth were decayed around the edges, as if she'd been eating Oreo cookies. Her cold must have been at its worst. Her forehead was lined and her eyes half squinted, like a magazine ad for sinus medication. Her nose was so stopped up she was forced to breathe through her mouth. In spite of all that, she managed to smoke, lighting up a Virginia Slim the minute we sat down.

"You should be home in bed," I said, and then wondered why I'd suggested such a thing. Billy and Lovella were currently back there groveling around on the floor, probably causing the trailer to thump on its foundations. Who could sleep with that stuff going on?

Coral put her cigarette down and took out a Kleenex to blow her nose. I've always wondered where people learn their nose-blowing techniques. She favored the double-digit method, placing a tissue over her hands, sticking the knuckles on both index fingers up her nostrils, rotating them vigorously after each honk. I kept my eyes averted until she was done, wondering idly if she was aware of Lovella's current whereabouts.

"What's the story on Lovella? She seemed distraught at the funeral."

Coral paused in her endeavors and looked at me. Belatedly, I realized she probably didn't know what the word distraught meant. I could see her put the definition together.

"She's fine. She had no idea they weren't legally married to each other. That's why she fell apart. Freaked her out." She gave her nose a final Roto-rooting and took up her cigarette again with a sniff.

"You'd think she'd be relieved," I said. "From what I hear, he beat the shit out of her."

"Not at first. She was crazy about him when he first got out. Still is, actually."

"That's probably why she called him the world's biggest asshole at the funeral," I remarked.

Coral looked at me for a moment and then shrugged noncommittally. She was smarter than Billy, but not by much. I had the same feeling here that I'd had with him. I was tapping into a matter they'd hoped to bury, but I didn't know enough to pursue the point.

I tried fishing. "I thought Lovella and Billy had a thing at one time."

"Years ago. When she was seventeen. Doesn't count for shit."

"She told me Billy set her up with Daggett."

"Yeah, more or less. He talked to Daggett about her and Daggett wrote and asked if they could be pen pals."

"Too bad he never mentioned his wife," I said. "I do want to talk to Lovella, so when you see her please tell her to get in touch." I gave her a business card with my office number on it, which she acknowledged with a shrug.

"I won't see Lovella," she said.

"That's what you think," said I.

Coral's attention strayed to the bartender who was holding a finger aloft. "Hang on."

She crossed to the bar where she picked up a couple of mixed drinks and delivered them to the one other table that was occupied. I tried to picture her flipping Daggett backwards out of a rowboat, but I couldn't quite make it stick. She fit the description, but there was something missing.

When she got back to the booth, I held up the high heels. "These yours?"

"I don't wear suede," she said flatly.

I loved it. Like suede was against her personal dress code. "What about the skirt?"

She took a final drag of the cigarette and crushed it in the metal ashtray, blowing out a mouthful of smoke. "Nope. Whose is it?"

"I think the blonde who killed Daggett wore it Friday night. Billy says she picked him up in here."

Belatedly, she focused on the skirt. "Yeah, that's right. I saw her," she said, as if cued.

"Does this look like the skirt she wore?"

"It could be."

"You know who she is?"

"Uh-uh."

"I don't mean to be rude about this, Coral, but I could use a little help. We're talking murder."

"I've been all tore up about it too," she said, bored.

"Don't you give a shit about any of this?"

"Are you kidding? Why should I care about Daggett? He was scum."

"What about the blonde? Do you remember anything about her?"

Coral shook another cigarette out of the pack. "Why don't you give it a rest, kid. You don't have the right to ask us any of this shit. You're not a cop."

"I can ask anything I want," I said, mildly. "I can't force you to answer, but I can always ask."

She stirred with agitation, shifting in her seat. "Know what? I don't like you," she said. "People like you make me sick."

"Oh really. People like what?"

She took her time extracting a paper match from a packet, scratching the tip across the striking area until it flared. She lit her cigarette. The match made a tiny tinking sound when she dropped it in the ashtray. She rested her chin on her palm and smiled at me unpleasantly. I wanted her to get her teeth fixed so she'd be prettier. "I bet you've had it real easy, haven't you?" she said, her voice heavy with sarcasm.

"Extremely."

"Nice white-collar middle-class home. The whole mommy-hubby trip. Bet you had little brothers and sisters. Nice little fluffy white dog . . ."

"This is amazing," I said.

"Two cars. Maybe a cleaning woman once a week. I never went to college. I never had a daddy giving me all the advantages."

"Well, that explains it then," I said. "I did meet your mom, you know. She looks like someone who's worked hard all her life. Too bad you don't appreciate the effort she made in your behalf."

"What effort? She works in a supermarket checkout line," Coral said.

"Oh, I see. You think she should do something classy like you."

"I'm sure not going to do *this* for life, if that's what you think."

"What happened to your father? Where was he in all this?"

"Who knows? He bugged out a long time ago."

"Leaving her with kids to raise by herself?"

"Skip it. I don't even know why I brought it up. Maybe you should get to the point and let me get back to work."

"Tell me about Doug."

"None of your business." She slid out of the booth. "Time's up," she said, and walked away. God, and here I was being friendly.

I picked up the shoes and skirt and dropped a couple of bucks on the table. I moved to the entranceway, pausing in the shelter of the doorway before I stepped out into the rain. It was 10:17 and there was no traffic on Milagro. The street was shiny black and the rain, as it struck the pavement, made a noise like bacon sizzling in a pan. A mist drifted up from the manhole covers that dotted the block, and the gutters gushed in a widening stream where water boiled back out of the storm drains.

I was restless, not ready to pack it in for the night. I thought about stopping by Rosie's, but it would probably look just like the Hub—smoky, drab, depressing. At least the air outside, though chilly, had the sweet, flowery scent of wet concrete. I started the car and did a U-turn, heading toward the beach, my windshield stippled with rain.

At Cabana, I turned right, driving along the boulevard. On my left, even without a moon visible, the surf churned with a dull gray glow, folding back on itself with a thundering monotony. Out in the ocean, I could see the lights on the oil derricks winking through the mist. I'd pulled up at a stoplight when I heard a car horn toot behind me. I checked my rearview mirror. A little red Honda was pulling over into the lane to my right. It was Jonah, apparently heading home just as I was. He made a cranking motion. I leaned over and rolled the window down on the passenger side.

"Can I buy you a drink?"

"Sure. Where?"

He pointed at the Crow's Nest to his right, a restaurant with exterior lights still burning. The light changed and he took off. I followed, pulling into the lot behind him. We parked side by side. He got out first, hunching against the rain while he opened an umbrella and came around to my door. We huddled together and puddle hopped our way to the front entrance. He held the door and I ducked inside, holding it for him then while he lowered the umbrella and gave it a quick shake.

The interior of the Crow's Nest was done in a halfhearted nautical theme which consisted primarily of fishing nets and rigging draped along the rafters and mariner's charts sealed into the table tops under a half-inch of polyurethane. The restaurant section was closed, but the bar seemed to be doing all right. I could see maybe ten tables occupied. The level of conversation was low and the lighting was discreet, augmented by fat round jars where candles glowed through orange glass.

Jonah steered us past a small dance floor toward a table in the corner. The place had an aura of edgy excitement. We were protected by the weather, drawn together like the random souls stranded in an airport between flights.

The waitress appeared and Jonah glanced at me.

"You decide," I said.

"Two margaritas. Cuervo Gold, Grand Marnier, shaken, no salt," he said. She nodded and moved off.

"Very impressive," I said.

"I thought you'd like that. What brings you out?"

"Daggett, of course." I filled him in, realizing as I summed it up that I'd had just about as much of Billy Polo and his ilk as I could take for one night.

"Let's don't talk about him," I said when I was done. "Tell me what you're working on."

"Hey, no way. I'm here to relax."

The waitress brought our drinks and we paused briefly while she dipped neatly, knees together, and placed a cocktail napkin in front of each of us, along with our drinks. She was dressed like a boatswain except that her high-cut white pants were spandex and her buns hung out the back. I wondered how long uniforms like that would last if the night manager was required to squeeze his hairy fanny into one.

When the waitress left, Jonah touched his glass to mine. "To rainy nights," he said. We drank. The tequila had a little "wow" effect as it went down and I had to pat myself on the chest. Jonah smiled, enjoying my discomfiture.

"What brings you out so late?" I asked.

"Catching up on paperwork. Also, avoiding the house. Camilla's sister came down from Idaho for a week. The two of them are probably drinking wine and carving me up like a roast."

"Her sister doesn't like you, I take it."

"She thinks I'm a dud. Camilla came from money. Deirdre doesn't think either one of them should take up with guys on salary, for God's sake. And a cop? It's all too bourgeois. God, I gotta watch myself here. All I do is complain about life on the home front. I'm beginning to sound like Dempsey."

I smiled. Lieutenant Dempsey had worked Narcotics for years, a miserably married man whose days were spent complaining about his lot. His wife had finally died and he'd turned around and married a woman just like her. He'd taken early retirement and the two of them had gone off in an RV. His postcards to the department were amusing, but left people uncomfortable, like a stand-up comic making mean-spirited jokes at a spouse's expense.

Conversation dwindled. The background music was a tape of old Johnny Mathis tunes and the lyrics suggested an era when falling in love wasn't complicated by herpes, fear of AIDS, multiple marriages, spousal support, feminism, the sexual revolution, the Bomb, the Pill, approval of one's therapist, or the specter of children on alternate weekends.

Jonah was looking good. The combination of shadow and candlelight washed the lines out of his face, and heightened the blue of his eyes. His hair looked very dark and the rain had made it look silkier. He wore a white shirt, opened at the neck, sleeves rolled up, his forearms crosshatched with dark hair. There's usually a current running between us, generated I suppose by whatever primal urges keep the human race reproducing itself. Most of the time, the chemistry is kept in check by a bone-deep caution on my part, ambivalence about his marital status, by circumstance, by his own uneasiness, by the knowledge on both our parts that once certain lines are crossed, there's no going back and no way to predict the consequences.

We ordered a second round of drinks, and then a third. We slow danced, not saying a word. Jonah smelled of soap and his jaw line was smooth and sometimes he hummed with a rumbling I hadn't heard since I sat on my father's lap as a very young child, listening to him read to me before I knew what words meant. I thought about Billy Polo lowering Lovella to the trailer floor. The image was haunting because it spoke so eloquently of his need. I was always such a stoic, so careful not to make mistakes. Sometimes I wonder what the difference is between being cautious and being dead. I thought about rain and how nice it is to sink down on clean sheets. I pulled my head back and Jonah looked down at me quizzically.

"This is all Billy Polo's fault," I said.

He smiled. "What is?"

I studied him for a moment. "What would Camilla do if you didn't come home tonight?"

His smile faded and his eyes got that look. "She's the one who's talking about an open relationship," he said.

I laughed. "I'll bet that applies to her, not you."

"Not anymore," he said.

His kiss seemed familiar.

We left soon afterward.

21

I drove to the office at 9:00. The rain clouds were hunched above the mountains moving north, while above, the sky was the blue white of bleached denim. The city seemed to be in sharp focus, as if seen through new prescription lenses. I opened the French doors and stood on the balcony, raising my arms and doing one of those little butt wiggles so favored by the football set. *That* for you, Camilla Robb, I thought, and then I laughed and went and had a look at myself in the mirror, mugging shamelessly. Amazing Grace. I looked just like myself. Where tears erase the self, good sex transforms and I was feeling energized.

I put the coffee on and got to work, typing up my case notes, detailing the conversations I'd had with Billy and Coral. Cops and private eyes are always caught up in paperwork. Written records have to be kept of everything, with events set out so that anyone who comes along afterward will have a clear and comprehensive résumé of the investigation to that point. Since a private eye also bills for services, I have to keep track of my hours and expenses, submitting statements periodically so I can make sure I get paid. I prefer fieldwork I suspect we all do. If I'd wanted to spend my days in an office, I'd have studied to be an underwriter for the insurance company next door. Their work seems boring 80 percent of the time while mine only bores me about one hour out of every ten.

At 9:30, I touched base with Barbara Daggett by phone, giving her a verbal update to match the written account I was putting in the mail to her. The duplication of effort wasn't really necessary, but I did it anyway. What the hell, it was her money. She was entitled to the best service she could get. After that, I did some filing, then locked up again, taking the green skirt and heels with me down the back stairs to my car, heading out to Marilyn Smith's. I was beginning to feel like the prince in search of Cinderella, shoe in hand.

I took the highway north, drinking in the newly washed air. Colgate is only a fifteen-minute drive, but it gave me a chance to think about events of the night before. Jonah had turned out to be a clown in bed . . . funny and inventive. We'd behaved like bad kids, eating snacks, telling ghost stories, returning now and then to a lovemaking which was, at the same time, intense and comfortable. I wondered if I'd known him in another life. I wondered if I'd know him again. He was so generous and affectionate, so amazed at being with someone who didn't criticize or withhold, who didn't withdraw from his touch as though from a slug's. I couldn't imagine where we'd go from here and I didn't want to start worrying. I'm capable of screwing things up by trying to solve all the problems in advance instead of simply taking care of issues as they surface.

I missed my off-ramp, of course. I caught sight of it as I sped by, cursing good-naturedly as I took the next exit and circled back.

By the time I reached Wayne and Marilyn Smith's house, it was nearly 10:00. The bicycles that had been parked on the porch were gone. The orange trees, though nearly leafless with age, still carried the aura of ripe fruit, a faint perfume spilling out of the surrounding groves. I parked my car in the gravel drive behind a compact station wagon I assumed belonged to her. A peek into the rear, as I passed, revealed a gummy detritus of fast-food containers, softball equipment, school papers, and dog hair.

I cranked the bell. The entrance hall was deserted, but a

golden retriever bounded toward the front door, toenails ticking against the bare floors as it skittered to a stop, barking joyfully. The dog's entire body waggled like a fish on a hook.

"Can I help you?"

Startled, I glanced to my right. Marilyn Smith was standing at the bottom of the porch steps in a tee shirt, drenched jeans, and a straw hat. She wore goatskin gardening gloves and bright yellow plastic clogs that were spattered with mud. When she realized it was me, her expression changed from pleasant inquiry to a barely disguised distaste.

"I'm working in the garden," she said, as if I hadn't guessed. "If you want to talk you'll have to come out there."

I followed her across the rain-saturated lawn. She tapped a muddy trowel against her thigh, distractedly.

"I saw you at the funeral," I remarked.

"Wayne insisted," she said tersely, then looked over her shoulder at me. "Who was the drunk woman? I liked her."

"Lovella Daggett. She thought she was married to him, but it turned out the warranty hadn't run out on his first wife."

When we reached the vegetable patch, she waded between two dripping rows of vines. The garden was in its winter phase—broccoli, cauliflower, dark squashes tucked into a spray of wide leaves. She'd been weeding. I could see the trampled-looking spikes scattered here and there. Farther down the row, there was evidence that the earth had been turned, heavy clods piled up near a shallow excavation site.

"Too wet for weeding, isn't it?"

"The soil here has a high clay content. Once it dries out, it's impossible," she said.

She shucked the gardening gloves and began to tear widths from an old pillow case, tying back the masses of sweet pea plants that had drooped in the rain. The strips of white rag contrasted brightly with the lime green of the plants. I held up the skirt and shoes I'd brought.

"Recognize these?"

She scarcely looked at the articles, but the chilly smile appeared. "Is that what the killer wore?"

"Could be."

"You've made progress since I saw you last. Three days ago, you weren't even certain it was murder."

"That's how I earn my pay," I said.

"Maybe Lovella killed him when she found out he was a bigamist."

"Always possible," I said, "though you still haven't said for sure where you were that night."

"Oh, but I did. I was here. Wayne was at the office and neither of us has corroborating witnesses." She was using that bantering tone again, mild and mocking.

"I'd like to talk to him."

"Make an appointment. He's in the book. Go down to the office. The Granger Building on State."

"Marilyn, I'm not your enemy."

"You are if I killed him," she replied.

"Ah, yes. In that case, I would be."

She tore off another strip of pillow case, the width of cotton dangling from her hand like something limp with death. "Sounds like you have suspects. Too bad you're short on proof."

"But I do have someone who saw her and that should help, don't you think? This is just preliminary work, narrowing the field," I said. It was bullshit, of course. I wasn't sure the motel clerk could identify anybody in the dark.

Her smile dimmed by a watt. "I don't want to talk to you anymore," she whispered.

I raised my hands, as if she'd pulled a gun. "I'm gone," I said, "but I have to warn you, I'm persistent. You'll find it unsettling, I suspect."

I kept my eyes on her as I moved away. I'd seen the muddy hoe she was using and I thought it best not to turn my back.

I cruised by the Westfalls on my way into town. I was going to have to show the skirt to Barbara Daggett at some point, but the Close was on my way. The low fieldstone wall surrounding the place was still a dark gray from the passing rain. I drove through the gates and parked along the road as I had before, pulling over into dense ivy. By day, the eight Victorian houses were enveloped in shade, sunlight scarcely penetrating the branches of the trees. I locked the car and picked my way up the path to the front steps. In the yard, the trunks of the live oak were frosted with a fungus as green as the oxidized copper on a roof. Tall palms punctuated the corners of the house. The air felt cool and moist in the wake of the storm.

The front door was ajar. The view from the hallway was a straight shot through to the kitchen and I could see that the back door was open too, the screen door unlatched. A portable radio sat on the counter and music blasted out, the *1812 Overture*. I rang the bell, but the sound was lost against the booming of cannons as the last movement rose to a thunder pitch.

I left the front porch and walked around to the back, peering in. Like the rest of the house, the kitchen had been redone, the owners opting here to modernize, though the Victorian character had been retained. There was a small floral print paper on the walls, lots of wicker, oak, and fern. The cabinet doors had been replaced with leaded glass, but the appliances were all strictly up-to-date.

There was no one in the room. A door on the left was open, the oblong of shadow suggesting that the basement stairs must be located just beyond. Two brown grocery bags sat on the kitchen table and it looked like someone had been interrupted in the course of unloading them. There was an electric percolator plugged into the outlet on the stove. While I was watching, the ready-light went on. Belatedly, I picked up the smell of hot coffee.

The music ended and the FM announcer made his concluding remarks about the piece, then introduced a Brahms concerto in E minor. I knocked on the frame of the screen door, hoping someone would hear me before the music started up again. Ramona appeared from the depths of the basement. She was wearing a six-gore wool skirt in a muted gray plaid, with a line of dark maroon running through it. Her pullover sweater was dark maroon, with a white blouse under it, the collar pinned sedately at the throat by an antique brooch. For effect, I decided not to mention the heels and wool skirt I'd brought.

"Tony?" she said. "Oh, it's you."

She had an armload of ragged blue bath towels which she dumped on a chair. "I thought I heard someone knock. I couldn't see who it was through the screen." She turned the radio off as she passed and then she opened the screen door to admit me.

"Tony's bringing groceries in from the garage. We just got back from the market. Have a seat. Would you like a cup of coffee? The pot's fresh."

"Yes, please. That's nice." I moved the pile of rags out of the chair and sat down, putting the skirt and shoes on the table in front of me. I saw her eyes stray to them, but she made no comment.

"Isn't this a school day for him?" I asked.

"They're giving the sophomores some sort of academic placement tests. He finished early so they let him go. He's got an appointment with his therapist shortly anyway."

I watched her move about the kitchen, fetching cups and saucers. She had one of those hairstyles that settle into perfect shape with a flick of the head. I butcher my own at six-week intervals with a pair of nail scissors and a two-way mirror, causing salon stylists to pale when they see me. "Who *did* that to you?" they always ask. I wanted perfect waves like hers, but I didn't think I could achieve the effect.

Ramona poured two cups of coffee. "There's something I probably should have mentioned before," she said. She took a ceramic pitcher from the cupboard and filled it with milk, realizing then that I was waiting for her to continue. Her smile was thin. "John Daggett called here Monday night, asking to talk to Tony. I took his number, but Ferrin and I decided it wasn't a good idea. It might not matter much at this point, but I thought you should be aware."

"What made you think of it?"

She hesitated. "I came across the number on the pad by the phone. I'd forgotten all about it."

I could feel a tingle at the back of my neck—that clammy feeling you get when your body overloads on sugar. Something was off here, but I wasn't sure what it was.

"Why bring it up now?" I asked.

"I thought you were tracking his activities early in the week."

"I wasn't aware that I'd told you that."

Her cheeks tinted. "Marilyn Smith called me. She mentioned it."

"How'd Daggett know where to reach you? When I talked to him on Saturday, he had no idea where Tony was and he certainly didn't have your name or number."

"I don't know how he got it," she said. "What difference does it make?"

"How do I know you didn't make a date to meet him Friday night?"

"Why would I do that?" she said.

I stared at her. A millisecond later she realized what I was getting at.

"But I was here Friday night."

"I haven't heard that verified so far."

"That's ridiculous! Ask Tony. He knows I was here. You can check it out yourself."

"I intend to," I said.

Tony thumped up the wooden porch steps, armed with two more grocery bags, his attention diverted as he groped for the screen door handle, missing twice. "Aunt Ramona, can you give me a hand with this?"

She crossed to the door and held it open. Tony spotted me and the green skirt at just about the same time and I saw his gaze jump to his aunt's face quizzically. Her expression was neutral, but she busied herself right away, pushing canned goods aside so he could set one bag on the table top. The second bag she took herself and placed on the counter. She sorted through and lifted out a carton of ice cream. "I better get this put away," she murmured. She crossed to the freezer.

"What are you doing here?" Tony said to me.

"I was curious how you were feeling. Your aunt mentioned that you had a migraine Monday night."

"I feel okay."

"What'd you think about the funeral?"

"Bunch of freaks," he said.

"Let's get these unloaded, dear," his aunt said. The two of them began to put groceries away while I sipped my coffee. I couldn't tell if she was deliberately distracting him or not, but that was the effect.

"You need some help?" I asked.

"We can manage," she murmured.

"Who was that lady who went nuts?" Tony asked. Lovella had made a big impression on everyone.

Ramona held up a soft drink in a big plastic bottle. "Stick this in the refrigerator while you're there," she said.

She released the bottle an instant before he'd gotten a good grip on it and he had to scramble to catch it before it toppled to the floor. Had she done that deliberately? He was waiting for my reply so I gave him a brief rendition of the tale. It was gossip, in some ways, but he was as animated as I'd seen him and I hoped to keep his attention.

"I don't mean to interrupt, but Tony does have homework to take care of. Finish your coffee, of course," she said. Her tone suggested that I suck it right down and scram.

"I'm due back at the office anyway," I said, getting up. I looked at Tony. "Could you walk me to my car?"

He glanced at Ramona, whose gaze dropped away from his. She didn't protest. He ducked his head in assent.

He held the door for me while I gathered the skirt and shoes and turned back to her. "I nearly forgot. Are these yours, by any chance?"

"I'm sure not," she said to me, and then to him, "Don't be long."

He looked like he was on the verge of saying something, but he shrugged instead. He followed me out on the porch and down the steps. I led the way as we circled the house. The path to the street was paved with stepping-stones spaced oddly, so that I had to watch my feet to gauge the distances.

"I have a question," I said as we reached the car.

He was watching me warily by then, interested but on guard.

"I was curious about the migraine you had Friday night. Do you remember how long that one lasted?"

"Friday night?" His voice had a croak in it from surprise.

"That's right. Didn't you have a migraine that night?"

"I guess."

"Think back," I said. "Take your time."

He seemed uncomfortable, casting about for some visual clue. I'd seen him do this before, reading body language so he could adjust his response to whatever was expected of him. I waited in silence, letting his anxiety accumulate.

"I think that's the day I got one. When I came home from school," he said, "but then it cleared."

"What time was that?"

"Real late. After midnight. Maybe two . . . two-thirty, something like that."

"How'd you happen to notice the time?"

"Aunt Ramona made me a couple of sandwiches in the kitchen. It was a real bad headache and I'd been throwing up for hours so I never had dinner. I was starving. I must have looked at the kitchen clock."

"What kind of sandwiches?"

"What?"

"I was wondering what kind she made."

His gaze hung on mine. The seconds ticked away. "Meatloaf," he said.

"Thanks," I said. "That helps."

I opened the VW on the driver's side, tossing skirt and shoes on the passenger seat as I got in. His version was roughly the same as his aunt's, but I could have sworn the "meatloaf" was a wild guess.

I started the car and did a U-turn, heading toward the gates. I caught a glimpse of him in the rearview mirror, already moving toward the house.

22

It's a fact of life that when a case won't break, you have to go through the motions anyway, stirring up the waters, rattling all the cages at the zoo. To that end, on my way into town I did a long detour that included a stop at the trailer park, in hopes that Lovella would still be there. It was obvious to me, as I'm not a fool, that toting a green wool skirt and a pair of black suede heels all over town was a pointless enterprise. No one was going to claim them and if someone did, so what? The articles proved nothing. No one was going to break down sobbing and confess at the mere sight of them. The pop quiz was simply my way of putting them all on notice, making the rounds one more time to announce that I was still on the job and making progress, however insignificant it might appear.

I knocked at the trailer door, but got no response. I jotted a note on the back of a business card, indicating that Lovella should call. I tucked it in the doorjamb, went back to my car, and headed for town.

Wayne Smith's office was located on the seventh floor of the Granger Building in downtown Santa Teresa. Aside from the clock tower on the courthouse, the Granger is just about the only structure on State Street that's more than two stories high. Part of the charm of the downtown area is its low-slung look. The flavor, for the most part, is Spanish. Even the trash containers are faced with stucco and rimmed with decorative tile. The telephone booths look like small adobe huts and if you can ignore the fact that the bums use them for urinals, the effect is quaint. There are flowering shrubs along the walk, jacaranda trees, and palms. Low ornamental stucco walls widen in places to form benches for weary shoppers. Everything is clean, well kept, pleasing to the eye.

The Granger Building looks just like hundreds of office buildings constructed in the twenties—yellow brick, symmetrical narrow windows banded with granite friezes, topped by a steeply pitched roof with matching gables. Along the roofline, just below the cornice, there are decorative marble torches affixed to the wall with inexplicable half shells mounted underneath. The style is an anomaly in this town, falling as it does between the Spanish, the Victorian, and the pointless. Still, the building is a landmark, housing a movie theater, a jeweler's, and seven stories of office space.

I checked the wall directory in the marble foyer for Wayne Smith's suite number, which turned out to be 702. Two elevators serviced the building and one was out of order, the doors standing open, the housing mechanism in plain view. It's not a good idea to scrutinize such things. When you see how elevators actually work, you realize how improbable the whole scheme is . . . raising and lowering a roomful of people on a few long wires. Ridiculous.

A fellow in coveralls stood there, mopping his face with a red bandanna.

"How's it going?" I asked, while I waited for the other elevator doors to open.

He shook his head. "Always something, isn't it? Last week it was that one wouldn't work."

The doors slid open and I stepped in, pressing seven. The doors closed and nothing happened for a while. Finally, with a jolt, the elevator began its ascent, stopping at the seventh floor. There was another interminable delay. I pressed the "DOOR OPEN" button. No dice. I tried to guess how long I could survive on just that one ratty piece of chewing gum at the bottom of my handbag. I banged the button with the flat of my hand and the doors slid open.

The corridor was narrow and dimly illuminated, as there was only one exterior window, located at the far end of the hall. Four dark, wood-paneled doors opened off each side, with the names of the professional tenants in gold-leaf lettering that looked as if it had been there since the building went up. There was no activity that I could perceive, no sounds, no muffled telephones ringing. Wayne Smith, C.P.A., was the first door on the right. I pictured a receptionist in a small waiting area, so I simply turned the knob and walked in without knocking. There was only one large room, tawny daylight filtering in through drawn window shades. Wayne Smith was lying on the floor with his legs propped up on the seat of his swivel chair. He turned and looked at me.

"Oh sorry! I thought there'd be a waiting room," I said. "Are you okay?"

"Sure. Come on in," he said. "I was resting my back." He removed his legs from the chair, apparently in some pain. He rolled over on his side and eased himself into an upright position, wincing as he did. "You're Kinsey Millhone. Marilyn pointed you out at the funeral yesterday."

I watched him, wondering if I should lend him a hand. "What'd you do to yourself?"

"My back went out on me. Hurts like a son of a bitch," he said. Once he was on his feet, he dug a fist into the small of his back, twisting one shoulder slightly as if to ease a cramp. He had a runner's body—lean, stringy muscles, narrow through the chest. He looked older than his wife, maybe late forties while I pegged her in her early thirties. His hair was light, worn in a crewcut, like something out of a 1950s high school annual. I wondered if he'd been in the military at some point. The hairstyle suggested that he was hung up in the past, his persona fixed perhaps by some significant event. His eyes were pale and his face was very lined. He moved to the windows and raised all three shades. The room became unbearably bright.

"Have a seat," he said.

I had a choice between a daybed and a molded plastic chair with a bucket seat. I took the chair, doing a surreptitious visual survey while he lowered himself into his swivel chair as though into a steaming sitz bath. He had six metal bookcases that looked like they were made of Erector sets, loosely bolted and sagging slightly from the weight of all the manuals. Brown accordion file cases were stacked up everywhere, his desk top virtually invisible. Correspondence was piled on the floor near his chair, government pamphlets and tax law updates stacked on the window sill. This was not a man you'd want to depend on if you were facing an I.R.S. audit. He looked like the sort who might put you there.

"I just talked to Marilyn. She said you came by the house. We're puzzled by your interest in us."

"Barbara Daggett hired me to investigate her father's death. I'm interested in everyone."

"But why talk to us? We haven't seen the man in years."

"He didn't get in touch last week?"

"Why would he do that?"

"He was looking for Tony Gahan. I thought he might have tried to get a line on him through you."

The phone rang and he reached for it, conducting a business-related conversation while I studied him. He wore chinos, just a wee bit too short, and his socks were the clinging nylon sort that probably went up to his knees. He switched to his good-bye tone, trying to close out his conversation. "Uh-huh, uh-huh. Okay, great. That's fine. We'll do that. I got the forms right here. Deadline is the end of the month. Swell."

He hung up with an exasperated shake of his head.

"Anyway," he said, as a way of getting back to the subject at hand.

"Yeah, right. Anyway," I said, "I don't suppose you remember where you were Friday night."

"I was here, doing quarterly reports."

"And Marilyn was home with the kids?"

He sat and stared at me, a smile flickering off and on. "Are you implying that we might have had a hand in John Daggett's death?"

"Someone did," I said.

He laughed, running a hand across his crewcut as if checking to see if he needed a trim. "Miss Millhone, you've got a hell of a nerve," he said. "The newscast said it was an accident."

I smiled. "The cops still think so. I disagree. I think a lot of people wanted Daggett dead. You and Marilyn are among them."

"But we wouldn't do a thing like that. You can't be serious. I despised the man, no doubt about that, but we're not going to go out and track a man down and kill him. Good God."

I kept my tone light. "But you did have the motive and you had the opportunity."

"You can't hang anything on that. We're decent people. We don't even get parking tickets. John Daggett must have had a lot of enemies."

I shrugged by way of agreement. "The Westfalls," I said. "Billy Polo and his sister, Coral. Apparently, some prison thugs."

"What about that woman who set up such a howl at the funeral?" he said. "She looked like a pretty good candidate to me."

"I've talked to her."

"Well, you better go back and talk to her again. You're wasting time with us. Nobody's going to be arrested on the basis of 'motive' and 'opportunity.' "

"Then you don't have anything to worry about."

He shook his head, his skepticism evident. "Well. I can see you have your work cut out for you. I'd appreciate it if you'd lay off Marilyn in this. She's had trouble enough."

"I gathered as much." I got up. "Thanks for your time. I hope I won't have to bother you again." I moved toward the door.

"I hope so too."

"You know, if you did kill him, or if you know who killed him, I'll find out. Another few days and I'm going to the cops anyway. They'll scrutinize that alibi of yours like you wouldn't believe."

He held his hands out, palms up. "We're innocent until proven otherwise," he said, smiling boyishly.

23

Waiting for the elevator, I replayed the conversation, trying to figure out what I'd missed. On the surface, there was nothing wrong with his response, but I felt irritated and uneasy, maybe just because I wasn't getting anyplace. I banged on the DOWN button. "Come on," I said. The elevator door opened partway. Impatiently, I shoved it back and got on. The doors closed and the elevator descended one floor before it stopped again. The doors opened. Tony Gahan was standing in the corridor, a shopping bag in hand. He seemed as surprised to see me as I was to see him.

"What are you doing here?" he said. He got on the elevator and we descended.

"I had to see someone upstairs," I said. "What about you?"

"A shrink appointment. He's been out of town and now his return flight was delayed. His secretary's supposed to pick him up in an hour so she said to come back at five."

We reached the lobby.

"How are you getting home? Need a ride?" I asked.

He shook his head. "I'm going to hang around down here." He gestured vaguely at the video arcade across the street where some high school kids were horsing around.

"See you later then," I said.

We parted company and I returned to the parking lot behind the building. I got in my car and circled the four blocks to the lot behind my office where I parked. For the time being, I left the skirt and shoes in the backseat.

There were no messages on my answering machine, but

the mail was in and I sorted through that, wondering what else to do with myself. Actually, I realized I was exhausted, the emotional charge from Jonah having drained away. I'm not used to drinking that much, for starters, and I tend, being single, to get a lot more sleep. He'd left at 5:00, before it was light, and I'd managed maybe an hour's worth of shut-eye before I'd finally gotten up, jogged, showered, and fixed myself a bite to eat.

I tilted back in my swivel chair and propped my feet up on the desk, hoping no one would begrudge me a snooze. The next time I was aware of anything, the clock hands had dissolved magically from 12:10 to 2:50 and my head was pounding. I staggered to my feet and trotted down the hall to the ladies' room. I peed, washed my hands and face, rinsed my mouth out, and stared at myself in the mirror. My hair was mashed flat in the back and standing straight up everywhere else. The fluorescent light in the room made my skin look sickly. Was this the consequence of illicit sex with a married man? "Well, I soitonly hope so," I said. I ducked my head under the faucet and then dried my hair with eight rounds of hot air from a wall-mounted machine that had been installed (the sign said) to help protect me from the dangers of diseases that might be transmitted through paper towel litter. Idly, I wondered what diseases they were worried about. Typhus? Diphtheria?

I could hear my office phone from halfway down the hall and I started to run. I snagged it on the sixth ring, snatching up the receiver with a winded hello.

"This is Lovella," the glum voice said. "I got this note to call you."

I took a deep breath, inventing as I went along. "Right," I said. "I thought we should touch base. We really haven't talked since I saw you in L.A." I sidled around my desk and sat down, still trying to catch my breath.

"I'm mad at you, Kinsey," she said. "Why didn't you tell me you had Daggett's money?"

"To what end? I had a cashier's check, but it wasn't made out to you. So why mention it?"

"Because I'm standing around telling you I'm married to a guy who'd just as soon kill me as look at me and you're telling me to call the rape crisis center, some bullshit like that. And all the time, Daggett had thousands of dollars."

"But he stole the money. Didn't Billy tell you that?"

"I don't care where it came from. I'd just like to have a little something for myself. Now he's dead and she gets everything."

"Who, Essie?"

"Her and that daughter."

"Oh come on, Lovella. He couldn't have left them enough to worry about."

"More than he left me," she said. "If I'd known about the money, I might have talked him out of some."

"Yeah, right. As generous as he was," I said drily. "If you'd gotten your hands on it, you might be dead now instead of him. Unless Billy's been lying to me about the punks from San Luis who were after him." I'd never really taken that story seriously, but maybe it was time I did.

She was silent. I could practically hear her shifting gears. "All I know is I think you're a shit and he was too."

"I'm sorry you feel that way, Lovella. John hired me, and my first loyalty was to him . . . misguided, as it turned out, but that's where I was coming from. You want to vent a little more on the subject before we turn to something else?"

"Yeah. I should have got the money, not someone else. I was the one who got banged around. I still got two cracked ribs and an eye looks like it's all sunk in on one side from the bruise."

"Is that why you freaked out at the funeral?"

Her tone of voice became tempered with sheepishness. "I'm sorry I did that, but I couldn't help myself. I'd been sittin' in some bar drinkin' Bloody Marys since ten o'clock and I guess

I got outta hand. But it bugged me, all that Bible talk. Daggett never went to church a day in his life and it didn't seem right. And that old fat-ass claimed she was married to him? I couldn't believe my eyes. She looked like a bulldog."

I had to laugh. "Maybe he didn't marry her for her looks," I said.

"Well, I hope not."

"When did you see him last?"

"At the funeral home, where else?"

"Before that, I mean."

"Day he left L.A.," she said. "Week ago Monday. I never saw him after he took off."

"I thought maybe you hopped a bus on Thursday after I left."

"Well, I didn't."

"But you could have, couldn't you?"

"What for? I didn't even know where he went."

"But Billy did. You could have come up to Coral's last week. You might have met him at the Hub Friday night and bought him a couple of drinks."

Her laugh was sour. "You can't pin that on me. If that was me, how come Coral didn't recognize me, huh?"

"For all I know, she did. You're friends. Maybe she just kept her mouth shut."

"Why would she do that?"

"Maybe she wanted to help you out."

"Coral doesn't even like me. She thinks I'm a slut so why would she help me?"

"She might've had reasons of her own."

"I didn't kill him, Kinsey, if that's what you're getting at."

"That's what everyone says. You're all wide-eyed and innocent. Daggett was murdered and nobody's guilty. Amazing."

"You don't have to take my word for it. Ask Billy. Once he gets back, he can tell you who it was for sure, anyway."

"Oh hey, sounds great. How's he going to manage that?"

There was a pause, as if she'd said something she really wasn't authorized to say. "He thought he recognized somebody at the funeral and then he figured out where he'd seen 'em before," she said reluctantly.

I blinked at the telephone receiver. In a quick flash, I remembered Billy's staring at the little group formed by the Westfalls, Barbara Daggett, and the Smiths. "I don't understand. What's he up to?"

"He set up a meeting," she said. "He wants to find out if his theory's right and then he said he'd call you."

"He's going to *meet* with her?"

"That's what I said, isn't it?"

"He shouldn't be doing that by himself. Why didn't he notify the police?"

"Because he doesn't want to make a fool of himself in front of them. Suppose he's wrong? He doesn't have any proof, anyway. Just a hunch is all and even that's not a hundred percent."

"Do you have any idea who he was talking about?"

"Uh-uh. He wouldn't tell, but he was pretty happy with himself. He said we might get some money after all."

Oh God, I thought, not blackmail. I could feel my heart sink. Billy Polo wasn't smart enough to pull that off. He'd blow it like he did every other crime he tried. "Where's the meeting taking place?"

"What makes you ask?" she said, turning cagey.

"Because I want to go!"

"I don't think I should tell."

"Lovella, don't do this to me."

"Well, he didn't say I could."

"You've told me this much. Why not the rest? He could be in trouble."

She hesitated, mulling it over. "Down at the beach somewhere. He's not dumb, you know. He made sure it was public.

He figured in broad daylight, there wouldn't be any problem, especially with other people around."

"Which beach?"

"What if he gets mad at me?"

"I'll square it with him myself," I said. "I will *swear* I forced the information out of you."

"He's not going to like it if you show up and spoil everything."

"I won't spoil it. I'll lurk in the background and make sure he's okay. That's all I'm talking about."

Silence. She was so slow I thought I'd scream. "Look at it this way," I said. "He might be happy for the help. What if he needs backup?"

"Billy wouldn't need backup from a *woman*."

I closed my eyes, trying to keep my temper in check. "Just give me a hint, Lovella, or I'll come over to the trailer and rip your heart out by the roots." That, she heard.

"You better never tell him I told," she warned.

"Cross my heart and hope to die. Now come on."

"I think it's that parking lot near the boat launch. . . ."

I banged the phone down and snagged my handbag. I locked the office in haste and ran down the hall, going down the back stairs two and three at a time. I'd had to park my car at the far end of the lot and once I got to the pay booth, there were three other cars in front of mine. "Come on, come on," I murmured, banging on the steering wheel.

Finally, it was my turn. I showed the attendant my parking permit and shot through the gate as soon as the bar went up.

Chapel is one way, heading up from the beach, so I had to turn right, take a left, and hit the one-way street going down again. I caught the light wrong at 101 so that delayed me. I didn't want to miss this one. I didn't want to show up two minutes late and miss the only chance I might have. I pictured a citizen's arrest . . . me and Billy Polo saving the day.

The light turned green and I crossed the highway. Two

blocks more and I reached Cabana where I took a right turn. The entrance to the lot I wanted was all the way around the bend near Santa Teresa City College. I got a ticket from the machine and threaded my way along the perimeter of the lot. I scanned the parked cars, hoping for a glimpse of Billy's white Chevy. The marina was on my right, the sun reflecting starkly from the white sails of a stately boat as it glided out of the harbor. The boat launch itself was at the very end of the parking lot, through a second parking gate. I pulled a second ticket and the arm went up. I found a slot and left my car, proceeding on foot.

Four joggers passed me. There were people on the boat dock, people on the walk, people by the snack shop and the public restrooms. I broke into a trot, searching the landscape ahead of me for some sign of Billy or the blonde. I heard three hollow pops in quick succession dead ahead. I ran. No one else was reacting, but I could have sworn it was the sound of shots.

I reached the boat launch, where the parking lot slants down into the water. There was no one in sight. No one running, no one leaving the scene in haste. The air was still, the water lapping softly at the asphalt. Two pontoon piers extend into the water about thirty feet, but both were empty, no boats or pedestrians in sight. I did a three-sixty turn, surveying every foot of the area. And then I spotted him. He was lying on his side by a boat trailer, one arm caught under him awkwardly. He struggled, gasping, and turned himself over on his back. I crossed the macadam rapidly.

A man in cutoffs had come out of a snack shop and he peered at me as I went past. "Is that guy okay?"

"Call the cops. Get an ambulance," I snapped.

I knelt beside Billy, angling so he could see me. "It's me," I said. "Don't panic. You'll be fine. We'll have help here in a second."

Billy's eyes strayed to mine. His face was gray and there

was a widening puddle of quite red blood spreading out under him. I took his hand and held it. A crowd was beginning to collect, people running from all directions. I could hear them buzzing at my back.

Somebody handed me a beach towel. "You want to cover him with this?"

I grabbed the towel. I let go of him long enough to unbutton his shirt, opening it so I could see what I was dealing with. There was a hole in his belly. He must have been shot from behind, because what I was looking at was an exit wound, ragged, welling with blood. The slug must have severed the abdominal aorta. A coil of his lower intestine was visible, gray and glistening, bulging through the hole. I could feel my hands start to shake, but I kept my expression neutral. He was watching me, trying to read my face. I made a pad of the towel, pressing it against the wound to staunch the flow of blood.

He groaned, breathing rapidly. He had one hand resting on his chest and his fingers fluttered. I took his hand again, squeezing hard.

He tilted his head. "Where's . . . my leg? I can't feel nothin' down there."

I glanced down at his right knee. The pantleg looked like it had caught on a nail. Blood and bone seemed to blossom through the tear.

"Don't sweat it. They can fix that. You'll be fine," I said. I didn't mention the blood soaking through the towel. I thought he probably knew about that.

"I'm gut-shot."

"I know. Relax. It's not bad. The ambulance is on its way."

The hand I held was icy, his fingers pale. There were questions I should have asked, but I didn't. I couldn't. You don't intrude on someone's dying with a bullshit interrogation like you're some kind of pro. This was just me and him and nothing else entered into it.

I studied his face, sending love through my eyes, willing him to live. His hair looked curlier than I remembered it. With my free hand, I moved it away from his forehead. Sweat beaded on his upper lip.

"I'm goin' . . . .I can feel myself goin' out . . ." He clutched my hand convulsively, bucking against a surge of pain.

"Take it easy. You'll be fine."

He began to hyperventilate and then his struggle subsided. I could see the life drain away, see it all fade—color, energy, awareness, pain. Death comes in a gathering cloud that settles like a veil. Billy Polo sighed, his gaze still pinned on my face. His hand relaxed in mine, but I held on.

24

I sat on the curb near the snack shop and stared at the asphalt. The proprietor had brought me a can of Coke and I held the cold metal against my temple. I felt sick, but there wasn't anything wrong with me. Lieutenant Feldman had appeared and he was hunkered over Billy's body, talking to the lab guys, who were bagging his hands. The ambulance had backed around and waited with its doors open, as if to shield the body from the public view. Two black-and-whites were parked nearby, radios providing a squawking counterpoint to the murmurs of the gathering crowd. Violent death is a spectator sport and I could hear them trading comments about the way the final quarter had been played. They weren't being cruel, just curious. Maybe it was good for them to see how grotesque homicide really is.

The beat officers, Gutierrez and Pettigrew, had arrived within minutes of Billy's demise and they'd radioed for the CSI unit. The two of them would probably drive over to the trailer park to break the news to Coral and Lovella. I felt I should ride along, but I couldn't bring myself to volunteer yet. I'd go, but for the moment, I was having trouble coping with the fact of Billy's death. It had happened so fast. It was so irrevocable. I found it hard to accept that we couldn't rewind the tape and play the last fifteen minutes differently. I would arrive earlier. I would warn him off and he could walk away unharmed. He'd tell me his theory and then I'd buy him the beer I'd promised him that first night at the Hub.

Feldman appeared. I found myself staring at his pantlegs, unable to look up. He lit a cigarette and came down to my level, perching on the curb. I hugged my knees, feeling numb. I barely know the man, but what I've seen of him I've always liked. He looks like a cross between a Jew and an Indian—a large flat face, high cheekbones, a big hooked nose. He's a big man, probably forty-five, with a cop haircut, cop clothes, a deep rumbling voice. "You want to bring me up to speed on this?" he said.

It was the act of opening my mouth to speak that brought the tears. I held myself in check, willing them back. I shook my head, struggling with the nearly overwhelming rush of regret. He handed me a handkerchief and I pressed it to my eyes, then folded it, addressing my remarks to the oblong of white cotton. There was an "F" embroidered in one corner with a thread coming loose.

"Sorry," I murmured.

"That's okay. Take your time."

"He was such a screw-up," I said. "I guess that's what gets me. He thought he was so smart and so tough."

I paused. "I guess you never know which people will affect your life," I said.

"He never said who shot him?"

I shook my head. "I didn't ask. I didn't want the last minutes of his life taken up with that stuff. I'm sorry."

"Well, he might not have said anyway. What was the setup?"

I started talking, saying anything that came to mind. He let me ramble till I finally took control of myself and began to lay it out systematically. After hundreds of reports, I know the drill. I cited chapter and verse while he nodded, making notes in a battered black notebook.

When I finished, he tucked his ballpoint pen away and shoved the notebook back into the inside pocket of his suitcoat. He got up and I rose with him, automatically.

"What next?" I asked.

"Actually, I got Daggett's file sitting on my desk," he said. "Robb told me you tagged it a homicide and I thought I'd take a look. We had a double killing, one of those execution-style shootings, up on the Bluffs late yesterday and we've had to put a lot of manpower on that one, so I haven't had a chance as yet. It'd help if you came down to the station and talked to Lieutenant Dolan yourself."

"Let me see Billy's sister first," I said. "This is the second brother she's lost in the whole Daggett mess."

"You don't think there's any chance she's the one who plugged him?"

I shook my head. "I thought she might connect to Daggett's death, but I can't picture her involved in this. Unless I'm missing something big. For one thing, he wouldn't have to meet her out in public like this. It was someone at the funeral, I'm almost sure."

"Make a list and we'll take it from there," he said.

I nodded. "I can also stop by the office and make some copies of my file reports. And Lovella may know more than she's told us so far." It felt good, turning everything over to him. He could have it all. Essie and Lovella and the Smiths.

Pettigrew approached, holding a small plastic Ziploc bag by one corner. In it were three empty brass casings. "We found these over by that pickup truck. We're sealing off the whole parking lot until the guys have a chance to go over it."

I said, "You might check the trash bins. That's where I found the skirt and shoes after Daggett was killed."

Feldman nodded, then gave the shells a cursory look. "Thirty-twos," he remarked.

I felt a cold arrow shoot up my spine. My mouth went dry. "My thirty-two was stolen from my car a few days ago," I said. "Gutierrez took the report."

"A lot of thirty-twos around, but we'll keep that in mind," Feldman said to me, and then to Pettigrew, "Let's hustle these folk out of here. And be polite."

Pettigrew moved away and Feldman turned to study me. "Are you all right?"

I nodded, wishing I could sit down again, afraid once I did I'd be stuck.

"Anything you want to add before I let you go?"

I closed my eyes for a moment, thinking back. I know the snapping sound a .32 makes when fired and the shots I'd heard weren't like that. "The shots," I said. "They sounded odd to me. Hollow. More like a pop than a bang."

"A silencer?"

"I've never heard one except on TV," I said, sheepishly.

"I'll have the lab take a look at the slugs, though I don't know where anybody'd get a silencer in this town." He made another quick note in his book.

"You can probably order one from the back of a magazine," I said.

"Ain't that the truth."

The photographer was snapping pictures and I could see Feldman's gaze flick in that direction. "Let me tend to this guy. He's new. I want to make sure he covers everything I need."

He excused himself and crossed to Billy's body where he engaged in a conversation with the forensic photographer, using gestures to describe the various angles he wanted.

Maria Gutierrez came up to me. "We're going out to the trailer park. Gerry said you might want to come."

"I'll follow in my car," I said. "You know where it is?"

"We know the park. We can meet you there if you want."

"I'm going to see if Billy's car is here in the lot. I'll be along shortly, but don't wait on my account."

"Right," she said.

I watched them pull out and then I worked my way through the lot, checking the vehicles in the area adjacent to the boat launch. I spotted the Chevy three rows from the entrance, tucked between two RVs. The temporary sticker was still on the windshield. The windows were down. I stuck my head in without touching anything. The car looked clean to me. Nothing in the front seat. Nothing in the back. I went around to the passenger window and peered in, checking the floorboards from that side. I don't even know what I was hoping for. A hint, some suggestion of where we might go from here. It looked as if Feldman might initiate a formal investigation after all, and glad as I was to turn it over to him, I still couldn't quite let go.

I stopped by my car and picked up the skirt and shoes, which I handed over to Lieutenant Feldman. I told him where to find Billy's car and then I finally got back in mine and took off. In my heart, I knew I'd been stalling to allow Pettigrew and Gutierrez a chance to deliver the news of Billy's death. That has to be the worst moment in anybody's life, finding two uniformed cops at your door, their expressions somber, voices grave.

By the time I got to the trailer park, the word had apparently spread. By some telepathic process, people were collecting in twos and threes, all staring at the trailer uncomfortably, chatting in low tones. The trailer door was closed and I heard nothing as I approached, but my appearance had generated conversation at my back.

A fellow stepped forward. "You a family friend? Because she's had bad news. I wasn't sure if you were aware," he said.

"I was there," I said. "She knows me. How long ago did the officers leave?"

"Two minutes. They were real good about it . . . talked to her a long time, making sure she was all right. I'm Fritzy Roderick. I manage the park," he said, offering me his hand.

"Kinsey Millhone," I said. "Is anybody with her now?"

"I don't believe so, and we haven't heard a peep. We were just talking among ourselves here . . . the neighbors and all . . . wondering if someone ought to sit with her."

"Is Lovella in there?"

"I don't know the name. Is she a relative?"

"Billy's ex-girlfriend," I said. "Let me see if I can find out what's going on. If she needs anything, I'll let you know."

"I'd appreciate that. We'd like to help any way we can."

I knocked at the trailer door, uncertain what to expect. Coral opened it a crack and when she saw it was me, she let me in. Her eyes were reddened, but she seemed in control. She sat down on a kitchen chair and picked up her cigarette, giving the ash a flick. I sat down on the banquette.

"I'm sorry about Billy," I said.

She glanced at me briefly. "Did he know?"

"I think so. When I found him, he was already in shock and fading fast. I don't think he suffered much if that's what you're asking."

"I'll have to tell Mom. The two cops who came said they'd do it, but I said no." Her voice trailed off, hoarse from grief or the head cold. "He always knew he'd die young, you know? Like when we'd see old people on the street, crippled or feeble. He said he'd never end up like them. I used to beg him to straighten up his act, but he had to do everything his way." She lapsed into silence.

"Where's Lovella?"

"I don't know," Coral said. "The trailer was empty when I got here."

"Coral, I wish you'd fill me in. I need to know what was going on. Billy told me three different versions of the same tale."

"Why look at me? I don't know anything."

"But you know more than I do."

"That wouldn't take much."

"Level with me. Please. Billy's dead now. There's nothing left to protect. Is there?"

She stared at the floor for a moment and then she sighed and stubbed out her cigarette. She got up and started clearing the table, running water in the tiny stainless steel kitchen sink.

She squirted in Ivory Liquid, dropping silverware and plates into the mounting suds, talking in a low monotone as she worked. "Billy was already up at San Luis when Daggett got there. Daggett had no idea Doug was related to us, so Billy struck up an acquaintance. We were both of us bitter as hell."

"Billy told me he and Doug were never close."

"Bullshit. He just told you that so you wouldn't suspect him. The three of us were always thick as thieves."

"So you did intend to kill him," I said.

"I don't know. We just wanted to make him pay. We wanted to punish him. We figured we'd find a way once we got close. Then Daggett's cellmate died and he got all that money."

"And you thought that would compensate?"

"Not me. I knew I'd never be happy till the day Daggett died, but I couldn't do it myself. I mean, kill someone in cold blood. Billy was the one who said the money would help. We couldn't bring Doug back, but at least we'd have something. He always knew Daggett lifted the cash, but he didn't think he'd get away with it. Daggett gets out of prison and sure enough, he's home free. He starts throwin' money around. Lovella calls Billy and we decide to go for it."

"So the guys up at San Luis never did figure it out," I said.

"Nope. Once Billy saw Daggett was in the clear, we decided to rip him off."

"And Lovella was part of it?"

Coral nodded, rinsing a plate, which she placed in the dish rack. "They got married the same week he got out, which suited us just fine. We figured if she didn't talk him out of it, she could steal it. . . ."

"And failing that, what?"

"We never meant to kill anyone," she said. "We just wanted the money. We didn't have much time anyway because he'd already spent part of it. He went through five grand before we could bat an eye and we knew if we didn't move fast, he'd blow the whole wad."

"You didn't realize he intended to give the rest of it to Tony Gahan?"

"Of course not," she said with energy. "Billy couldn't believe it when you told him about that. We thought most of it was still around somewhere. We thought we could still get our hands on it."

I watched her face, trying to compute the information she was giving me. "You mean you set Daggett up with Lovella so you could con him out of twenty-five thousand bucks?"

"That's right," she said.

"You were splitting it three ways! That's a little over eight grand apiece."

"So?"

"Coral, eight grand is nothing."

"Bullshit, it's nothing! Do you know what I could do with eight grand? How much do you have? Do you have eight grand?"

"No."

"So, all right. Don't tell me it's nothing."

"All right. It's a fortune," I said. "What went wrong?"

"Nothing at first. Billy called him up and said the guys at San Luis heard about the money and they wanted it back. He told Daggett they were coming after him, so that's when Daggett split."

"How'd you know he'd hightail it up here?"

"Billy told Daggett he'd help him out," she said with a shrug. "And then when Daggett got into town, Billy started working on him, trying to get him to fork it over to us. He said he'd act as a go-between, smooth it all over and get him off the hook."

"He'd already given it to me at that point, right?"

"Sure, but we didn't know that. He acted like he still had

it handy. He acted like he might turn it over to Billy, but that was all crap. Of course, he was drunk all the time by then."

"So he was conning you while you conned him."

"He was just stringing us along!" she said indignantly. "Billy met him Tuesday night and Daggett was real cagey. Said he needed time to get his hands on it. He said he'd bring it in Thursday night, so Billy met him at the Hub again, only Daggett said he needed one more day. Billy really laid into him. He said these guys were getting very pissed and might kill Daggett anyway, whether he gave 'em the money or not. Daggett got real nervous and swore he'd have it the next night, which was Friday."

"The night he died."

"Right. I was working that night, and I was supposed to keep an eye on him, which I did. Billy decided to come late, just to make him sweat, and before I knew what was happening this woman showed up and started buying him drinks. You know the rest."

"Billy told me you took some kind of cold cap and crashed in the back room. Was that true?"

"I was just laying low," she said. "When I saw Daggett leave, I knew Billy'd have a fit. I already felt bad enough without putting up with his bullshit."

"And Billy finally figured out who she was?"

"I don't know. I guess. I wasn't here this morning, so I don't know what he was up to."

"Look. I have to go down to the police station and tell Lieutenant Dolan what's been going on. If Lovella comes back, please tell her it's urgent that she get in touch. Will you do that?"

Coral wedged the last clean dish against the pile in the rack. She filled a glass with water and poured it over the lot of them, rinsing off the few remaining suds. She turned to look at me with a gaze that chilled. "Do you think she killed Billy?"

"I don't know."

"Will you tell me if you find out it's her?"

"Coral, if she did it, she's dangerous. I don't want you in the middle of this."

"But will you tell me?"

I hesitated. "Yes."

"Thank you."

25

I had a brief chat with the manager of the trailer park. I gave him my card and asked him to call me if Lovella came back. I didn't really trust Coral to do it. The last I saw of him, he was tapping at her door. I got in my car and headed over to the police station. I asked for Lieutenant Dolan at the desk, but he and Feldman were in a section meeting. The clerk buzzed Jonah for me and he came as far as the locked door, admitting me into the corridor beyond. Both of us were circumspect—pleasant, noncommittal. No one observing us could have guessed that mere hours ago, we'd been cavorting stark naked on my Wonder Woman sheets.

"What happened when you got home?" I asked.

"Nothing. Everybody was asleep," he said. "We have something in the lab you might want to see." He moved down the hall to the right and I followed. He looked back at me. "Feldman had the guys check the trash bins at your suggestion. We think we found the silencer."

"You did?" I said, startled.

He opened the half-door into the crime lab, holding it for me as I passed in front of him. The lab tech was out, but I could see Billy's bloody shirt, tagged, on the counter, along with an object I couldn't at first identify.

"What's that," I said. "Is *that* it?" What I was looking at was a large plastic soft drink bottle, painted black, lying on its side with a hole visible in the bottom.

"A disposable silencer. Handmade. A sound suppressor, in effect. It's been wiped clean of prints," Jonah said.

"I don't understand how it works."

"I had to have Krueger explain it to me. The bottle's filled with rags. Take a look. The barrel of the gun is usually wrapped with tape and the bottle affixed to it with a one-inch hose clamp. The soda bottle has a reinforced bottom, but it's only effective for a few shots because the noise level increases each time as the exit hole gets larger. Obviously, the device works best at close range."

"God, Jonah. How do people know about these things? I never heard of it."

He picked up a paperbound booklet from the counter behind me, flipping through it carelessly so I could see. Every page was filled with diagrams and photographs, illustrating how disposable silencers could be made out of common household objects. "This is from a gun shop down in Los Angeles," he said. "You ought to see what you can do with a length of window screen or a pile of old bottle caps."

"Jesus."

Lieutenant Becker stuck his head in the door. "Line one for you," he said to Jonah and then disappeared. Jonah glanced at the lab phone, but the call hadn't been transferred.

"Let me take this and I'll be right back," Jonah said. "Hang on."

"Right," I murmured. I leaned toward the silencer, trying to remember where I'd seen something similar. Through the hole in the bottom, I caught a glimpse of the blue terrycloth filling the interior. When I realized what it was, my mental processes clicked in, and the interior machinery fired up. I knew.

I straightened up and crossed to the door, checking the corridor, which was empty. I headed for my car. I could still see Ramona Westfall coming up the basement stairs with an armload of ragged blue bath towels, which she'd dumped on the chair. The plastic bottle had been filled with a soft drink which she nearly dropped as she passed it to Tony to refrigerate.

I stopped by the office long enough to try the Westfalls' number. The phone rang four times and then the machine clicked in.

"Hello. This is Ramona Westfall. Neither Ferrin nor I can come to the phone right now, but if you'll leave your name, telephone number, and a brief message, we'll get back to you as soon as possible. Thank you." I hung up at the sound of the tone.

I checked my watch. It was 4:45. I had no idea where Ramona was, but Tony had a 5:00 appointment just a few blocks away. If I could intercept him, I could lean on him some about her alibi since he represented the only confirmation she had. How had she pulled it off? He had to be on heavy medication for the migraine, so she might have slipped out while he was sleeping, adjusting the kitchen clock when she got back so she'd be covered for the time of Daggett's death. Once she was home again, Tony had wakened—she'd probably made sure of that so she'd have someone to corroborate the time. She'd fixed the sandwiches, chatting pleasantly while he ate, and as soon as he went back to bed, she changed the clock again. Or maybe it wasn't even as complicated as that. Maybe the watch Daggett wore had been set for 2:37 and then submerged. She could have killed him earlier and been home by 2:00. Tony may have realized what she'd done and tried to shield her when he understood how close my investigation was bringing me. It was also possible that he was in cahoots with her, but I hoped that wasn't the case.

I locked my office and went down the front stairs, trotting up State Street on foot. The Granger Building was only three blocks up and it made more sense than hopping in my car and driving all the way around to the parking lot behind the building. Tony might still be hanging out at the arcade across the street. I had to get to him before she had a chance to intercept. I didn't want him going home. She had to realize things were getting hot, especially since I'd shown up at the house with the shoes and skirt. All I needed from him was an indication I was on the right track and then I'd call Feldman. I thought about the Close, which I knew would be gloomy with the gathering twilight. I didn't want to go back there unless I had to.

I checked the arcade. Tony was at the rear, on the right-hand side, playing a video game. He was concentrating fully and I didn't think he was aware of me. I waited, watching small creatures being blasted off the screen. His scores weren't that good and I was tempted to have a try at it myself. The creatures suddenly froze into place, random weapons firing off here and there without regard to his manipulations. He looked up. "Oh hi."

"I need to talk to you," I said.

His eyes moved to the clock. "I got an appointment in five minutes. Can it wait?"

"I'll walk you over. We can talk on the way."

He picked up his package and we moved out to the street. The fading afternoon sun seemed bright after the darkness of the arcade. Even so, the fog was rolling in, November twilight beginning to descend. I punched the button at the crosswalk and we waited for the light to change. "Last Friday . . . the night Daggett died, do you remember where your uncle was?"

"Sure. Milwaukee, on a business trip."

"Are you on medication for the migraines?"

"Well, yeah. Tylenol with codeine. Compazine if I'm throwing up. How come?"

"Is it possible your aunt went out while you slept?"

"No. I don't know. I don't understand what you're getting at," he said.

I thought he was stalling, but I kept my mouth shut. We'd reached the Granger Building and Tony moved into the lobby ahead of me.

The elevator that had been out of order was now in operation, but the other one was immobilized, doors open, the housing visible, two sawhorses in front of the opening with a warning sign.

Tony was watching me warily. "Did she say she went out?"

"She claims she was home with you."

"So?"

"Come on, Tony. You're the only alibi she has. If you were zonked on medication, how do you know where she was?"

He pressed the elevator button.

The doors opened and we got on. The doors closed without incident and we went up to six. I checked his face as we stepped into the hallway. He was clearly conflicted, but I didn't want to press just yet. We headed down the corridor toward the suite his psychiatrist apparently occupied.

"Is there anything you want to talk about?" I asked.

"No," he said, his voice breaking with indignation. "You're crazy if you think she had anything to do with it."

"Maybe you can explain that to Feldman. He's in charge of the case."

"I'm not talking to the cops about her," Tony said. He tried the office door and found it locked. "Shit, he's not here."

There was a note taped to the door. He reached up to snatch the piece of paper, turning the movement into an abrupt shove. Next thing I knew, I was on my hands and knees and he'd taken off. He banged on the elevator button and then veered right. I was up and running when I heard the door leading to the stairway slam back against the wall. I ran, banging into the stairwell only seconds after he did. He was already heading up.

"Tony! Come on. Don't do this."

He was moving fast, his footsteps scratching on the concrete stairs. His labored breathing echoed against the walls as he went up. I don't keep fit for nothin', folks. He had youth on me, but I was in good shape. I flung my bag aside and grabbed the rail, starting up after him, mounting the steps two at a time. I peered upward as I ran, trying to catch sight of him. He reached the seventh floor and kept on going. How many floors did this building have?

"Tony. Goddamn it! Wait up! What are you doing?"

I heard another door bang up there. I stepped up my pace.

I reached the landing at the top. The elevator repairman had apparently left the door to the attic unlocked and Tony had shot through the gap, slamming the door behind him. I snatched the handle, half expecting to find it locked. The door flew open and I pushed through, pausing on the threshold. The space was dim and hot and dry, largely empty except for a small door opening off to my right where the elevator brake, sheave, and drive motors were located. I ducked my head into the cramped space briefly, but it appeared to be empty. I pulled out and peered around. The roof was another twenty feet up, the rafters steeply pitched, timbers forming a ninety-degree angle where they met.

Silence. I could see a square of light on the floor and I looked up. A wooden ladder was affixed to the wall to my right. At the top, a trap door was open and waning daylight filtered down. I scanned the attic. There was an electrical panel sitting on some boxes. It looked like some kind of old light board from the theater on the ground floor. For some reason, there was a massive papier-mâché bird standing to one side . . . a blue jay, wearing a painted business suit. Wooden chairs were stacked, seat to seat, to my left.

"Tony?"

I put a hand on one of the ladder rungs. He might well be hiding somewhere, waiting for me to head up to the roof so he could ease out and down the steps again. I started up, climbing maybe ten feet so I could survey the attic from a better vantage point. There was no movement, no sound of breathing. I looked up again and started climbing cautiously. I'm not afraid of heights, but I'm not fond of them either. Still, the ladder seemed secure and I couldn't figure out where else he might be.

When I got to the top, I pulled myself into a sitting position and peered around. The trap came out in a small alcove, hidden behind an ornamental pediment, with a matching pediment halfway down the length of the roof. From the ground, the two of them had always looked strictly decorative, but I could see now that one disguised a brace of air vents. There was only a very narrow walkway around the perimeter of the roof, protected by a short parapet. The steep pitch of the roof would make navigating hazardous.

I peered down into the attic, hoping to see Tony dart out of hiding and into the stairwell. There was no sign of him up here, unless he'd eased around to the far side. Gingerly, I got to my feet, positioning myself between the nearly vertical roofline on my left and the ankle-high parapet on my right. I was actually walking in a metal rain gutter that popped and creaked under my weight. I didn't like the sound. It suggested that any minute now the metal would buckle, toppling me off the side.

I glanced down eight floors to the street, which didn't seem that far away. The buildings across from me were two stories high and lent a comforting illusion of proximity, but pedestrians still seemed dwarfed by the height. The streetlights had come on, and the traffic below was thinning. To my right, half a block away, the bell tower at the Axminster Theater was lighted from within, the arches bathed in tawny gold and warm blue. The drop had to be eighty feet. I tried to remember the velocity of a falling object. Something-something per foot per second was as close as I could come, but I knew the end result would be an incredible splat. I paused where I was and raised my voice. "Tony!"

I caught a flash of movement out of the corner of my eye and my heart flew into my throat. The plastic bag he'd been carrying was eddying downward, floating lazily. Coming from where? I peered over the parapet. I could see one of the niches that cut into the wall just below the cornice molding. The frieze that banded the building had always looked like marble from the street, but I could see now that it was molded plaster, the niche itself down about four feet and to the left. A half shell extended out maybe fifteen inches at the bottom edge and it held what was probably meant to be some sort of lamp with a torch flame, all molded plaster like the frieze. Tony was sitting there, his face turned up to mine. He'd climbed over the edge and he was now perched in the shallow ornamental niche, his arm locked around the torch, legs dangling. He'd taken a wig out of the bag he carried, donning it, looking up at me with a curious light in his eyes.

I was looking at the blonde who'd killed Daggett.

For a moment, we stared at each other, saying nothing. He had the cocky look of a ten-year-old defying his mom, but under the bravado I sensed a kid who was hoping someone would step in and save him from himself.

I put a hand on the pediment to steady myself. "You coming up or shall I come down?" I kept my tone matter-of-fact, but my mouth was dry.

"I'll be going down in a minute."

"Maybe we could talk about that," I said.

"It's too late," he said, smiling impishly. "I'm poised for flight."

"Will you wait there until I reach you?"

"No grabbing," he warned.

"I won't grab."

My palms were damp and I wiped them on my jeans.

I squatted, turning to face the roof, extending a foot tentatively down along the frieze. I glanced down, trying to find some purchase. Garlands of pineapple, grapes, and fig leaves formed a bas relief design that wound across the face of the building. "How'd you do this?" I asked.

"I didn't think about it. I just did it. You don't have to come down. It won't help."

"I just don't want to talk to you hanging over the edge," I said, lying through my teeth. I was hoping to get close enough to nab him, ignoring visions of grappling with him at that height. I steadied myself, tucking a toe into the shallow crevice formed by a curling vine. The niche was only four feet away. At ground level, I wouldn't have given it a thought.

I sensed that he was watching me, but I didn't dare look. I held onto the parapet, lowering my left foot.

He said, "You're not going to talk me out of this."

"I just want to hear your side of it," I said.

"Okay."

"You won't try to kill me, will you?" I asked.

"Why would I? You never did anything to me."

"I'm glad you recognize that. Now I feel really confident." I heard him laugh lightly at my tone.

I've seen magazine pictures of a man who can climb a vertical cliff face in a pair of tennis shoes, holding himself with the tips of his fingers tucked into small cracks that he discovers as he ascends. This has always seemed like a ludicrous pursuit and I usually flip to an article that makes more sense. The sight of the photographs makes me hyperventilate, especially the ones taken from his vantage point, staring down into some yawning crevasse. Maybe, if the truth be known, I'm more anxious about heights than I let on.

I allowed my right foot to inch down again as far as the lip of the niche. I found a handhold, down and to the right. Felt like a pineapple, but I wasn't sure. Pinning my safety to a phony piece of fruit. I had to be nuts.

The hardest part was actually letting go of the coping once my foot was resting safely in the recess. I had to bend my knees, turning slightly to the right, sinking little by little until I could take a seat. Tony, ever gallant, actually gave me a hand, steadying me until I eased down next to him. I'm not a brave soul. I'm really not. I just didn't want him flying off the side of that building while I looked on. I locked my left arm around the torch, just below his, holding onto my wrist with my right hand. I could feel sweat trickle down my sides.

"I hate this," I said. I was winded, not from effort but from apprehension.

"It's not bad. Just don't look down."

Of course I did. The minute he said that I had an irresistible desire to peek. I was hoping somebody would spot us, like they always do on TV. Then the cops would come with nets and the fire engines would arrive and somebody would talk him out of this. I'm an organism of the earth, a Taurus. I was never born of air, of water, or of fire. I'm a creature of gravity and I could feel the ground whisper. The same thing happens to me in old hotels when I'm staying on the twenty-second floor. I open a window and want to fling myself out.

"Oh, Jesus. This is such a bad idea," I said.

"For you maybe. Not for me."

I tried to think back to my short life as a cop and the standard procedure for dealing with potential suicides. Stall for time was the first rule. I didn't recall anything about hanging your ass off the side of a building, but here I was. I said, "What's the story, babe. You want to tell me what's been going on?"

"There's not much to it. Daggett called the house on Monday. Aunt Ramona made a note of the number so I called him back. I dreamed about killing him. I couldn't wait. I had fantasies for months, every night before I went to sleep. I wanted to catch him with a wire around his neck and twist till it bit into his windpipe and his tongue bugged out. It doesn't take that long. I forget what that's called now . . ."

"Garroting," I supplied.

"Yeah, I would have liked that, but then I figured it was better if it looked like an accident because that way I could get away with it."

"Why'd he call?"

"I don't know," Tony said uncomfortably. "He was drunk and blubbering, said he was sorry and wanted to make it up to me for what he did. I go, 'Fine. Why don't we meet and talk?' And he goes, 'It would mean so much to me, son.'" Tony was acting out the parts, using a quavering falsetto for Daggett. "So then I tell him I'll meet him the next night at this bar he's calling from, the Hub, which didn't give me much time to put together this getup."

"Was that Ramona's skirt?"

"Nah, I got it at the Salvation Army thrift store for a buck. The sweater was another fifty cents and the shoes were two bucks."

"Where'd the sweater go?"

"I tossed it in another trash can a block away from the first. I thought it would all end up at the dump."

"What about the wig?"

"That was Aunt Ramona's from years ago. She didn't even know it was gone."

"Why'd you keep it?"

"I don't know. I was going to put it back in her closet where I got it, in case I needed it again. I had it on at the beach, but then I remembered Billy already knew who I was." He broke off, obviously confused. "I might have told my shrink about the whole thing if he'd been here. Anyway, the wig's expensive. This is real hair."

"The color's nice too," I said. I mean, where else could I go with this? Even Tony recognized the absurdity and he flashed me a look.

"You're humoring me, right?"

"Of course I'm humoring you!" I snapped. "I didn't come down here so we could have an argument."

He did a half shrug, smiling sheepishly.

I said, "Did you actually meet him there Tuesday night?"

"Not really. I went. I had it all worked out by then, only when I walk in, he's sittin' at this table talking to some guy. Turned out to be Billy Polo, but I didn't know it at the time. Billy was sitting in this booth with his back to the door. I saw Daggett, but I didn't realize he had company till I was right there in front of him. I veer off the minute I spot Billy, but by then he's had a good look at me. I'm not worried. I figure I'll never see him again anyway. I hang around for a while but they're really into it. I can tell Billy's leaning all over him and isn't likely to let up so I take a hike and go home."

"Was this one of the nights you had a migraine?"

"Yeah," he said. "I mean, some are real and some are fake, but I have to have a pattern, know what I mean? So I can come and go as I please."

"How'd you get down to the Hub, by cab?"

"My bike. The night I killed him, I rode down and left it at the marina and then I called a cab from a pay phone and took it over to the Hub."

"How'd you know he'd show up?"

"Because he called again and I said I'd be there."

"He never twigged to the fact that you'd showed up the first time in drag?"

"How was he going to know? He hadn't seen me since way before the trial. I was twelve, thirteen, something like that, a fat boy back then. I figured even if he guessed, I'd do it anyway, kill his ass . . . and once he was dead, who would know?"

"What went wrong?"

His brow furrowed. "I don't know. Well, I do. The plan went fine. It was something else." His eyes met mine and he looked every bit of fifteen, the blonde wig adding softness and dimension to a face that was nearly formless with youth. I could see how he'd pass as a woman, slim, with a clear complexion, sweet smile on his wide mouth. He looked down at the street and for a moment I thought he meant to swing out into space.

"When I was eight, I had these pet mice," he said. "Really sweet. I kept 'em in this cage with a wheel and a water bottle hanging upside down. Mom didn't think I'd take care of 'em but I did. I'd cut up strips of paper in the bottom of the cage so they could nest. Anyway, the girl mouse had these babies. They couldn't have been as long as this." He was indicating the end of his little finger. "Bald," he went on. "Just little bitty old things. We had to go out of town one weekend and when we got back the cat had tried to get in the cage. Knocked it off the desk and everything. The mice were gone. Probably the cat got 'em except for this one that had been laying in all these paper shreds. Well, the water had spilled so the paper was damp and the little thing must have had pneumonia or something because it was panting, like it couldn't breathe good. I tried to keep it warm. I watched it for hours and it just kept getting worse and worse so I decided I better . . . you know, do away with it. So it wouldn't suffer anymore."

He leaned forward, swinging his feet back and forth.

"Don't do that," I murmured anxiously. "Finish the story. I want to know what happened next."

He looked over at me then, his tone of voice mild. "I tossed it in the toilet. That's the only way I could think of to kill it. I couldn't crush it, so I just figured I'd flush it away. The little thing was half dead anyway and I thought I'd be doing it a favor, putting it out of its misery. But before I could do it, that little tiny hairless baby started struggling. You could tell

223

it was in a total panic, trying to get out of there, like it knew what was happening . . ." He paused, dashing at his eyes. "Daggett did that and now I can't get away from the look on his face, you know? I see it all day long. He knew. Which was fine with me. I wanted that. I wanted him to know it was me and his life wasn't worth two cents. I just didn't think he'd care. He was a drunk and a bum and he killed all those people. He should have died. He shoulda been glad to go. I was putting him out of his misery, you know? So why'd he have to make it so hard?"

He fell silent and then he let out a deep breath. "Anyway, that's how that went. I can't sleep anymore. I dream about that stuff. Makes me sick."

"What about Billy? I assume he figured it out when he saw you at the funeral."

"Yeah. That was weird. He didn't give a shit about Daggett, but he felt like he should get part of the money if he kept his mouth shut. I would have given him all of it, but I didn't believe him. You should have seen him. Swaggering around, making all these threats. I figured he'd start bragging one night about what he knew and there I'd be."

The edge of the niche was beginning to cut into my rear end. I was hanging on so tightly that my arm was getting numb, but I didn't dare ease up. I couldn't figure out how to get us out of this, but I knew I'd better start talking fast.

"I killed a man once," I said. I meant to say more, but that's all I could get out. I clamped my teeth together, trying to force the feelings back down where I'd been keeping them. It surprised me that after all this time, it was still so painful to think about.

"On purpose?"

I shook my head. "Self-defense, but dead is dead."

His smile was sweet. "You can always come with me."

"Don't say that. I'm not going to jump and I don't want

you to either. You're fifteen years old. There are lots of other ways out."

"I don't think so."

"Your parents have money. They could hire Melvin Belli if they wanted to."

"My parents are dead."

"Well, the Westfalls, then. You know what I mean."

"But Kinsey, I murdered two people and it's first degree because I looked it up. How'm I gonna get away with that?"

"The way half the killers in this country do," I said with energy. "Hell, if Ted Bundy's still alive, why shouldn't you be?"

"Who's he?"

"Never mind. Someone who did a lot worse than you."

He thought for a moment. "I don't think it would work. I hurt too bad and I don't see the point."

"There isn't a point. That's the part you invent."

"Could you do me a favor."

"All right. What's that?"

"Could you tell my aunt I said good-bye? I meant to write her a note, but I didn't have a chance."

"Goddamn it, Tony! Don't do this. She's had enough pain."

"I know," he said, "but she's got my Uncle Ferrin and they'll be okay. They never really knew what to do with me anyway."

"Oh, I see. You've got this all worked out."

"Well, yeah, I do. I've been reading up on this stuff and it's no big deal. Kids kill themselves all the time."

I hung my head, almost incapable of framing a response. "Tony, listen," I said finally. "What you're talking about is dumb and it doesn't make any sense. Do you have any idea how crummy life seemed when I was your age? I cried all the time and I felt like shit. I was ugly. I was skinny. I was lonely. I was mad. I never thought I'd pull out of it, but I did. Life is hard. Life hurts. So what? You tough it out. You get through and then you'll feel good again, I swear to God."

He tilted his head, watching me intently. "I don't think so. Not for me. I'm in too deep. I can't bear any more. It's too much."

"Tony, there are days when none of us can bear it, but the good comes around again. Happiness is seasonal, like anything else. Wait it out. There are people who love you. People who can help."

He shook his head. "I can't do that. It's kind of like I made a deal with myself to go through with this. She'll understand."

I could feel my temper snapping. "You want me to tell her that? You took a flying leap because you made a fucking *deal* with yourself?" His face clouded with uncertainty. I pressed on in a softer tone. "You want me to tell her we sat up here like this and I couldn't talk you out of it? I can't let you do it. You'll break her heart."

He looked down at his lap, his eyes remote, face coloring up the way boys do in lieu of tears. "It doesn't have anything to do with her. Tell her it was me and she did just great. I love her a lot, but it's my life, you know?"

I was silent for a moment, trying to figure out where to go next.

His face brightened and he held up an index finger. "I nearly forgot. I have a present for you." He shifted, letting go of the torch with a move that made me snatch at him instinctively. He laughed at that. "Take it easy. I'm just reaching in the waistband of my jeans."

I looked to see what he'd produced. My .32 lay across his palm. He held his hand out so I could take it, realizing belatedly that I couldn't free up a hand to reach for it.

"That's okay. I'll put it right here," he said kindly. He set it in the niche, behind the ornamental torch I was clinging to.

"How'd you get it?" Stalling, stalling.

"Same way I did everything else. I used my head. You put your home address on that business card you gave Aunt Ramona, so I rode over on my bike and waited till you got home. I was going to introduce myself, you know, and act like this real polite kid with good manners and a nifty haircut and stuff like that. Real innocent. I wasn't sure how much you knew and I thought maybe I could steer you off. I saw the car and you almost stopped, but then you took off again. I had to pedal my ass off to keep up with you and then you parked at the beach and I saw a chance to go through your stuff."

"You killed Billy with that?"

"Yeah. It was handy and I needed something quick."

"How'd you know about disposable silencers?"

"Some kid at school. I can make a pipe bomb too," he said. Then he sighed. "I gotta go soon. Time's nearly up."

I glanced down at the street. It was really getting dark up here, but the sidewalk was bright, the arcade across the way lit up like a movie house. Two people on the far side of the street had spotted us, but I could tell they hadn't figured out what was going on. A stunt? A movie being shot? I looked at Tony, but he didn't seem to be aware. My heart began to bang again and it made my chest feel tight and hot.

"I'm getting tired," I said casually. "I may go back up, but I need some help. Can you give me a hand?"

"Sure," he said. And then he paused, his whole body alert. "This isn't a trick, is it?"

"No," I said, but I could hear my voice shake and the lie cut my tongue like a razor blade. I've always lied with ease and grace, with ingenuity and conviction and I couldn't get this one out. I saw him make a move. I grabbed him, hanging on for dear life, but all he had to do was give his arm a quick twist and my hand came loose. I reached again, but it was too late. I saw him push out, lifting off. For a moment, he seemed to hover there, like a leaf, and then he disappeared from my line of sight. I didn't look down again after that.

I thought I heard a siren wailing, but the sound was mine.

I billed Barbara Daggett for $1,040.00, which she paid by return mail. It's nearly Christmas now and I haven't slept well for six weeks. I've thought a lot about Daggett and I've changed my mind about one thing. I suspect he knew what was going on. From a distance, Tony might have passed for a woman, but up close, he looked like exactly what he was . . . a young kid playing dress-up, smart beyond his years, but not wise enough by half. I don't think Daggett was fooled. Why he went along with the game, I'm not sure. If he believed what Billy'd told him, he must have figured he was dead either way. Maybe he felt he owed Tony that last sacrifice. I'll never know, but it makes more sense to me that way. Some debts of the human soul are so enormous only life itself is sufficient forfeit. Perhaps in this case, all of the accounts are now paid in full . . . except mine.

—Respectfully submitted,
Kinsey Millhone

Sue Grafton
'A' is for Alibi £4.99

Nobody mourned murdered Laurence Fife, ruthless hot-shot lawyer
and two-timing husband. A lot of people might have wanted him
dead, but it was his young wife, Nikki, who they put on ice for
homicide.

Eight years later, Nikki's out on parole and hiring her own investigator
to find the real killer. Which is how Kinsey Millhone picks up a trail
that's eight years cold, hunting someone clever enough to get away
with murder . . .

'Smart, well-paced, and very funny' NEWSWEEK

'B' is for Burglar £4.99

The expensively wrapped client didn't look the type who was longing
for a family reunion when she asked Kinsey to find her sister. It
looked routine, but routine jobs still pay the bills.

The missing sister had gone missing headed for Florida in a $12,000
lynx coat. When Kinsey got to Florida, the case that looked routine
was filled with fire-raising, burglary and murder. Not so routine after
all . . .

'Tough, fetching, Kinsey Millhone in swirling Florida waters of murder
and arson. "A" was for Alibi and on the evidence to date the rest of
the Grafton alphabet could be well worth waiting for'
THE OBSERVER

Sue Grafton
'C' is for Corpse £4.50

'Violent death is like a monster. The closer you get to it, the more damage you sustain . . .'

The doctors could do something about the damage to Bobby Callahan's body – but not for the broken bits of his brain. The car crash was no accident. Somebody wanted him dead and he can't remember who or why . . .

Three days later, whoever was trying to kill Bobby Callahan came up with the winning ticket. Kinsey Millhone had never worked for a dead man before, and she didn't need the money. But she cared . . .

. . . cared enough to try to make sense of the whole savage joke . . .

'E is for excellent, Ms Grafton' THE SUNDAY TIMES

'Quiveringly alive' THE DAILY TELEGRAPH

'C is for classy, strong characterization and a tough cookie heroine' TIME OUT

'Private-Eye-ette Kinsey Millhone gets more interesting by the book' THE TIMES

'E' is for Evidence £4.99

'I could feel my face heat, the icy itch of fear beginning to assert itself. I said. "This isn't the report I saw . . ."'

It was a routine job – and it was Christmas. All things considered, a neutral verdict looked like a good bet.

But when a mystery well wisher weighs in with an unmarked bank deposit for $5,000, Kinsey Milhone's suspicions are finally aroused.

Too late to avoid the set up – and fighting for her life against the oldest trick in the book . . .

'A woman to identify with . . . a gripping read' PUNCH

'Kinsey Millhone is going to have herself a bright literary future' STANLEY ELLIN

Sue Grafton
'F' is for Fugitive   £4.99

A Kinsey Millhone Mystery

'I slammed the phone down before the guy got out another word. Sat straight up, heart thudding. Floral Beach. Already I was wishing I'd never come . . .'

It was an old man's dying wish. To clear his son's name and reunite his family. But Bailey Fowler had been missing for sixteen years and there was more than one person in Floral Beach who didn't want him found.

Until the cops turn him up – by accident. And suddenly murder is the hottest game in town all over again. Kinsey Millhone was summoned for the fairy tale ending . . .

And arrived at a tragedy – starring herself . . .

'Quiveringly alive' THE DAILY TELEGRAPH

All Pan books are available at your local bookshop or newsagent, or can be ordered direct from the publisher. Indicate the number of copies required and fill in the form below.

Send to: Pan C. S. Dept
               Macmillan Distribution Ltd
               Houndmills Basingstoke RG21 2XS
or phone: 0256 29242, quoting title, author and Credit Card number.

Please enclose a remittance* to the value of the cover price plus: £1.00 for the first book plus 50p per copy for each additional book ordered.

*Payment may be made in sterling by UK personal cheque, postal order, sterling draft or international money order, made payable to Pan Books Ltd.

Alternatively by Barclaycard/Access/Amex/Diners

Card No.

Expiry Date

Signature:

Applicable only in the UK and BFPO addresses

While every effort is made to keep prices low, it is sometimes necessary to increase prices at short notice. Pan Books reserve the right to show on covers and charge new retail prices which may differ from those advertised in the text or elsewhere.

NAME AND ADDRESS IN BLOCK LETTERS PLEASE:

....

Name

Address

6/92

Mariah glanced at him.

Held his gaze in the moonlight illuminating the room.

And...he wanted to make love to her.

What the hell!

Harper was settled down.

Michael sat up, intending to go upstairs, to take the steps three at a time, but the little girl lifted up.

Frowned at him.

And he lay back down, pulling the fleece around him and turning his back to the two females who were upending his entire life. One bringing out all kinds of protective instincts and a soft but fierce love. The other...well, he had no idea what all Mariah was doing to him, but he knew he had to ignore it.

Every heavenly-appearing twist and turn on that road would lead him straight to hell.

Dear Reader,

I'm so excited to welcome you to Sierra's Web! This brand-new series centers around a firm of experts who travel all over the United States to help people in tough situations. The firm was founded by seven college friends who were bound together for life when they helped solve the murder of one of their close friends, Sierra. Each of the friends are now experts in their own fields, and the partners also hire experts from all over to fit client needs. Some stories are suspense and will be published by Harlequin Romantic Suspense, and some, like this one, are emotionally intense family and relationship stories, all published by Harlequin Special Edition. Every book in the series stands alone—and yet they're all connected by a love that never dies. *His Lost and Found Family* is proof of that love and is the perfect book to show you what Sierra's Web is all about. I look forward to the long-standing friendships we're all about to embark upon together!

Tara Taylor Quinn

His Lost and
Found Family

———

TARA TAYLOR QUINN

HARLEQUIN

SPECIAL
EDITION

Recycling programs
for this product may
not exist in your area.

ISBN-13: 978-1-335-40831-0

His Lost and Found Family

Harlequin Enterprises ULC
22 Adelaide St. West, 41st Floor
Toronto, Ontario M5H 4E3, Canada
www.Harlequin.com

Printed in U.S.A.

Having written over ninety novels, **Tara Taylor Quinn** is a *USA TODAY* bestselling author with more than seven million copies sold. She is known for delivering intense, emotional fiction. Tara is a past president of Romance Writers of America and a seven-time RITA® Award finalist. She has also appeared on TV across the country, including *CBS Sunday Morning*. She supports the National Domestic Violence Hotline. If you need help, please contact 1-800-799-7233.

Visit the Author Profile page
at Harlequin.com for more titles.

For Jeanine—you've been gone too many years but remain as alive in my heart as always. From reading our first Harlequin romances together before we were old enough to drive, to weddings and then being godmother to each other's daughters, you are my best friend forever.

Chapter One

Michael O'Connell collapsed. Straight down, with a hard thump, to the high-backed leather chair behind his desk. Knees weak, using his free hand to loosen the knot of tie at his neck, he just stared at the registered letter that had been waiting for him upon his return to the States. It dangled, limply suspended, from his shaking fingers.

June was dead.

He'd wondered. Suspected. But to know for sure...

His sweet baby sister turned into a drug addict by their abusive drunk of a father...

His thoughts didn't complete. Just reached stopping points and hung there.

Pointing to a fact that was always with him. He should have done more.

What, he didn't know.

But something.

More.

June was dead.

The letter teetered there at the end of his drawing hand. Bearing unread revelations. Late on that early-September Thursday afternoon, he wasn't ready to hear about the where, or how. Didn't want to know if she'd been arrested for drug possession and prostitution and God knew what else, if she'd died in prison like the old man should have done.

Didn't want to know he was too late to give her a proper burial.

He most definitely didn't want to look at the years during which he'd climbed to the top of his profession without being in touch with her.

Didn't matter that that choice had been hers. And hers to make.

Or that the last time he'd tried to see her she'd called the cops and threatened a restraining order if he didn't leave her alone.

He'd wanted her to complete the rehab program he'd enrolled her in. She'd wanted the right to make her own damned choices.

Her right had trumped his love for her and he'd been forced to walk away.

Leaving her with his cell phone number.

And never leaving home without the phone.

Not ever. In all the years since, she'd never called.

But he did stop procrastinating. Lifting the letter, he read it in its entirety. Twice. Parts of it a third time. And grabbed that phone he was never without to call his own lawyer.

"Len, I got a certified letter here from an attorney in Marietta, Oklahoma. Says I'm guardian to a four-year-old child. Can that be right? Can I be made a guardian without consent? Or knowledge?"

"What kid?" Len asked, and followed the question with, "Whose kid?"

"June's."

What in the hell was June thinking? She of all people knew that he was no good for raising a child. Or being family to anyone.

And a four-year-old girl? Heels bopping a mile a minute, his feet were held in place by the soles of his hand-tailored black business shoes pressing into the floor. He felt the blood drain from his face as Len said, "In answer to your question, yes. Though it's not at all advisable to do so without prior conversation and agreement, for obvious reasons, it is legal to appoint a guardian in the event of death and to do so without said guardian's knowledge."

There was a pause. Michael hung there with it until Len asked, "June's dead?"

He swallowed. Jutted his chin. And eventually said, "Yeah."

"Wow, man. I'm so sorry."

"Yeah."

"Okay, so mandates vary state by state, but for the most part requirements stipulate only that the guardian be a minimum of eighteen years of age, be of sound mind and not be in prison."

He could do a stint in prison. Should do one for having abandoned his little sister to their abusive father in order to accept the full-ride academic scholarship he'd earned. Didn't matter that the old man had never raised an angry hand to her prior to Michael's leaving. Didn't matter that he'd been the only one to earn his father's ire, that he'd been the cause of all the anger in their home, and he'd hoped to give June a more stable home life by vacating. Or that she'd chosen to run away and live on the streets over telling Michael what had been going on after he'd left.

What mattered was that he hadn't gone home himself to find out. And that he'd left town in the first place, taking away her immediate access to him.

Running a hand through his hair, he ended the silence that had fallen on the line. "Yeah, uh, Len, I need you to find out what it takes to transfer guardianship."

"Seriously, Michael? This is June's kid you're talking about. You've spent ten years hating yourself for leaving her alone with your old man, ten years trying to gain back her confidence, to help her, ten years of throwing money away on rehab and tuition she never used, and now you're going to give up her kid?"

He made a mental note, reminding himself to get a new attorney. One who wasn't his former roommate and didn't know every damned thing about him.

"Just get me whatever paperwork there is, tell me what I need to do, and how soon I can sign to make it happen." He'd screwed up on a fifteen-year-old girl. No way he was taking on a four-year-old.

No way he could even figure out what June was doing, giving the child to him. Trying to trap him? Make him pay for leaving her?

She hadn't been thinking clearly. The answer came to him quietly.

Grasping hold of a thought that finally made sense to him, his wave of return to sensibility diminished as Len said, "You'll need to have someone else to name as guardian before any paperwork can be created, signed or filed."

Whom did he know whom he could ask to permanently take in a little kid? To love her as though she was their own?

No names came immediately to mind. Except…

"What about you and Sarah?"

"We were going to wait to tell you until dinner over the weekend, but Sarah's pregnant, Mike. They think it's twins…"

His friends had been trying for years…to the

tune of half a dozen miscarriages. His own challenges disappeared as he pictured the sorrow he'd seen on Sarah's face the last time she'd lost a child. The three of them had been having dinner together and, her face ashen, looking stunned, she'd dropped her fork and run for the bathroom…

No way he was going to add any stress to a new pregnancy. "How far along is she?" he asked, knowing all of the pertinent markers from the last six attempts.

"Four months." The jubilance in Len's voice was a bit subdued, but Michael heard it. "We waited this time…haven't told anyone…"

"Well, hallelujah," he said, grinning. "Congratulations, man!"

"You're going to be an uncle." Because Len sounded as though he was grinning from ear to ear, Michael didn't disabuse him of the moniker.

Neither did he take it on.

He was a friend. *Only* a friend.

In his own personal world, family meant screwups and pain. He wasn't going to repeat the pattern. He'd promised himself, the last day he'd seen June, that he'd never, ever bring anyone else into a family with him.

The O'Connells just didn't know how to do it right. His grandparents had split. And then his parents. And even when it had just been their dad and him and June, Michael had mouthed off, or forgotten something, or given a wrong look pretty much every day. June would tell him how good things were when he was away spending the night with a friend. And urge him to try to stay out of the way when he got home so they could all live in peace.

He hadn't been able to do so. He'd been too busy thinking he had all the answers.

"Maybe she's all you've ever needed," Len's voice came softly, referring to June's child—as though just because they'd been friends for so long the guy thought he could read Michael's mind. "She could be a big cousin in five months and we can fill the house with kids' excitement on Christmas morning instead of just the three of us drowning in mimosas."

He looked forward to the mimosas. They were a tradition that didn't hurt. And he only went there because Len and Sarah didn't have any family close, and they put up a tree. Michael didn't own a single ornament. And liked it that way.

He'd seen enough of them broken as a kid.

He'd also seen enough of the travel wrinkles in his gray chinos. He should shower. Change.

"Get going on the paperwork," he said, more curtly than he should have done. "I'll find someone to take her."

He rang off, but didn't put the phone down.

Instead, he clicked and scrolled with one thumb, coming up with the name he'd wanted within seconds.

"Dan, yeah, Michael O'Connell here. I've got a job for you…" He'd pay whatever it took to be at the top of the man's list.

Sitting impatiently, silent through the private detective's greeting, nodding at the ten years it had been since they'd last spoken, he then said, "I need you to find out who fathered Harper Blackstone, a four-year-old girl living in Marietta, Oklahoma. And get me everything you can find on the guy and his family. By tomorrow, if possible."

The child was in a shelter in Marietta. Michael had to claim her. Find someplace for her to stay, preferably with him for only an hour or two. One night at the most. He'd book a room in a hotel with a nanny service.

The little one would likely be afraid of him, a six-foot total stranger. And it wasn't like he had one iota of experience when it came to dealing with kids. He'd have no idea how to assuage fears, or know what she should eat, or how to put a kid that age to bed. Did they just go? Did you have to…

"This have anything to do with June?" Dan's question rescued him from his speeding thoughts.

"Yeah, the kid is hers." Kid. Not little girl. Not

child in need. Definitely not niece. Nothing that would make him feel personally protective of her.

He already knew he'd fail that one.

"You been in touch with her since we spoke last?"

Dan had been the one to find June every single time Michael couldn't get a hold of her. He'd been there that last day, when June had called the cops.

"Nope."

"How do you know about her daughter?"

Daughter. His baby sister had a daughter. Throat tight, he shook his head. He wasn't going there.

And knew how to stay away. You controlled your thoughts. Ruled your mind instead of letting it rule you.

"I heard from her legal representation. She named me guardian of the child in event of her death."

"June's dead." More confirmation than question.

The PI didn't sound surprised. Michael didn't blame him.

"Apparently."

"You want me to find out what happened?"

He'd been trying to avoid the obvious. Knew it wasn't going away. And couldn't waste valuable brainpower on fighting it. "I want to know everything she's had to eat in the past ten years," he said. Or, at the very least, how she'd died.

He hoped to God she hadn't suffered long.

"But I need the other first," he said, standing at the high-rise window in his office, looking out over the city of Little Rock. "Find the father. And get me a dossier on his whole family."

"By tomorrow, right, I got that," Dan said. "You do know I own my own firm now, right? I've got a staff of people I can put on this."

He hadn't known. Should have known.

"I'll pay you all double what you'd normally make," he said.

And hung up a second time without saying goodbye.

He wasn't ready to say goodbye.

Not to anyone.

But whether he said the words or not, he wasn't going to change the facts.

"Where's Mama?"

Slowing the rocking chair, child specialist Mariah Anderson looked up from the disaster relief resource book she'd been reading to see the small-boned but well-fed four-year-old—with her head still on the pillow of her temporary shelter bed—staring straight at her. Her big brown eyes bore shadows that Mariah would give anything to erase.

No matter how many times Harper asked the

question—and she'd asked many times a day—the answer remained the same.

"Mama died," she said softly, leaving her book on the rocking chair and brushing her hair back over her shoulder. She sat on the edge of Harper's little cot and then adjusted the lightweight-fleece purple-and-white-heart-print blanket up to the preschooler's chin. After three days of sharing the space with other displaced preschoolers, Harper had the room to herself as of that morning. All of the other children her age had been collected by parents who'd been treated and released or by other approved family members.

"What's 'died'?" The little voice struck a hole clear through Mariah's heart. She was in too deep with this one. Couldn't seem to find her professional distance.

She picked up one of Harper's tanned little hands and lowered the blanket to put that small palm on the little girl's unicorn-shirted chest. "You feel that beating?"

Harper nodded, still meeting Mariah's gaze as they went through a process they'd repeated many times in the three days since they'd met. It was almost as though Harper knew she'd broken through the barriers that Mariah had to have in place in order to do her job. The young child just kept climbing deeper inside Mariah's heart.

Without boundaries, Mariah would hurt too much to be able to do her job week after week, year after year.

"That's your heart," she continued softly. She moved Harper's hand atop her green-shirted larger chest. "You feel my heart beating?"

The child's nod was quick.

"That's my heart. Bodies need hearts to beat to stay alive. Mama's heart stopped beating," she said then.

"When will she be back?"

Another question she'd answered multiple times. And one Harper would likely continue to ask repeatedly in the coming months. But for some reason, knowing that the girl was exhibiting typical behavior didn't make the questions any easier to hear. Or answer.

"She's not coming back."

It wasn't Mariah's first bereavement. It wasn't even her fiftieth.

But it was her hardest yet. And she couldn't figure out why. It wasn't like the other kiddos she'd been called on to help through crises were any less special than Harper Blackstone. She'd even had other cases where both parents were suddenly deceased.

"I want Shadow." Another sentiment she'd heard over and over.

Both hands on the thighs of her cotton capri

pants now, she said, "I know, sweet Harper, and the people who are cleaning up your house will be bringing us everything they can find from your room, okay? We just have to wait for them to get done." She'd managed to find out, through a series of questions and drawings and reading stories in picture books, that Shadow was a stuffed cat—not a real one, who likely would have been killed during the tornadoes and storms that had ravaged the small town of Marietta three nights before.

With four-year-old imaginations, things like *stuffed* and *alive* weren't always clear. Especially when concerning a personal companion.

Whether or not Harper would ever be reunited with her Shadow wasn't clear at the moment, either.

"When they bring us all the things, we'll look through them together and see if we can find Shadow, okay?" It was the best she could offer.

"Okay."

Mariah waited for the "Where's Daddy?" question that should be coming up next. They'd talk about breathing, then. About how Harper breathes, and Mariah breathes. Maybe play a game of blowing on each other. And then get to the part where Daddy had stopped breathing.

It was way more than a child should have to deal with, but Mariah didn't get to choose what happened to the kids in her care. She only got to help them through what did happen as best she could. And direct honesty was the healthiest way to do that. Esoteric comments like "in heaven" were too ethereal for Harper to grasp. Telling her her parents were "sleeping" was a huge unfairness—lying to her would only instill mistrust for the future.

Harper wasn't asking about her father. She also wasn't nodding off to sleep as Mariah had hoped she would. The little tyke hadn't had more than three or four hours of sleep a night without waking up in tears. And neither had Mariah.

"I want Mama."

Mariah brushed the curly blond bangs from Harper's forehead. "I know, Harper." Mention of the girl's name was purposeful—giving her a sense that she was known.

"I don't want that man to take me away."

And there they had it.

Mariah had been trying for a day and half, through storytelling, drawing exercises, building block and stick figure play, coloring and point-blank questions, to get Harper to talk to her about going to live with her uncle. She'd explained that he was her mama's brother, which made him her family, too. That she was a lucky little girl to have him. And that her mama had grown up with him and had chosen him to be the one to come get Harper, but the child had shown no reaction at all.

"Why don't you want him to come get you?"

"I don't like him."

"Why not?" Harper had finally opened the door for exploration. It was Mariah's job to keep it open.

The little girl shrugged.

"Maybe you will like him when you meet him." No one in Marietta had ever met Michael O'Connell. Mariah had looked him up on the internet, though, the first night she'd met Harper. He didn't seem to do social media at all, but had a nice, clearly professional website. And a ton of articles written about him with pictures of impressive buildings he'd designed.

There'd been some pictures of the architect, too, and she hoped she hadn't just imagined the kindness she'd thought she'd seen in his eyes.

"I want Mama."

"I know."

"When's she coming to get me?"

"She's not coming to get you. Mama died. Your uncle is coming."

With a sigh, Harper turned her back.

And five minutes later was snoring softly.

Chapter Two

The five-and-a-half-hour drive from Little Rock to Marietta wasn't nearly long enough. Up at four thirty that next morning, Michael was pulling into town, adjusting the knot on the navy-and-white thin-striped tie at his neck, a full hour before his 11:00 a.m. appointment with June's attorney. He'd meet with whoever he had to see from there, sign what he had to sign, and then…

He drew a blank.

The child was at a church being used to shelter storm victims. Did he just pick her up, put her in his car and go?

Would he have a better shot at finding someone who would adore raising her if he looked around in Marietta? Maybe someone there already loved her to pieces?

Dan, as good as always, had already been back in touch three hours into Michael's unexpected road trip. Harper's father had a name. Blaine Ryan Blackstone. He went by Ryan. Had worked as a warehouse manager in Marietta for a national chain of stores, making above-average money for the area. Had been June's husband for the past five years.

Died lying right next to her when a beam fell on them as they slept in their bed the night of the storms.

And, having grown up in the foster system, Ryan Blackstone had no other family.

Michael's baby sister had been completely clean, sober and married. For five years. And hadn't been in touch with him. Because she'd built the family she'd always said they could be.

And she'd known he hadn't fit the picture she'd had in her head.

He'd never felt compelled to put family first.

Or even to have one.

He also knew, then, why she'd named him guardian of her only child—because there hadn't been anyone else. In the event of the unthinkable, she'd wanted her child with family.

As far as family went, he was it. And June's dream to make the life she wanted, to be part of a real, healthy, happy family, had apparently survived the drugs and the streets, after all.

He was pleased she'd done that.

Proud of her.

And was having difficulty swallowing as he thought about her losing it all. Fate was such a fickle, confounding thing, taking loving parents away from a small girl and leaving behind a man who couldn't possibly give her the home she should have. He'd have changed places with the young couple if the option had been presented to him.

Instead, less than two hours later, in dark blue dress pants that were generously unwrinkled, he was parking in the lot of a large church building just outside town, with the name of a social worker to ask for. When they'd spoken on the phone from the attorney's office, Sandra Larson had had questions for him which he'd readily answered. She was expecting him. Would provide him with the mandatory car seat.

And would have Harper ready.

Trouble was, in all of the conversations he'd had over the past couple of hours, no one had asked if *he* was ready.

Or seemed to care that he most definitely was not. He'd catch on quickly, he'd been assured.

No one appeared to understand, in spite of his spoken doubts and questions regarding others who might love Harper, that it was in the child's best interests to be with someone who was not him.

And it could just be that their hands were tied. He was Harper's legal guardian, and unless there was reason to prove him unfit—he hadn't had time

to get his ass in prison—the state had an obliga-
tion to deliver Harper to him.

And after that… All anyone could do was hope
for the best.

Harper's uncle was on the way. Sandra's text
came just as Mariah and Harper were having
lunch. Peanut butter and jelly sandwiches because
they were what Harper wanted. Most of what was
happening to and around the little girl was out
of her control. Mariah was trying to give her all
the choices she could. To give her some sense of
power and control.

Spiraling into her own sense of loss of control
at the imminent arrival was not anywhere on her
agenda. And yet there she was, unable to swallow
past the lump in her throat or take anything more
in her stomach. She worried that the skinny black
jeans, white top and tennis shoes she had would
make her appear unprofessional to the stranger
soon to be in their midst. Putting down her half-
eaten sandwich, she focused on what she knew—
her job—and talked to Harper about the color of
jelly. It was purple, Harper's favorite—the color of
the cushy-soft brand-new teddy bear she'd given
the child at bedtime the night before.

The child had named the bear Ryan. "After
Daddy," she'd said, because Daddy brought her

Shadow and so when Shadow came home the toy would like Ryan, too.

If Shadow was not returned intact, the idea was Ryan would already be in place to help Harper through the many transitions coming in her young world. And the next moments were likely to present one of those times.

They'd had a talk at bedtime about Harper hugging Ryan anytime she got scared or lonely and Harper had held the bear tight as she'd fallen asleep.

Pushing Ryan a little closer to Harper on the bench they were sitting on, she knew she'd done all she could to help the sweet little girl in the time she'd had, but wasn't at all sure she'd prepared Harper for all that she had before her. How could she have? Harper's entire world was drastically changed forever and Mariah had only had three days. During most of that time, she'd had other charges as well.

There was no reason to feel as though she'd failed the little girl.

And yet...

"Your uncle Mike is on his way to see you," she said, naming him as he'd just instructed. Sandra had asked the question due to Mariah's recommendation that she do so, and then texted the response. "He'll be here in a few minutes." She'd been told the man was expected sometime that day. She'd hoped she'd have a few more hours with Harper. Had some activity sheets she'd planned to do with her to help with the transition to a new home, in a new state.

"Mikey?" Harper looked at her, her little nose all scrunched up as she asked the question.

"You know him?"

Relief simmered through her nerve endings. There'd been no indication Harper had ever met the man. Not in anything anyone in town had known or said. And not in recognition from the child, either, during all of the mentions of him made over the past couple of days. Always as Uncle Michael.

But word from Sandra was that he'd been Mike to his sister and should be referred to as Uncle Mike. Had they just been getting the name wrong? Was there less to fear in this transition than she'd thought?

"I don't know Uncle," Harper said seriously, shaking her head. "Just Mikey. In the picture with Mama. He's a boy, not a uncle. You wanna see?"

The little girl got up. Turned to the room. And stopped. She wasn't at home eating lunch. There were no familiar pictures there.

But Mariah was suddenly determined to stick around long enough to see if someone could find at least that one photo Harper had in mind in the rubble of lives lost that the storm had left behind. It could serve as a critical transition from old life to new for one very special little girl.

He was a coward, Michael knew. Being academically gifted had covered for his failing most of his life, but being valedictorian, graduating college with highest honors, earning his doctorate and making millions designing famous buildings weren't going to matter a whit to a four-year-old.

A coward and a failure when it came to committed relationships. His intelligent mind didn't seem to get when to stand up and fight and when to sit down and shut up where his loved ones were concerned. So he'd quit having anyone around to whom he was committed.

It hadn't been that difficult, really. He'd known from an early age that he wanted no part of the marriage-and-kids plan.

June had made it work, though. She'd always been different. Special.

And this Ryan guy she'd married... From what he'd been told over the past two hours, the man had been pretty much a saint. He hoped the reality in their home had been even half as good as the perception they'd given others. With that, it still would have been a hundred times better than what June had known growing up.

Tucking in the edges of his white shirt, adjusting his tie one last time, he pulled open the heavy church door, appreciating the old, probably hand-carved woodwork. And the structural beams that were visible. He'd widen the doorway a bit if he were designing it. Raise the ceiling some. And definitely add a larger vestibule. The small space he stepped into, while lovely with all of the natural oak, seemed far too small to contain his panic.

Sandra didn't leave him there long enough to test the theory. Within seconds, she'd met him, shaken his hand and was leading him through a series of hallways to Sunday school rooms and a nursery.

While the halls were busy, and most all of the rooms that he could see into were alive with television, a card game, exercise activities, a group of people sitting in a circle, the place seemed well organized. Clean.

And bustling with people trying to cope while dealing with tragedy. Some of them had lost homes, he learned. Would be waiting for insurance monies, or family to come get them. Others had nowhere to go while roofs were being replaced. Sandra's string of conversation never paused as she kept walking past every door.

He realized he'd stopped wondering if the next one was it, had managed a deep breath or two as he'd put his mind to the trials of others, rather than focusing only on himself, when she finally stopped.

"You ready?" Her gaze seemed empathetic when she looked over at him.

"No." Maybe he'd finally met someone who could see that the child's best interests weren't being served.

She nodded. Gave a sad, though understanding, smile. And opened the door.

The man who entered, Harper's uncle, Michael O'Connell, won Mariah's forever gratitude the second she saw him. His gaze searched, not to see the room, but for only one person in it: his niece. It didn't stop moving, not on Mariah, not on anything, until it found Harper.

His expression softened, his whole face seemed to lose some stress, and his gaze...concerned, but filled with real warmth...eased Mariah's own tension a bit. He appeared to have heart. Harper's chances of being well loved had instantly grown exponentially in Mariah's estimation.

Not that the little girl would get that point. Or would understand if she had.

"Not Mikey." Harper, in beige leggings and

a matching cotton top with orange horses on it, stood from the bench at the little plastic picnic-type table. Before Michael entered, they'd been sitting in the playroom of the two-room suite where Mariah's young charges had been staying. Grabbing up Ryan, the purple bear, Harper hugged him. Tight.

She'd been told to do that when she was frightened or feeling lonely. The latter didn't seem pertinent to the moment.

The little girl was scared. And yet, earlier in the day, she'd remembered her uncle with happiness, wanting to show him off in the picture.

Sandra's phone rang, and with a questioning glance at Mariah, she nodded, excused herself and closed the door behind her.

"I'm your uncle Mike," the tall man said, not moving from the step he'd taken inside the doorway while introductions were made. His beard was freshly trimmed, his eyes were blue, not brown like Harper's. His hair color matched his niece's. Mariah wished he'd get down on his haunches, sit on the little bench they'd just vacated, somehow lower himself to the little girl's level, but he just stood there. A big figure towering over the room.

"He's not Mikey," Harper said, looking up at Mariah like she'd made some kind of mistake.

"He's your uncle Mike," Mariah said, sitting

back down on the bench just a foot or so from where Harper stood. It was either that or grab the child up in her arms, and the action wasn't appropriate to the situation. She couldn't intervene to help Harper. Michael O'Connell was the one who was going to have to do that. "You want to introduce him to Ryan?"

"No."

While she felt a bit of compassion for the man standing there—he must've just been told of his sister's death and was finding himself a sudden parent to a four-year-old who was rejecting him outright—her job was to help Harper cope through the transition.

"Then let's get that ice cream we talked about having for dessert after lunch," she said, taking Harper's hand and leading her over to the refrigerator standing next to a counter and sink along the far wall of the room. "You said you wanted chocolate, right?"

Distraction was in order before the situation imploded. And a return to the plans they'd had for the next few moments was the distraction she had to offer.

"Ryan did." Harper stood next to her, clutching her new bear, staring up at the freezer door. "He wanted chocolate."

It was as though the stranger wasn't in their midst.

"What about you? I thought you wanted chocolate, too."

Harper nodded.

"Here's yours." Mariah pulled the tab to remove the lid from the miniature cardboard bowl and handed the ice cream to Harper with a little wooden spoon, repeating a habit they'd formed a few days before. If Harper ate all her food, she got an ice cream treat. "Ryan's is…"

"Make-believe," Harper said, cramming her bear between her elbow and her ribs and taking her bowl over to the table, as she'd been taught the first day they'd all been together. But instead of putting the bowl on the table and sliding onto the bench, facing it, she held the bowl in her hand, sitting with her back to the table—and to the man still standing just inside the door.

Mariah tried to catch his gaze. To signal for him to hang on, to somehow let him know that she could help, but his attention never wavered from the child.

"Your mom, June, used to eat ice cream with a fork." He spoke as though making small talk in a boardroom. As though Harper were one of his peers.

Harper's legs swung back and forth as she ate.

"She liked chocolate, too." He could have been musing to himself or another adult in the room.

But the content was good. Mariah couldn't have coached him any better.

"She'd even put chocolate syrup on chocolate ice cream."

He hadn't moved. Not his body, nor his gaze, holding steadfast on that little back. From Mariah's vantage point, in front of Harper, the scene transpiring in front of her was heartbreaking. The man's expression slightly lost. And the child's stone-like.

"Have you ever had chocolate syrup on ice cream, Harper?" Mariah asked.

The small shoulders shrugged big.

"I never have," Mariah continued, glancing between girl and man, unsuccessful at drawing either gaze to her.

"Maybe, if we eat dinner with Uncle Mike, and we eat all our food, we can both have chocolate syrup on chocolate ice cream."

An established rule—ice cream treat when you finish eating—and her safe person—currently Mariah—still in the picture. She should have checked with Michael first, but trusted that he wanted what was best for Mariah.

"Dinner?" he asked. "We have a five-hour drive to Little Rock ahead of us."

Harper stopped eating. Her legs stilled. Mariah noted, and then, staying close to the child, said, "I thought maybe it would be fun to stay in town for another day or so," she said in a cheerful tone, thankful when the man finally looked in her direction. She gave a pointed glance toward the bent blond head in front of her. "Maybe you and Harper and I can talk some."

You'd have thought she'd thrown a rope to a drowning man, the way his gaze widened and filled with something less panicky looking. "Okay, good," he said, in a more cheerful tone as well. "I can get a hotel room for us…" With another glance at the small back turned to him, he seemed to flush a bit.

"Harper can stay here with me one more night," she offered, knowing the child would benefit from some continuity as she adjusted to her new family member. And when Harper went to bed, Mariah would have a chance to counsel with her uncle.

"Oh, well, okay. Good." He almost smiled at her. She almost smiled back. Their gazes held and Mariah breathed a little easier as the preschooler's legs started to swing again, with less agitation this time. Harper took another bite of ice cream while the adults in the room made decisions that would affect the rest of her life.

Chapter Three

She looked just like June, Michael mused as he drove back to his hotel later that day. Michael had been seven when June was four—a wise-in-the-ways-of-the-world seven, to her still mostly cheerful innocence. He remembered so clearly. The way her little mind would sum up circumstances in her own world, and the fantasy would usually be far better than reality. Or she'd do as Harper had done just moments ago when he'd said he was taking her away—she'd go inside herself and refuse to engage.

Even if no one else got it, that little girl knew that going home with him wasn't in her best interests. Problem was, he couldn't find an alternative that satisfied him.

No way he was making her a ward of the state. And without a suitable guardian to appoint, that, so he'd been told, was his only other option.

Harper had announced naptime as soon as she'd finished her ice cream. As though she'd been plotting and planning all the while she'd spooned in the cold treat. She'd scooted down off the bench with definite purpose, dropped her cup and wooden utensil in the trash and, with shoulders back and head high, had made her declaration and marched her little body through a door to the left of the trash. He'd followed far enough to see that the room she'd entered held several small cots, and one larger one for Mariah.

The adult one he expected, having been told the city had hired the child life expert to oversee the toddlers and preschoolers who'd been left without family during the crisis. There was nothing distinguishable about that bigger cot, though. Made up with a generic blanket and white pillowcase, it could have been slept in recently or not.

When Harper climbed onto the only made-up smaller cot, pulled a fleece blanket up over her shoulders, leaving her bottom half without covers, turned her back and hugged her bear, he moved to the outer door through which he'd entered the suite. The intelligence that had stood him in good stead all his life had allowed him to recognize his window of escape; he was getting the hell out of there before he'd be expected to tuck the child in or something.

"I'll call you," Mariah had said softly, winning her more of his gratitude. She'd take care of Harper, watch over her and call him with updates.

It wasn't often that he felt…gifted…in his personal life. Usually his abundances came professionally. But then, he focused 98 percent of his existence in the professional world.

As he would do again. As soon as he found someone he trusted to love and protect Harper. To teach her how to live a happy life. To give her what he and June hadn't had, but what June had provided for her—healthy, loving people surrounding her.

He needed a family for Harper.

Whatever it took. Whatever the cost.

He'd been back in his luxury SUV less than fifteen minutes when his phone rang with a Phoenix, Arizona, area code.

Grateful for the momentary distraction, he picked up.

"Hi, Michael, this is Mariah Anderson."

Of course it was. The woman had a job to do—pass the last of her charges off to family. She was a professional. Just like him.

Except that he wasn't one at the moment. And wasn't sure how to deal with that, either.

He'd come home expecting a day of laundry, a workout at the gym, some quiet time in his office before meetings. Instead, life was spinning on a dime and he couldn't see where he was going.

"If you aren't doing anything, I thought maybe

we could use this time while Harper's asleep to discuss her transition..."

He didn't want to discuss a transition. He wanted to know how to keep from damaging that little one further while he found a home for her.

He also felt a little safer in this woman's calming presence, though. She'd been the first person to make him feel as though he'd be heard, and possibly even understood, since he'd opened the envelope on the certified letter the day before. "Of course I'm not doing anything," he told her. The lunch he'd been seeking out could wait. Food wasn't nearly as important as getting Harper's life on track as soon as possible.

So when she suggested that he return to the church so they could talk in person, he took the first opportunity to make a U-turn.

Something about the woman...from the long red curls and green gaze to the specific warm look in those eyes, as though they saw and understood what one didn't say, while remaining firmly cloaked in professionalism...called to him.

Only an ignorant person would ignore that call.

And one thing Michael O'Connell knew was that he had never been ignorant.

Mariah's heart rate sped up the second Michael stepped back into the makeshift nursery. There was no reason in Marietta for her to have such an emotional response to this man, at least not on a level to elicit heart rate escalation.

Not unless it was fear based, but she knew the danger to life and limb had disappeared elsewhere on its destructive path before she'd arrived on the scene.

She didn't feel at all afraid. To the contrary, she felt deeply…moved.

"Thanks for coming back," she said, showing him to an older but clean couch-and-chair arrangement in a far corner of the playroom. She was the facilitator, and an advocate, not a parental figure. Motherhood, again, was not in the cards for her. And though she felt underdressed with him in professional wear and her in her casual clothes, she reminded herself their meeting was not about her.

"Are you kidding?" He took the chair and she settled in the corner of the couch farthest away from him. "You're like the one drop of hope in a seemingly hopeless situation here."

A drop of hope. The words moved her some more.

Which did frighten her a bit.

Personal involvement in a case wouldn't necessarily mar her judgment. The opposite could occur, if a wide-open heart allowed her to tune in more deeply to a child's stress. But that open heart could also be debilitating for her when it came time to walk away, which was also a critical part of her job. Walking away. As a child life specialist, she knew those boundaries were what allowed her to do what she did.

"I'm sorry about your loss," she said, wanting him to know that he mattered, as well as Harper.

He nodded. Looked like he was going to say more, but didn't.

During her stint as a child life specialist at Phoenix Children's Hospital, she'd worked with families and kids, helping them all cope, while helping the parents to lessen effects of trauma for their children anytime she could.

Her quick assessment of the gorgeous man sitting across from her showed her someone who was more than just uneasy. Harper would sense panic, even if she didn't have a definition for it.

"First, I don't know what all they've told you about me…"

"Your name and the general role you've had here and in Harper's life specifically. But I looked you up while I was waiting for June's attorney to process paperwork. You're one of seven partners in an impressive firm of experts, with reviews that name you one of the best in your field."

Right. False modesty wasn't her way, but neither was shining a light on herself. She'd asked the question for Harper's sake. One of the reasons she was so good at her job was because she much preferred focusing on others to thinking about herself. She'd moved on from the pain and loss in her own life, but it would rise up and bite her if she gave it too much freedom. "So you understand that anything I might recommend, I do so with one goal only—to give Harper the best chance of successfully navigating extremely difficult life changes."

"I do. And I want you to know that I'm almost desperately eager for your assistance." A shard of highly unprofessional pleasure shot through her at the thought of him desperately eager for her. Not in a sexual sense, although, in another place and time she'd most definitely be eager for that, but just having something that he needed, being able to help him—that excited her. What *was* it with her and this case?

"Just to be clear, I'm not a doctor, a psychiatrist or a counselor. I'm a certified child life specialist, with a doctorate in child development. I specialize in easing emotional stress in children of all ages, and teaching age-specific, as well as child-specific, coping mechanisms for dealing with physical and emotional hardships, both now and in the future."

"Got it. I didn't know the profession existed before this morning, but then, I'm not a family man. I'm an architect and I use technical computer programs, and occasionally still a drawing board, to design stationary structures that aren't even in the realm of emotional *anything*." He was making it very clear he had no childrearing experience. Funny that he'd come running the second he'd returned to the States—from she knew not where, just that his late arrival was due to the fact that he'd been out of the country—and heard that Harper was his. To her way of thinking, the instinct that had him in Marietta, and already having legal custody of his niece, was the first important part of successful childrearing. That instinct would have him put Harper first when and where it mattered.

Her time with him was limited and she wanted to give him as much help as she could… There was so much she could teach him…

"You'd never met Harper before today," she said, feeling her way.

"No."

"Can you tell me a little bit about that? It might help me to know the family history as we talk to Harper. While it's good to speak in simple terms to a child her age, we also need to speak the truth in what we do say. You give her the ability to trust you by doing that."

He paused, as though making a mental note, and then said, "The truth is, knowing who she was, and seeing how she ended up, I'd guess that June put my name down because I'm probably the only living family either she or Ryan had. Of course, she didn't think, in a million years, that anyone would ever be looking me up to actually care for her daughter. That's what I've been trying to explain all morning. I was constantly raising our father's ire, which caused pure hell for her in our home when we were growing up and later, when I tried to help her, she called the cops on me. I'm not the guy everyone seems to think I am. What I need is some help finding a loving family who needs Harper as badly as she needs them."

She heard the panic more than the words. And took a few big steps back, too. The man wasn't going to take Harper?

Her heart lurched.

"So why is it that you hadn't met your niece?" she asked again, softly. Kindly. Drawing on her professional expertise to offset her own feelings. She had to know more to know how to proceed.

Adoptions didn't happen as quickly for older kids as they did for babies.

"I haven't seen June in almost ten years."

That long? No wonder he was so shell-shocked, with less than twenty-four hours to process everything that had come at him. His sister being married, having a child, her tragic death. His becoming an overnight parent.

Could it explain what he'd just said about giving Harper up? Pray to God he hadn't really meant those words. That he wasn't going to abandon the child who'd just been so tragically orphaned.

"What happened that last day you saw your sister?" Her job meant asking the difficult questions necessary to best help Harper cope. What had June told the little girl about Michael—or Mikey? Ordinarily she'd be asking a parent about Harper's previous encounters with stress, but that wasn't an option here.

He sat forward, elbows on his knees, hands hanging as though he didn't know what to do with them. Stared at the commercial-grade gray linoleum floor and then looked up at her. "I'd paid for a rehab program for June and got a call from her therapist saying that she'd checked herself out. I went to one of her favorite areas—an old parking lot by a river where kids, mostly homeless, hung out and got high. Found her there, scoring a fix, and tried to get her into my car to take her back to rehab. She pulled out the cell phone I bought her and called the police instead. Said I was harassing her and trying to kidnap her. When all was said and done, bottom line was, unless she'd been ordered into rehab on a condition of probation, which she hadn't, then she was free not to go and if I tried to force her I could be charged with kidnapping. She tried to get a restraining order against me, but the judge didn't grant it. He did, however, warn me to stay away from her unless she initiated contact. I gave her my number, and have kept my phone on me every second of every day since…"

The way he spoke, with obviously difficult emotions lacing his voice, made her wonder how much of what he was telling her, he'd told others. She'd guess not much, if at all.

"Sounds like you loved her a lot."

"She was my baby sister. But it was more than that. I blame myself for her ending up on the streets. If I'd just learned to keep my mouth shut, if I'd quit standing up to my old man, she wouldn't have grown up in a home filled with anger and violence. Wouldn't have had anything to run away from to begin with."

Her gut tightened as she staved off the emotion pushing at her from the inside out, wondering how much he wasn't saying. Wanting to reach out to him. To help him process his grief, if nothing else.

Their time was limited, though.

And she'd been hired to help Harper.

Encouraging Michael to hand the child over to the state would be better than sending her home with a man who didn't want her, but she wasn't çonvinced that he didn't want his niece so much as he didn't think he'd be good for her. What Harper needed more than anything was love, and he seemed to care a lot. The way he'd stared when he'd first seen her. The fact that he was there at all. Trying.

Baring his soul.

From her research, she'd learned this man was renowned in his field. Successful beyond most measures. And he was humbled by the surprise of a child in his life.

He could have saved himself the trip to Marietta and just signed her over to the state without missing a beat in his daily routine. Instead, he was meeting with Mariah.

"You see why it's not in her best interests to come home with me."

She didn't. To the contrary, she saw a man who was exhibiting signs of having loved Harper before he'd even met her. Because he'd loved June so much.

It wasn't a lot to go on, but it was all she had.

Drawing a long breath, she took a chance on the deep caring she thought she saw in him. "If you put her up for adoption, she goes in the system, and there's a good chance she'd grow up a ward of the state, in and out of foster homes, like her father."

"Whoa, wait a second, who said anything about putting her in the system?" He sat up straight, cocking his head, a look of indignation shining from those expressive blue eyes. "I was talking private adoption. You know, to someone who's been completely vetted and who can convince me that they'll love her as though she was their own."

Her tension eased a small bit and Mariah thought about Harper's best interests. "Did June call you Mikey?"

With a shrug, he said, "When she was little. Before I left for college, probably, still. The last couple of years I was in her life, through various rehab attempts, it was mostly 'you bastard.'" He smiled, but the gesture was tinged with sadness. "Mikey. I haven't heard that in a long time."

Energy coursed through her. She took a second to calm, and then said, "Harper said it this morning." Just fact. Like, *it's raining outside*.

"She what?" His frown held nothing but confusion.

She relayed the incident, and then said, "Apparently your sister kept a picture of the two of you out in the house. Harper knew it was Mama and Mikey, but Mikey was a boy."

When his gaze grew moist, Mariah knew that she had to move hell and high water if that's what it took to help this little family.

Bringing happiness to others was what made her life worth living.

Chapter Four

Didn't matter how he felt; he couldn't condemn a four-year-old to life with him. Michael could feel Mariah Anderson, with her nurturing ways, trying to make sure he took his niece home, but it wasn't going to happen.

"I'm quick to understand things," he told her. "I speak to others as though they get them, too, and don't slow down enough to realize when they don't." When he realized she probably had no idea what he was talking about, he added, "Those are a few of my faults. I'm also gone more than I'm home, I put work first without even realizing it, and sometimes, when a building is in construction and a site challenge arises, I have to travel on a moment's notice."

As she'd said, they didn't have a lot of time. He had to get through to her. She was smart. She'd catch on if she'd just listen. The woman was a walking load of compassion. She'd protect Harper once she saw the true picture.

"I think I know best, often because I do, but I

have a tendency to expect others to accept what I say as right, and that tends to frustrate people," he continued when she remained silent. "And then, sometimes, to anger them."

"You anger your clients?"

"Not generally, no, unless I have to tell them that the design options they want don't meet safety codes."

"You have friends?"

"Yes."

"You anger them?"

"They're used to me. And they only deal with me in spurts."

She nodded, seeming more like the counselor she'd said she wasn't. He knew how they worked, sitting there, thinking if they waited long enough he'd spew.

And he knew he had to spew and do it quickly if he had a hope in hell of accomplishing the goal in front of him.

"When I know I'm right, I shut down on other perceptions." That's what had angered the old man the most, he'd finally figured out. That fact that Michael wouldn't admit that he was wrong when he wasn't. That he wouldn't admit the old man was right when he wasn't.

He hadn't known then that he had a higher IQ than normal. Hadn't understood that his father hadn't had one. He should have just listened to the man—who'd been trying to do his best raising two kids after his wife was killed in a car accident—agreed with him even when he knew he was wrong or, at the very least, just shut up. It would have kept the peace from the beginning. He got it all now. With the hindsight of an adult.

"And when others know they're right, do you allow them the same privilege?"

He'd never been asked the question before. Considered it. "I guess so." Usually, if it dealt with an area of expertise with which he was unfamiliar, he got familiar with it. And then ended up in agreement. Maybe. From what he could recall. But... "People don't often argue with me."

There was no threat, or warning to his words. Just fact.

She smiled.

His groin twitched.

What the hell? He was there to see to the welfare of his sister's kid and he was attracted to her advocate? Another sign that he wasn't a family man.

One he'd most definitely be keeping to himself.

"I'm a pressure cooker."

With a frown that only heightened those big green eyes, she said, "You have a problem with your temper?"

Like his old man?

Would that get Harper off his hook?

"No." He wasn't going to lie. "I somehow manage to stay calm when others get riled, which only riles them further," he told her. "I'm told it's infuriating and that it seems like I have a superiority complex."

In Harper's mother's own words.

"At least you're aware and can work on that."

He could. Did, actually. But was she willing to risk Harper's future on the chance that he'd get it right?

"Back to the pressure cooker. Explain, please."

"I expect a lot from myself, and apparently from those within my sphere as well. Talk to any of the people who work for me. I have a real issue with slacking off. I get impatient with excuses for laziness and don't tolerate procrastination well, either."

"Just at work?"

"No." June had pointed that flaw out to him, too. Back when she was about eight and he'd told their father that if he'd just take the time to put things back where he got them then he wouldn't have to waste so much time looking for them or getting mad when he couldn't find them. Michael had mumbled the words under his breath after taking a slap to the back of the head for supposedly having moved the pair of pliers his father swore he'd put in the kitchen drawer; only later, his dad had found that he'd left them in the bathroom when he'd gone in to fix a running toilet.

His father had unfortunately heard the muttered comment and given him a backhand across the mouth. There'd been dozens of other instances in his life where his overachieving tendencies made others look bad, but it had been June's words to him, that last day, that had struck the deepest.

We aren't all like you, Michael. You expect too much. Maybe if you didn't put so much pressure on me to be perfect, I wouldn't have to try so hard to convince you I'm not.

"Do you have a high turnover among the people who work for you?"

"No. None in the past five years." And before she could find some kind of sainthood to put on him for that, he added, "I have a great office manager who runs interference for me."

Tried to mother him was more like it. But the office ran smoothly. The work got done. His employees were happy. And so was he.

Because he kept his distance, he felt sure.

"What about friends?"

"What about them?"

"Do you have any?"

"You already asked me about friends."

"I'm asking again."

"Sure, I have friends. They don't have to live with me."

She sat there, all beautiful woman in those jeans that showed the shape of her legs, the top that hugged her lovely breasts—and he had no business noticing either. Not in that venue. Maybe, if he came on to her, she'd get the point he was trying to make. He thought about doing so for a hot second. Thought about what it would be like to ask her to dinner.

Something told him she wasn't a fling type of woman, and flings were all he had.

He didn't want her to walk out on Harper's case, most definitely not because he'd made a sexual advance.

"I drove my father to drink." He had to get this done.

"Your father was a grown man. You were a child. The onus was on him."

"I never saw him drunk until after my mom died and he didn't know what to do with me."

"Your mom knew what to do with you?" Those green eyes changed. Grew more alert, not that she hadn't been fully taking him in to begin with. Talking with Mariah was akin to being under a microscope. She'd just upped the magnification. Odd, though, that he didn't mind being there.

"I remember having long conversations with her

about things that interested me. I remember a talk once about birds being able to stand on two skinny little stick legs that managed to hold and balance all of their weight. We discussed the physics of it, as best as a kindergartner could, I guess. Another time I was wondering about cell phone signals, wanting to know why we couldn't see them. She drew them for me on a piece of paper."

"Was she some kind of scientist?"

He shook his head. "Didn't even go to college. Though she read all the time. And I'm not saying her depiction was correct. She just answered my question to the best of her ability."

"Your parents, they got along?"

He shook his head. "It's the O'Connell curse," he said. Except, apparently, for June and Ryan. He hadn't processed that one yet. "My parents hardly said a civil word to each other. Same with my grandparents. They married too young. Should have divorced, but instead stayed together and made each other miserable. There were never huge fights between my parents, like there were with my grandparents. They just went their separate ways. I can't ever remember sitting down to the dinner table with both of them there. Or being in a car with both of them at the same time."

He was whining like a baby. Saying things he'd

never articulated before. Pulling out every single stop he could come up with.

Because Harper's future depended on him finding a stable home for her.

And he was certain that his was not it.

Every word this man said convinced her further that he was just what Harper needed. And the little girl was probably what he needed, too. More than anything else in the world.

Her daily work had her applying studied theories with young children in crisis in an attempt to help them grow into healthy, successful adults, in spite of trauma and stress. What she was looking at was a healthy, successful adult who'd made it through years of severe trauma, apparently without much help at all.

Michael O'Connell was the finished product. Who better to help a little girl who had some tough times ahead of her?

And the memories…

"No one but you can keep June's memory alive for Harper. You have so many stories to tell, many she wouldn't have heard yet. You have new ways for her to know her mom, and her grandmother, invaluable truths that will help sustain her through lonely moments…"

"Have you not heard anything I've said?" His

eyes widened some, giving him a somewhat panicked look again.

He didn't raise his voice, but she felt his tension encapsulate their situation.

"I've listened very carefully to every word," she replied calmly, allowing her professional persona to carry her perfectly over the hump. "And here's what I know. Everyone has faults. Some people are lazy. Some aren't. Some people are good with money, others aren't. Some have obvious talent, while some search their whole lives and never find any. But all of them can be good parents."

With his chin jutting like it was and his entire face tightening, she figured he was probably gritting his teeth.

"Some people are aware of their faults, and others aren't," she said softly, holding his gaze. "Those who are aware are less likely to let those faults harm those around them."

"Exactly." He sat forward, rubbing his hands together. "And the way you do that is to keep yourself out of situations where you might do damage."

"Harper is going to be dealing with more pain than she'll be able to process or even begin to understand. She's going to feel like she did something horribly wrong. She'll think she's bad. That it's her fault that her parents were taken from her. It's illogical to you and me, but that's how children her age process these types of situations. She'll be unbearably lonely. It seems like you're more likely to get all of that because you've lived through it yourself. As a kid. And you thrived in spite of it. You could be the only key to that child's best shot at a great life." She wasn't selling him anything. The words were pouring straight from her heart.

"You know what to guard against, so you can try to stop these faults from becoming an issue."

"I don't. That's what I'm telling you. I can look back on a situation and see it, but I don't at the time."

"She needs to belong. She needs stability. She needs family."

"Family is more than biology and I've never been a part of a healthy one, nor do I have a desire to become a part of one. The opposite, in fact. I've always known I wouldn't marry or have kids. I fill my life in other ways. And adopted families are great," he said. "My attorney and best friend, he was adopted. I've spent Christmas with his family, and he's one of them, completely. And successful and thriving. As a matter of fact, he and his wife are pregnant with twins." He said the words as though he'd just proved the last point to be made.

He'd thought things through, that much was obvious. As were the flaws in his logic.

Mariah barely missed a beat. "You don't have

a family ready to adopt her. She needs security right now. Not later. This instant. And she's lucky enough to have a biological uncle with sweet memories of her mama. Someone who knew June as well as or better than she did."

He was *there*. Harper was legally in his custody. Those actions spoke more loudly to her than his worries. When he had no immediate comeback that time, she feared she'd sent him back into panic mode, and immediately moved into her *calming the parent* mindset.

"You know what not to do, Michael. I listen to you talk and what I hear is someone who is aware, conscientious, determined, smart, willing to learn, accountable. And most of all, I hear how desperately you care about Harper in your fight to see her well-loved and also protected from what you see as your inabilities. That love is all she really needs. Or needs more than anything else."

"She's clearly afraid of me. That's not love."

"That's a traumatized four-year-old meeting a stranger who's many feet taller than she is. I'm not saying that her fear will immediately, or even easily, dissipate. She's going to find it difficult to trust you, or anything, having just had everything she knew completely ripped away from her. But if you'd squat when you talk to her, bring your eyes to her level, it would help."

"She seems to trust you."

"I'm her safe person," Mariah explained, wishing she could wrap her arms around Michael. He looked so alone. Was obviously trying so hard. "I got the honor by default, simply by being here when she was brought in. By caring for her immediate needs. It's natural for her to find someone to cling to during the first shock and aftermath. Just as she'll naturally learn to cling to you when you're the one caring and providing for her."

"You said she's your last client here?"

"Yes."

"Come home with us."

"Excuse me?" Was he asking her to be a part of their family? A total stranger? He couldn't be. Who did that? Unless he really was less together than she'd thought.

"I want to hire you. At least until I can wrap my mind around even half of this. Clearly I know nothing about taking care of a young child, let alone a little girl. My home is not prepared for kids. I have no place for her to sleep and wouldn't know how to go about setting that up, even temporarily. She's needy right now. It's not like she's going to hold on a second while I get up to speed. She needs your support and I need your guidance. I'll double whatever fee you normally charge."

She couldn't go home with him. She'd get in too deep. Was already in too deep.

And yet she wanted to go more than she'd wanted anything in a long time. More than she'd wanted anything since...Joey.

Harper had her heartstrings all tangled up. And Harper's handsome uncle had her attention, too. Not just in child life terms.

Going home with them was out of the question.

"You really want to put her in a donated car seat in the back of my SUV and send her off? Because, based on how hard you're advocating for her, I don't think that's the case."

"It's my responsibility to advocate for her."

"Do you have another assignment you have to get to?"

"My job doesn't work like that. Crises don't wait for me to be available. Either I can be there when they call or I send someone else who works under me. I'm one of seven partners in a firm of experts. Sierra's Web is a nationally renowned firm that offers expertise in pretty much any area of need. All seven of us have other expert employees that we've vetted in our fields, and there are other experts in their own fields who work on commission..." That was it. "I think Cheryl Downs is free. She's a little older than me, has been a child life specialist for fifteen years, and she's been with Sierra's Web the longest. You can hire the firm and I'll send Cheryl."

"She won't be Harper's immediate safe person, though," he said. "I'm fine to hire Sierra's Web, but I want you. You've just told me that the right now, how this next day is handled, how she's helped to cope with the stress of this transition, could affect her for a long time to come, if not her whole life."

She hadn't outlined it quite that clearly. And wasn't used to parents or guardians actually hanging on to her every word. Or using them against her.

"Are you going to tell me that having you along in my SUV as we drive home wouldn't be a huge benefit to Harper?"

"It could build expectation that I'm going to be her forever person, and I'm not."

"Couldn't we tell her that you're not staying, that you're only helping us get settled, starting right away, and repeat it over and over? And then when you leave, she'll trust us both for telling her the truth."

She sat back, her mind scrambling, and her heart in a jumble, too. She had to think. To tune in to what she knew.

She needed to call Kelly, one of her closest friends, a Sierra's Web partner and their expert psychiatrist.

"See what I mean about pressuring people?" Michael's voice dropped softly into the silence that had fallen between them.

Surely he hadn't just been testing her, trying to prove his theory that his being pressured into being a parent was a bad idea. If so, he was a jerk. And she'd read him all wrong and...

Right up until he'd let her off the hook by acknowledging what he'd done. She liked this man. Not as Harper's guardian, or uncle. Just as a person.

"Do you manipulate people on purpose?" She had to ask.

"Not usually."

"Did you just now, with me?"

"Absolutely not." His answer was a good one. "I was sincere about my desperate need to have you stay with us."

Her stomach took a leap at that. "When do you manipulate people on purpose?" she blurted, attempting to keep herself on task.

"When my attorney and I are verbally sparring and he's close to getting too close."

"Too close to what?"

"Things better left unsaid."

Mariah had no idea what that meant. And badly wanted to know.

Which was why she had to talk to Kelly.

"So, will you come with us?"

"I need to make some calls before I give you an answer."

"Fair enough. But...this does mean that you're considering my request?" His gaze met hers. Her insides melted.

She knew she had to tell him no.

And instead, she nodded.

Chapter Five

Every built-in safety mechanism Michael had was sending off vital signals. It was like a series of buzzers and sirens and bright blinking lights were alerting inside him.

He had custody of June's four-year-old daughter. It was fact.

He was going to have to do something with her.

He'd die before knowingly hurting her.

And only the woman sitting across from him could dim the cacophony. A fact that brought its own set of alarms, but ones he could more easily manage. He'd deal with his own personal situation.

"If today's anything like the past couple of days, Harper's going to be awake soon," Mariah was saying. "And there's something else I wanted to talk to you about. I was wondering if you had access to whatever things have been salvaged from her house. If anything's actually been done with the place yet. If we could get that photo of you and June, it could be a dealmaker in many ways as you take her home. I'm thinking it must have been framed and displayed because Harper was going to take me to show it to me. And if her stuffed cat, Shadow, is in any way salvageable, it would help tremendously for you to give it to her to take with her in the car. She can hold it during the drive. She talks to it, though I don't know if she conducts the conversation in silence or aloud, but her being able to have that connection could be a godsend for her."

He stood, nodding. Eager to have something concrete to do to help Harper. Eager to be out of there and have some time to let his mind make some sense of…any of it.

"I already arranged to have someone go through the place, box up anything that's salvageable and ship it to my home. June and Ryan owned the property and I plan just to hang on to it for now. If the house is fixable, I'll have it repaired. If not, it'll be torn down as early as next week," he said, knowing he was rambling. Something he tended to do when he was feeling penned in.

Mariah had risen, too. Was only a couple of feet away from him. Close enough that he could touch those curls at her waist if he reached out a hand.

He most definitely did not do that.

"I'll head over there right now and talk to the couple I hired, at the sheriff's recommendations, to take care of things. And stay with them until we find what you need." He pulled out his wallet, retrieved a card and handed it to her. "My office number is on there, too, if you can't reach me on my cell. Call me if she needs anything else, mentions anything else, if you can think of anything else…"

Or if anything else came up…

Because he sure as hell didn't have anything else to offer.

But she did.

She could accept his job offer and help him save a little girl's future.

Mariah checked in on Harper after Michael left. Cleaned up the rest of the lunch crumbs off the table. Looked in the freezer for dinner because it would be good for Harper to have her first meal with her uncle in the place that had been home to her in her new life, not out in the town she'd recognize from her old one.

And when an hour had passed and she'd read the same sentence half a dozen times, at least, without remembering what she'd read, she set the book down in the rocking chair she normally occupied as Harper slept and crept out to the other room. Pulling the door only partially closed behind her, she called the woman who'd become more sister than friend to her. More family than the brother and parents with whom she spent some holidays.

She and Kelly caught up on each other's assignments for the first few minutes, with Mariah mentioning that Harper's uncle wanted to hire her as the child transitioned into his home, and then, without any kind of segue, she unloaded.

"I'm in a situation with this job, Kel. Feeling things I haven't felt since…Joey died." The name stuck in her throat, hung heavy on her tongue. And she thought of the little girl sleeping so unusually soundly and pushed forward. "When I'm with Harper, I don't just give help. I get something, too. More than that great feeling of knowing you're helping someone else. It's like she's helping *me*, which is absurd, I know, but it's how I felt when Joey was growing inside me. I wasn't just giving him life—he was adding a whole new dimension to mine."

"How do you feel about that?"

"Like I'm losing professional focus." It was a first. But she couldn't pretend it wasn't happening. She wasn't one to push away reality.

"You don't feel like you can give Harper what she needs from a care perspective?"

"Oh, no, that's not what I meant. I know I can do my job. Maybe even better than ever because I'm so in tune with her. It's just that I'm not sure I'm maintaining proper boundaries…"

"To her detriment?"

She thought about the times she'd wanted to pull the little girl into her arms and cradle her to sleep—and had, instead, sat beside her, given her a bear to hug, talked gently to her. Done activities to help Harper to express herself. And the time the little girl had raised her arms and she'd given her the hug she'd requested.

"No," Mariah responded.

"To yours?"

The two words hit home. *She* was making it about herself. "So the problem is only that I'm likely going to be hurt if I take this job. When I have to leave her."

"*Likely* might be an understatement."

"You think I should send someone else?"

"Do you?"

"Don't play therapist on me here, Kel. I'm talking to my friend."

"Who happens to be a therapist—not yours, but I can't just turn off half my brain. What you've been through, the way we all lost Sierra… We can't deny that it's had an effect on all of us." Thinking of their college friend whose murder the Sierra's Web partners had helped solve strengthened her resolve to help Harper and Michael, not weaken it. Sierra's memory was why they'd all dedicated their lives to helping others through their toughest spots.

"Add to that your compassionless ex-husband, telling you it was all for the best when Joey died…"

Yeah, that had been a bit brutal. But she and John had already been struggling by that point.

"I can't help thinking like a therapist at the moment."

"Okay, as a therapist, you think I shouldn't take the job."

"I think I want you to answer my question. Do you believe you should send someone else?"

"As long as I can do my job, no. Michael was right. Bringing in another stranger at this point, while transitioning her to a new state to live with a man she's only just met, wouldn't be her best-case scenario." She shuddered even thinking about it. And knew that this eventuality had been at the crux of her discomfort about Harper this whole time. She just hadn't been in a position to invite herself along.

"And if you get there and the job gets too difficult, you call in someone else." Kelly stating what they both already knew she'd do still helped. Sometimes things carried more weight when you heard them from outside your own head.

But…

"The uncle, Michael O'Connell. He's getting to me a little bit, too." Maybe a lot, if she'd let herself think about him for more than a second or two at a time. Distracting kids from pain for a living gave her a lot of tools for self-survival as well.

"It's natural to feel compassion for him, as you do with many of the parents you help in dealing with their child's trauma." Right.

She paced the big room, in it but not really taking it in at the moment.

"It's different with him." The compassion was there, of course. Tenfold. But an accelerated heart rate when he walked in the door? Excited anticipation at the thought of traveling with him, seeing his home, staying there? "I haven't felt anything close to it since John. And it's more intense than it was when I first met John."

She was turned on by the guy. So what? It happened. To some more than others, to others more than her, but she didn't have to make a big deal out of it.

"You find him sexy?" Kelly's voice changed. Became all soft-spoken and friendly.

"Yeah." She almost held her breath after making the confession.

"So… That's a bit of complication." Trust her friend to not make a big deal out of the fact that Mariah's sex drive, which most often rested in Park, would choose such an ironically inopportune moment to gear up.

Mariah smiled, so thankful she'd called Kelly. "A bit."

"You able to handle it?"

"Of course. Just wondering… Do you think it's because he's Harper's uncle? Am I feeling so attached to the child so I'm transferring familial bonds to other members of her family?"

"You mean, do I think your psyche is somehow trying to make a family out of the three of you?"

She had thought, at first, that that was what he'd been asking…

"It's only been a few hours here, but in a less drastic sense, yeah, that's what I mean."

"Highly doubtful, Mar. It's possible, of course, but transference generally has an emotional base. What you're describing is an instant physical attraction."

That sounded about right. "I *was* moved by him, emotionally," she added. She had to give full disclosure if she was going to be able to trust Kelly's advice.

"I know, and understandably so. But you've been moved by other cases as well, worked with traumatized newly single fathers, but that emotion hasn't ever led to physical attraction, has it?"

"Of course not." Kelly knew Mariah would have told her if it had.

"If you go, would you be open to exploring those feelings?"

"With him?" Her voice rose on the last word and she had to remind herself to keep it down because of the sweet child sleeping in the other room. Harper had had very little restful sleep since Mariah had met her.

"Of course with him. Who else?"

No one. She just… "No. Of course not. He'd be my employer. And if it went bad, it could affect my relationship with Harper. That can't happen. Not over something that could be easily prevented if those of us who care for her make responsible choices."

And there was another reason. And maybe the reason she'd really needed to call her friend.

Walking to the far door of the playroom, with her face to the corner to preclude any possibility at all that the child sleeping in the next room could hear, she lowered her voice and said, "He doesn't want to keep Harper."

Silence hung on the line. A telling silence. An expression of a deeply personal understanding. One that had absolutely nothing to do with Harper Blackstone's emotional health, her transition or her future.

"It's not like I get turned on on a regular basis," she said, equally soft. "Is something wrong with me that the two times it's significant—this one being way more so than John—" it seemed key to make that point "—that the guys I'm attracted to would make me miserable in the same way? By rejecting a child I care about?"

She'd married in haste the first time around, having been so thrilled to have sex be more than body parts and occasional minimal pleasure. She'd briefly mentioned that she wanted kids as a first on her list, had heard his reply of "sure, sure" in response. Had never in a million years figured him for a man who'd thought it for the best that their son...

She shook her head. Knowing that she couldn't do her job to the best of her ability if she dredged all that up right then. Nor was it fair to Harper.

"Michael's made it very clear that he never wants to have kids or be part of a family," she said as Kelly remained silent, letting Mariah work herself through the moment as she usually did.

"I'd say that should take care of any worries that you'll get in over your head there, then," Kelly said, her tone equally soft. And, again, Mariah's tension eased. She'd known she'd just needed a check-in.

"So what do you think?"

"I think that choice is yours. You'll do your usual great job if you go, and maybe end up with another break in your heart when you have to leave Harper. And if you choose not to go, it's completely understandable, too. You've already done so much for Harper, getting her through these first few days. Chances are, when she looks back at this time in her life, as we both know she'll be doing for the rest of her life, she'll remember kindness and caring alongside the debilitating fear and loss, and that was your goal."

"I want to go." Personally, she wanted to do the job. And do it so well that Harper grew up happy and healthy, in spite of the tragic turn her young life had taken.

"Then go."

"Really?"

"As a psychiatrist and as a business partner, I say yes. I know you'll do a great job and call for backup if you find yourself struggling to give Harper your best."

"And as one of my best friends?"

"I don't want your heart hurting anymore, Mar. At the same time, if by some miracle you're coming fully back to life, and somehow this little one is instrumental in that, then even if it hurts now, it would be worth it for you to be able to live more fully."

"I'm fully alive." Not everyone had to be passionate to get the most out of their existence.

"This isn't a conversation we need to be having on the phone. Just…promise me one thing?"

She'd promise Kelly anything if it were in her power to make it happen. "What?"

"If you get into trouble, you call me again. Friend me, not partner or therapist me."

"You don't even have to ask that one. I would think you'd know that. And besides, you've been telling us all since we got our degrees that you couldn't be our therapist, as it wouldn't be ethical."

"I want your promise anyway."

"I promise to call you if I get into any trouble."

She promised a second time. Told her friend she loved her and hung up.

She had one more phone call to make before her new charge woke up.

And couldn't help the smile that spread across her face as she glanced toward that partially closed door.

Hand shaking, Michael stared at the wobbling picture he held. Ruth and Phillip Morris, the local antique storeowners the sheriff had recommended to him, were in the front room, giving him time alone to search through the rubble in June and Ryan's bedroom. The photo had been lodged under a pressboard nightstand, protected by the base, and was completely intact.

How that could be when the rest of the room was unsalvageable, he didn't know. Two people had lost their lives there, and the frame's glass was still intact.

The image blurred, and for a moment, he let it. Remembering the day the picture had been taken. Their dad, a medical technician, had been called into work and they'd spent the whole day playing video games, vying for an overall win that would have the loser doing the other's chores for an entire week. They'd been seven and ten at the time. Home alone all day.

He'd let June win, but she'd come close to doing it on her own.

They'd made dinner together. Boxed mac and cheese. And had leftovers waiting when their dad got home. They'd done the dishes, too—June's suggestion. And their dad—he'd been proud of them. Or grateful, at least. And had snapped the picture on the brand-new flip phone—complete with a camera that was .3 megapixels and could only hold twenty pictures—that he'd won at a raffle at work. The old man had loved that phone.

Michael had been fascinated by the technology.

They'd gone to the print shop in town to print out the picture at some point. Their dad had framed it.

Wiping tears from his eyes before they could

fall, he sucked in his bottom lip. There'd been a good moment or two.

But the picture told him something else, too. June didn't name him guardian of her child because she thought Michael was up to the task. She'd named him guardian because she must have somehow gone backward in time, remembering from the perspective of a seven-year-old. Because that same picture had come into play later, too. When she'd screamed at him, with tears streaming down her face, asking him why he couldn't be the guy he'd been at ten. Why couldn't he just be like that?

Maybe at seven she hadn't been aware of their dad getting drunk, getting mad at Michael for messing with his cell phone and backhanding him across the face.

The old man had told him to leave the damned thing alone. There was no way they could afford to get it fixed or replace it if Michael broke it. But he'd had to get his hands on it. To explore its functions. Try to figure out the design of the pieces inside, to know how they all fit together, worked together. He'd had the back off when his dad had found him with the device.

The only damage done had been to his jaw, but he'd never touched the phone again.

Grabbing a piece of clothing left on a hanger in

the closet, a red shirt that had to have belonged to June, he carefully wrapped the photo. He'd already found the stuffed cat. A lot of Harper's things had been unscathed by the storm, just as she had been. Phillip and Ruth were going to pack up the entire room and have everything shipped to his place.

They'd gone through the rest of the house already. Some things they'd put in storage until he figured out what to do with them until Harper was old enough to take possession. Dishes and other personal things would also be shipped to him. If Harper wanted to eat off those dishes while she was with him, if it would make her transition easier, he'd put them in his cupboard.

He didn't have to stay any longer, and yet he wasn't leaving.

When his phone rang, he answered almost as eagerly as a drowning man grabbing for a life raft.

"Michael? It's Mariah." Her number was already programmed on his phone. He knew who was calling. And his heart started to thud.

"Is Harper okay?"

"She's still asleep, actually. This is the longest she's gone without waking up since I've been here. I think knowing you're here, knowing that she has someplace to go and someone to belong to, might have put her at ease."

"Or she's just exhausted and her body is just

giving up the fight." He didn't live in a land of nicety-nice and hoping for the best. He went with facts and truth and most of the time, in his experience, the first two—niceness and hope—were lacking.

So if there was no change with Harper, was she calling to tell him she'd work for him? Or that she wouldn't?

"Did you find the picture? Or Shadow?"

"I found both. And cleared out her dresser and closet, too, so she'll have all of her own clothes." Would that win him enough points with her to get her to come to work for him?

"Great call. And thank God for Shadow and the picture. Let's introduce Shadow tonight. Bring her when you come for dinner and you be the one to give her to her. And then tomorrow, before she leaves with you, we'll give her the picture and explain that you're Mikey all grown up, just like her mother grew up from the little girl in that picture."

The woman had a way of making everything seem so simple. And doable.

A way of putting him at ease.

He wasn't used to that. Found it a bit off-putting. And nice in an odd kind of way.

He didn't like, at all, the *before she leaves with you* phrase.

"I thought it best that we have dinner here," she said next, giving more sound reasoning.

"And I've decided to accept your job offer," she continued right on without pause. "With conditions."

His knees went weak. He wanted to weep. And to shout a hallelujah. "Bring them on," he said, not the least bit concerned. Whatever they were, he'd honor them.

"It's only for a short time. Not more than a week or two. As soon as Harper is settled and acclimating, I have to go. We can't give her the impression that I'm a permanent part of her life."

He didn't like it. At all. Would rather play it by ear. But… People could change their minds. "Fine."

"And I have to be in the background. You'll need to take on her care, communicating with her, cooking for her, from the very beginning."

He didn't like that one, either. "I assume you'll be coaching me on all of it."

"Of course. I just need it clear that I'm not a nanny. I'm a child life specialist, there to assist you both as you adjust to your new normal. I am not there to be a part of that normal."

The woman was giving him a headache. But he needed her.

And, again, people could always change their minds.

Or he could get lucky and find a new family for Harper within the week or two Mariah was giving him. "I understand."

"Okay, good. So, I suggest that we leave early in the morning, at dawn or just before, and take the back roads out of town so that Harper doesn't start the trip by staring at all of the destruction. She's seen so much already, and we want to minimize the lasting impact at this point by giving her as few memories of the storm's physical aftermath as possible."

In a matter of hours, he would be taking physical custody of a four-year-old child. Putting her in his car with the bags of her belongings he was loading into it now. Bringing her home to live with him for the time being. Exposing her to his lack of familial capabilities.

We.

Mariah had said *we.*

And because of that, he knew he could allow the rest to take place.

Chapter Six

The five-and-a-half-hour drive from Marietta to Little Rock provided far too much time for Mariah to question her choices. What was she doing, sitting in a luxury SUV with a man whose hands on the wheel seemed to be connected invisibly and directly to her libido? Every time he slid those fingers and palms along the leather covering, she imagined them sliding along her body.

And each time she'd glance back at Harper, who was sound asleep in her car seat, and reset herself. The little girl hadn't let go of Shadow since her uncle had handed the stuffed cat to her the night before, other than to set her on the edge of the tub when Mariah helped her with her bath.

The last bath she'd be giving her. It would be up to Michael to run her water and help her wash her hair from then on. She'd coach as needed, but nothing else.

Boundaries had to be firmly established and held.

Even as Harper slept, she clutched the toy between her elbow and her side. Protected.

Ryan, the purple teddy, was on the seat beside her. At Harper's insistence.

The picture Michael had given her early that morning after he lifted Harper up into the back seat of his car was back there, too. On the seat where she'd set it. Upside down, so the photo didn't show.

Remembering how Michael had explained that he was Mikey, all grown up, and seeing the preschooler's nose scrunch up in question, and then soften into a frown as she rejected his statement, brought a lump to Mariah's throat even hours later. He'd repeated himself four times. Explaining that just like Mama grew up, so did Mikey, but she'd just kept shaking her head. Saying, *No, Mikey, not him*, and pointing to the photo.

"It'll come in time." Mariah broke the silence that had been hanging for close to half an hour as she watched miles and miles of cornfields, some already harvested, some not, flying by on that balmy early-September Saturday. "She'll accept that Mikey and Uncle Mike are one and the same."

"Or she won't." He shrugged, as though it was no big deal either way, but she knew differently. She'd seen how hard he'd tried, seen the tension on his face, followed by disappointment when Mariah had intervened, and he'd finally given up trying to convince Harper that he was telling her the truth. For all she knew, they'd still be standing back in a church parking lot in Marietta if she hadn't distracted the two of them from their adamant stances.

"There are going to be a lot of times that you're right, but Harper won't accept what you say as truth. Some of that comes with the territory of a little one testing boundaries as they explore their worlds, but in Harper's case, she might reject a lot of what's coming at her right now. It's not personal. It's just her way of maintaining some kind of control over her life.

"It'll help if you just let things go after the second try. Just kind of make a rule. You try twice and let it go. Unless it has to do with her health or safety, of course."

"Don't pressure her, you mean."

Shrugging, she stared out the front windshield, rather than at the man in second-day clothes, looking as delicious to her wrinkled as he had the day before when he'd been pristine. The hotel had had all necessary toiletry essentials. But those wrinkles... Something about them called out to her.

They were kind of like the man himself... When you first met him, he seemed so put together, you'd think you'd never met anyone who was so balanced and right all the time. But when you spent a day with him, other things started to show.

Like how hurt he'd been when Harper had rejected him as "her" Mikey.

"Another thing that will help is to give her a choice anytime you possibly can, rather than just making all decisions for her." She was there to work. And work she would.

His chin jutted as he nodded. And then, not taking his gaze from the freeway, said, "An example, please?"

"When you drove through for breakfast, instead of just ordering the kids' meal, you could have given her a choice of say, three things from the menu that you wouldn't have minded her having."

"There was only one breakfast kids' meal."

"So offer her a biscuit and egg sandwich off the regular menu. She won't finish it all, if she chooses it, but leftover food is a small price to pay for building her sense of control by allowing her to make the choice. As you get better at it, maybe you adjust your own order to compensate for what you know she won't finish, and then you do."

He glanced over at her. Seemed about to say something, and then glanced in the rearview mirror, obviously considering his niece in the car, not wanting her to possibly overhear, and remained silent.

Taking his cue, Mariah remained silent as well.

Future conversations regarding Harper would take place without the child present. Which would give them something to talk about anytime they might find themselves alone over the next week or two.

A good plan.

One she needed to remember. And stick to.

No matter what.

Mariah had one suitcase. A big duffel on rollers. Michael started for it first as soon as he'd put his SUV in Park in his three-car garage and turned off the engine. As though the presence of her bags in his home could somehow make her stay as long as he needed her.

"What is this place?" He heard Harper's question as he got one foot out the door.

Mariah stopped him with a hand on his arm before he'd put any weight on that foot. And then she said, "Harper asked you a question."

Not really, she hadn't. She just put it out there. Not specifying either of them.

"It's my house," he told her, turning around to give her a smile. And felt his heart lurch when those big brown eyes framed by wayward blond curls stared him down. So much like her mother, he had to look away.

"It's your new home," Mariah backed him up. "Yours and Shadow's and Ryan's."

He watched the little girl from the rearview mirror. She clutched the stuffed cat tightly to her chest, her little lower lip stuck out in a way he recognized as not good. Funny how he'd remember such a thing from so long ago. How it seemed familiar to him.

"Come on, let's go show Shadow her new room. You want to?" Mariah continued, sounding as cheerful as a day on the beach as she remained turned awkwardly in her seat, facing Harper.

Shadow's new room. Not Harper's.

He caught the distinction. Obviously, Mariah knew the frown, too. From Harper? Or because all kids got similar looks, not just June and now her daughter?

"It's a big-girl room with a bed and dresser. I brought all your clothes and you can show me where you want them in the drawers." He latched on to the clues Mariah was handing him.

"Where's Mama?"

He gulped. Couldn't speak.

"Mama died." Mariah's words seemed harsh to him. Too harsh. Ready to tell her so, he remembered that the child would also hear and remained silent.

"What's *died*?"

What the hell? Hadn't they told her...? He was sure he'd been told she knew...

Up on her knees, Mariah leaned over to the back seat. Michael watched her take Harper's hand and place it on her chest. "You feel that beating?"

Harper's gaze locked to Mariah's, the little one nodded.

"That's your heart beating. Mama's heart isn't beating anymore. That's died."

He couldn't breathe. Couldn't do this. Not any of it. A four-year-old child needing to learn about the death of her mother, Mariah being such a calming force in the face of such awfulness.

Why in the hell hadn't they told her?

"When will she be back?" Oh, God. The constrictions on his throat tightened. There was a plethora of work waiting for him. Stacks of it. Literally. Requests for his services.

Thinking about building projects calmed him. Reminded him of who he was and what he did.

And what he most certainly had to do immediately.

Find a permanent, loving, healthy and safe home for his sister's daughter.

"She's not coming back." Mariah's words fell softly between them.

Harper harrumphed. He saw her disgruntled expression in the mirror. And then she said, "Maybe let's show Shadow a room." And Michael's heart cracked a bit more.

Mariah stopped short at the door to the room Michael showed them to, calling it the place where Shadow could sleep. Not Shadow's room. The word choice hit her hard as they followed him up a wide, winding, carpeted staircase, but she pushed the unease aside, not yet ready to worry about him not giving Harper a permanent home, as she caught a glimpse of the space he'd shown them. Harper had clutched her all the way up the stairs, having refused to take the hand Michael held out to her and grabbing Mariah's. Now the little girl dropped her hand and stepped into the room. Turning a circle as she looked around her.

"I don't get it," Mariah said. Mouth hanging open, she shook her head and looked again.

From the single-size white, antique-looking press wood bed to two matching dressers, and a small rocking chair with a doll in the corner, the room made no sense to her at all.

Even with all his money, no way he could have had all of that done from Friday night to Saturday afternoon. And why would he, when he didn't plan to keep Harper?

Unless... Had he moved mountains because he'd changed his mind and was committed to raising his sister's child?

Harper had moved to the little rocking chair. Was kneeling in front of it, speaking softly in her little voice. Mariah couldn't make out all the words, but it sounded like she was asking the doll something. Shadow sat upright beside her, also facing the chair.

"June was in rehab for the third time," Michael said quietly, "when our father died. He was just renting the house and had to be out, so I had everything moved into storage. I told June that her things were waiting for her, when she got well, but she never did. Not while I was around," he corrected himself. "After she made it clear I wasn't ever to contact her, I had her things moved here. Well, to the house I had then. Just in case. I know it's a teenager's room, not a four-year-old's, the bed's high and there aren't any safety bars or anything, but..." He shrugged.

"It's been, what, ten years since you told June her things were waiting for her?" He'd obviously moved up in the world. Moved to a new home. And he still had the room waiting?

He shrugged. "I told her to call." And was never without his phone. He'd said that before.

"You'd still have taken her in."

"Of course."

"You don't believe you're family material." Did he not see the ludicrousness of that assertion? That his actions spoke a far different truth?

"I was the one who screwed up her life. I owed her."

He had it all worked out. Was diligently stick-

ing to his perception of the facts. And she didn't
see them his way at all. The man had a room in
his home allotted to his younger sister who'd never
once visited. She couldn't get over it.

But she got one thing clearly even if he didn't—
family mattered to him.

There were no sheets on the bed. No sheets
in his home that fit it. June's had been eaten by
moths long ago. The covering didn't really fit, either. He'd found it in an old trunk of his mother's
and figured June might know the history of it.
Because it appeared homemade, he'd kept it out
of storage.

And because a service cleaned his house, and
he'd never laundered the quilt when he did his own
stuff, he couldn't be sure if the thing had been
washed in the five years he'd owned the home.

The room had been tidied regularly, but never
used.

Mariah had assured him the room, the furniture, was just fine for Harper.

As a rule, the door was kept shut. It faced the
front of the house, got afternoon sun. As did his
own large suite at the other end of the upstairs
loft, but his faced the back of the house, too, with
a view of the lake and a balcony.

He'd given Mariah the other lake-view bedroom, also because it was directly across from Harper's room.

They didn't linger there, though. Instead, the three of them went shopping for sheets and a comforter for Harper's room. Michael was fine after Mariah's suggestion to let Harper make her own choices regarding the room. Anything to make her happy and feel like she had some ownership of her surroundings. It would just have to be a condition of her adoption that the new parents be willing to let Harper use the same sheets and comforter on her bed in their home. Until Harper no longer needed them.

For that matter, he'd send the whole bedroom set with her, since Mariah deemed it appropriate for the child.

There was no longer any reason to maintain a room for a sister who could never come back.

He knew how to make a bed and volunteered for that task once they'd returned home, but Mariah redirected him, making the bed herself and suggesting he help Harper move her things into the drawers, letting his niece tell him where they should all go. It went well. Following directions, he could do. And she didn't want him touching her things. He'd pick them up in piles from the bags he'd packed, and Harper would hurry to take them from him, telling him she could do it. Dropping one pile on the floor to get to another, if she had to keep him from taking her possessions.

Once he caught on, the process went much better. He didn't unpack another pile until she'd put the previous stack where she wanted it to go.

All in all, she did a fairly usable job as far as he could tell. The underthings and socks were spread over three drawers. Shirts and pajamas were stuffed in one big one.

And pants and shorts each had a drawer.

Shoes had a drawer, too. He'd set them on the carpeted floor of the closet and she'd retrieved them and put them away.

Fine with him. The drawers were all going with her. Made sense that her things be in the same place in her new home as they were in his temporary one.

Another note for the new parents. They had to agree to leave her drawers arranged as she wanted them until she was exhibiting behaviors of having taken ownership of her new home.

"When's Mama coming?" she asked when he'd finished one big bag and had moved on to the second. Michael froze.

Mariah, who'd been finishing up on the other side of the room, didn't miss a beat, though. "She's not coming back," she said, then Harper shut her finger in the drawer. He was there immediately, wanting to take a look, wrapping an arm around her as he knelt by her side, but, crying, she pushed past him and ran to Mariah.

He didn't blame her. Was maybe even relieved.

He'd laid his angst at Mariah Anderson's feet as well.

But was not at all happy with himself when he started to wonder how much better he'd feel if the woman would wrap her arms around him, too.

Chapter Seven

Being in Michael's home, watching the way he'd avert his eyes and yet stay present with every slight Harper handed him, Mariah was having a hard time maintaining control of her emotions.

More than she'd ever struggled on a job before.

In some ways, Michael O'Connell was as vulnerable as Harper. His emotional hurricane was current and blistering, and yet it extended far back into his past, too. From the time his own mother had died, most likely. It didn't sound like anyone had been around to help him back then like she and he were helping Harper.

Funny, how life didn't always work out fair and square.

To do her job, she had to set him up for rejection again and again, stepping back and watching him acclimate to the situation, and to his niece, until Harper felt emotionally safe enough to allow him to help her.

And each time he tried to pretend that her rejection didn't hurt him, she hurt for him. It was like there was some bizarre tie between his heart and hers and every time his heart ached, hers felt it, too.

With Harper it was even worse. She felt like the child was part of her. She didn't just want to help Harper through her trauma; she wanted to guide her through life, be there for her, do all she could to protect the little girl from whatever pains she could spare her.

These were the maternal stirrings she'd felt while carrying Joey—which had made sense back then. Feelings that she'd welcomed, gloried in, opening her heart wide to let every ounce of that love inside.

Those feelings made no sense now, so many years later. For a child that wasn't hers. One she'd known less than a week. Kelly had intimated that it was possible that it was just time, that her heart had been slowly awakening, and this was the case when it roused itself fully, but it didn't feel that way. When she'd tried to imagine getting pregnant again, having a child of her own, her emotional barriers had been as high as ever.

Michael took a dress still on a child-sized hanger out of the bag. Harper took it from him— not impolitely, but with definite purpose—and walked to the closet.

Holding the hanger, she glanced up at the rod,

clearly way too high for her to reach, and then hung the dress on the door handle. With a second garment in hand, Michael approached, took the first one off the handle, and reached up to put both dresses on the rod.

"No!" Harper started to cry. "I wanna do it myself."

Sitting on the floor, she bent her legs, wrapped her little arms around her shins and lowered her face to her knees.

Looking shocked, and worried, Michael quickly took the dresses off the rod and glanced at Mariah, as though expecting her to come save the day.

She couldn't keep saving either of them. She could teach and counsel and suggest, but during these moments that flared up, he had to be able to pull from within himself to manage.

More, she sensed that Michael *could* manage. His memories of the past he'd shared, most particularly with his sister—they were filled with his empathy. His insights.

He was a smart man.

Knew how to problem-solve.

As Harper cried and Michael stood there, looking like he might join his niece on the floor—or bug out—she made herself remain still. Silent.

Michael looked from Mariah to the dresses to the curl-covered bent head. And sat down. Not to bury his head in his lap, though. Instead, he laid the dresses down on the floor at Harper's feet. "The way I see it is, we have two choices here." His voice was calm. Even. And sounding as though he was speaking to a room of businessmen.

Mariah's stomach cramped. Her throat clogged up with tears.

She didn't cry on the job. Never had.

Until Harper.

And now Michael.

Staring toward the bent head, Michael continued. "We either get you a step stool that you'll have to climb up and down every time you want to get a dress down or put one up. Or we put in a second bar that's low enough for you to reach standing on your own."

Harper didn't look up. Didn't respond at all.

But she'd stopped crying.

"You can make the choice. If you don't, I'll have to make it for you. Because there are a lot of dresses and coats in there that have to be hung up on your hangers."

It was more four-year-old logic then thirty-something, the being-on-your-hangers part, but Mariah had a feeling that it was really Michael's logic at the moment. He knew he shouldn't change things that didn't need to be changed. That Harper needed as much of her world to remain the same as possible as she transitioned. They'd talked about it the night before after Harper was asleep and he was back in his hotel room.

Harper seemed frozen. Completely aware and listening, but not moving. Her unnatural stillness said as much. Whether or not Michael got the translation, she didn't know.

"So what's it going to be?"

"Nothing."

"Well, then, since they have to be hung up, I guess I'll just put them on the high bar until you tell me differently." He started to rise.

"No!" Harper turned a wet face up to him, but the jutted chin and frown spoke more of standing her ground than giving in to it.

"Then what do you want to do to solve the problem?"

The little girl stood, arms crossed as she walked purposefully into the closet. "The step first, and a bar, too."

She wanted both.

Not one of the options given to her. One she'd come up with on her own.

Because she was taking ownership, one little decision at a time.

Mariah wanted to whoop at the top of her lungs.

Instead, tearing up, she slipped from the room.

They'd stopped at the grocery store and Michael hadn't even had to be told to defer to Harper in terms of what she wanted for dinner. No way was he going to take a chance on serving up the wrong thing.

She ate every bite of her macaroni and cheese, and even asked for seconds. Asked Mariah, of course. And when the woman deferred to him, telling Harper to ask him, as he was her family now and she'd be leaving, Harper just insisted, "You ask him."

Michael didn't wait for the situation to be resolved. Harper was eating. If she wanted more, she'd have it. He spooned up a second helping and put it in front of her.

She looked at the bowl, not at him, and then pulled it toward herself and dug in.

As far as he was concerned, that was the win, her eating.

Bonding with him wasn't going to matter any more than her bonding with Mariah would. They were both temporaries in her life.

But as he sat in his study after Harper had gone to bed—choosing not to have a story read to her as she had on each of the previous nights she'd been with Mariah—he realized just how critical the timeline had become in terms of finding his niece's forever home.

He was scrolling through a horrendously long list of contacts, waiting for inspiration, for something right to click, when Mariah knocked on the open door.

"We said we'd have a meeting each night I'm here, to discuss anything that can't be said in front of Harper." She reminded him of one of the employment guidelines they'd worked up on the phone the night before—him in his hotel room and her at the church with Harper.

"Right." He stood, grabbed the monitor receiver; that had been a part of another one of their purchases earlier, so he could hear if Harper woke up. It wasn't a good idea for him and Mariah to be alone in the seclusion of his office with only a child sleeping upstairs as chaperone.

"Let's head out to the deck."

It was oversize. Held handmade rockers that he'd commissioned from a client a few years back, along with an entire wicker ensemble with couch and table, and a high-top glass table for four with wicker seating.

Turning on the landscape lighting, he also ignited the gas torches lining the deck, illuminating the immediate vicinity with a soft glow. He barely glanced at the lake that was visible only by a streak of moon glow on the water.

He was heading for a rocker.

His bobbing foot wouldn't be as noticeable in the event that she put him under her microscope again, if he was using it to keep his chair moving.

And a rocker clearly was meant for one person only. Alone. Him.

She took the matching chair. And suddenly he saw a couple of grandparents—not his—sitting together on a balmy September evening, with years of happy memories between them. Maybe their hands would connect, his on top of hers, on the arm of one of the chairs and they'd rock slowly in unison.

And maybe he'd sprout a halo and magically exterminate all of the pain in the world.

Or, better yet, a red-and-blue cape and he'd fly around and stop crime.

"I'm sorry for how hard this must be for you," she started in as soon as they were seated. He'd offered her a beer. She'd declined.

He had one anyway. Just one. That he'd nurse for as long as he could make it last.

"Sorry, I don't have any wine to offer you," he said, in lieu of acknowledging her first comment. She had no reason to apologize to him.

And he didn't like feeling like one of her victims needing solace.

Even if a part of him craved solace. A far different kind of solace than she'd been giving his niece by the gallon full. Harper needed all of that kind she had to give.

No way he'd take any of it away from her.

"I don't drink on the job."

Her words probably weren't meant as a slap in the face. He felt it anyway. Not because of his beer, but because of the reminder that while he could use a friend, she was there as an employee.

An employee who had the upper hand and bossed him around. In her kind and gentle way, of course.

That in itself was a novelty—the bossing. And probably the gentleness, too, though he'd dated women over the years who were quite nice and soft-spoken.

And not at all what he was supposed to be thinking about. They were having a meeting. A business meeting.

He took a sip of his beer—a long one—remembering too late that he was trying to make it last.

He looked through the darkness toward the glow of the lake at the end of his acre of grass and few feet of beach. A flip of a second switch would illuminate, to the immediate right, the dock he'd built a few years back for the boat he was going to get. As soon as he decided what he wanted it for so he'd know what kind to get.

He wasn't much of a fisherman. Speeding around, getting whiplash from bouncing on the water, didn't seem like something he'd do much of. Pontoons were more for gatherings, and he had some of those.

But everyone on the lake who had one, that he knew of, seemed to have family attached to it.

He'd always thought the idea of having a boat was cool. He'd built the dock based on a kid's perception of life. And there it sat.

"You did great today." Mariah's voice broke into his pleasant boat reverie. His pondering of a problem he could actually solve anytime he chose.

The very next day if he so chose. Even with it being a Sunday. Maybe the speedboat to start with. He didn't have to run it at Mach.

But probably should run that quickly from the desire slowly building within him every time she touched those long, red curls of hers. And he knew how badly he wanted to stroke them, too.

"At the grocery store, you knew instinctively what to do. And the hanger thing, that was brilliant."

He had a higher-than-average IQ. Had been deemed brilliant a time or two in his professional world.

The hanger episode definitely was not brilliance.

It was a last resort. "I didn't appreciate you leaving me there hanging out to dry. The poor thing was sobbing." And he'd hired Mariah to help with exactly that kind of thing.

"I told you, Michael, I'm only here to guide you.

I'd have stepped in if you'd bungled the situation, but you didn't. You handled it as well or better than I could have scripted. You gave her the choice, you provided reason for the choice on a level she could process, then you established firm boundaries and set consequences in the event that she didn't respect the boundaries."

He hadn't done any of that. He'd solved a problem presented at the last minute of closing an important deal.

Or getting clothes put away, as the case might be.

"Adults have a tendency in traumatic situations with little ones to coddle to the point of giving them whatever they want. Spoiling them."

So, yeah, he was definitely guilty of that. Macaroni and cheese at the grocery store and again at the dinner table, as cold hard proof.

"The guardians don't realize that all that really does is set the child, and them as trusted authority figures, back further. Children need boundaries. These not only establish a means by which little ones learn to live within a society, but they also give them security. A four-year-old can know what she wants in the moment, but she can't possibly know what's best for her. Her brain isn't capable of reasoning to that level yet. She'll eat an entire chocolate bunny if you let her, not caring that it will likely make her sick to her stomach. Her feelings of safety come in knowing that someone is there to tell her what she can and can't do while still giving her autonomy wherever possible."

He hadn't known any of that. He'd simply looked at a bar that was too high, a little girl who had to hang her clothes. And come up with a logical solution. Could be that the next logical solution wouldn't work out so well for Harper.

"That said, depending on what happens tomorrow, I might head out at the beginning of the week. The sooner I can get out of her life, the better for both of you."

Not for him. Absolutely not for him.

And not for Harper, either. How could Mariah not see that?

"I'll be going back to work on Monday." He threw out what occurred to him first.

"I don't recommend that. Do you have any vacation time coming?"

"Not that I can take at the moment. I have to wrap up the business I was traveling for this past week." A huge European project that had been awarded to him. He'd promised more detailed preliminary designs to be passed among those in charge of funding. "I need at least a couple of days…"

"So Wednesday, then."

Wednesday was better than Monday. And still

far too soon. That gave him three days, one being Sunday, to find a new family, vet them, get paperwork done enough for them to take custody, get them introduced to Harper so Mariah could work her magic... He was brilliant. He wasn't a magician.

"I said at least a couple of days. It could take longer." He had to have more time. It was the biggest problem in front of him at that moment.

"Hire a nanny. You'll need one, anyway, or some other child care arrangements, for when you go back to work."

Back to work? He wasn't *leaving* work. Sipped beer. Tried to relax the tightness in his chest. The meeting wasn't going at all well. Generally, when that happened, he ended it. Gave everyone time to think. Reassessed the viability of the project on the table.

Harper was most definitely viable. Didn't need time to reassess that one. And, for her sake, he couldn't afford to lose this deal.

"You want me to introduce yet another stranger into Harper's intimate space before she's even acclimated to me?"

Didn't she get that he needed her? For more than just Harper? Did she feel none of the chemistry between them? Was it all him? Yeah, there was some bit of need on his part, because of Harper, but the chemistry—that had nothing to do with his niece.

He'd been studying Mariah as he'd had the thought and she moved, more like squirmed. As though she'd read his thoughts.

Did she feel something, too?

And if she did... He had absolutely no idea how she'd feel about that. Had no idea if she was free to ponder such feelings, if indeed they did exist mutually between them, or if he was willing to explore them. Big *if*s. Coupled with another huge one—if she was willing to explore them.

He didn't know because he knew nothing about Mariah Anderson other than what he'd read online about Sierra's Web, and the partner bios on their website—and what he'd experienced firsthand. He'd asked her to come home with him, to move into his home, to stay an indeterminate amount of time—for Harper's sake—and had no idea what kind of sacrifices doing so was causing in her own personal life.

"Is it too late to add another fault to my long list?" he asked.

"What?" Frowning, she shook her head a little, like she was confused. Which he supposed she should be, not having been along on the thirty-second mental ride he'd just taken.

"Single-mindedness. I consider the problem right before me. And I set about solving it without taking time to look around and see what else might be needing attention."

"That's a character trait, and one that's not all that uncommon in highly intelligent people. It's not necessarily a fault."

He wasn't letting her let him off the hook.

"I've just realized that I haven't even considered how being here is affecting the rest of your life," he told her. "I'm sorry, Mariah. As much as I want you here, as much as I see that Harper needs you, I should have asked you what kind of hardships this might bring upon you. Instead, I did what I do. I saw the best solution to the problem before me and I pressured you, with your own logic and fact, to go along with me."

"I'm not here because of any pressure you put on me," she said, not so quickly that he could read instinctive denial instead of truth. "I'm a big girl, Michael. I know how to handle pressure. If I didn't think my being here was the right thing, I wouldn't be here."

He started to relax. To smile even. To take a long deep breath. And a smaller sip of beer.

Until he saw the way her brows came together. The tightness in her clasped hands.

And sensed there might be a *but* coming.

Chapter Eight

He'd changed clothes before they'd gone to the grocery store. The jeans and T-shirt did not help her libido calm down. To the contrary, that butt, those thighs...

How cruel was fate to bring on the most intense sexual feelings she'd ever had in her life at such an inappropriate time? For a man she couldn't have?

He wanted her to stay.

She wanted to stay.

She couldn't stay.

"We do need to be working on an exit plan, though, not a settling-in time. I thought I made that clear yesterday. I'm only here to help you and Harper transition. Nothing more."

"Is there someone waiting at home for you? Someone you need to get back to?"

The glint in his eye made her belly squirm in a delicious way. Better than any food she'd ever consumed. The question was...normal enough.

He was being kind. Thinking of her instead of just what was in front of him.

And yet it felt so personal.

Another sure sign that she had to go.

"I live alone," she told him.

"Where?"

Definitely not a work question.

Though, to be fair, Sandra, the social worker, had asked the same question when they'd been chatting late one night. As had some of the parents who'd come to pick up their children from her.

"I currently own a condo in New Orleans, and I have an apartment in Phoenix, too." She told him what she'd told them.

"You have two homes?" He sounded as though she'd told him she lived on Mars.

She shrugged, feeling defensive all of a sudden. They were more like stopping places where she stored belongings. "The apartment in Phoenix is a studio. I don't keep any personal mementos there. Just some generic pictures I bought for the walls, toiletries and clothes, of course, and a kitchen filled with my choices. Our home office is there and so I spend a lot of time in the city."

Shut up. Stop talking. You don't have to justify anything to him. If he thought her lifestyle odd, he did. His approval of her personal choices wasn't part of their plan.

"The New Orleans place is larger, six rooms. And has a whole room filled with books." She smiled. She'd always loved to read. Just knowing the books were there, with her grandmother's rocker in the corner, made her feel better.

"Are you seeing anyone?"

"No."

She'd answered too quickly. Shouldn't have answered at all.

"Where do you go from here?"

"Wherever the next job takes me. Schools are all back in session for the year and we typically get calls from administrations experiencing problems with bullying. Clients call the firm, and off we go. Sierra's Web took off in a way none of us had expected and we are constantly taking on new experts just to handle all of the business."

"Has there ever been a time when you've had more work than you can take on?"

His interest felt…good. And engaged her thinking with nonsexual thoughts.

"Not yet." She held up crossed fingers. "I have a staff of specialists who work for me full-time, as experts in court cases, in schools and hospitals, as well as emergency trauma situations. And I've got a list of vetted experts for one-time contracted use as well."

"How much time do you spend at home in any given year?"

Getting a little more personal. A little less safe

for her current state of mind. Regarding him. Or Harper.

"Mostly just weekends in New Orleans, and I'm there fairly often. During the week when I have downtime, I'm in Phoenix at the home office."

"What about holidays?"

"I have family, my parents and an older brother, who's married. They all live in Ohio. I go there sometimes. But truthfully, my Sierra's Web partners and I spend a lot of our holidays together." She smiled. "We took a cruise once over Christmas and New Year's. It was odd, but good."

As good as a time could be after losing your heart, your child and your marriage. Her friends had planned the cruise specifically for her. And she'd made it through the holiday intact.

His gaze took on a new look, an interested look, and she took note. And precaution. She didn't need him curious. Or interested.

She needed him to respect her judgment, do as she said, get it together for his niece and let her get out of there. Before that departure hurt her more than she could bear.

She'd stay long enough for him to grow enough confidence to know that he was exactly what Harper needed. That he was enough.

And that the love he so obviously felt for Harper was the healthiest thing he'd ever be able to give her.

Because she was certain of all of that.

"So, there's really no reason you can't stay a little longer...if necessary."

Statement more than question. Alarms went off, but she didn't think they were professional ones. Had to weigh what she could take versus what was best for the job.

In Marietta, that reading had been pretty clear to decipher. In Michael's home, things were growing cloudier by the second. He said he wasn't into family, but the home he'd built—not just the structure, which he'd told her he'd designed and had constructed, but inside—was the warmest, most beautiful home she'd ever been in. She was already feeling a part of it and she hadn't even slept there yet.

"I can't guarantee that I'll be here more than a few more days," she told him. "That's all it should take for you and Harper to get used to each other, accept each other, enough for me to fade out. The timing is critical," she reminded both of them. "If I'm here too long, she'll grow too attached to me and not need you as much."

"She wouldn't even let me read her a bedtime story," he said. "Nor would she look at me at the dinner table. Her security is clearly still one hundred percent with you."

And she was a mother figure. It didn't need to

matter, but clearly, with Harper, it did. "I'm guess-
ing her dad left a lot of Harper's daily care to her
mom. Which is why it's most important that I defer
to you in all things."

"So, if we work together, you defer, I do as
much as she'll let me, will it be better for her if
you hang around a few extra days, or better for
her to have you leave before she can look at me?"

He'd know the answer to that. Because it was
right there in his words. The logic was unmistak-
able. Obviously, it would be better for Harper to
feel comfortable with Michael before Mariah disappeared out of her life.

"What's not going to be better for Harper is
for her to sense how much I care. And I'm honestly not sure I can prevent her from feeling that."
There. She had her own issues. And logic that went
with them.

He frowned. "I don't understand. You never
spend more than a few days with any one child?
I got the impression from what I read that you've
spent up to a month on a case before."

There'd been mention on the Sierra's Web site
about a project she and a team of her people had
taken on, helping with children at the border who'd
been orphaned.

She had to tell him. He deserved to make an

informed decision. Harper was his. "Harper's different."

"Different?" He'd set his beer down, cocked his head to the side as he frowned. "You've cared for plenty of orphans. Why is she different?"

"She's not different. I'm different around her."

"How so?"

Really? Her gaze implored him.

His held steady on his quest.

And she wished to God she knew why Michael and Harper were bringing forth feelings from her that, while completely different, were inundating her with things she'd never expected to feel again.

Things she seemed to need, suddenly, like the air she breathed.

Which was not logical.

She wasn't herself. Was overreacting.

Her whole life was about coping with drama. Not causing it or wallowing.

"I'm feeling things around Harper that I only felt once before in my life." More information than she should have shared.

"What kind of things?"

"Mother type things." There she'd said it. Let it go.

"You felt them once before? With another client?"

"I lost a child." The words blurted out of her. She felt them coming. Let them. "A baby."

His mouth fell open. He leaned forward, his elbows dropping to his knees abruptly, as if he'd gotten that far and didn't know what to do. His gaze, warm and clear blue, never leaving hers.

If he were a man who was too selfish to care for anyone else, wouldn't he be sitting there wondering why she'd blurted what she had rather than showing compassion?

Could her heart handle his showing that to her on top of all of the other feelings she was fighting where he was concerned?

She'd known him two days.

Why did it feel like two months, two years, two lifetimes?

"Can you tell me about him?"

She shouldn't. Could she stop herself?

"His name was Joey."

Joseph Winchester Anderson.

"How old was he?" His gaze never left hers. She couldn't seem to pull hers away. Whatever storm had arisen inside her wasn't diminishing.

Like a hurricane, it just kept coming with threats of severe flooding.

"Eight months ges…tation." She stumbled over the word. Her little guy hadn't even had a chance to breathe a single breath of life. "I was eight months pregnant when he was stillborn."

"Oh, my God, Mariah. I'm sorry. I'm so sorry."

She tried to smile. Wanted to tell him, as he'd earlier told her, that it wasn't anything to do with him. Instead, she teared up. Shrugged.

And when she could, when he continued just to sit there with her, focused on her, she said, "He had some problems. They knew he had Down syndrome, but otherwise appeared completely healthy. They were monitoring him so closely and I wanted him so badly." The Down diagnosis, while hugely saddening in one perspective, if she thought about the limitations, hadn't bothered her at all in another. Most Down children were extremely happy and loving, and what mattered on earth more than anything was that her child would be happy. He'd love and in so doing, bring love upon himself.

She'd been ready for the adventure. Ready for him. To be his mom.

And then...

"My husband... We'd only been married a short time before I got pregnant. Turned out, we didn't know each other as well as we'd thought we had."

She shook her head. Broke eye contact.

"He wasn't there for you."

She shook her head. Could feel him still watching her but couldn't meet his gaze. She looked toward the lake instead. Had spent some time gazing at it from her balcony before she'd come down for the meeting. Had watched the last of the sunset from there while giving Michael some playtime with Harper before she'd gone to bed.

When she'd come out of her room to join them, they'd been in Harper's space across the hall. Michael had been sitting on her bed, scrolling on his phone and she'd been in the corner with a very expensive tablet, watching a video. Harper had found his tablet in his office—why they'd been there, Mariah didn't yet know—and had evidently taken it without asking, gone upstairs to her room and found the video on her own. Michael had followed right behind her.

That had been Mariah's agenda item for the evening's meeting. The conversation they needed to have about letting her do whatever she wanted to do.

Not Joey.

Not any of the rest of it.

"He probably was," Michael said softly, his words lingering in the balmy night air. "He probably just didn't know what to do. How to show you."

His words sent a wave of alert through her. Michael was speaking from experience. With June? Not knowing how to help and being unable to care for family members were two entirely different things.

"He showed me just fine how he felt, and seemed

to do exactly what he intended," she said now, opening up parts of her she'd never intended to share. But if showing what John being a real jerk had done to her family would illuminate for Michael that that wasn't him, then she was willing to open up. "He was there in the emergency room when I delivered," she said. "And as soon as they left us alone for a moment, with Joey on my chest, giving us a moment with him, to say goodbye, my ex-husband's words of comfort, right before he said he had to get back to work, were, 'It's for the best.'" She didn't tear up.

She choked on the word, instead.

Michael wanted to pick up Mariah right out of her chair and carry her away to some brilliant place where the air was spiked with happiness. He'd send Harper with her.

Everyone could just quit hurting.

Of course, that place didn't exist.

He didn't have any words that could make anything better. No way to solve the pains in either Harper's or Mariah's hearts.

What it seemed to him was that they could do that for each other, though.

Maybe… Could it be that his solution was sitting right in front of him? Would Mariah want to adopt Harper?

"I can't stay if my personal feelings continue to escalate." Mariah broke the silence that had fallen after her emergency room recitation. "It's not fair to Harper, first and foremost. And it's not good for me, either. I need to be able to do my job without my personal past getting in the way."

He searched for words. Drew a blank. Felt like he was failing her. Wanted to take her hand and just hold on.

He was her employer, even if her job was to tell him what to do.

"I can't make it better." He gave her what he had. "I would if I could, but I can't." Which was why he focused on what he could excel at—work. Giving the world the talent with which he'd been blessed. And staying away from the areas where he was lacking.

She nodded.

"For what it's worth, I think your ex is too vile to be rat food."

She looked up, smiled at him. You'd think he'd scored a grand-slam home run at a playoff game, the way his adrenaline started racing. He wished it was from something as uncomplicated as baseball.

"I married him without knowing him well enough."

"That doesn't sound like something you'd do." Not that he knew her. And yet, he was fairly certain he *did* know her. In times of trouble, actions said far more than words, and she was there, in his home, because one small girl had been orphaned by a storm.

"Ordinarily it isn't," she agreed. "There were… extenuating circumstances." Her gaze took on a dark glow and she seemed to be studying him.

"What were they?" She'd brought them up.

"Something to talk about another time," she told him, her tone suddenly professional as she sat up straighter in her chair.

Bringing attention to her breasts as they strained against her shirt. Her nipples were taut. And it wasn't at all cold outside.

"I just want to make sure that you're going to facilitate my leaving as soon as possible."

Her words should have been a cold shower on his fascination with those nipples. They were more of an irritant. Like a fly at a picnic. He wanted to brush them away.

But he had responsibilities, Harper being the most urgent and important.

"I've already started the search for someone to adopt her," he assured Mariah. "I'll be up late tonight putting out feelers and hope to have news for you in a day or two. In the meantime, I'll do everything I can to help Harper feel safe enough with me for you to leave us."

He hated the words.

And hated even more the quick nod she gave him. The way she stood with a thank-you. And then a good-night.

Like there was any chance he'd be having one of those.

Chapter Nine

She'd had to get away from him. She was too raw.
Was in unprofessional territory. Was flooding with
desire for a man who'd just reiterated that he was
going to give away his niece.

Right after she'd told him about John being relieved that their son had died.

The two things weren't one and the same.

Michael was trying to protect Harper. Because
he didn't believe he could give her a happy home.
But it could also be that he couldn't see her happy
with him because he didn't want a family.

Not everyone wanted children.

John certainly hadn't—a key fact she should
have known before they'd married. Before he'd
agreed, when she'd suggested it one night, that
they could go without birth control.

They'd been on vacation. Having such a good
time together, sharing a half carafe of wine. Until
the next morning when he'd awoken stone-cold
sober and half-panicked, telling her that they

couldn't take a chance like that again. Couldn't have sex without birth control.

That had been the morning she'd really met her husband. He'd had a vasectomy scheduled before they'd even returned home.

And it had all been downhill from there.

She'd married in haste because John had been the first person who'd ever been able to instill full jump-your-bones passion within her.

Michael was number two. And it was much more intense the second time around.

For a moment down there, she'd actually wanted him to hug her. And to do a lot more.

In some ways she was a stranger to herself. Living in her own skin, but it was covering another woman's body.

She checked quickly on Harper and shut herself in the bedroom she'd been allotted way down the hall from Michael, on the other side of the stairs. Because the unusual home featured an upstairs loft, the two rooms were mirrors of each other, the huge expanse between them featuring a hallway that looked down over the great room below.

Still buzzing with unshed tears mixed with a heavy dose of unrequited desire, Mariah put on the light purple cotton, capri-length pajama bottoms and matching top she'd packed in the to-go bag she'd grabbed quickly for the Marietta trip, and climbed into bed. She'd been up since four. Was running on empty in so many ways.

After a good night's sleep, she'd feel like herself again. Be ready to give Harper exactly what she needed from her. The gentle, watchful distance to notice Michael.

And yet... As she lay awake in the dark, listening to the silence of his house, smelling the fresh-air scent of the sheets upon which she lay, she wondered about helping Harper attach to Michael. If he was really going to give the child away—and she was believing more so that it might happen—then it was only going to harm Harper further to start to find family again, only to have him also stripped away from her.

She couldn't take Harper from Michael. But she didn't want to leave her with him, either.

Eventually, sometime after she'd heard a door close in the distance, she knew he was in his room, and wondered if he'd remembered to bring the monitor receiver upstairs with him.

They'd left Harper's door open so she could come find them if she woke up. But did Michael remember to latch the gate he'd installed at the top of the stairs that afternoon to prevent Harper from falling down the stairs in the middle of the night?

They were wide, carpeted steps. She probably wouldn't roll far. Had seemed to enjoy playing on them when they'd first arrived at the house and were carrying things in.

But in the dark…

She got up, opened her door so slowly it took forever, tiptoed out into the hall far enough to see the gate securely closed and made her way back to her room.

Still no guarantee he had the monitor with him.

She left her door open partway, just in case, and drifted off to sleep.

Or thought she did.

One second she was worrying about Harper; the next she was sitting straight up in the dark, hearing the little girl cry out.

The sound had awoken her every night for the past four nights, and she was out of bed, across the hall, before she'd fully opened her eyes.

And stumbled into the man standing a foot away from Harper's bed, as though frozen, facing the little body that, half-covered in blankets, was turned toward the wall.

Michael didn't even seem to notice when Mariah's hand hit his side, while the other landed somewhere near his chest. She felt hair. Quickly stepped back, warm, alive and also relieved, as she studied Harper.

The nightmares were upsetting, but they were natural, too. The good news was, Harper appeared to be sleeping through the current one, despite her whimpers. A definite sign of improvement.

And her uncle was taking his responsibility to heart.

Also good. She wasn't going to make too much out of that. Didn't mean he'd keep Harper. To the contrary, being awoken in the night by a little girl's cries might make him more rushed to find her another home.

Still, he was there. And not leaving or stepping away, even with Mariah's arrival.

Backing slowly out of the room, she left Michael to his vigil, her hands still tingling with warmth from his skin.

And spent the rest of the night squirming for his body.

Awake. And in her dreams.

He'd been through his entire contact list. Twice. Once before bed, and once just after dawn, before he got in the shower that morning. Nothing had clicked in terms of a family for Harper. There were agencies, but he'd already decided he didn't want to give her up to a complete stranger. He wanted connection between them.

Wanted to know her family.

He wanted to play a distant role—as he'd have

done if June had really wanted him in Harper's life. If she'd ever once contacted him.

Tackling the problem before him was the only way he knew how to live. Most particularly when his world was resting on a time bomb.

Mariah was going to go. *Had* to go.

For her own sake. For Harper's. And for his, too.

Those fingers of hers against his skin...no way to solve that problem, which meant he had to walk away from it. Just as he'd had to walk away from June.

Just because you wanted something didn't mean you pushed for it until you got it. Not when it involved you interfering in someone else's life.

And the fire Mariah had lit within him with those fingers on his chest would definitely burn her if he didn't walk away from it. It would have him pursue her. And even if she wanted him, too, even if the sex was mind-numbing perfection, even if he wasn't her boss and she wasn't leaving, it would still burn her. She might still want a family. Maybe she was going to do something about it. Maybe she'd be in limbo with pain from what she'd lost, for the rest of her life, but one thing was clear. She'd already been unbearably hurt by a man who didn't want a child. No way another such man would be a good thing in her life.

He heard the preschooler talking as he came out

of the shower—having an entire conversation as though she had a lot to say, but he couldn't make out the words. Could just hear the tone of the sweet voice. Easy. No fear. No worry.

Just chatting.

He dried quickly. Kept glancing toward the monitor receiver, had turned it up actually, and could still hardly hear even at full volume. Pulling on jeans and a black polo shirt, he slid into black leather slip-ons and headed out the door in search of that voice.

Was she talking to Shadow?

Was it wrong of him to want to eavesdrop? To have this little window into her mind so that he could better help her be happy?

He stepped slowly along the carpeted hallway, not wanting to alert her to his presence lest she clam up the cheerful conversation, and then stopped completely.

The monitor hadn't been picking up Harper's voice well because she wasn't in her room. The voice was coming from Mariah's room, and when he heard the woman's voice say, "I think we should get up, don't you?" he very quickly soft-stepped it down to his office.

Harper needed Mariah. And he had a strong sense that she needed Harper, too.

He should ask Mariah to adopt Harper.

The idea he'd had the night before returned with a vengeance, and he knew he'd landed on the right answer to his problem. He didn't jump for joy. He'd miss them both. Even after only knowing them a couple of days, he knew they'd leave a void. One that would kick him in the ass at first. But he'd stay in touch. And Harper would thrive.

That's all that mattered. Not his own wayward heart.

He'd call Len, find out what the legalities entailed, and then talk to Mariah.

It was the best answer for everyone.

And he was glad he'd found it.

Sunday passed mostly in a blur. For some reason Michael decided he had to buy a boat and when the man made a decision, he apparently didn't waste any time implementing it.

By midafternoon he had a four-seater speedboat, a trailer to pull it, life jackets, including a child size, and had the whole ensemble hooked up to his SUV and was hauling it home. Except for the small life vest. Harper was holding that looped over one hand, with Shadow up against her side, as she napped in the car seat.

"I think you scored big with this day," Mariah told Michael as they took the freeway out to the lake. "I suggested a distraction. I didn't mean purchasing a thirty-five-thousand-dollar boat."

"I've been planning to get one. The dock's empty. Harper asked why it was there. The first question she's asked me directly, though I'm sure you noticed. Made sense to show, rather than tell her. She needs solid concepts, you said. And it was a good deal. A year old and half of what it would have cost retail."

He wasn't just all talk, that was for sure. The man did what he said he was going to do.

And hadn't mentioned the night before at all. Her hands on his naked skin.

He was right to pretend it hadn't happened. Could be he hadn't even noticed. It wasn't like a guy as hot as him, as kind as him, as successful as him, wouldn't have women willing to touch him anytime he felt the need.

Just because she was in the middle of a rare physical phenomenon didn't mean that anything between them would be any different for him. That was a key piece that she'd missed with John.

Based on her physical reaction to her ex-husband, based on the fact that he'd been the only person who'd ever been able to arouse a fully excited sexual reaction within her, she'd assumed they had something special. That he was the only one for her.

She'd been one of many for him. Why he'd married her, she still couldn't figure out. Except maybe to get ahead in his career. He'd needed a wife.

And she'd been eagerly willing.

Pathetically willing.

And it was now all water under the bridge.

"You do what you say you're going to do," she said aloud, returning to her earlier thought. "That's good for Harper. Will help her learn to trust you. If you tell her you're going to turn off the television if she doesn't stop throwing toys, then you have to turn off the television if she doesn't stop throwing toys. It's important that you not try to bribe her into doing something she doesn't want to do, but that you know she has to do. Like taking a bath or eating. You can tell her that when she takes a bath she can watch one more show on television. That's a reward. But you can't tell her that if she wants to watch one more show on television, she has to take a bath. That's a bribe." Feeling a bit desperate, needing to be at work, not living a day in her own life, she started in on a new parent lesson, as much because it was what she needed as because he was paying her for the information.

And because she had to teach him everything she could, as quickly as she could, so she could be ready to leave as soon as Harper showed signs of being emotionally okay with him.

The day had been a great start. Noticing her

curiosity about the dock and keeping her interest in a big way.

Who did that?

Who went out and bought a boat to answer a little girl's question?

A guy who didn't seem to be listening to a word she said. Michael was staring out the windshield, occasionally glancing at the boat visible in his side mirror, and not reacting to her at all. Because he didn't plan to keep Harper?

Panic built within her for a second. How did she prepare Harper for possibly being abandoned a second time?

She wanted to call him on it. To make him see how important it was that Harper have stability. Sameness. To get him to look at himself from a different perspective and see all of the things that he was doing right with Harper. How much he had to offer her. To admit how much he cared, and to realize that love was what mattered most.

But the truth was, not all kids got everything they needed.

Not all good, caring people wanted children.

And there was only so much she could legally do.

So she talked about dealing with four-year-olds. Giving him what insights she could because that was what he'd employed her to do. And as the miles passed, she was growing more and more certain that he wasn't paying any attention.

Until he said, "You'd make a good mother."

And she shut up.

Michael was used to deadlines. People paid big money for designs and had to have them by specific times for those who'd be implementing them. So many players were involved in the creation of a stunning building, with inspections and approvals, permits, contractors, governmental meetings a lot of times... If he was late, he affected all of them.

Which was why he'd never been late.

And here he was with the deadline of his life—finding permanence for Harper—and not at all confident Mariah would see the world, this particular portion of it, as clearly as he did.

He'd hoped, for a few minutes there, when they'd been working with the salesman during the purchase of the boat and Mariah had stepped up to mother Harper while Michael did business. The man had assumed they were husband, wife and daughter. That they were a family.

And he'd had an adrenaline high, thinking his plan could work. Mariah could adopt Harper and he'd still be in their lives.

Harper had been so excited by the boat. Begging to sit in it, and then not sitting still at all once she was up there. She'd kept asking to go for a ride on the water.

He'd bought the vessel on the spot, wanting her to have something positive to remember him by. A reason to want to see him again.

And then all the way home Mariah had been talking as though she still thought he could keep Harper himself. As though she hadn't heard, or understood, a word he'd said.

He'd spent a good part of the drive picturing her with Harper. With a husband and child of her own. And wanted it for her. How could he not, after hearing her talk about her past the night before? Her calm, nurturing personality… Who wouldn't crave that? Respond to it?

Seeing her legs so perfectly outlined in the black leggings and the way her white, midthigh shirt rode up a lot farther as she sat in his SUV… He wanted some of her himself.

And couldn't go there. Even if she'd be open to it, and she might very well not be.

Their waters were already far too muddied and he might have his faults, but he was no masochist.

He did, however, have phenomenal self-control. A very good thing as no way could he see a future for Harper without Mariah in it.

Or a future for Mariah without Harper in it, either, he realized yet again as the two of them sat on the speedboat. Maybe she didn't want to try again, to risk hurting as she had when she'd lost Joey, but seeing her with Harper, how happy she was… it didn't take a genius to figure out that they belonged together. With Michael's back to them as he steered, Harper seemed to consider him absent and jabbered up a storm. Asking questions. Making statements like when she said that fish knew that boat motors could hurt them and so stayed away from them. And the tone of Mariah's voice as she responded—her voice raised to be heard over the motor—lightening with every mile of water they covered. He turned once, to see where Harper was pointing when she exclaimed "Look!" but he never did follow the little finger to its visual destination. He'd been caught by the pure joy on Mariah's face, the huge smile, red hair blowing behind her as she sat with one arm around the little blonde girl with her own head of curls.

It was a vision he knew he was going to remember forever. His own personal Madonna portrait.

And then, when he grilled burgers for dinner to go with the French fries Harper had wanted, Mariah fixed a plate and headed toward the door into the house, saying something about some reading she needed to do upstairs.

"No!" Harper called. She wore pink shorts and a matching unicorn T-shirt—the child seemed to be obsessed with the creatures and, based on clothing choices, June must have pandered to the obsession. The little girl froze with a fry halfway to her mouth.

The tone was different from before—not scared. Just…adamant.

Michael wondered how Mariah would handle that—a four-year-old demand. Did you do as you were told, or explain that you had other things to accomplish?

He knew why Mariah was going upstairs. She was purposely leaving the two of them alone together for a family dinner after a day of Harper softening toward him over the boat expedition.

He didn't want Mariah going any more than Harper did, but until they talked about the adoption, he couldn't express his desire to have her stay.

Mariah had barely turned around when Harper continued. "It's law. You eat together," she said.

Mariah took a step back toward them. "Whose law?" she asked.

"Mama and Daddy's law. You eat together. At a table, not on the couch. Remember?"

Remember. As though the "law" applied to everyone, not just the Blackstone household. Mariah had told him on the drive home about children's perception. What Harper knew from her life at home applied to everyone in the world, not just her.

Standing with his own full plate, ready to sit at the table, he waited. Tried not to smile.

And took a big bite of his burger to cover the grin failure when Mariah lifted a foot over the bench and settled down next to Harper.

Maybe June's kid knew more than she was letting on.

He hoped his little sister was watching over them.

And smiling, too.

Chapter Ten

Harper wanted to shower by herself, like Mama. When Mariah asked if she'd ever done it before and discovered the June had taught her daughter how to wash her own hair—"but Mama checked it for getting all the soap out"—she deferred the decision to Michael, who immediately complied. And then insisted he be the one to make sure the preschooler got all the soap out.

She went out to the hallway when she heard Harper's little "I'm ready" come through the door, just in case an issue arose, but when Michael peeked behind the shower curtain to check his niece's hair, Harper didn't say a word.

She was warming to him. He had to see that.

Mariah couldn't be certain what he perceived, but she very clearly saw the moisture in his eyes as he walked out of that bathroom door a few seconds later, avoiding her gaze.

And was still thinking about it an hour and a half later, when she joined him on the outside deck for their nightly meeting. She almost went back in for a beer, when she saw the bottle in his hand, but didn't. She never drank when she was on assignment. Even if the job took a month.

And the fact that she felt like she needed alcohol was even more reason to wrap things up.

She needed to talk to him about her exit date. After the day they'd just shared, she was feeling internal pressure to remove herself from the picture before Harper grew any more attached to a Mom-and-Dad image of them. The dinner table episode had shown her the danger loud and clear.

She ached at the thought of leaving. Wanted to believe she was still needed.

But she knew that those reasons were precisely why she had to get out.

The previous night, she'd given him until Wednesday due to his work deadline. She sat down with him—she in her rocker, he in his—to nail down her firm leave date.

"Today went really well," she started in immediately, taking charge. She just had to keep her mind firmly on Harper's needs and not let her own feelings for the little girl, or her uncle, have any brain time. The heart she couldn't help, but the head… She had some say there.

And her heart wasn't all one-sided. Even as it hurt, it was telling her she had to get out of there. Maybe the fear induced walls around her heart would leave someday, or maybe not. All she knew was that she wasn't ready to think about another try at her own family.

He leaned forward, elbows on his knees, hands clasped together, and looked up at her. "I need to talk to you," he said. The tone brought an inexplicable constriction to her throat. And she waited. "And I need you to hear me out before you respond."

"Okay." She shrugged. "I'm generally a good listener," she added.

"Hear me with an open mind," he added.

He was kind of scaring her. A *lot* scaring her, as she considered that he might have found a family for Harper. He'd been scrolling on his phone at various times throughout the day. Had been texting some, too, his expression serious as he'd read responses and then typed.

"I've never had anyone give me an indication that they find me closed-minded." The words were a bit defensive. She hadn't meant them to be. They were fact.

"I'm sorry. I'm not meaning to indicate you are." Shaking his head, he gave a small grimace and sat back, scooting down a bit in his chair, ankle resting over opposite knee, and took a sip of beer. "The truth is, I'm nervous," he told her.

"Nervous? Because of me?" That hadn't occurred to her.

She had to matter to him in some way to have the power to make him nervous.

The idea was a little intriguing. But mostly nerve-wracking.

He held all of the cards. He had custody of Harper. He could choose whatever he wanted, within the law, for her future. And his own. All Mariah could do was wish them well and say good-bye.

And wonder now and then. Or a lot.

"I've carefully analyzed and evaluated this entire situation with Harper. What I know. All that you've told me. What I've perceived in the more than sixty hours since I first made contact. And I've reached a conclusion that is best suited to giving her a healthy and happy future."

Her heart sank. *Here it comes.* She'd take it. Remain professional. And spend the next couple of days doing all she could to help Harper with yet another transition.

The last one, hopefully, until she became an adult and could direct her own life choices.

Michael's blue-eyed gaze locked with hers, serious intent shining clear. "I think you should adopt Harper."

She heard him. From a distance. Stared. Knew her heart was pounding. Didn't move. Let her mind catch up. Couldn't wrap it around anything.

And tried for professional distance. Her boundaries had long since deserted her.

"I believe you love her." Michael had started talking again, so she listened. She'd told him she would. "When you talk about her and talked about your Joey... It's clear that for some reason Harper has touched you in the same deep way. Your bond with her is obvious."

He didn't need to convince her of that. She already knew. Had known before she'd even met him.

He wasn't going to pressure her into making his way easy.

It wasn't about what he wanted. Even less about what she wanted.

It was about what *Harper* needed.

"It's also very clear that she's bonded with you in much the same way. Child to mother, rather than mother to child, of course."

No. She shook her head. "That's not fair, to put that on Harper. Given the situation, she'd have bonded with whoever happened to be first in line to tend to her. It just happened to be me." She knew her job. Knew her words to be true. Couldn't dare allow herself to read more than was there, especially when she wasn't sure if she could be a mother again.

He didn't argue. Just sat quietly until she thought she might explode, just sitting there. Trying to take deep breaths, but they wouldn't move through the constriction in her chest.

"Your life choice was to have a child of your own. You lost yours. Harper's most critical need is to have a mother, a family—and she lost hers. You share something that a lot of people wouldn't understand, even if she doesn't know it yet."

That was not a reason to consider his suggestion, though, she admitted to herself.

"The trauma of this situation… She's coming through like a star, but another transition, as you've said a few times, could set her back tremendously. I can't keep her here. But if she went with you, that problem would be solved even better than if she stayed with me."

That part was irrefutable at the moment, while Harper was still clinging to her.

"I'd like to remain a part of her life. From a distance. I've already talked to my attorney about setting up a college fund for her. And can offer any other financial support she'd ever need."

That made her angry. Because she had to release some of the emotions ready to explode inside her and fury was the only one she could handle.

"None of this is about money," she snapped. "From what I've seen, her parents weren't rich, but Harper clearly lacked for nothing that she needed. Right now, she needs family. That's you. And if I were ever to have a child of my own, naturally, or by other means, I would support that baby on my own. It will have what *I* can provide."

There. That felt better. For a hot second.

Until she saw his knowing look. Like he thought he was so smart he could read her mind like one of his books.

"The money is negotiable," he said, holding her gaze as though they were speaking a silent language as well. "And my part in her life is as well, if it came down to what was best for her. I'd just like to remain an uncle, if I could. I got ahead of myself there, and I apologize."

She wanted to shake him. And lay her head on his shoulder and cry. She wanted to kiss him and pretend that they'd met in another world and he was a man who wanted to raise a family as badly as she did. A man who wanted her as badly as she did him. To see what could happen between them.

She wanted to have sex with him and see if the feelings swarming through her, just being close to his body, were real. Would culminate in a full, mind-blowing completion. She'd just seen the tip of the iceberg with John but she knew there could be so much more.

And then to see if the feelings vanished afterward.

Or if they could last awhile.

Mostly she wanted to think about those feelings so she didn't have to face the heartache in front of her, leaving Little Rock and her current client family behind.

"She belongs with you, Michael," she said softly, calmly after several minutes. "That's her mother's choice."

"Only because I'm the only biological family left. And because she didn't know you or see Harper with you."

"You love her."

"Yes. Enough to give her away."

"But…"

He shook his head abruptly. "I loved June, too, Mariah. And I believe our parents, both of them, loved us, and probably each other. Sometimes that isn't enough."

It had to be.

Her whole world depended on that truth. Love could always find a way. If one was willing to walk every hard, hot, blistery mile to be able to live with the joy.

And it dawned on her. He didn't know that. There was a hole in the genius's knowledge base and the emotion part had leaked out, dripping a trail of pain behind him.

It wasn't a hole that could be filled with words or knowledge learned. It had to be experience that

taught him. And Harper didn't have time for that...
unless Mariah could convince him to give the little
girl six months in his home. To see that there were
things he didn't know, missing pieces that left serious kinks in his logic.

As soon as she had the thought, she knew it
wouldn't work. He couldn't let Harper move in,
find a home and then six months later upend her
again. Let her learn to love him and then lose
him, too. Mariah didn't think that would happen,
didn't think Michael would still want to give her
up by then, but she'd never in a million years have
pegged John for saying that their son's death was
for the best.

He'd had Down syndrome, not a painful, terminal disease. Could have lived a long, happy life.

And as she sat there, feeling hopeless, she just
had to ask. "Why, Michael? What happened with
June, it was horribly, painfully unfortunate, I get
that, but you couldn't possibly have foreseen...
Your father had never unleashed his anger on
her when you were around. How could you have
known that it wasn't just because you pissed him
off, but because he'd just needed a punching bag?
How could you have known that he'd turn to June
once you were gone? Or that she wouldn't tell you
when he did?"

His expression changed in a heartbeat. Face

tight. Those blue eyes glaring. He lifted his chin. "I could have known if I'd been more aware outside my own frame of reference."

"You were a kid. Being self-centered in terms of how you view the world is natural and normal behavior for kids. Until we get out in the world, we don't see firsthand the other stories out there that are vastly different from our own."

"Or it could be that I'm just like my old man."

His shoulders dropped, his face fell, losing all fight, after he spoke. And then, in an entirely different tone, he continued. "When I was little everyone said how much I was like him. I looked like him. Had mannerisms the same as his, apparently even when I was still a baby—according to his parents. Everyone who knew us would say how uncanny it was, how alike we were. Now, I've never had a wife. I've never had kids. So I have no idea how I'd be if my wife died and I was left alone raising two children who were challenging me at every turn. I don't think I'd pick up a bottle and try to drown myself, but how do I know that? I haven't worn those shoes. What I do know, and have grown to understand through the perspective of years, is that my father wasn't always like that.

"As the bad memories fade some, I've remembered some good ones, too. Ones like today, out on the lake with Harper. And that man who took me fishing, took me everywhere with him until I started to talk about things he didn't understand, changed. People change. Life changes them. I'm sure if you'd asked my father, while he was walking into the hardware store with me on his shoulders, if he'd ever get drunk and beat the hell out of me, he'd have said, 'Absolutely not.' More, if you'd asked my mother if he was capable of doing such a thing, she'd have said the same. And if I'm as much like my father as everyone says, I could become him. I say not, but I won't take that kind of chance with that little girl's life. My father failed me. I failed June. I will not put that legacy on Harper."

She wanted to argue. To show him possibility. Another whole side to that story. She wanted to talk about legacy and heredity versus environment. To remind him that he'd been a little boy when his mother had died, and really had no idea what she'd have said in answer to his hypothetical question to her. No idea what had gone on between his parents in their private relationship.

She wanted to say so many things.

But his *if* effectively rebutted every single word she could have said.

There was always an *if* in life. And he'd made a conscious choice not to gamble with this one.

His words saddened her to the core. She needed

to go upstairs to her room and cry all the tears that were pushing for release. Years' worth of them. His. Hers. Little Harper's now and in the future, as she remembered the past week. And slowly forgot so many of the memories of life with her parents.

But she was there for Harper.

And the little girl's time was running out.

Michael was apparently not going to keep her. No matter what.

She couldn't, either. Not as a hired expert on a job.

And as a woman?

Could she really even be asking herself the question?

Watching the man seated across from her, close enough for their knees to touch if they coordinated their rocking, she couldn't not ask the question. The O'Connell/Blackstone family was more than a job to her. Had been since she'd first laid eyes on Harper.

She didn't understand it. Had no rational explanation for it. Wasn't sure she even trusted her feelings when it came to Michael...but Harper?

"I need some time to think about this." She heard the words at the same time her brain was processing them.

Not to say yes. Just to think. About all of it.

"My lawyer is already drawing up paperwork,

in the event you say yes," Michael told her quietly, scaring the crap out of her.

And igniting a small spark of excitement, too.

Could she really adopt Harper Blackstone? The idea was so far-fetched. So not even in the realm of normal or expected that she couldn't fully grasp the concept.

"There'd have to be formal proceedings," she told him, just because it was something she knew to be true. "Each state is different."

He opened his mouth as though to speak, she saw it and ran on right over what he'd been about to say. "In Arkansas, a single person can adopt as long as they aren't cohabitating with a sexual partner and unmarried." She was calling up a mental list. It helped her.

"You've looked up Arkansas adoption laws?"

She shook her head. "Not recently, so I suppose that could have changed. I learned the state laws in college as part of my child development undergraduate degree. I went to university here in Arkansas. In Searcy."

"That's just an easy hour's drive from here."

She nodded. Had thought about taking a side trip while she was so close, but wasn't sure about revisiting old wounds when she was feeling so raw.

"My professional partners and I… We were all

close friends in college. There were eight of us then."

"The eighth one didn't want to join the firm?"

She didn't know why she was telling him. Just needed to backpedal from him thinking she could adopt Harper.

"She's the reason we formed the firm," she told him. "She was murdered and the seven of us each used our own areas of expertise and what we knew of Sierra and helped the police find her killer. He's now doing life without parole."

His study of her seemed to grow more focused, not less. "You keep tabs on him?"

"Every year, on the anniversary of her death, one of us checks to make sure he's still locked up and reports to the others of us. We try to all meet in Phoenix as close to the date as we can, based on current jobs."

"They sound more family than business partners."

"They feel that way, too."

"So you'll need to talk to them before you commit to adopting Harper."

"Stop." She stood. "Don't get ahead of yourself, Michael. And don't pressure me. I said I wanted time to think, not time before I say yes. You need to proceed as though my answer is no."

His lips pursed, he closed his eyes for a moment, but nodded. And then, still seated, looked up to her and said, "Just to be clear, you aren't actually saying no." Picking up his mostly full beer, he took a long sip and set it carefully back down beside the monitor receiver he'd once again carried out with him.

She didn't know what she was doing. She should be saying no. Would be saying no. "Not tonight."

He seemed satisfied with that, and she knew him well enough already to assume that he was counting on her to get to the right answer eventually. The right answer in his world.

"Have you thought about the fact that I live in New Orleans?" she asked him, standing her ground rather than leaving as she'd fully intended to do. "You said you wanted to be in her life, so surely you aren't thinking I'm going to move to Arkansas."

"That's not a choice for me to make," he said, infuriatingly calm. "I accept that you'd have the right to take her to live anywhere you want."

"And that doesn't bother you?"

It had to. How could it not? She knew he loved her.

"I'm thinking about Harper here," he told her, completely firm as he held her gaze. "Not myself."

And it occurred to her that there was a major

difference between Michael and her ex-husband, because John had only ever thought about himself.

"And what about the fact that I travel for my job? I'm on the road all the time."

"I figured you had a plan worked out for that since you were going to be raising a son."

A special needs son. He wasn't homing in on that fact. John had. All the time. Every single conversation.

"I was going to take on more of a managerial role, only, expanding Sierra's Web's child life division, and hiring at least one more full-time expert. I'd still travel, just not as much. The idea was that John would be there when I was not."

Which had been part of the problem between them those last months of her pregnancy, too. John hadn't wanted to be left to care for Joey single-handedly on a regular basis.

He stood then. "I understand there's a lot to think about. Would you consider staying here under my employ until we get this worked out?"

Nothing had changed. She had to go.

And yet...

"I've currently got the job length down as open ended with a two-week estimate. I'll leave it there for now." She had to think about his request. Had to think about Harper. And herself, too. She needed time to do that. She'd still end up having to leave Harper, but somehow, knowing that he'd give her the little girl to raise as her own settled her heart some.

The choice would be hers—for Harper's best interest, not one forced on Mariah without choice.

She just had to make certain that Harper knew her staying wasn't permanent. She'd told her. They'd both told her. Multiple times.

The little girl, though, was more apt to believe what she saw in the moment, not what she heard about the future. The future was a concept too nebulous for her to fully grasp.

And the emotional danger of living in Michael's home with him…tending to a devastated child with him… She'd deal with that one moment at a time. As the moments came.

She couldn't be in the same house as him, sleep with him, *and* adopt Harper. The state's law said so very clearly. Even though she wasn't prepared to adopt, the thought of doing anything that would prevent the option seemed inconceivable at the moment.

She needed some rest. And to talk to Kelly. Telling him good-night, she turned to go.

"Mariah?"

When she turned around he was sitting again, rocking slowly, beer bottle in hand. "Yeah?"

"It's just under seven hours' drive between here

and New Orleans. An hour-and-thirteen-minute flight, nonstop."

"You looked it up?"

He didn't say he had, but... He knew. Her heart fluttered as she headed upstairs. He already knew how long it would take him to get to Harper if he got his way and Mariah adopted her.

He cared.

A lot.

Which made her care about both of them even more.

Chapter Eleven

Michael forced himself to settle into a routine as much as possible over the next couple of days. Having an energizing work project to complete helped, but didn't entirely eradicate the sense of disruption in his life.

Or the temptation to want more from both Harper and Mariah.

He knew better. That last day with June, when she'd called the police on him, and he'd been warned never to contact her again… It had changed him forever.

Shown him that he couldn't make everything better.

That day had taught him what it felt like to be truly powerless. To hurt and have no ability to improve anything.

It had shown him that knowing what was best in a situation didn't necessarily solve the problem. In fact, sometimes knowing made it worse when he was dealing with others who had the right to their own choices and couldn't see what he saw.

Not that he saw everything. He'd never pretended to do so. He just struggled when solutions were so clear to him and yet he had to defer to others.

Take Mariah, for instance. He didn't just want her to take Harper for Harper's sake. He wanted it for hers, too, even though he couldn't say for sure what was right for Mariah. She had already given her vulnerable heart to his niece. She'd pretty much admitted as much.

The woman was a marvel to him. She looked like she was out of a fairy tale. All that long, red hair, the china-delicate features, fair skin and totally sexy body.

He needed to see her get her happy ending. He hadn't seen June's; his sister hadn't lived long enough for them both to heal the rift.

It somehow felt as though Harper was the key. She'd given June the best life, clearly. And was doing the same for Mariah. If he could just find a way to facilitate the healing of Mariah's broken heart, and fill Harper's, too, he'd somehow gain something important.

His life would be worth more to him.

Tempted to call from his office on both Monday and Tuesday nights and say he had to work late, giving Mariah as much time as Harper's sole nurturer as he could, Michael kept his word and went home early instead. He couldn't manipulate her. Pressure her.

Just as with June, he had to stand back and let others choose their own paths.

Still, after Harper was in bed Tuesday night, after two more dinners with the three of them together, plus Mariah reading her a story with Michael in the room, Michael was feeling hopeful. Mariah was keeping her distance from him, keeping things completely professional, but he'd intercepted some stolen glances at Harper.

And a few that had come his way as well.

And she was no longer pushing the child onto him. Had apparently accepted that he wasn't meant to have children or a family of his own.

Wild how a part of him was disappointed. As though, somewhere, in the back of his subconscious, there'd lingered a bit of hope that he'd been wrong.

He'd known he wasn't. Had spent years watching over himself—and analyzing past mistakes. He'd found peace with the answers he'd found. A way to live a satisfying, productive, positive life.

Mariah had had two days to think about his suggestion that she adopt Harper, and she hadn't told him no.

They'd had their nightly meeting, and as was becoming routine, he took a walk down to the lake,

monitor receiver in hand, after she went upstairs.
Needing some cool air, some distance, to calm
the desire that raged through him anytime he was
alone with Mariah. And not finding enough of it as
sprinkles and a distant roll of thunder forced him
back inside. He puttered in the kitchen, emptying
the dishwasher. Spent of bit of time on the computer in his office. Answered an email from over-
seas, where the business day was just beginning.

And when he was satisfied that both of the ladies in his home were in bed asleep, he made his
own way upstairs, to shut himself in at the opposite end of the house.

Mariah had had two days to think, and she
hadn't told him yes, either.

The thought was causing him unease as he settled back against his headboard in the dark, hands
behind his head.

Ideas popped around, ways he could try to affect the situation, and he consciously, forcibly,
pushed them away. Refusing to entertain them
long enough to determine their feasibility.

At work, he was the boss.

Outside work… He was just one man in a world
of free-to-choose human beings. A man who had
to bite his tongue more than some.

He must have drifted off to sleep on that
thought, still propped up. The next thing he knew

he was sitting straight up in bed, heart pounding, and not sure why.

A flash of lightning through the glass doors leading out to his balcony settled him for a moment. The storm that had been threatening had moved in was all.

Generally, he slept through them, but with the current state of his affairs, nothing was happening normally.

Then he heard it again. A scream. Followed by a whimper. He was out of bed, hand on the doorknob of his door, by the time he'd recognized the last for what it was. In a pair of the cotton pajama pants he'd been sleeping in while he had houseguests, he hurried down the hall and in through Harper's open door, unable to see clearly in the darkness until another flash illuminated the room.

Mariah was there, on the side of the twin bed, obviously having arrived just before he did, with Harper climbing up to sit on her lap, little hands wrapping tightly around Mariah's neck.

He turned to go, to leave them to what they needed, and Harper screamed, "No!" There wasn't any kind of command in her tone, only stone-cold, debilitating fear. Her eyes were open; he could see glints of light from her gaze pinned on his body. But he wasn't sure she was really seeing him.

Her mouth hanging open, she was crying, clinging, clearly shaking. If he didn't know better, he'd think she was having a seizure. He grabbed a fleece throw from the chair, and, standing at Mariah's back, draped the fleece around Harper. Mariah held it in place, still rocking the little girl.

Lightning flashed again and Harper screamed again.

"We need to get her out of this room." Mariah stood, wrapping the blanket more securely, including Shadow in the bundle, as she headed with her armload to the door. "You said that couch in your family room is a sleeper pullout. Let's get her down there."

"Let me carry her down." He reached for Harper, under her arms, intending to cradle the little body against him, but she wailed animalistically and clutched her arm more tightly around Mariah's neck.

Stepping quickly in front of Mariah then, he stayed just one step ahead of her the entire way down. If she stumbled, he'd catch them.

He tossed the pillows from the couch and had the bed pulled out in less than a minute, then spread and tucked sheets and a comforter down. But when he tried to take Harper, to lay her down, she screamed such a high, shrill sound he couldn't believe it had come from such a small body.

Mariah scooted herself fully onto the bed.

He wasn't sure why the couch bed was any different from the one upstairs, but didn't question Mariah's dictate. Nor did he know what to do next.

Did he get Harper some water? Seemed like she'd choke at the moment if she tried to drink.

Harper cried softly. She hiccupped. Sometimes it seemed as though she was falling asleep, her head cradled on Mariah's breast as she took a deeper breath and shuddered, but then thunder would sound or lightning would flash and the child would flinch, cry out, clutch frantically at Mariah again.

Mariah didn't look at him. Didn't even seem to know he was there as she gently rocked against the back of the couch, crooning to Harper. Letting her know, not that it was going to be okay, but that she was right there.

"When you get afraid, you need to try to think about not being afraid," she said. "Think about being happy. Hug Shadow, because that feels good, huh?"

Harper sniffed.

"And find something that feels safer. Like now. The bed was scaring you because of the last time, so now we're not in a bedroom. And it's a different kind of bed. See? It's not the same. We changed it. And fear, it's not as smart as us. It doesn't know that when we change things it can't hurt us as badly."

Truth. Always tell her the truth. But only as much of it as she can comprehend. She'd told him that the first day he'd met Harper.

"It's going to be over soon," he spoke while still standing, not sure what to do with himself. How to help. "And it's not the kind of storm that hurts," he added. It was possible Harper had always been afraid of thunder and lightning, but it was also pretty obvious to him that the recent supercell storm that had torn through her house and taken her parents from her was terrifying her still.

"This kind of rain is called a single cell," he told her, and then remembered Mariah's mandate about keeping it simple. "It's like a kitten storm instead of a cat storm. Like if Shadow had a baby." She'd be less afraid of a baby, right? "It only lasts a little while, no more than an hour—which is about two of the *StoryBots* show you watched last night. Remember how quick that went?" She'd been told she could watch one before getting ready for bed. The episode had passed so quickly she'd tried to bargain for two.

She hadn't succeeded. She had to be able to rely on the fact that when they said something, they'd follow through on it.

Mariah's grateful-looking glance, the small nod she gave him, had him scrambling for more to say.

Harper didn't seem to be listening, but what did he know?

"This baby storm just blows little winds, like when you blow out birthday candles. And the drops of rain are smaller and soft, kind of like soap bubbles, only a little heavier. It's that kind of storm." His niece seemed to be breathing more evenly and he stayed silent, not wanting to wake her if she'd fallen back to sleep. Five minutes passed. Lightning streaked again and she didn't make a sound.

Turning, Michael took a step as slow and light as he could make it toward the staircase.

"No!" The little voice cut clear through him.

Harper's head still lay on Mariah, on her shoulder now, but her eyes were wide open, staring at him.

"Mama and Daddy died," she said with a whimper and another hiccup. "I don't want any more died."

"We're all going to be fine," he told her, his tone soft.

"No!" she said again, starting to cry harder. "No more died!" Lightning streaked, thunder sounded, but farther in the distance, and Harper cried out, "No more died! No more beds! No more died!"

Was she afraid for him to go back upstairs?

Or did she just not want him to leave her?

Didn't really matter, either way.

Michael moved to the other side of the couch. Sat down on the mattress. "I'm here," he told her. "Would you do something for me?"

She didn't acknowledge him.

"Would you be willing to try to lie down right here, with me on one side and Mariah on the other, and we'll all three be safe together?"

Harper lifted up her arms. With both hands on Mariah's shoulders, she stared hard into her face, their noses almost touching.

"We can have a sleepover," Mariah said. "A baby-storm sleepover. Would that be okay?"

Harper nodded. Slid down to the mattress and under the covers. Michael grabbed some small throw pillows off the other couch and distributed them to Harper first and then Mariah, before dropping his own down right up against the arm of the couch. By the time he was settled, intending to stay atop the covers and use the fleece throw from the rocker, Harper was already draped over Mariah, an arm over her upper chest, and a leg over her hip, her eyes closed.

Mariah glanced at him. Held his gaze in the moonlight illuminating the room.

And... He wanted to make love to her.

What the hell!

Harper was settled down.

He sat up, intending to get his ass upstairs, taking them three at a time, but the little girl sat up.

Frowned at him.

And he lay back down, pulling the fleece around him and turning his back to the two people who were upending his entire life. One bringing out all kinds of protective instincts and a soft, but fierce love—the other… Well, he had no idea what all Mariah was doing to him, but he knew he had to ignore all of it.

Every heavenly appearing twist and turn on that road would lead him straight to hell.

She'd never slept next to a little one. Didn't think she *would* sleep. Most particularly not with Michael O'Connell just feet away, sharing the same mattress. And yet, with her senses abuzz and her heart bubbling with emotion, she floated off with a tiny body wrapped around her and slept better than she had in years. Deeply. Peacefully.

And woke up, completely disoriented, before dawn, to see Michael rounding the end of the pullout bed and heading toward the stairs. She knew it was for the best. Waking up together, all three of them in the same bed, would create an intimacy they couldn't afford in their situation.

She cried a little, though, lying there in the dark with a small head digging into the side of her rib cage and a hand on her stomach. Was she being a fool? Refusing to seriously consider her option to adopt Harper because of professional boundaries and obligations? There was nothing that said she couldn't fall in love with a child she met through work, or seriously consider taking that child in as her own if it was the employer's request that she do.

Or had she already been seriously considering doing so and holding up the actual consideration with a professional boundary that was crumbling that night, in that bed?

She didn't know if taking Harper was the best thing for the little girl. Had to think in-depth and with no blinders on about the logistics of becoming an overnight mother to any four-year-old child— let alone one who was going to need extra careful attention over the coming months as she moved on from a horrendous tragedy.

If she was in Phoenix, that part would be easier. Mandy Faith was there. A wife, mother of a toddler and a fellow child life specialist who worked part-time at the children's hospital and part-time for Sierra's Web. Mandy was top on Mariah's list of contracted child life experts. If Mariah asked her, she'd be available to watch Harper, keep her overnight even, when Mariah had to be gone. For the first month, at least, she'd need to stay put, but there was also a pile of administrative work she'd been meaning to get done at the Sierra's Web home office. And the partners were all in and out of Phoenix, using an apartment the firm owned for just that purpose. Mariah's was in the same complex. She'd just wanted her own because she was in town more than some of them. Any one of them in town would happily bop over and stay at her place if necessary. They were her family.

For that matter, anyone who was available would fly to Phoenix for just that purpose.

Harper sighed. Flopped over, turning her back to Mariah, her butt pressed up against Mariah's thigh now. And as Mariah watched night fade through the blinds, watched the child, she found it a little harder to breathe. Reined herself in. In the cover of darkness, she'd gone off on a wild tangent there, getting way ahead of herself. In the dawning light of day, she knew she was going to seriously think about all angles of adopting a child. Actually call Kelly, instead of just thinking about it.

But her decision had absolutely not been made.

For one very clear and undeniably strong reason. Michael O'Connell. June had given Harper to her brother because she'd thought that was best for Harper. Michael might not think so, but Mariah believed it with all her heart. A mother who loved a child as well as Harper had clearly been loved would make that choice with most utterly serious consideration. Because once June had signed her name on that paperwork, she'd needed her heart to be at peace.

And Michael… Her heart ached just thinking of him losing Harper. He might not see it yet, but he needed that little girl as much as Harper needed him.

How did she become a player in a scenario that prevented their eventual union as a family?

And how long before the lack of permanence in a decision regarding Harper's future started to be a detriment to the child herself?

Another day or two?

A week?

Or had they reached that point already?

Harper was taking on her new life. Insisting that everyone eat together at the table. Laughing as the water sprayed her face on the boat. Moving her clothes in, and insisting, each morning, that she pick the ones she was going to wear that day.

Finding solace in bed with the new people in her life.

Mariah didn't know the answers, just knew that she had to find them.

Fast.

Chapter Twelve

Michael went to work Wednesday with a tic inside his bones, tasing his nerve endings. He worked fast, so focused he didn't notice time passing, and when he was done with what he absolutely had to do, he embarked on the search that would find a home for Harper. No more wondering. No more time to search or wait for Mariah.

The little girl was claiming him, settling in, and the night before, in that bed with her and Mariah, he'd wanted them both to stay. Had been unsure if he could really let Harper go.

But he had to.

June had been everything to him as a kid. The one bright spot in a lousy life. She'd symbolized hope to him. Her existence had spurred him to make something of himself. Her smile was proof that faith existed. And he'd blown it with her. Just as their father had blown it with both of them.

In terms of hurting those he loved, he was more like his father than he'd ever thought he'd be, with one major distinction.

A real man, a decent man, took accountability.

And he made damned certain he didn't turn his blind, selfish personality loose on anyone else he cared about. The day the police had led him away from June, he made that promise to himself. That he would never be a core member of another family. Would never give himself the opportunity to damage the life of someone else he loved. That promise was the only thing guaranteeing that Michael didn't completely become his father.

And so he made phone calls, and then followed up on referrals from there. Found an agency that had been in business for fifty years and had testimonials from children who'd been adopted through them. This was one of the first agencies to allow contact with a biological family post-adoption. And they had a list of vetted families waiting for a child. By the time he'd headed home, he'd read through the twenty-family dossier and had put out feelers with three of them.

Dan was running private investigative searches on them. Michael had spoken with two of the mothers and fathers via videoconference, and sent an email to the third, requesting the same.

His heart was breaking, but he would not fail Harper. That sweet, precious piece of him was going to have the best life a girl could have. June must have known that he'd move hell and mountains to find her daughter a fairy-tale life in the event that June wasn't there to raise her. At least she'd trusted him that much. He was not going to let her down again.

And to guarantee that he wouldn't weaken, wouldn't listen to his own pain, he had to get it done as quickly as humanly possible.

To guarantee that Harper didn't bond with him and his home any further, he had to get her out of there immediately, and to a permanent family that would give her a healthy, happy, loving existence, in spite of the tragedy she'd suffered.

Children were resilient. Mariah had told him that. Harper was young enough to get through the storm that had ripped up her life and still be trusting. Still have faith in the world around her.

She could still view the world with wide-open eyes and believe that she could be whatever she wanted to be. To do whatever she wanted to do. To reach the stars if she so chose.

And if he was lucky, he'd find a family who'd be willing to take on a distant uncle on Harper's behalf. To send him pictures. And, maybe, when she was adjusted and doing well, he could even visit now and then.

As he drove home, loosening the knot of the black tie he'd donned that morning to match his mood, feeling like it was choking him, his mind finally won its daylong battle and focused on Mariah.

He'd had no right to use the affection he saw in her for Harper to pressure her into taking on what he could not. No right to expect her to make such a permanent, all-encompassing change to her life.

He'd been thinking of himself, again. Because he was so drawn to the woman, and could see that Harper was, too, it would have been easier for him to give up his niece to her.

And he'd been fairly certain that he could play a regular role in the little girl's life if Mariah had her.

It got even worse than that, he acknowledged as he pulled onto his street and felt the anticipation that had been hitting him the past three nights as he arrived home from work. Having Mariah adopt Harper meant that Michael would still have this woman in his life.

He'd known her one day short of a week, yet Mariah had a hold of him like none other. Which meant it was for the best that she be out of his life as well.

Because it wasn't just children from whom he had to protect himself. The O'Connells didn't do marriage well, either. They didn't do family well.

And he was not going to be responsible for creating another dysfunctional one.

But with Mariah safely ensconced as Harper's

mom, he could have seen her now and then. Just as he saw Harper.

It had been the perfect solution.

For him.

And from there, he'd convinced himself that it was best for Mariah and Harper, too.

It was all about perception. Seeing what you wanted to see instead of what was really there.

He got out of the car slowly, half dreading, half savoring the moment when he walked into his usually empty house and heard noise of life. Maybe the television. Or Mariah and Harper talking. Maybe smell something cooking.

He'd always been content, coming home. He would be again.

Or he'd build another place that pleased him. That's what he excelled at. Designing buildings.

Nothing was cooking.

Dropping his keys on the counter and emptying the pocket of his black dress pants in the corner jug set for that purpose, he listened for some clue as to what he was walking into.

Possibly to avoid it.

Or maybe pop in to say hello, and then practice avoidance until dinner.

He'd cook dinner. Chicken on the grill. With more mac and cheese. They hadn't had it for a couple of days and it made Harper happy. She gobbled the stuff up.

Rolling up the cuffs of his white shirt, he finally heard the faint sound of the television coming from the family room. Not the one in the living room where they'd watched shows previously.

Had Harper adopted a new space after the previous night's storm?

He'd lain down in bed with Harper and Mariah in that room. The feeling of that mattress, listening to them breathe as he'd tried to sleep, giving up on getting rest and using the time to shore up memories; instead, he'd pushed all of that as far away as he could.

Walking back into that room wasn't on his want-to-do list.

So he peeked his head in long enough to see Harper in front of an educational show, with Mariah off in the corner, speaking on the phone. She glanced up, saw him. He waved. She nodded, and he hightailed it out of there. Harper gave no indication of having noticed him.

But she hadn't wanted him *died* the night before. One thought followed the other, equally soothing him and throwing him further into a quagmire. If she didn't notice him, transitioning away from him shouldn't be difficult for her.

But knowing she didn't want him to die...sent warm feelings all the way through him.

He felt it was no mistake when his phone rang and he recognized the number he'd tried to call earlier. Corrine and Dale Swanson. The third family.

Entering his office, he took the call. Switched to video. And, with his back to the door, to the household out there, he went through his bevy of questions by rote.

Liking some of their answers, but not others. And even while he was still on the phone with them, following through with a complete interview because he was that thorough and open to finding out what he didn't know, he knew they weren't the family for Harper. The first two couples he'd interviewed had both passed with high scores. As soon as he had Dan's reports, he'd make his choice between those two.

After the Swansons answered the last question, he gave them the same information he'd given the other two couples, that his lawyer would be calling them to discuss any further details and share his final decision. He was relieved to end the call. Turning to drop his phone to his desk, he saw Mariah standing in the doorway to his office, mouth open, her face pale.

Harper. Heart stabbing his throat, he came

around the desk, expecting her to hit him with bad news, ready to take action.

His words of alarm, asking what was wrong, all froze in his throat before taking flight as she just stood there and shook her head. In the same tight black jeans, white short-sleeved shirt and tennis shoes she'd had on the first day he'd met her, those long red curls resting along her hips, she looked young and sexy and athletic, ready to jump on his boat and ride to the ocean where they could sail away...

Until his gaze came back to those wide green eyes, glaring as though he'd somehow betrayed her. And he realized she'd overheard his conversation.

He'd already planned to discuss everything with her that evening. Had even hoped she might help him choose between the two couples to which he'd narrowed down his search.

"It's done!" Harper's voice came from the distance, and then, closer, again. "It's done. Can I watch another?" Shadow and Ryan were hugged to either side of her as she appeared, in light green jeans and a pink-and-white-striped shirt that seemed a little big and did not match.

He'd missed a question on his parental survey. Would they let her choose her own clothes, even if they didn't go together, to honor her right to make what choices she could, as long as they didn't hurt her?

Although, he'd asked if they'd be willing to work with the child life expert who was taking care of her, and to comply by her recommendations during the transition, which kind of did cover the clothes.

Mariah had just finished telling Harper that the deal had been one show and then off.

"I'm hungry," Harper said then, not sounding the least bit put out about the lack of more television. And Michael sprang into action.

"I'm just getting ready to grill some chicken and make another pot of mac and cheese. How does that sound?"

Screwing up her little nose in a way that twisted Michael's gut every time, Harper said, *"Gooood."* She drew out the word. "But just no black junk on it, okay?"

"Black junk?"

"Sometimes when Daddy did it, the stuff had black junk on it."

"Grilling you mean?" Mariah asked, sounding like her usual, calm nurturing self as she addressed the child. "Sometimes the meat had black on it when he took it off the grill?"

"Yeah." Harper's nod was full-out. Chin to

chest and then head fully back, her little neck exposed. "That's what I meaned."

"Got it," Michael said, already heading for the door. "No black stuff on it." And when he reached Mariah, who'd ushered Harper out toward the family room to pick a book to read—news to him that there were four-year-old-capacity reading books in that room—he stopped. Grabbed Mariah gently by the elbow.

Dropped his hand the second she looked up at him. "We'll talk tonight," he said.

She nodded.

Everything was fine.

So why did he feel as though he'd just signed the warrant for his own death sentence?

He was interviewing a family to adopt Harper.

Mariah made it through the motions of sitting for dinner, ate a bite or two, chewing a long time per bite and swallowing slowly. Aware, constantly aware, hugely aware, that Michael was interviewing a family to adopt Harper.

The knowledge hung there like death, hovering over every breath she took. She could hardly look at the little girl without tearing up.

Not for herself, but for Harper.

And for Michael, too.

And maybe a little for herself, actually. If Michael had hung on long enough to see that he was good for Harper rather than a hindrance, if he'd kept Harper, she'd have had the possibility of a chance to stay in touch with the little girl. To know that she was growing up happy and healthy. If Michael welcomed the contact. She'd thought he probably would.

He'd found a potential family for Harper.

Mariah wanted to be angry with him. She just wasn't. Fury had helped her get through those first days of dealing with John after Joey's death.

Michael wasn't doing anything wrong. From his perspective, and out of love, he was doing what he thought was best for Harper.

She was grossly disappointed, though. And she hurt worse than she had in recent memory.

Feeling helpless, as she had after she lost Joey, she'd still been able to help Harper through a major breakdown after dinner. The child had been talking about her parents having stomach issues and, obviously realizing all over again that June and Ryan weren't there, had started to cry. Saying she missed Mama and Daddy. Asking when they were coming back.

Mariah had made it through the conversation same as always, in tune with Harper, delivering age-appropriate responses, pausing at times when Michael volunteered age-appropriate answers as well.

That's when she'd had to fight her own tears. Hearing him right there in the fire with them. Fighting the flames together.

She'd known she was in too deep.

And pulled on her professional boundaries with a vengeance, staying in her room as Michael stood by for his niece's shower, checking Harper's hair when called. Intending to remain absent, but with her door open, available if needed, during story time, too.

Until Harper, in a purple short-sleeved unicorn-emblazoned nightgown, came into her room and straight to the chair where Mariah sat. Book in one hand, Harper picked up Mariah's hand with the other and asked, "Are you mad?"

"No."

She could see Michael across the hall, sitting on the edge of Harper's bed, head bent toward the carpeted floor.

"Was I bad today?"

Sitting forward, Mariah brought her eyes level with Harper's. "No, sweetie!" she said, in a fervent tone and with a smile. "You were the best girl today. Just like your mommy taught you."

"Then why don't you want to read with me?"

"Because it's Uncle Michael's turn. You know how everyone has to take turns at things sometimes."

Harper nodded. "But I want you to be a turn, too. He said it's okay."

Still just *he*. Mariah had yet to call Michael by name. Any name. But she'd asked her uncle's permission for something. She'd made the choice to engage with his position of authority in her life. A major sign of acceptance.

A step Mariah had been praying for.

No way she was going to let that end badly. "Well, then, since it's okay with Uncle Mike, of course I want to listen to the story."

She wouldn't read it. But to solidify Harper's small sense of power, she'd be there. As soon as the book was done, she leaned down, kissed Harper's forehead, wished her a good-night and headed straight outside to the location of the regular meeting.

Sucking in desperately needed fresh air, Mariah stood at the deck's rail, shoulders back, looking out to the moon glow on the water in the distance, and waited.

The silhouette took his breath away. Slender, straight, natural curls hanging to her hips on both sides, curves lining inward from there on down...

He'd never wanted a woman more than he wanted Mariah Anderson in that moment.

Had never before continued to hunger after anyone he knew he couldn't have.

Dreading the upcoming meeting, he allowed himself a second or two to just stand there. Shoring up his strength, or wallowing, he wasn't sure. Probably some of each.

She'd been perfectly amenable over dinner and afterward, but he'd felt her distance like a man in the desert without water. There'd been no glances between them over Harper's head. No shared smiles when she came out with her innocent and sometimes amusing observations. Like when, as they left the table, she'd said, "I farted. Daddy's farts stink, but Mama's and mine don't stink."

Mariah's back had been to him as she'd responded to the little girl, something about daddies having bigger bodies, and, though Michael had waited, Mariah hadn't thrown him one of the backward glances she'd been sending him over the past few days.

They'd lain on the same mattress the night before. The child in between them. A strange kind of trust had come from that where he was concerned.

They hadn't spoken, just the two of them, since. Because, by mutual agreement, they saved all personal conversation for their nightly meetings—focusing only on Harper when the preschooler was around.

Did she know he was standing there?

She was upset by the phone call she'd over-heard. He'd seen the look on her face when he'd noticed her there. He just wasn't sure what about it had bothered her. The fact that he hadn't waited for her final answer before starting his search? Or because he hadn't told her he'd started it?

"I told you from the beginning that I tend to put pressure on people when I see what I believe is the best solution for a problem," he said, stepping out onto the deck and standing a couple of feet behind her. No beer bottle to occupy his hand. He'd forestalled getting one when he'd seen her standing out there.

And apparently no rocking chairs, either. He could see her hands on the deck rail, imagined they were turning white from the pressure she was currently applying. She didn't turn around or say anything.

"And though I'm aware of that, and try to be ac-countable, it happens anyway. As is firmly substan-tiated by the pressure I put on you to adopt Harper."

Her hands, still on the rail, slid a little closer to her body. No other response.

Frustrated, Michael needed to make things right and figured he'd just stand there, shooting out pos-sible antidotes as long as it took. And as long as he had honest explanations left to give.

"After last night, the way Harper needed to know we were both with her and safe, I got very clearly what you'd been saying about her growing attached, taking ownership, and realized that I was doing her a huge disservice, hurting her, with every day that I put off finding her a permanent home."

Her shoulders seemed to stiffen, to pull back even straighter.

"Up until then I didn't calculate much danger in that regard, in that we've been telling her all along that you're a health worker, like a nurse, and only there to help for a little while, and because she rejects me at every turn. It didn't seem at all likely that she was forming any kind of attachment to me. Or that she'd be upset if I was gone."

His breath came easier, or at least one breath did as her head cocked a bit, but her hands never left the rail.

"Upon recognition of the acuteness of the situation, I couldn't waste another whole day. It wasn't fair for me to continue putting off finding a solution, other than you adopting her, with you knowing that every day I didn't do anything would make it harder for Harper to transition to new strangers. I was only putting further pressure on you to do something I should never have asked in the first place. So I went through the list of agencies Len had vetted for me, made inquiries, narrowed them down and followed up with contact. All of which I planned to tell you tonight, right now, as this is the first opportunity I've had for private conversation with you since my enlightenment. I'd narrowed the search to three families, all three of whom were willing to work with you and abide by your recommendations, but the one I was interviewing in my study tonight is out of the running. That leaves two. I recorded their complete interviews and was hoping you'd watch and let me know what you think."

That was it. He'd given her all he had.

And stood there completely at her mercy.

Chapter Thirteen

She wasn't going to let him see her cry. No good would come of it.

And didn't know how to wipe her eyes without him knowing that she'd been standing there consumed with pain, rather than being a part of the solution, which was what he was paying her for.

Mariah listened to every word he said. Took them in, took them to heart. And mentally cried out against some of them, too.

Physically, she was drawing her professional persona like a cloak around herself, dragging boundaries back up and into place.

When he fell silent, Mariah hoped she'd done a good enough job, and turned to face him. Harper deserved every chance to live with her uncle. Her mother's choice for her.

Taking a moment to steady herself as she looked at the handsome, vulnerable, sexy man standing there just a few feet away—while her heart told her they were miles and miles and miles apart— her psyche glommed onto the fact that he hadn't changed out of the black dress pants, white shirt and tie he'd come home in that afternoon.

A sign that their relationship was a business one?

Her heart added that they were so in tune, they'd turned up matching—black pants, white shirt—as though they'd somehow known what colors the other was reaching for when they'd separately dressed that morning.

She couldn't afford to rely on ethereal ideas of almost spiritual connections.

Mariah pushed that aside for the ridiculous and purposeless nonsense that it was, and said, "I'll be happy to go over the interviews."

His head jerked back, almost, but not quite, imperceptibly. As though she'd taken him by surprise. "Thank you." He pulled out his phone. Scrolled. Typed with flying thumbs. And said, "I just sent them to you."

Her phone binged its receipt of a new text message even before he'd completed his sentence.

"I'm sorry for putting you in an untenable situation, expecting you to take on Harper. It was unprofessional, and possibly even unethical of me to have done so with you in my employ."

"Not given the circumstances." Mariah had to correct him on that one. "We're in the midst of a tragic situation, doing our best to keep a four-year-old girl afloat. There aren't rules and regulations specific to something like this. You have to rely on good sense, on judgment and on instincts sometimes. It's part of what makes us human, instead of robots." Kelly had said much the same to her that afternoon when, during Harper's naptime, she'd called her friend and business partner. "You've been honest from the beginning, as have I, and I think we're doing pretty good, considering."

Not perfect. That human element again.

Getting in the way all over the place, apparently, she thought, as she caught herself looking him in the eye for too long and ended up with trembling lips.

Michael moved over to the railing beside her, gripping it much as she'd done, facing the water, and she leaned back against the same board, looking over at him.

"I swore to myself, the last day I saw my sister alive, that I would never put myself in a position where I could do to another human being what I had done to her. I think that's why she left Harper to me. She knew I'd find her the best home possible."

Maybe. Mariah didn't think so, but there was no way of knowing if she was right. There was logic in Michael's thinking. He made sense.

There was loyalty, too, to the sister he'd adored.

And reliability, responsibility, ethics in his determination to honor June's wishes.

But there was also deep pain emanating from him and Mariah knew firsthand that that kind of insidious fire could force people to shield themselves in a seemingly impenetrable armor in order to survive.

She'd also recently discovered, personally, that *seemingly impenetrable* didn't mean that it *was* impenetrable.

"June ended up with a good husband, a loving family, in a community where they were known and loved," she pointed out softly, working with a troubled parental figure, advocating for Harper's future. "From what you say about the childhood you two shared with your father and what she suffered when you left, the only example she ever had of what to look for in a good man had to have come from you. You set a standard for her, and it sounds like she didn't settle down until she found someone who lived up to it."

He was shaking his head even before she finished speaking. "If I'd been there for her, none of it would have happened. She was still full of faith and hope when I left, certain that the two of us would be family forever. Be there for each other forever." He turned then. "I swore to be a better man as the cops led me away from her. I stood next to the police car and watched June loop her arm through her pimp's and walk away. A good man doesn't get over something like that."

He'd built himself a box of iron and closed the lid.

Maybe he was right to have done so. Mariah's heart wasn't convinced. But it wasn't her heart that had the ability to unlock his self-made prison.

Still, she had to try. "Who do you think taught her to take control? Or showed her how to come from your world, from your father, and build a good life?"

"Ryan," he said without pause. "I spent a good bit of time with their lawyer, the first day I was in town, and heard a lot of things. Ryan came up from nothing, had been through worse than June and I could probably imagine, and he fought his way out. Worked his way through a technical diploma, and from there worked all day and went to night school to get a management degree. He met June when he was volunteering at an addiction clinic, a former addict, washing dishes in his free time just to help out. He's the one who pulled her up and out. Not anything I did."

"She made it to the clinic for him to find her. Because you'd seen in her an ability to make it clean. You'd seen, and had shown her, a value worth saving. So when she was ready, she got herself help." She didn't know if it had gone down that way. But she knew, from all of her studies of children's psyches and how critical formative relationships could be to the future, that it was likely that there was truth to her words.

"I hope to God you're right," he said, sighing. "And that's even more reason not to let her down now. Bring up those videos. Let's look at them together and I can let Len know tomorrow what we've decided."

Her body seemed to freeze. Inside first, and then out. She heard his words, but didn't reach for her phone.

He wasn't even going to consider keeping Harper. He wasn't going to see another side.

He'd told her he had an inability to consider other perspectives when he knew he was right, and he was correct about that, at least.

She wasn't going to be able to save him from himself. No matter how much her heart, her instincts, were telling her he needed it.

Kelly had told her to listen to her heart as much as her head. That only with the two working equally together would she find the solution she was seeking. She had to use her brain so she didn't lose sight of what was best for Harper. And her emotion was necessary so she didn't lose herself. Because Michael's request for her to adopt

Harper had made the girl's future personal. Not just business.

He'd pulled out his phone. She felt the warmth of his arm brush against hers in the process, felt his shoulder just behind hers as he moved in closer, holding the phone in front of them so they could both see. As if in slow motion, she saw his thumb moving to the half-diamond shape on the screen that, once pressed, would start a video interview.

"No." She grabbed the phone. Slid it into the left back pocket of her jeans.

"That's fine. If you'd rather watch on your own…" He was frowning, face turned toward his empty palm, as though trying to figure out why she'd just stolen his phone out of it.

He'd want the answer before he'd determine what to do about it. She might not have known him long, but she knew her assessment was right. Because she knew him.

And that…the moment where he stood there assessing before acting…was the solidifier. The final determiner.

"I want to adopt Harper." No emotional preparation for him in her delivery. No lead-in. Just the bald statement.

"What?" He shook his head.

"I don't want to watch the videos," she said, taking hold of that empty hand, meaning to set it gently back on the rail beside him, but ending up with it wrapped around hers instead. She let him hold on to her, held on to him, too, as she said, "I don't want to choose between two other families. I want you to call your attorney and tell him that I want to adopt Harper."

Her eyes filled with tears. Relieved ones. Ecstatic ones. And sad ones, too. Because her unbelievable gain would be his loss. Her heart, personal life and home would be filled.

Leaving all of his empty.

And she felt his pain as if it were her own.

Stunned, Michael had to know. "Are you sure?"

In the business world, he was respected. Even revered. He had mentees out the wazoo. Was often invited to speak to full auditoriums on elite college campuses.

But his personal life never worked out the way he expected. The solutions he saw as clearly the best options weren't shared by others. He never got his way. Not for himself, or for those he loved.

Still holding Mariah's hand, loath to let go of it for fear she and her glorious words would slip away and fade into the ether, he moved them slowly to the rocking chairs. Sat down together. And met her wide-open gaze.

"Yes, I'm sure." Her smile was the Madonna-like one. Almost serene. With a hint of giddiness.

"You aren't just reacting to the moment?"

She pulled out her phone, dialed someone with one push and said, "Kel, I'm here with Michael O'Connell. Can you please assure him that I've given Harper's adoption an incredible amount of thought, including legal research and preliminary child care preparations, and that I want more than anything to have her as my daughter?"

With only a slightly challenging look to him, she flung the hand holding her phone in his direction.

Michael took it. Somewhat fascinated. A bit slow on the uptake as he sat there watching the proceedings through literal, logical eyes, while dealing with a vagary of emotions. Relief. Amazement. Hero worship. All tarnished by the sadness that he knew he'd never be able to dispel. The constant companion he'd had with him since that final walk away from his little sister.

"This is Michael O'Connell. With whom am I speaking?"

"Dr. Kelly Chase, MD, psychiatrist and expert partner at Sierra's Web." Her voice held strength. Confidence. And a wealth of emotion, too.

If he continued to speak with her, would she know that he was riddled with conflicting feelings? That, like a high school kid, he was eager to "meet" Mariah's friend, even just by phone? Just because Mariah was so close to her, and he wanted to be a part of Mariah's life?

"I have been in contact with Mariah," Kelly said, "throughout this assignment, both in Marietta and with you in Little Rock. I am fully versed on the situation, both professionally and personally. I can assure you that Mariah doesn't ever say anything she hasn't fully thought out or doesn't mean. Beyond that, maybe as proof of her very serious intent, you should know that she's already spoken with all six of the partners, who've all signed on to help with child care in the event that Mariah is unavoidably called out of town. Her apartment in Phoenix is adjacent to the one owned by the firm and used by all of us who don't live in Phoenix. Harper isn't just getting a mother, Mr. O'Connell. She's getting a ready-made family of people who are all excited to have her grow up in our midst. You're more than welcome to conduct your own investigation into all of us."

"I've already done so." He told her something he hadn't told Mariah. But this was business. The business of ensuring his niece's future health and happiness.

"Then you know that Harper's getting a mother that will surpass most."

"I do." Harper was going to Mariah! His niece was going to be happy about that! Maybe she had no current idea about how close she'd been to losing the woman she'd instantly adored, but someday, she'd know.

There would be no further painful transition in front of his little preschooler, other than the one she was already facing. His body flooded with relief.

"Is there anything else you need from me?"

Not at the moment. In the future, maybe. He had no idea. "No."

"You want to put Mariah back on?"

He wanted to hang up. To have Mariah to himself for a moment or two while he adjusted to so many things.

Getting what he'd been so certain he wanted more than anything, for one thing. Harper's future was secure. He could hardly believe he'd managed to pull it off.

"Yes," he said, simply, and handed the phone back to the woman he'd been locking gazes with since the conversation began.

There was much to be said, to be done. But as soon as Mariah ended her call, he stood. "Take a walk with me?" he asked, and when she bit her lower lip and nodded, he picked up the monitor receiver he'd set on the table as he'd come out, took her hand and led her down the deck steps over the grass and toward the lake before she changed her mind.

He just needed a few minutes with her. To soak her in and get himself straight. Could her agreement to adopt Harper allow him to stay in his niece's life?

Either way, as soon as he could make it happen, the adoption was a done deal. He could hardly let himself believe that Harper wasn't going to lose her. All day, as he'd contemplated taking Harper from Mariah and giving her to strangers, he'd felt sick at heart, knowing what that would do to the little girl in the moment.

But the thought of taking love from her again…

That thought was now off the table. He could relax. Breathe easily for the first time since returning home the previous week to a lawyer's shocking epistle. Harper's little heart was secure; her future was secure.

But did it include him? Was Mariah open to having him on the outskirts of their lives?

Was a brand-new future opening up before them? Between them?

He'd be fine, no matter what. Harper was going to have the best home he could possibly have given her. Anything else, he could handle, he insisted to himself.

When he'd asked Mariah to adopt Harper, he'd put in the caveat that he could see his niece, be a part of her life. Mariah seemed to think it so important—that Harper know her biological family.

So... Was he in?

He had to know before they proceeded as it could change the legalities somewhat. If he wasn't a part of the deal, he was putting a trust fund for Harper in there instead. He could leave her money on her parents' behalf, if nothing else.

They'd taken several steps, on grass that had just been mowed the day before and still smelled fresh. The air was balmy. Cool, but not with a chill. The night clear. Moon-filled. With stars shining in dots of splendor. He wanted to hold her hand again.

To run his hands through her hair, kiss her until he could only feel the desire coursing between them. Knowing that even if he never saw her again, they'd still be forever tied by his biological attachment to her daughter...made the wanting in him fiercer than ever.

"No pressure. I swear, either way, she's yours, I just need to know, before this goes to Len to start formal proceedings, if you intend for me to remain a part of her life."

She stopped. Faced him. Darkness held them, shrouded them, but the moon cast a spotlight on her face as she gazed up at him. With a hand on his arm, she said, "Always, Michael. You are her family. Her mother's choice to watch over her. I'll be her parent, the one who makes the decisions for her life because it's important for her to have consistency and stability in that area, but you are her uncle and will always be welcome in our home."

Tears sprang to his eyes. He wanted to thank her. But could only stand there, lost in her gaze, and nod as his heart overflowed.

No words would come.

Somehow, by some miraculous twist of fate, his sister had given him another shot at being a part of a family. In a peripheral way he couldn't as easily screw up.

He wasn't going to blow it a second time.

Chapter Fourteen

The man was killing himself. Eaten up with guilt over something that hadn't ever been his responsibility, something he might not even have been able to prevent had he made different choices. Mariah needed so badly to help him. To show him that what he had to give was more than enough.

And she needed to get her intense desire for him off the table. To her, mind-blowing desire and physical ecstasy were fairy-tale fantasies.

The constant tingle down below that she felt whenever Michael was near, the swirling in her groin... Those were real. And facing a life with him in it, no matter how menially, meant she needed those feelings gone.

In her mind it was the last hurdle between the present and her future with Harper. The legalities Michael worried about, while completely necessary, were no more than a fly at a picnic to her. An irritant that you had to endure, something that came with the territory.

But wanting to see the man naked, to touch him

and know that he was big with desire for her...
That was a major stumbling block.

He started to walk again, still toward the lake,
not back to the house, and she was glad for more
time alone with him.

Time to figure out whether or not she was going
to try to seduce him.

Whether or not she'd tell him why.

Whether or not he'd even want to have sex with
her.

"When do we tell Harper?" His question caught
her off guard. And sent a different kind of thrill
through her, too.

Tell Harper. She was going to be a mother
again! The reality had nowhere near set in.
Strangely, though, once she'd talked to her friends,
there was no panic at the thought. None of the fears
she'd faced the first time she'd become a mom.
None of the doubts. She'd make mistakes, assur-
edly. But she could do this.

She wanted to do it.

Badly.

"As far as telling her that I'm going to be her
mother, we need to wait until we know what we're
facing legally and set that in motion. Just in case.
Under normal circumstances, she might be told at
this point, but with her having just lost her birth
parents, I don't advise giving her new ones until
the day it's being done."

He nodded. "Makes good sense." And then, "So do we at least stop telling her that you're going to be leaving?"

She liked the idea. For Harper most of all. Thought about things closer than adoption and the future. "I can always apply for guardianship," she said slowly. "It's just a court filing, there'd be a hearing, and with you there, it could be done within minutes. I suspect your attorney could get the hearing scheduled almost immediately. That would let me take her to Phoenix and we could do the rest of the adoption from there."

It could let her leave within the week.

Take Harper from him almost immediately. She didn't want to do that. To either of them. He wanted to be permanently in Harper's life, so it wouldn't hurt the little girl to spend more time with him. And it could give him more time to see that he'd make a great father figure.

But for the child's sake, the more quickly they could get a permanent arrangement in place, the better it would be.

"I'll talk to Len first thing in the morning. Have him draw up whatever you need to sign and get it filed."

"Tomorrow I won't mention that I'm going to be leaving, as I've done every day since we've been here. And tomorrow night, maybe we have a celebratory dinner—she loves cheese pizza—and tell her that I'll be a permanent part of her life, too."

"Too?"

"She needs to know she isn't losing you."

"But we'll be telling her that she'll be living with you. Not staying here." His words were more adamant than question.

"Yes," she said, wanting to shake him. And to hold him and let him feel wanted. He had so much love to give. And to receive. "But if it's okay with you, I'd like to tell her that her room will be there for her, and that she'll be visiting. Even if, down the road, you no longer want to keep the furniture, or want to repurpose the room, it would best for her to have a picture of it in her mind, to know it's there waiting for her, as are you, as I move her to a new home in a new state."

"It's been sitting that way for years," he told her, slowing as they drew close to the water. His new boat bobbed there, as though inviting them to take a spin. "I see no reason to change it."

Which wasn't exactly denoting it as Harper's room. Just a room that would remain as it had been.

She caught the distinction. Wanted to do something to rattle him. To make him feel everything that he was keeping battened down inside him. It was there. She could see it in his eyes. Feel his pain.

Frowning, he stood there, hands in his pants

pockets, looking at the boat he'd purchased to make a grieving girl happy for a few hours. He may have had other reasons, no way for her to know, but pleasing Harper on Sunday had definitely been part of his motivation.

A man didn't do that unless he cared deeply.

And the more proof she had of his emotional involvement, the more she wanted him. It was like everything that made him different from John was an aphrodisiac to her.

A cruel twist of fate.

Why couldn't she just be satisfied to finally have what she wanted most in the world? A child of her own to love.

But she knew the answer.

Because Harper was Michael's child more than hers. And he needed her as badly as she did.

So she'd invite him to spend holidays with them. Invite him for weekends. Maybe even ask him to babysit for a weekend if she was on a short job. Just as all of the Sierra's Web partners were going to be Harper's extended family, Michael could, too.

She just had to get the sex thing out of her system.

One time was all it would take. Her wimpy libido would be sauntering off before they even got to completion.

And without her response, even if Michael

found her attractive, he wouldn't stay interested. Not in that way.

The solution was clear. She had a tentative plan. Assuming Michael was willing to go along with it.

The only thing left was to figure out when and how to implement it.

Michael left work before Harper and Mariah were up the next morning. The way she'd insisted that he be the primary caregiver when she'd been hoping he'd keep his niece, he knew that, now that Harper was hers, Mariah had to be the one Harper expected to see first, and tend to her the most.

He also had an early-morning appointment with Len, set up late the night before. Len was due in court first thing, so they met for breakfast down the street. And by the time Michael walked through the doors of the downtown office building he'd designed and into the penthouse suite that served as his offices, he'd officially started the process to give Harper a great future. Len would be speaking to a family court judge later that morning and, based on the tragic circumstances, his attorney found it feasible that Mariah could be Harper's legal guardian by the end of the week.

He was thinking maybe he'd celebrate with a week's vacation someplace filled with sunshine, adults and noise. Someplace far away from home. Monte Carlo, maybe.

Unless…no… He didn't want to be that far, just in case there was an issue with Harper, with the ongoing transitioning. Maybe he should stay put for the first month or so, at least.

Feeling better about that plan, he cleared his desk of the things that couldn't wait and made it home a couple of hours earlier than he had the previous few days.

He had to make sure that she got everything from him that she needed before she left. And to hopefully put more glue on a solid friendship between him and Mariah.

To spend time with the two women who'd crashed into his world, spun him dizzy and were leaving him better for it.

He'd miss them like hell when they were gone. Maybe even worse than that.

But he was going to sleep at night, knowing he'd done the right thing.

Knowing that he'd kept his promise to himself, his silent vow to June.

And if his heart broke some more, it did.

He knew how to live with that.

For all the momentous change taking place in her life, Mariah had an incredibly low-key day.

Caring for Harper, reading with her, coloring and doing some math in a book, and playing games while completing worksheets Mariah had to help Harper deal with trauma and change, she passed from one hour to the next with an odd sense of normalcy. Calm. Interspersed with moments of wanting to grab Harper up, squeal and spin them in circles. She was that happy to be gaining a daughter.

And aware, too, that Harper was missing the mother who'd given birth to her. The mother whose right it had been to raise her to adulthood.

Everything she did with the little girl was made brighter by the knowledge that her time with Harper wasn't coming to an end. That they were building a forever, one minute, one memory at a time. As she thought about the apartment in Phoenix, the home in New Orleans, about what would be Harper's rooms in each place, and about needing to probably choose one city to call home as Harper started school the following year, Mariah's stomach ballooned with butterflies.

Excited ones. But still nervous ones. So much to do. And there she sat, coloring in balloons.

In Michael's house.

She'd been disappointed when she'd arisen that morning to find him already gone. She'd purposely gotten up and ready early—dressing in the one flowing, patchwork-quilt-style skirt she had with her, pairing it with a short-sleeved, close-fitting top because she thought them the most physically appealing of any of the outfits in her go bag—hoping to have a few minutes alone with him before Harper woke up. Instead, she'd found half a pot of the coffee they both liked sitting on the warmer. And had had her first cup alone, out on the deck, monitor receiver in hand so she'd know when her soon-to-be daughter woke up.

Michael was such a conundrum to her. And the one part of the life-changing plan that was still making her uneasy. Feeling his pain as though it were her own… That wasn't normal. It spoke of something more than compassion or empathy.

She wouldn't call it love. It was too soon for that. But it was something powerful. And coupled with the way she got wet just thinking about him, that could create serious friction in the future they were carving out if she didn't find a way to get him out of her system.

She was enjoying the process of figuring it out—of thinking about different ways she might get him to go to bed with her—far too much.

Did she tell him that halfway through she'd probably lose desire, but not to worry, that he should go ahead and finish anyway?

Tell him that once they did it, she wouldn't get those feelings for him anymore?

Let him know that he was only the second person in her entire life who'd turned her on?

If she did admit that she wasn't the type to date a lot, at least he could rest assured that she wouldn't be leading a parade of men in and out of Harper's life.

Yes, he definitely should know that.

Before or after she tried to seduce him?

She didn't consider the possibility that he'd turn her down. It was there, of course. She just didn't dwell on it. He'd looked at her a time or two over the past week the way a man looked at a woman when he was thinking about sex. He was healthy. She was attractive. To her knowledge, not many unattached men would turn down a no-strings offer for a one-night stand.

Or an afternoon of it?

She was out on the deck again, rocking with a book in her lap as Harper napped, gazing out at the lake that went on as far as she could see, when she heard a sound behind her and turned to see Michael, in gray dress pants, a black shirt and white, gray and black-striped tie, stepping outside to join her.

Heart rate speeding up, she tried not to stare, but her gaze followed him as he took a seat on a wicker love seat, rather than in his usual rocker. "You're home early."

Home early. Listen to her. She sounded like a housewife. Like she was privy to his regular schedule, when, in fact, she only knew about a few days out of time when he'd had an important deadline to meet.

"I just wanted to be available. In case you had any concerns or questions as we move forward on things," he said. And then, with a sideways tilt of his head, gave a half smile. "I was finding it a little difficult to concentrate in the office. I met with Len this morning. He spoke with a family court judge he knows well, and we've got a hearing scheduled, you and I, for Friday morning to grant you full guardianship. Once you get to Phoenix and start adoption procedures, I will, of course, cooperate fully on this end."

Her stomach jumped. With excitement, mostly.

And some dread, too. Now that she knew Harper's future was secure, and she was going to be in it, she wasn't in such a hurry to head out. To leave Michael in his big house all alone.

"I know it's best for Harper that you get her settled into her permanent residence as quickly as possible. Or what will be one of them, anyway."

"I was thinking about that," she started slowly, not sure where she was going exactly, but said,

"Harper's going to be starting school next year, and while having dual residences is fine for me, I'm not sure it would be a good idea for her."

"What are you saying?" His gaze grew worried. Then panic-stricken. "Are you changing your mind?"

Did he believe so little in things working out?

"Of course not. I'm just contemplating buying a house. A single permanent home for her. I just have to choose which city to start looking in."

Sitting back, he lifted an ankle over the opposite knee, and nodded. "I'd think Phoenix," he said, "since your support system is there. And speaking of which, have you told your parents yet? Your brother?"

She should have. She'd meant to call them that afternoon. She'd come out to the deck to think about sex with him instead.

"I think it's better to wait, at least until I have guardianship, because knowing my mother, she's not going to rest without at least a video call to meet her granddaughter, and that's not fair to Harper. Not until Harper's had time to process, and until we've established legal custody," she said on the fly. All good and true points. Just not ones she'd given prior thought to. She'd been too busy processing it all herself.

Her entire life was about to change forever.

She wanted it. More than ever.

And still had to take it all in.

To learn how to bring Michael into her life, figure out where to keep him, in a way that didn't have her constantly hurting for him.

Or longing for his company.

She didn't want to live in Phoenix. Or New Orleans. Not permanently.

"I was thinking about buying a place here," she said. "In Little Rock." Not really. She hadn't been thinking about it. But she was then. The idea hung there in front of her like an ultra-white lightbulb.

"I'll still take her to Phoenix, to the apartment, when I'm working at the office and she's not in school. But if my base is in Little Rock, then when I have to travel, she can stay here, with you. Her room's upstairs. She's accepted this place as home. And you'll have time with her without worrying about being a bad parent or letting her down. You'll only be counted on to babysit." The words started out in a trickle but turned into an outpour.

He stood. Walked to the deck rail. Turned. Came to the empty rocker beside her and went back to the rail. Both hands on the rail behind him, as though propping him, he stared her down.

She held his intent gaze. Seconds passed. She wasn't budging.

"You're doing this for me."

"No, actually, I'm doing it for Harper *and* for me. If I'm going to have a child, I want a real home. And because you love Harper already, and you're also family, I want her to have more than occasional access to you."

"What about New Orleans? That's where you spend weekends and the majority of your nonworking time. Isn't that home to you?"

"Honestly, I chose the city because of Katrina. Because of the need. Because of the number of storms that pass through the area. But I'm finding myself working all kinds of cases, fewer storms than other things, and can fly in there if and when I'm needed. I've got friends there, but just casual, hangout friends. No one I'm particularly close to." She shrugged as it all just came out, as aspects of the changes her life was taking became clear to her. "I'm going to have a family now. My needs are different."

And being close to Michael, knowing that she wasn't taking his last relative from him, made the sky seem bluer and the sun shine brighter.

It made her feel good inside.

Felt right.

"But Little Rock? Out of all the cities in the United States?"

"I lived in Searcy for four years, remember? Up until Sierra died, they were the four best years of my life. My friends and I, my partners now, used to come to Little Rock on the weekend to hang out, go to the movies, eat out. In some ways, this city already feels like home to me. A home filled with good memories." The idea had been planted, taken root and blossomed. Maybe the seeds had been put in the ground when he'd first mentioned adoption. She'd spent some significant time over the past days sitting with what-ifs.

He wasn't going to talk her out of it.

She wanted to make sure he didn't think he had cause to try.

"If you happen to benefit from my being here, then that's okay," she said, noting the defensiveness in her tone, but letting it remain. "It's my choice, not something you hinted at. Or in any way suggested you'd like. Maybe you don't want it. Either way, I think it's my choice and I think it's for the best."

His nod was slow, so was his smile, but when it reached full capacity, aimed right at her, it took her breath away.

The man was unlike anyone she'd ever met. And she welcomed him into her life.

Chapter Fifteen

For all the major upheaval in the adults' lives going on around her, Harper seemed surprisingly blasé about the whole dinner announcement. Mariah wasn't going to be leaving. Harper took a bit of pizza as she listened. Nodded. Chewed and swallowed.

Then, when her mouth was empty, said, "Hey, guys, I got a idea. How 'bout we go on a boat ride?"

And so, of course, they did.

Michael found himself humming an old tune his mother used to sing, *Michael, row the boat ashore, hallelujah. Michael, row the boat ashore, hallelujah,* as he set the coffee for the morning and grabbed a beer while Mariah put her new daughter to bed.

Her daughter. Hers and June's. It felt…damned good.

And Ryan…the father. Who would be that figure in Harper's life? The question came and he immediately shoved it away. He was not going to ruin the night, or the plan, by overthinking.

Things were working out. He had to let them happen, not get in the way.

Taking his beer out to the deck, he waited for Mariah to join him. Was eager to hear her plans regarding house hunting. Moving.

She could stay with him as long as she liked, of course, but he knew she was looking forward to getting Harper into her permanent home.

Maybe they'd go to Phoenix, as planned, so her friends could meet Harper and Harper could see the apartment that would be a second home to her. Maybe Mariah had work to do there and would need to go.

He'd be amenable to whatever worked for them.

And sit in the glow of knowing that they'd be back. That he was getting what he'd always wanted, family, without breaking his word to himself or to his sister.

Mariah's colorful skirt flowed around her as she came out through the door and his penis sprang to immediate attention, as it had been doing on and off for days in her presence. Holding his beer bottle in such a way to camouflage the response, as he'd also been doing, he said, "I got a package from Marietta today, from June's attorney. It contained the papers for the trust I asked him to set up for Harper. He emptied their bank accounts into it and will add any money transpiring from sales of their possessions. He shipped some personal stuff that should be arriving by the weekend. Apparently, there's a lockbox at the bank there, too. I need to be present, with a key found in June's things, to retrieve the contents."

He was rattling on and knew it. He was just so damned glad to have her sitting there next to him. To know that she'd always be in his life, along with his niece. The monitor sitting right beside her seemed far more symbolic that night than it had every other night they'd been out there. The monitor was the tie binding Mariah and Harper.

And they were going to be right there in town.

"Let's look through it all without Harper at first, just to make sure she's not exposed to something that should wait. Since we didn't pack the boxes and have no idea what might have been found in their home. Maybe a picture of her parents with the frame broken. That kind of thing."

He nodded. Loving how attentive she always was to the possibility of someone else being hurt. Always looking outward. Not inward, like him.

He'd have to be careful to maintain enough distance, to make certain he didn't start seeing fairy tales around the three of them, but he was nothing but diligent when it came to how hard he was on himself. No letting up. Not ever. Anytime he was tempted, all he had to do was see his little sister with her arm threaded through that pimp's...

But he couldn't help feeling satisfied that he'd done something good for June's daughter. He couldn't help loving Harper more than life.

"I need to talk to you about something...completely off topic...and...intensely personal."

With those words, he couldn't help the flood of sexual desire he felt for the woman who'd pretty much worked miracles in his and his niece's lives. Out there on the deck, with the large expanse of yard and empty lake encasing them in a darkness that suddenly seemed like their own little world.

"I'm listening."

"I'm struggling with one aspect of our future. I have a solution. It's guaranteed to work. But it involves you."

"I'm not going to co-parent with you. This only works if you adopt Harper and I'm just the uncle she sees sometimes." He noticed the upgrade from "once in a while." Kept his mind on the bigger issue at stake. Her problem couldn't be that he wasn't keeping Harper himself.

"Yeah, I got that," she said. And then, "Can I go on?" She smiled, but her lips were trembling.

Feeling more intrigued than like the ass he'd just been called out to be for jumping to conclusions, he nodded in her direction. Keeping his mouth shut before it got him into further trouble.

"I'm…" She stopped. As though words failed her.

Needing to help her, because…it was Mariah… he said, "Just tell me how it involves me." She didn't need to give him more than was comfortable for her. He'd do whatever she needed, without question or explanation. He trusted her that much.

"I need you to have sex with me."

While he immediately grew hard, ready to comply on the spot, his upper half went into apoplexy. Heart pounding, he choked on the sip of beer he'd just sent down. Sent another after it, to force the first down, and then put down a third, just for good measure. And to stall.

"Right now?"

"Preferably. It would be good to get it over with."

How could he be so turned on with such a lackluster comment? The more she talked, the more he wanted to take her to bed. To take her wherever. However.

"Here? On the deck?"

She looked around. Her gaze landed on the chaise lounge up against the bars of the far side of the deck. The three-inch outdoor weather pad on it wasn't bad. He'd slept on it a night or two one summer when his air-conditioning was out.

But… She wasn't serious. She was testing him. They weren't really going to do it.

Except that… She stood. Moved toward the chaise, pulling her top over her head as she did so. He shook his head. Looked again, and yeah, right there, just feet away, the woman who'd been monopolizing his dreams lately was showing a lot of flesh.

He still trusted her implicitly. Waited.

She turned so that she was facing him front-on in the moonlight.

Her bra wasn't sexy. White. Run-of-the-mill. Seeing her in it had him practically done before he'd begun, though. He'd never been with a woman so hot that she made the mundane seem like it was triple-X-rated.

He sat there, fascinated, ramrod straight, feeling a need to rut. Waiting to see what was next.

"This isn't intended to be a one-person show," she said. "You going to join me?"

His tie came loose with one hard jerk from one hand as he set his beer down with the other. All ten fingers were fumbling buttons next, and then he had his shirt pulled free from the waistband of his pants. He wasn't sure how far she wanted him to go, but figured he'd just keep on keeping on until she stopped him.

It was like every fantasy he'd ever had rolled

into one. And happening so fast there was no thought.

He didn't know the purpose. Didn't know how far she was going to go before she stopped him. Didn't care. When she said stop, they were done. No questions asked.

And he'd deal with the physical consequences on his own.

Was that it? She needed to know that no matter how turned on he might get, she was safe with him. That he'd have the wherewithal to stop.

He'd dropped his shirt to the deck. Watching her watch him made him ache to the point of touching himself to relieve a bit of the pressure. By the time he'd taken a breath, she was there, her fingers tangling through his chest hair. Finding and teasing his nipples.

His fingers twitched, needing to find hers, to return the pleasure, but he wouldn't let them move from his sides. He was not going to fail her.

With a hand behind her, holding his gaze the whole time, she unclasped her bra and slid the straps down both arms, letting the garment fall to the floor. He didn't look. He wanted to look. Ached to. But he held her gaze.

He'd pass whatever test she gave him.

As she stepped closer, rubbed her nipples

against his chest, he sucked in a breath. Then groaned.

"You don't want to?" she asked, her tone oddly vulnerable, given how brazen her behavior was.

With a voice clearly strangled with desire, he croaked, "Want to what?"

"Do this?"

"Yeah, I'm fine."

"You're not participating."

"I'm waiting for you to tell me what you need."

"I need you to have sex with me. That means I touch you and you return the favor. You know, sex."

The woman set an almost impossibly high bar.

"I generally start with a kiss," he said then, knowing that he could give her his best, his all, and still stop on command.

Her lips parted, and he moved in. The first kiss should have been tentative. A "Hello, how do you do?" An introduction to his taste, his touch. Instead, it was openmouthed, tongue dueling with tongue, by his design, or hers, he knew not. Cared not.

Pulling her tightly to him, he kissed her until he needed air. Greeting. Exploring. Promising. When he started to feel light-headed from need, he moved them back toward the chaise, lifted her down with him and broke the kiss to look at her, lying there with him. He'd known her breasts were large; he just hadn't pictured them quite so perfectly shaped, with nipples that were large and utterly responsive to his touch.

She groaned and squirmed, spreading her legs and lifting her hips as he teased both nipples at once. She grabbed for his waistband, pulling at his belt.

Fine with him. Whatever she needed. He helped get the belt out of the way, and she unfastened the pants, not hesitating or fumbling at all. The woman's experience was as much a turn-on as everything else. He was wet when she opened his fly, pushed his underwear down and sprang him free.

So was she, he quickly discovered as he lifted her skirt and slid his hand in her panties. Soaked. Ready.

He lowered the panties, waiting for her to stop him. Dreading the stopping. She moved her legs and, using her feet, got the panties down past her knees, off one ankle, and spread her legs for him.

From there, he didn't know. She moved. Or he did. They kissed. Touched. He pulled his wallet from the back pocket down around his lower butt. She found the condom, slid it on. And he slid inside her. It wasn't pretty. Wasn't slow or tender. Just him jammed deep inside her, moving back and forth with her. Feeling her convulse around him quickly, coming with an orgasm unlike any he'd ever felt around him, and he followed suit almost immediately.

It wasn't until he was breathing again that he realized she hadn't stopped him.

He hadn't stopped.

He'd just done the most selfish act he could have done. He'd had mind-blowing, intense, one-of-a-kind sex with his niece's adoptive mother.

The type of woman you fell in love and got into a relationship with—leading to eventual tension and breakup. Or the kind you walked away from and never looked back.

If he did either, Harper lost.

Standing, he pulled his pants in place, condom and all, fastened the top clasp. And stood at the rail of the deck, breathing hard, looking out at the lake.

Hating himself.

The cool air hit her like a shower when Michael vacated her body, and the chaise, all in one motion. Still reeling from being catapulted into a world she'd never even imagined in her wildest dreams, Mariah sat up, covered her breasts with one arm and went to collect her top. Prosaic things. Covering oneself. Putting a top on right side out and tag in the back.

When she realized her panties were lying on

her foot covered by the bottom of her skirt, still attached to one ankle, she took care of that situation, too, all the while keeping an eye on the straight naked back Michael was presenting to her.

Clearly, he wasn't over the moon with how great the sex had been.

Was he feeling used? Like he was part of a convenient exchange of goods? Like she'd taken advantage of their situation to get some quick thrills on the side?

She owed him an explanation. He needed to know that the sex had been a means by which they could be friends with no messy, desire-filled tension between them all the time.

Kind of hard to convey her point when the facts didn't support them.

How on earth could she have known that she wouldn't lose interest halfway through? That she'd actually have a full-blown orgasm?

Inappropriate as it probably was, she itched to call Kelly. Right then and there. What did it mean?

"So, that didn't go as planned." Michael wasn't just any man. She had to fix this.

His hands gripped the railing. She saw the movement, not the white grip. Those were in shadow.

Until he turned around. Then she could see his hands. See him flexing his fingers back and forth as they hung at his sides. Her gaze rose, intending to seek his, but met a roadblock at his chest. Lingered there, remembering her own fingers traveling freely over the expanse.

His shirt. Putting it on would give his fingers something to do. The simple task of getting dressed had helped her.

His covering up would help her.

She reached for the garment and handed it to him. Turned her head as he shrugged those strong shoulders into it.

And still stood there imagining what it would feel like to lay her head on his shoulder and fall asleep.

"I apologize for my extreme selfishness, my lack of control, even knowing that an apology cannot undo what's done."

Her gaze shot to his at his words, the ominous tone of voice. What?

"Excuse me?" she shot back. "I'm the one who came on to you, stripping to get your attention, and you somehow think this is on you?"

How dare he?

Gentlemanly of him, but… She'd done this. Well, okay, they both had done *it*, but she was the one who'd started it.

"I told you that I needed this one thing from you in order to get rid of the last stumbling block to our best future," she reminded him, jutting her chin out defensively.

Frowning, he studied her intently. Once again, she stood up to that look. "You aren't trying to tell me that I'm part of the agreement, I hope," he said. "Trying to show me that you and I would be good together and so we should do a package deal..."

She might have had a moment or two of wondering, later that night, lying alone in bed with him down the hall and that incredible sex having just happened, but she hadn't gotten that far yet.

And fantasy had nothing to do with what she'd done. "Absolutely not," she said, with no faltering whatsoever. "The opposite, in fact..."

His gaze softened, head tilting as he watched her. Saying nothing.

Waiting for her to continue?

"When I met John, wow, it was like a miracle to me, that I felt stirrings just looking at him. I felt a physical pressure to touch, and to have him touch me. I thought I was just a late bloomer. That I'd finally have the same temptations as my friends had been talking about for years. But it was just John. So I married him. He needed a wife for a promotion he was angling for and, based on the feelings he raised in me, I figured I'd met my soul mate. Everything was lining up perfectly. So...leading up to now... The first day I met you, it was like John all over again, only on steroids. I was swamped with this sweet energy that's been building ever since and... I knew that the feelings could get in the way, but that me being me, they didn't need to. I knew how to get rid of them. I just had to act on them and they'd fade throughout the process. And then any desire you might have for me would fade, too. John's did almost immediately. So, you see, it was the perfect solution, except..."

"Except I want you again, even more now than I've ever wanted a woman in my life."

Her crotch got warm all over again. She didn't get it. Couldn't believe it.

"So, I made things worse," she said. Or better? If he wanted her so badly, more than anyone else, and she wanted him, could fate possibly be giving them both a second chance at a family?

He shook his head, almost as though he'd read her thoughts. But he said nothing. Scaring her.

"Do you want to change our plans? To find a different family for Harper?" She held her breath, knowing she had to abide by whatever choice he made. Not just legally, but ethically, too.

And knowing that her heart would never fully recover from the loss.

"Of course not! You're Harper's best future. I trust you implicitly." Relief made her weak in the knees, and brought a surge of happiness, with a dose of panic right behind it. Harper needed him as part of the plan.

Maybe Mariah needed him, too.

More than she'd realized.

"You trust me implicitly?" She wanted to fight with him, to rattle him and get him to see that there might be something good to be had right there between them.

His shrug couldn't be sexy, not in the circumstances, and it still made her want to be naked with him, chest to chest, holding each other.

"I was making an assumption based on the information I had," he told her. "And it wasn't a matter of not trusting you, even then. You've been completely open regarding your opinions about my place in Harper's life. You've said from the beginning that you believed I was her best shot at happiness. Anything you might have done, here tonight, would have been, in my mind, just you trying to do what you thought was best for Harper and I. That's who you are."

She didn't want him to know her that well.

And his knowing her that well brought tears to her eyes.

She took a step forward. He stepped back.

"I trust you, Mariah. It's myself I don't trust. No matter who came on to whom, I knew that I had to stop before it went all the way, and I didn't stop."

"I was a willing partner, Michael. I'm as culpable as you are." She couldn't push. If she did, she became what he'd assumed she'd been—a woman who wanted to convince him to give them a chance.

"You were trying to get desire out of your system. I was merely taking advantage of it."

The man was going to hate himself until he died, apparently. Holding himself accountable for the actions of an abused kid with a chance at a future, and the belief that he was the cause of the strife.

"I'll be staying away over the next day or so, until we can transfer guardianship. I'll leave early and come home after Harper's bedtime. You can tell her that I'm working late. There will be no more nightly meetings. We no longer need them as you're going to be sole guardian, so all choices and advice are yours to make and implement. As soon as the paperwork is finalized, I think it's best that you take Harper and go to Phoenix, as you'd planned."

He was *banning* her?

"My plan is to buy a home here, in Little Rock."

He wiped a hand through his hair. "Go to Phoenix," he said. "Please. Look into adoption there, as you already have residency established. Tell Harper you're going on a vacation if you want to. We need some time, Mariah. I need some time. We need to look at things logically, for the long term, and set parameters that will work for all three of us. I can't do that with you here."

But... What about the fact that she'd just had the first real orgasm of her life? The thought popped in and then out. When it came to Harper, and the little girl's future, Mariah's sex life truly didn't matter to her.

Her heart did, though.

And as she nodded, agreeing to pack up and go, she knew that she'd be leaving a part of her heart behind. That there'd be a hole in it in Phoenix.

She would never have chosen to fall in love with a man who didn't want a family. Never would have chosen to fall for Michael. She'd liked to have had a say in the matter.

But it was too late.

Chapter Sixteen

Michael was good on his word, out of the house the next morning long before anyone else was stirring.

Arkansas adoption regulations stipulated that unmarried people living together and having sex couldn't adopt a child. Or some such. Mariah had rattled it off to him days ago. He could look up the specifics. Call Len, even, if he wanted his friend to know what an irresponsible ass he'd been. Instead, he used the existence of such a statute to justify his current course of action. To strengthen him.

While he hadn't actually seen Mariah since they'd had sex, they'd been communicating by text message.

She'd texted, telling him that Harper had asked where "he" was three times.

After which he'd called Mariah's number, had asked to speak to Harper, which he'd done, and after which, he'd hung up. And buried himself in work so he didn't have to think about the hole the tyke was going to leave in his life. Was already leaving. It had only been a day or so since he'd seen her, and he missed his niece.

It was nice, though, in a weird, out-there kind of way. Missing her meant he had her in his life. He had someone to miss. And he'd be seeing her—and her caregiver and soon-to-be adoptive mother—again soon. They were leaving his home, not his life.

He was all set to go to court that afternoon when he got a phone call from Len telling him that the guardianship hearing had been canceled. By the petitioner. His friend wouldn't tell him anything else, just kept saying he needed to talk to Mariah.

Had Mariah changed her mind about taking Harper?

And she'd called his attorney instead of him?

They'd already told Harper that Mariah wasn't leaving her. Now what?

Panicked, he left his office, made it to his vehicle and speed-dialed her number.

She picked up, but only long enough to tell him that she'd talk to him when he got home.

Home.

So, she was still there. At his house?

Relief passed through him before panic returned and he headed in her direction. Of course she was still there. She wouldn't have abandoned a four-year-old child.

Nor would she have left and taken Harper without proper authority to do so.

His mind returned in spurts during what was turning out to be one of the longest rides of his life. She'd been planning to bring Harper to court with her. And then, by his instruction, they were to have been out of his house.

Mariah was in the kitchen when he came in through the garage door. In the black skinny jeans and white top again. Looking sexier than any woman had a right to. He was growing hard before he'd even shut the door behind him. "Harper's asleep," she said, her tone professional. If she noticed him at all, other than a body in her presence, she gave no indication of it.

He wanted to take a kiss or two. To hold her just for a second before either of them said anything else.

"I told her she needed to take an early nap."

No explanation for that, but he noticed the suitcases at the bottom of the staircase. Her rolling duffel and one that he didn't recognize. She glanced in their direction.

"You laid down your law, and you've darn well stuck to it, avoiding us completely." If that was meant to make him feel guilty, she'd failed.

But then, he'd done such a number on himself in that department—ensuring that he didn't get weak and fail again—that there probably wouldn't have been anything she could have said to make it worse.

"So now I'm laying down mine," she continued without missing a beat. Or giving him any personal acknowledgment whatsoever. She was looking at him, but without any particular recognition. He could have been any employer or client, one she'd never even met before.

His gut clenched so tight it hurt. She was leaving. He didn't need suitcases to tell him so.

And she'd canceled the hearing.

"I spoke to Len—he's quite nice, by the way—and he had a bit to say about you."

He was going to fire the guy. Best friend or not.

"He tells me that you can write a letter of permission, allowing me to travel with Harper, and to get medical attention for her if necessary."

She was still taking Harper.

He slowed down from the inside out. Took a breath. But didn't respond. Not until he knew what was going on. When he had the facts, he could form his hypothesis.

"I'd like you to write and sign that letter. I have a flight booked for the two of us to Phoenix this evening and Kelly's scheduled to pick us up from the airport."

She was leaving.

She was taking Harper with her.

As he'd mandated.

"In order to adopt a child in Arkansas, you have to petition and then before it becomes final, you have to live in your home with the child for six months. My law is this. I'll give you the time apart from us. I think both you and I need it at this point. I know I have things to work out."

He waited for her to say what they were. She didn't, which was more than bothersome.

"While I'm gone, I plan to look for homes here in Arkansas. I'll want to move as soon as possible after we get back, obviously. And once Harper and I are in the new home, I'll petition for adoption to get the six months rolling. But I don't want to petition for guardianship. Instead, I'd like you to specify, by whatever legal means necessary, that I am to be her guardian in the event that anything was to happen to you."

He opened his mouth to ask why she'd changed her mind. But she just kept right on stipulating her insanely long and obviously well-thought-out "law."

"I want to adopt Harper with all of my heart. I've taken her on as my own and will always be here for her. However, I cannot take her from you without more time between losing June and giving up custody of the daughter she bequeathed you. Maybe you don't need the time. Maybe nothing will change. But I can't do this without leaving the space there for you to change your mind."

"I'm not going..."

"I'm not going to discuss this, Michael. It's either this, or..." She shrugged.

She didn't have an *or else*.

He wanted to know what she'd do if he challenged her. But no way in hell he was going to rock her boat just to find out.

"How long are you planning to be in Phoenix?"

"A week. Maybe two. I'll be going into the office, some, and will still be in charge of assigning experts to child life cases, but I'm taking vacation time for the next month, at least in terms of traveling."

"Fine." He stepped past her, fast, lest his feet get stuck on the tile floor right in front of her. "I'll go write the letter." He stopped just before she was out of his sight, faced her. "I have one caveat of my own."

Her chin jutted, making him ache to kiss her. "What?"

"That I drive you to the airport."

She nodded. And for the first time since he'd walked in the door, he saw softening in those bold green eyes.

* * *

As great as it was seeing her partners, being wrapped in the warm embrace of the friendship that would sustain them all for life, watching them hover around Harper, and seeing the little girl blossom in their fold, Mariah languished a bit that next week, too. Part of her life was flourishing in ways she'd never imagined it would again.

Bringing her more joy than she'd even hoped she could find. She'd wake up in the morning and remember that Harper was right next door—or once, in bed next to her—and every single time it was like Christmas morning to her. Exciting. Unbelievable. Bone-deep happy.

And even as all of the miracles unfolded inside her, another part of her, one newly born and helpless, just lay there. Unrequited. She'd talked to Kelly about Michael, of course. By phone first, and then in person once Mariah got to Phoenix, and discussing it just made the issue grow larger.

Kelly warned that there was always a chance that she'd lose some of the feelings Michael had brought to life inside her, counseling that most couples lost the rush of immediate need over time, but there was a good chance that he'd also always be able to give her orgasms into the unseeable future. If he ever cared to try again.

As she lay awake at night, warm and fuzzy with

the knowledge that Harper was nearby, she imagined a life somewhere down the road where she and Harper were a family in their own home, and Michael would come to dinner—and stay awhile after Harper went to bed.

She wouldn't be introducing any confusing strange relationships to the traumatized little girl. Michael belonged as Harper's uncle. What would it hurt for the two of them to have their own private bond as well?

But Mariah knew what it would hurt. Her heart. And eventually his, too. He knew her well enough to read her already; no way she'd be able to forever hide her yearning for him. And then he'd start to feel guilty for his inability to be the family she needed and he'd quit coming around.

Or maybe, like a divorced father, he'd simply take Harper out of her home for their time together. Have sleepovers at his place. Go do fun things with just the two of them.

Divorce without the marriage.

Or…some great memories before they went their separate ways.

It could happen that way, couldn't it?

She'd texted him the second they'd landed in Phoenix, and when they were with Kelly and once more at the apartment. She'd sent pictures all six days they'd been gone, all of Harper, in her room at the apartment, with each of the partners who were in town, once at a restaurant. He'd responded every single time. Emoji-only responses. A thumbs-up. A smiley face. A couple of times, when Harper was at the Phoenix Children's Museum, wearing a chef's costume and pretend cooking with a huge grin on her face, he'd sent smiley faces with red heart shapes for eyes.

On Friday, a week after they'd left Little Rock, Mariah found a house listed on the internet that was only a few miles from Michael's. With a swimming pool—surrounded by a six-foot wrought iron gate to keep unattended preschoolers from the water—a wall of windows looking out to the pool and woods at the back of the grassed acre lot, the place was lovely. Four bedrooms, the master suite the size of her Phoenix apartment, walk-out balconies upstairs and an eat-in kitchen, formal living and dining rooms, family room and library downstairs that looked like something from a magazine. She wanted it.

The school district was the one she'd already determined was the best for Harper's needs—she'd started her home search with that check and narrowed the candidates to the area.

Harper, who'd been playing with Kelly, came into Mariah's office at Sierra's Web, saying she was hungry and Aunt Kelly said she could have a cheese and cracker if it was okay with "Riah."

Her heart jumping with delight as she heard the little voice behind her, Mariah turned, leaving the image of the house on the screen. If the four-year-old saw it, there'd be some familiarity for her if everything worked as planned, and she bought the place.

"Of course you can have cheese and crackers." They kept packages of snacks in the suite's kitchen.

"She said okay!" Harper called in a definite outside voice, heading back out to the carpeted hall as though she'd never had a care in her life.

Mariah knew differently. Harper had screamed out in panic the night before, culminating in the two of them snuggled together for the rest of the night.

Watching that little back, not able to tear her gaze away while Harper was still in sight, Mariah saw Harper's frown as she turned back around.

"When's Mama coming?"

"She's not coming, sweet Harper." Endearments wanted to drool off her tongue, and her training told her to use the little girl's name when referring to her to solidify Harper's identity in her whole-new world. With the trip to a new town, a new place to sleep, even though she was happy and having fun, Harper was going to suffer through moments of insecurity.

The little girl stood still, out in the hallway, her nose scrunched up and her blond curls framing her face. "When's he coming?"

"Who he? Daddy?" She asked about her father's return occasionally, but after the first few days, not as often as she asked for her mother.

Harper shook her head.

"Who, then?"

"You know. *Him* he." She didn't stomp her foot, but her little voice sounded as though she'd wanted to do so.

"You mean Uncle Mike?"

She nodded.

"He's not coming here for our vacation," she told Harper, her heart leaping and aching at the same time. "He's at his house, and going to work at his office every day, like when we were there, remember?"

She nodded.

And Mariah couldn't hold back. "You want to go back to Little Rock?"

Harper nodded again.

And so did Mariah.

As soon as the little girl was down the hall, she called Michael. He didn't pick up.

But she left a message. Told him what his niece

had just asked. The desire she'd relayed to head back to Little Rock. And told him about the house she'd found, giving him a logical task. She needed him to drive by. To check it out for her, and make sure that the listing wasn't making it appear better than it was. She asked that, after he'd done so, he let her know.

And when she hung up, she called the Realtor who had the house listed. Told her she wanted to make an offer. She'd have twenty-fours to change her mind in the event Michael's report came back negative.

And if he didn't?

She might just have a new home for herself and Harper.

Chapter Seventeen

Michael listened to the voice mail immediately. He'd been waiting to see if she'd leave a message from the second he'd seen Mariah's call coming through.

It was best that they not chat about life happenings, but if something had happened to Harper, if she needed anything...while he was still her guardian, he had to know.

As her uncle, he was always going to want to be aware, even if he had no right to do anything to help.

Mariah's voice had his system overloading before he'd even heard what she had to say. Life without her and Harper had been rough over the past week. There was an adjustment period. He knew the process. Soon, his loneliness would begin to dissipate. As soon as he was able, he'd take an extended trip—accepting a number of the invitations that came through his office on a weekly basis.

He left work early that Friday afternoon to make a drive by the address Mariah had left him. He was going to tell her he didn't think she should buy the place. He knew that before he was even in the neighborhood. It was too close to his house. She really should be across town.

No point in tempting temptation. Once the adoption was final and they'd all settled into routines, once his psyche was back on track with the life he'd chosen and wanted for himself, then they could have casual drop-ins. See each other more.

Until then, he was on house arrest—away from them.

Every night since Mariah had left he'd woken up having dreamed of her. Sometimes he took cold showers. A couple of others, he just lay there hard and ached until he eventually drifted back to sleep.

He'd shed some tears the night he'd come home to an empty house after dropping Mariah and Harper at the airport, waiting to watch their flight take off. But no one other than him was ever going to know that. He'd be expressing the loneliness in his heart, not thinking of them.

Since then, he and Mariah had been communicating by text message until the day's phone call.

She'd texted, telling him that Harper had asked where "he" was once.

He'd called Mariah's number, had asked to speak to Harper, which he'd done. And buried himself in work so he didn't have to think about the hole the tyke was going to leave in his life. Was already leaving. It had only been a few days and he missed her hugely.

Every morning when he woke up, he thought about June's furniture down the hall, about the absence in that room that had finally known life.

He'd closed the door the very first morning after they'd left.

But every evening, over his solo dinner, usually standing in the kitchen because he didn't want to see his back deck, let alone venture out there yet, he scrolled through the text conversation filled with Harper's pictures and couldn't help but smile.

That's when he'd known he could do it. He could be an uncle from a distance. Harper would be happiest that way. And he could still love her full-out without fear of screwing up. Letting her down.

From what Mariah had relayed in her voice mail, Harper wanted to come back to Little Rock. Had asked when he was going to be back, much the same way she'd been asking about her mother.

That meant something huge. Only a fool would miss that point, and while he'd been an ass, selfish, single-minded, he was no fool.

With Harper in mind, he called Mariah the second he was back in his car after a thorough walk-through of the house and property she wanted to buy. He'd let her call go to voice mail. It was only polite to maintain the distance they'd determined they needed.

She didn't return the favor.

"C-can you talk?" He stumbled through a first line when she picked up on the first ring.

"Yeah. Harper's asleep in the other room. She just went down for her nap."

Early afternoon in Phoenix was closer to dinnertime for him. Time was only one of the many differences separating him and Mariah. He had to remember them all, keep them in the forefront of his mind. Her voice had him hard already.

Maybe he was barking up the wrong tree, there. Maybe it wasn't Mariah having that reaction on him. Maybe he needed to get himself in to see his doctor. He'd find that he had a testosterone imbalance that could be easily treated with medication.

"I saw the place," he told her. Went on to describe structural design choices, support beams, natural lighting, open space, character, views, even from an attic dormer window...

"Wait," she finally interrupted. "You checked out the attic?"

"How else would I get a close-hand look at the structural support?" There were always the building plans registered with the city. He'd seen them, too, but sketches being inspected and approved didn't absolutely guarantee that there'd been no flaws in the workmanship.

The building inspections and approvals said there'd been no flaws. He would not give his word without firsthand inspection.

"You called the Realtor?"

"She doesn't know I was looking on your behalf, though you might want to tell her that, so she doesn't think she has a second interested buyer and advise the seller to hold firm on the price. It's a little high."

"You've been through the entire place."

"I'm an architect. I design buildings. Including my own home, by the way. I thought that was why you called."

"I was just hoping you'd drive by. Make sure the place wasn't an island in an unsafe area, or that there wasn't, you know, business zoning next door and across the street."

So maybe he'd gone a little overboard. "I'm not going to fail you or Harper."

"I know that, Michael." Her tone had softened. "You're the only one who doubts you."

"I learn from past mistakes," he told her, feeling inexplicably weary as he pulled into his own driveway and sat, vehicle running, outside his opened garage door. "Rather than repeating them."

"It's possible that your intense focus on not

repeating past mistakes is causing you to create brand-new ones."

God, he hoped not. "We made a mistake," he acknowledged. "Are you telling me that we can't get past it?"

It was the first either of them had acknowledged the incredible few minutes of sex they'd shared on that chaise, but he'd known it had to come up. The elephant on their table.

"Maybe your mistake is on insisting we get past it."

What was she saying? Tense, wanting a beer, a cold shower—maybe a shower of lake water as he sped through the waves—he remained silent. There were some things a guy shouldn't touch. Not when he was trying to make sure no one got burned.

"I'm an adult, Michael, fully in possession of my faculties. I've done a lot of thinking this week, and have checked myself, too, talking to Kelly."

"Your friend knows we had sex." Not good news.

"Yes, she does. And I'm currently facing uncharted territory."

"Uncharted in terms of adopting Harper." He said the words aloud as much to get his mind back where it belonged as anything.

"Uncharted in terms of how much I can't stop thinking about your body. About your hands on mine. About how I've gotten wet down there every single day since we did what we did, just by thinking about it. That type of desire is new to me, Michael. Utterly, completely, kind of gloriously new to me."

What did he do with that? His repertoire of self-talk, of self-discipline, had absolutely nothing regarding the topic.

Dry. Her words made his throat dry. Too dry to speak. Even to swallow.

"I've become pretty strongly impressed with the idea that, as long as we keep it separate and apart from our time in front of Harper, we could…come together physically…now and then…for as long as it suits us both."

"Am I to assume your friend is in on that impression?" He choked the words out.

"No, I came up with that one all on my own. But it's growing on me, more and more, every day. Worst that can happen is that we end up not wanting to spend time alone together because it stopped working out, and then we proceed like any two people living separately who both care about the same child. Like a divorced couple, kind of, except that Harper won't be caught in the middle because she'd never have known us together to begin with."

He adjusted his fly. Told himself he absolutely

could not contemplate her theory with any eye to taking it seriously.

"And you can't blame yourself, or hate yourself, when I'm the one, with the time apart you rightfully specified, to have reached this conclusion."

The woman was a challenge on every level.

"I honest to God don't know what to do with this. Or you." The last emerged painfully.

Her chuckle had him loosening his belt enough to unfasten the button on his fly. "I'll take that for now," she said. "At least I have hope that I get to spend some time in my life knowing what all the fuss is about. Heck, for that matter, thanks to you, I already know. I'll be forever grateful to you for that."

Now him screwing up was making her grateful? Had the world become utterly out of control?

"You were...pretty incredible yourself." He spat out the words against his will.

"I find that hard to believe, given my lack of any internal drive guiding my education in that area, but I'm glad, considering my current situation, that you feel that way."

He wasn't.

And yet... He was.

"Don't go imagining, or hoping, that we're going to end up one happy family," he said, dead serious on that one.

"I said separate and apart from Harper." Her tone was as stern. "Just tell me you'll think about it."

Like he could somehow forget that he'd suddenly become a top contender for the world's best prize? "I'm not saying yes."

"But you aren't saying no."

He didn't say anything. Not that he'd think about it. Not that he wouldn't. How could he, all tongue-tied up with desire?

"I've booked a flight for Harper and me to return tomorrow. We get in at three. Can you be there to get us or do you need me to arrange a ride?"

He sat up straight at that. She was coming back? So soon? She didn't have a house yet. Putting the vehicle in gear, he got it into his garage. Pushed the button to shut the door behind him. "You're coming here?" In less than twenty-four hours?

He hadn't done dishes in a few days. For the first time in his life, he'd left them dirty in the sink.

"I've rented a furnished apartment for a month," she said. "It can go longer if I can't get through escrow in that time. But I think it's best that Harper see you right away. And that we come get her things. If that's okay with you, of course. You're still her guardian."

The week away had accomplished one of his goals. The most important one. She was taking full charge of Harper.

"Of course I'll pick you up. Give me your flight number and I'll be waiting at baggage claim." He wanted to tell her that she could forgo the apartment lease, too.

But he didn't.

Even if the moon were to turn purple and he somehow decided to have sex with her again, it had to be separate and apart from Harper. And there was no way he could have Mariah in his house, leaving her scent in the air, knowing she wanted him as badly as he wanted her, and keep his aching body to himself.

There was a renewed buzz in his veins, though, as he memorized the necessary flight information, even as she said she'd text it to him, and went inside to roll up his sleeves and get intimately acquainted with suds.

He knew what he couldn't allow in his personal life, but if fate wanted to show him a different kind of good—maybe some happiness he'd never imagined for himself—he was smart enough to keep his mind open to it.

Or foolish enough to hope that he could actually have a tiny slice of the pie without hurting anyone.

Harper jabbered for the first half hour of the flight, mostly about the things she was going to tell "him" about her week in Phoenix, slept for an hour and then talked nonstop for the rest of the trip, a lot of the time wanting to know if they were close yet.

She was certain that he would take them on a boat ride when they got back, no matter how many times Mariah explained that it would be too close to dark by the time they got their luggage and got back to Uncle Mike's house. "He will long as I ask him to," she'd said more than once.

Mariah's breath squeezed a bit more out of her lungs every time. She didn't want Harper hurt. And couldn't trust that Michael wouldn't shun her if she demanded too much.

And there it was. A jolt to the brain as the pilot maneuvered a bumpy touchdown. She finally understood, while Harper's eyes lit with excitement as she gazed out the window, what Michael had been telling her all along. He'd never knowingly do anything to hurt Harper. Or her, either, for that matter. To the contrary, he'd do everything in his power not to do so. Including barring himself from them. Because he knew his limitations.

As smart as he was, he didn't get all of the nuances. But because he was so smart, he thought he did.

Where that left them, she didn't know. But while they waited to deplane, she texted him, as she'd said she would, to let him know they were on the ground.

And then sent a second message. We have to take the boat out tonight. Even if it's just for a quick spin. Harper's counting on it.

By the time they'd deplaned and were on their way to baggage claim, he still had not responded.

As soon as Michael got the text saying they'd landed, he shoved the phone he'd had in his hand for the past twenty minutes into his pocket and started watching the passengers coming down from the gates.

He was a single man, who would live alone, but he had family. From a distance, fine. But he had family.

Harper had asked when he was coming to join them in Phoenix. "He" didn't have a name, and that was fine. He wasn't immediate family. But *he* was one of her people now. From a distance. The loving uncle.

Anticipation was like jet fuel propelling him higher and higher until he was almost floating on air. Members of his family were going to be appearing any second.

And then they were there and his heart flipped clear over. In jeans and matching Sierra's Web T-shirts, they were holding hands as they walked. Mariah's gaze sought his. He saw her looking. And the second she connected, the smile…hit him in the groin and everywhere else he could feel. Then, desire abated as emotion coursed through him.

Her body jerked slightly to the side, and as she glanced in that direction, he did, too, and saw Harper pulling toward him, trying to run.

How could a man be so lucky?

The thought barely processed as tears hit him again. Every day since that last day he'd seen June, no tears. And in a couple of weeks, he'd become a crybaby?

Then that thought flew by the wayside, too, as Harper marched up to him, tilted her head up, arms crossed over her body, and said, "I knew you'd come."

There were no hugs. His tears had been quickly blinked back before they'd been seen. They greeted as though they'd met up after a quick trip to the restroom. But as they left the terminal, him pulling one bag and Mariah the other with Harper helping her, he stopped at the curb before crossing a thoroughfare and hoisted the child up to his hip to get her safely across.

Or just to hold her close for a second.

Chapter Eighteen

They got to Michael's house, where Harper ran immediately upstairs to her room to say hello to her things, and then they took the boat ride she'd asked for on the ride home and Michael had immediately agreed to. By the time they fed the self-professed starving child, Harper was barely able to keep her eyes open.

Not good timing for introducing her to yet another new space. Or asking her to sleep in an unfamiliar place without having a chance to acclimate herself with it.

Had she been a child secure with her parents with whom she'd grown up, arriving so late for their first night at the apartment could have been an adventure. But in Harper's situation, not only was that not a great idea, but it was also grossly unfair to the child. Most particularly since she'd been so happy to reunite with the room that held most of her earthly belongings.

And so it was that, though she'd thought it wouldn't happen again, Mariah found herself spending another night in Michael's home. She opened her suitcase, pulled out the toiletry bag that she'd packed with tears in her eyes a week before, set it on the shelf where she'd kept it in the bathroom attached to her room.

Then didn't know what to do. He'd said no more nightly meetings after the one that had led to sex on the deck. It was too early for bed. There was no television in the room. In a matter of minutes, Harper was sleeping so soundly she was snoring. And with the monitor receiver in hand, Mariah could hear her darling girl from anywhere in the house and on most of the grounds.

She'd found the receiver in Harper's room, next to the monitor.

Michael had turned over custody of it.

He'd given her his niece in action and would do so legally as soon as possible.

He was nothing if not true to his beliefs.

She owed him an apology.

The thought propelled her out her bedroom door, receiver in hand, and down the stairs. He wasn't in his office—the only other place she'd found him in the evenings, other than out on the deck. Or the kitchen, either.

Checking the family room, having to go through the formal living room to do that, she came up empty.

Was he out on the deck after all? In spite of the no-meeting mandate?

Was he expecting her to join him? Or to stay upstairs and leave him to his peaceful evening out there?

Should she?

Maybe. As soon as she found him and knew he was okay. A man didn't just vanish. If he'd...what? Fallen and hurt himself? So badly he couldn't call out?

Even in the midst of major emotional upheaval, she got the ridiculousness of that one.

Maybe she'd just peek out on the deck, from the corner of the drape hanging at one end of the sliding glass door. Make sure he was okay.

And maybe she'd stand there awhile, watching him, once she saw that he was, physically at least, just fine.

He wasn't in the rocker, either of them. Or on the chaise, either. He was sitting on the top step leading from the deck down to the yard, still in the jeans and button-down shirt he'd worn to the airport earlier in the day. Since she hadn't changed, either, she figured they had that in common, at least.

Day-weary jeans.

Forearms resting casually over his knees, he had a beer bottle dangling from one hand. Mariah wanted one, too. Beer sounded good. Might make her sleepy. She could take it upstairs with her. Boot up her computer. Maybe reading would help her be ready to rest.

The thought was good. She approved of it. Got herself the beer. Opened it and took a sip. Walked past the sliding glass door, leaving his back-facing view behind her.

Had one foot on the stairs. Knowing that she was about to spend her last night, maybe ever, in Michael O'Connell's house.

She acknowledged that last thought as she glanced behind her and then found her feet pacing off the path she'd seen. One that led to the door, and then out to the deck. She didn't stop until she'd reached the top step, and then, since she was there, put her butt down a few inches from Michael's.

"This isn't a nightly meeting," she said inanely.

He might have nodded. She couldn't be sure. She was looking out toward the lake. She took a sip of beer. Liked how it felt when the cold liquid traveled through her. Peeled at the bottle label for a moment or two, but had nowhere to go with the paper she'd removed and shoved it with two fingers into her pocket.

"I think I'm in love with you." There. She'd admitted it. To herself. To him. To the night. Who the hell cared? "I know it's only been a few weeks. I know I have no track record that would in any way make my feelings seem legitimate, and yet, it's my track record that tells me that I'm right. What I feel for you, when I'm with you, when I'm not... It's painful and incredible. It brings me peace and panic at the same time."

Her face grew hot, and the cool air chilled it. She was an idiot. And yet doing what was right.

"This isn't going to work if we aren't completely honest with each other. And by this, I mean me adopting Harper and you being an active family member to her." Because that was the bottom line. That which mattered more than anything else. Including anything either of them might be feeling. "Anything we hide is going to rear up and smack us at some point, and chances are, Harper would be hurt."

He still hadn't spoken.

"So there, that's it. All I have to say. I'm in love with you. Good night."

She stood, headed back toward the door.

"You're in lust, not love." His words stopped her. She turned. Stared a mean gaze into his back. And when it seemed to have no effect at all, rejoined him on the step. Took a long sip of beer.

"No. As smart as you are, you don't get to just magically know my deepest heart, Michael. What I feel for you, it's like what I feel for Harper, and yet, completely different. I hurt when I think you're hurting. I worry about how something I do, or Harper does, is going to make you feel. I know I'd willingly die for either one of you."

And when that got no response, added, "I'd gladly never have sex with you again, too, if it meant that you'd be my friend again."

He gave her a long sideways glance. "Does that mean your…feelings…have dwindled, then?"

Did he have to sound so damned hopeful about that? He really wanted to condemn her to a life of no exquisite joy?

She'd just expostulated on how important honesty was to the success of their mutual love for Harper. "No, it doesn't mean that. In fact, just sitting here close to you… Well, I'm already ready… down there. I just don't want to lose you because of it."

As though she'd ever had him. Her mistake hit her with a new load of panic as soon as she uttered the words.

"You say you love me, but you didn't trust me to understand how important it was that, if Harper asked, I grant her the boat ride she wanted."

"Loving you doesn't mean I think you're perfect. I wasn't sure if you'd pick up on the importance of the request. And I had your back. That's what love is."

"For your information, I didn't see that text

until you'd taken her upstairs to bed." He sounded petulant.

Michael? Petulant?

She tried not to break out in a full-blown smile. Only partially succeeded.

"What?" he asked, nudging her with his elbow.

"You like us, too."

"Of course I like you. Harper... She's my sister's child. And you... I wouldn't be giving her up for adoption to you if I didn't hold you in the highest esteem."

There was that. But... "You like me, like me."

They needed honesty. Or it wouldn't work.

"Yeah."

"So, can't we just leave it there for now?"

"I'm not sure."

"Why do you have to borrow trouble from the future?"

"Because it's not the future I'm worried about at the moment. I'm looking at the trouble that's square in my face. You say you love me. I feel... pretty strongly toward you, too. And yet... I don't feel good about that."

"What do you feel?"

"A million warning sirens going off inside me. Like I'm about to let myself down. And weeks from now or a year, or two years... I'll have nothing but ashes and regret, and I'll have hurt you and Harper in the meantime."

"You might. We might hurt you, too. It's all a part of life, Michael."

She wanted so badly to help. But knew that she couldn't. She could love him. She could be there for him.

But his past, his regrets, his pain over the things his sister had done, the life she'd lived for a while? Those were his to find peace with.

Or not.

She'd said what she had to say.

And, with a hand on his shoulder, and a kiss on his lips, she stood and went upstairs to bed.

In his house. With Harper across the hall.

Crawling beneath the sheets, she counted her many blessings. Feeling thankful for every single one of them. And as she closed her eyes, to go to sleep, she felt adrift. Set apart. Alone.

And lonely, too.

But not just for herself. She hurt for the man sitting on the deck of the house he'd designed, refusing to allow it to become a real home.

Michael knew better than to believe that Mariah was in love with him. By her own admission, she'd fallen practically overnight for her ex, too. He wouldn't take advantage.

He'd have her back.

Because that was what people who loved each other did.

Her words repeated themselves from his own thought process as he lay awake long into that night, savoring the feeling of knowing that his house was full again. He didn't want to waste a second of the time with sleep. There'd be years' worth of nights to sleep when Mariah took Harper and left the next morning.

It was one of the last thoughts he remembered having.

He hadn't expected to sleep at all, and then, was suddenly shocked awake by the sound of a child's voice screaming, "No!"

Out of bed and down the hall before he'd fully opened his eyes, he stopped at the doorway to Harper's room. He'd expected to find her in bed in the dark, having a nightmare. Instead, her room was illuminated with sunlight. Harper was up, dressed in purple pants and a matching, short-sleeved unicorn top, and standing next to Mariah, also dressed, in black leggings and a white short-sleeved blouse he hadn't seen, who was sitting on the floor packing some of Harper's things in one of the boxes he'd provided to her the evening before while she'd been getting Harper ready for bed.

"No!" Harper said again, stomping her foot right by Mariah's leg.

"We talked about this, Harper. If you're going to live with me in the new apartment, we need to pack up your things so they can go with you."

Standing back a bit, not sure he'd been noticed by either one of them, Michael wondered how late it was, and wished he'd slept in a T-shirt, too, instead of just cotton pajama pants. He felt grossly underdressed. But couldn't make himself go back to his room.

"No." Harper wasn't backing down. Reminding him of a young June. Fascinated, he smiled, and then stopped himself. The unfolding scene wasn't funny.

"Do you want to live with me?"

"Yes." There was no doubting the validity of that response.

"Then why don't you want me to pack your things?"

"Because."

"Don't you want to have them anymore?"

"Yes."

"And you want to live with me."

"Yes."

"Okay, then you need to help me here. I'm not understanding. Use your words."

"I did."

"Use different words."

"I don't want you to put those books in a box."

"You want to pack them in something else?"

"No."

"Do you want some milk? You still have half a cupful left over from breakfast. We could go down to the refrigerator and get it." He recognized Mariah's attempt to distract Harper from a moment that was leading only to further frustration.

Because he'd learned a thing or two.

And felt so strongly for her, not only for the lessons to him, but for the patience and understanding she seemed to have in unending wells for his niece.

"Okay." Harper's tone had changed. Grown a little weepy.

He saw Harper slip a hand into Mariah's as Mariah stood, and he got his butt back inside his door before they'd exited Harper's.

But he'd barely brushed his teeth and made it into a pair of jeans before he heard screaming again, followed by little feet coming stomping up the stairs.

Waiting until he heard Harper shut the closet door in her room, Michael ventured out of his own in time to see Mariah, looking strangely weary, coming slowly back upstairs.

"Sorry, I overslept," he said inanely. As though he wasn't fully aware of the drama unfolding. He was, of course, just had no idea what to do about it. How to help.

"It's not that late," she said. Yeah, he'd seen the time. Eight thirty. A couple of hours past the time he normally rose. "Harper was just up early, and hungry, and I figured the earlier we get her to the apartment, the more time we'll have there for her to get acclimated before bedtime tonight. It's in a nice enough area, but furnished apartments aren't like a home."

"You're welcome to stay here, if that's what she needs."

Mariah opened her mouth, but no sound came out as she cocked her head, instead, as though listening.

He heard it, too. A young voice talking softly. He was right beside her as she crept down the hall toward Harper's room, stopping just before they reached the open doorway. Leaning forward, she peeked in, and then motioned for him to do so as well.

Harper sat, in the middle of the books she'd apparently taken out of the box, holding Shadow.

"She's our second mama," she was saying to the stuffed toy, as earnest as anybody could be. "We want to live with her forever and ever."

"She's feeling guilty or afraid," Michael whispered, in case Mariah's hurt feelings hadn't allowed her to access that point yet. She nodded, put a finger to her lips.

And then, leaning backward, her lips at his ear, sending tingles all through him as she whispered, "She's using a coping device I taught her. She's telling Shadow what's bothering her. More specifically, what she's afraid of."

He'd been worried about hurt feelings and she'd been…parenting. She'd probably already figured out that Harper was afraid that she'd made Mariah mad. Afraid that Mariah would leave without her.

He'd felt that way with his dad in the early days of pissing the old man off.

"But we can't leave, Shadow. We can't leave him."

He drew back. Stung. With a slice straight through him. Mariah was there. He could feel her, but had attention only for the little girl sitting on a floor of his house, talking to the stuffed cat he'd pulled out of the ravages of a storm.

"We can't leave Mikey, Shadow," she said, as matter-of-fact as any adult he'd ever heard. "What would happen to him? Mama loves Mikey. She said so from in the picture." He couldn't move. Was frozen in a moment that might never end.

Mariah had no such problem. She turned to him. Took his hand.

And… That was all.

She didn't go to Harper.

She didn't offer advice.

Gave him no answers.

She didn't even look at him.

She just stood there. Holding his hand.

Because that was what people who loved each other did...

Coughing with exaggerated loudness, because if he was Harper he'd want a moment's warning before someone barged in on a private conversation, Michael kept hold of Mariah's hand as he walked into the room he'd built for his little sister.

"Harper, there you are. I have a favor to ask." The little girl didn't acknowledge him, any more than she ever had.

And that was okay. He had her number. Or at least the beginnings of it.

She was as guarded as June had been when it came to laying out her heartstrings in times of need. As self-sufficient, apparently.

"I was really kind of lonely when you guys were gone, and I was hoping maybe you could stay awhile longer."

"I dunno," she said. "Ask my second mama. Maybe she'll say yes if you ask her." Harper's gaze was locked on Mariah more than him.

"Hang on a second," he told the child, driven by something bursting from somewhere so deeply within him, he'd missed its presence for a long, long time.

His entire body was trembling as emotion exploded inside him. A dam had burst, and he was the flood. The fact hit him hard. Stunned him.

Mikey.

And he knew...you didn't get to choose love. It chose you. Heart over brain. June had said that once to him, too.

Turning to Mariah, he took her other hand as well, facing her. "Mariah Anderson, I love you, for better or what might be a lot of worse on my part, but I don't want you to go. Ever. Will you stay here, you and Harper, and live with me forever and ever?" He borrowed the child's words shamelessly. He was in Harper's world. In Mariah's. And needed all the help he could get.

"You're sure?" Mariah's voice broke, and there were tears in her eyes.

"I've never been surer of anything in terms of wanting you both here. Wanting to be a family— Mom, Mikey and the kid. Wanting to marry you, too, for that matter. I'm not at all sure that I'll get it right most of the time. Or even half the time. I'm uneasy and scared to death that I'm going to let us all down. I'm breaking a promise I made to myself, so I don't know if it means anything, but I want to promise you that if I let you down, I'll always come back and try to fix it in any way I know how."

He was falling apart inside all at once. Crumbling. In seconds, because of a little girl talking to her cat about Mikey and Mama, years of self-control, of rigid discipline, were disintegrating. And he was left with a young man whose only family, his adored younger sister, had called the cops on him. Or rather, left him alone with the heart full of love he'd had for her.

And now for her daughter. And for the woman who'd saved that daughter.

Mariah wasn't answering. Maybe he'd come on too strong. He'd seen the solution and gone forth, in front of the child, without giving Mariah a chance to process from her own perspective.

She'd said she loved him.

She wanted a family.

Wanted to be Harper's mother.

The solution had been obvious to him.

But...

He'd rent an apartment. Give Harper his house. He'd go anywhere he had to go. If that's what they needed.

And he'd stay, too, if they'd have him.

Because that was what people who loved each other did.

"I want to stay here and get married." Mariah

looked at him, and then at Harper. "Okay?" she asked the little girl. "If we stay, it's forever and ever."

"Until I get growed up and go to college," Harper said, as though an adult speaking to a child. "That's what Daddy says. And then Mama always says that I can stay forever and ever."

"And so you can," Michael told her, bending down until his gaze was even with hers. "You can stay forever and ever until you grow up and go to college and then you can come back anytime you want, forever and ever. How's that?"

Reaching out a hand, Harper touched a finger to Michael's cheek. Drawing a line down it. "Mikey," she said, meeting his gaze head-on.

"Ye—" he started, but the word broke as tears filled his eyes.

"Yes, Mikey, from the picture, but all grown up," Mariah finished for him, kneeling beside him, pulling the little girl into her embrace. And somehow including him, too.

Two female arms wrapped around him, one on one side, one on the other, one big and one small.

And he knew he'd die for either one of them.

Because that's what people who loved each other did.

He'd messed it up before.

He'd learned.

And this time, this second chance, he was going to get right.

Wrapping his arms around both of them, he formed a circle, bonding the three of them together.

Forever and ever.

Epilogue

The lockbox was at Manhattan National Bank in downtown Marietta. Mariah hadn't been sure about bringing Harper back to her hometown after only seven months since the tragedy. Michael and Mariah had married and adopted her together, and when Harper had asked if she could see her pre-school friend, Angela, and show her her second Mama and Mikey, there'd been no answer but yes. It might be too much. Too soon.

But the call had to be Harper's. At least the first time. Until they saw how it went.

Mariah had called Angela's mother, Carmen, and made arrangements for the two girls to have a playdate at a park not far from Angela's house, someplace Harper had never been to before.

The girls hugged and then played for an hour, while Carmen talked nonstop to Michael about June and Ryan—a couple she'd clearly adored. The visit ended with promises to stay in touch. With an invitation to Carmen for her and her husband

and Angela to come to visit them in Little Rock and go boating.

And then, before leaving town, they finally got to the lockbox that June had reserved at the bank. Michael let Harper work the key. And then the little girl showed Shadow the other boxes, telling the cat about Angela coming to boat with them, as Michael pulled out a single envelope from the box on the table. It had his name on the front. No address, just his name.

Mariah's heart pounded as she noticed the shiny gold band on his left ring finger when he opened the envelope. Twisting her own matching wedding band, she prayed that Michael would share with her whatever his sister had to say to him. She'd never have believed she could be so happy. In love, not just with the sex that continued to be unbelievably phenomenal, but with the man, the companion he was to her, the daddy he was to Harper. He was always thinking of them, and she was still working on getting him to believe that he was thought of as highly. As much. That he mattered.

And she prayed that June's last words to him wouldn't send him back to the hell from which he'd fought so hard to emerge.

He started to read. Blinked a couple of times. Reached for Mariah and pulled her to him to read alongside him.

She tried. Her vision kept blurring. She kept trying.

Didn't make it all the way through before Harper turned and said, "Hey, guys, I got a idea. You want to get ice cream?"

"Forever and ever," Michael said.

He could have been telling Harper that he'd always want to get ice cream, but Mariah knew differently.

He'd just read aloud the last line of the letter.

A letter that told him how ashamed June had been of herself when he'd come home from college to surprise her with a visit and found her passed out in bed with a man she didn't know. How ashamed she'd been every time he got in touch with her. Unable to bear how he must think of her. She wasn't him. She wasn't as smart and strong as he was. All those years he'd taken the beatings for both of them, and she'd let him.

And when he'd finally taken his one chance in life, taken his own chance, she'd blamed him, started drinking, doing drugs. Had run away the second time their father had beaten her. And had been lost.

Until she'd met Ryan. Told him about Michael.

And Ryan had helped her see that Michael had never stopped loving her or seeing value in her. He'd never stopped believing in her. His continued attempts to help her were proof of that. Ryan had suggested that she call the number Michael had left her. And she had. Many times over the years. Always using a pay phone and hanging up as soon as he'd answered.

She hoped that she'd be giving him the letter in person, when she felt able to do so without falling apart, but if she wasn't, she just needed him to know that she loved him.

Forever and ever.

Just as he'd loved her.

And would love her daughter.

"Yeah, we're getting ice cream!" Harper cried happily, mostly to Shadow, but to the room in general, too. Mariah smiled, looked up at Michael, and was about to tell him that what they were having was a perfect moment.

Before she said anything, Harper came over to them, wrapped her arms as far around both sets of legs as they could reach and, looking up, said, "I love you guys."

"We love you, too, punkin," Mariah said.

But Michael, he was the one who remembered to bend down to her eye level, and said, "I will love you forever and ever, Harper. Don't you ever forget or doubt that."

She touched his nose. And said, "Does that mean I can have anything I want?"

"Probably. What do you want?"

"A baby brother. Mama said brothers are the best thing you can ever have in the whole wide world, except Daddies and Harpers, of course."

Michael choked. Mariah joined him on the floor and told Harper that she and Uncle Mike had already talked about that and would do everything they could to grant her wish, and then explained that babies didn't just happen. Things had to be just right for a family to get lucky enough to have a new baby.

She explained in terms appropriate for a four-year-old, but hoped liked a kid herself that Harper's wish would come true. A couple of times over.

But knew that no matter what the future might bring to them, they'd have each other. Her and Harper and Michael.

They hadn't started out together, but they were a family.

Forever and ever.

* * * * *

#2887 A SOLDIER'S DARE
The Fortunes of Texas: The Wedding Gift • by Jo McNally

When Jack Radcliffe dares Belle Fortune to kiss him at the Hotel Fortune's Valentine's Ball, he thinks he's just having fun. She's interested in someone else. But from the moment their lips touch, the ex-military man is in trouble. The woman he shouldn't want challenges him to confront his painful past—and face his future head-on...

#2888 HER WYOMING VALENTINE WISH
Return to the Double C • by Allison Leigh

When Delia Templeton is tapped to run her wealthy grandmother's new charitable foundation, she finds herself dealing with Mac Jeffries, the stranger who gave her a bracing New Year's kiss. Working together gives Delia and Mac ample opportunity to butt heads...and revisit that first kiss as Valentine's Day fast approaches...

#2889 STARLIGHT AND THE SINGLE DAD
Welcome to Starlight • by Michelle Major

Relocating to the Cascade Mountains is the first step in Tessa Reynolds's plan to reinvent herself. Former military pilot Carson Campbell sees the bold and beautiful redhead only wreaking havoc with his own plan to be the father his young daughter needs. As her feelings for Carson deepen, Tessa finally knows who she wants to be—the woman who walks off with Carson's heart...

#2890 THE SHOE DIARIES
The Friendship Chronicles • by Darby Baham

From the outside, Reagan "Rae" Doucet has it all: a coveted career in Washington, DC, a tight circle of friends and a shoe closet to die for. When one of her crew falls ill, however, Rae is done playing it safe. The talented but unfulfilled writer makes a "risk list" to revamp her life. But forgiving her ex, Jake Saunders, might be one risk too many...

#2891 THE FIVE-DAY REUNION
Once Upon a Wedding • by Mona Shroff

Law student Anita Virani hasn't seen her ex-husband since the divorce. Now she's agreed to pretend she's still married to Nikhil until his sister's wedding celebrations are over—because her former mother-in-law neglected to tell her family of their split!

#2892 THE MARINE'S RELUCTANT RETURN
The Stirling Ranch • by Sabrina York

She'd been the girl he'd always loved—until she married his best friend. Now Crystal Stoker was a widowed single mom and Luke Stirling was trying his best to avoid her. That was proving impossible in their small town. The injured marine was just looking for a little peace and quiet, not expecting any second chances, especially ones he didn't dare accept.

"I won! I won!"

"That you did," he said, laughing and trying to climb out of his own tube. With his long legs, he was having a hard time getting out on his own, so I reached out my hand to help him up. As soon as he grabbed me, we both went soaring, feet away from the slides. I was amazed neither of us fell onto the ground, but I think just when we were about to, he caught me midair and steadied us.

"Okay, so a deal is a deal. Truth. Do you like me?"

"I can't believe you wasted your truth on something you already know."

"Maybe a girl needs to hear it sometimes."

"Reagan Doucet, I will tell you all day long how much I like you," he said, bending down again so he could stare directly into my eyes. "But you have to believe me when I do. No more of that 'c'mon, Jake' stuff. You either believe me or you don't."

"Deal," I said, grabbing hold of the loops on the waist of his pants to bring him even closer to me. "You got it."

"Mmm, no. I've got you," he whispered, bringing his lips centimeters away from mine but refusing to kiss me. Instead, he stood there, making me wait, and then flicked out his tongue with a grin, barely scraping the skin on my lips. It was clear Jake wanted me to want him. Better yet, crave him. And while I could also tell this was him putting on his charm armor again, I didn't care. I was in shoe, Christmas lights and sexy guy heaven, and for once I was determined to enjoy it. Not much could top that.

"Now, let's go find these pandas."

I reached out my hand, and he took it as we went skipping to the next exhibit.

Don't miss The Shoe Diaries *by Darby Baham,
available February 2022 wherever
Harlequin Special Edition books and ebooks are sold.*

Harlequin.com

HSEEXP0122A

Get 4 FREE REWARDS!

We'll send you 2 FREE Books plus 2 FREE Mystery Gifts.

Harlequin Special Edition books relate to finding comfort and strength in the support of loved ones and enjoying the journey no matter what life throws your way.

FREE
Value Over
$20
